J.A. KERLEY

Little Girls Lost

HARPER

Harper
An imprint of HarperCollins*Publishers*
77–85 Fulham Palace Road, London W6 8JB

www.harpercollins.co.uk

A Paperback Original 2009

5

A catalogue record for this book
is available from the British Library

ISBN 978 0 00 734228 0

Set in Sabon by Palimpsest Book Production Limited,
Grangemouth, Stirlingshire

Printed in Great Britain by
Clays Limited, St Ives plc

*To my son, John, proof that evolution
can make dazzling leaps*

LITTLE GIRLS LOST

1

*"The Gumbo King is stepping out,
and all the pretty women gonna jump and
shout . . ."*

Her eight-year-old heart pounding, Jacy Charlane
crouched behind a table of turnips and tomatoes
in front of the small grocery and watched the
Gumbo King approach. He was singing, his king-
sized voice bouncing between storefronts and
apartments on the four-lane avenue.

*"The Gumbo King, he's so fine,
kissing all the women and blowing their minds."*

The Gumbo King was a white man, big, but
not fat. He was wearing a yellow felt crown and
a purple vest. His tee shirt and jeans were black.
Jacy found it strange that if the Gumbo King wasn't
singing, you never heard him coming, like cotton
balls were glued beneath his shoes.

Whenever the Gumbo King turned his brown eyes on Jacy Charlane, they stole her voice and turned her knees to pudding. The Gumbo King was scary, and in the past she'd always run when she saw him coming.

But today was different: Someone in the city was stealing little girls. Gone, like they'd been snatched by goblins. One disappeared last week. Another got took just last night. People were whispering about it on the street.

"The Gumbo King is struttin' down the street . . .
all them gumbo lovers know Gumbo King's got the treats . . ."

Jacy thought a king might be able to help find the girls. Especially one who owned his own place to eat and a humungous window sign with THE GUMBO KING written in red light beside a flashing gold crown.

The Gumbo King walked closer. Jacy swallowed hard and stepped from behind the table, blocking the king on the sidewalk. He stopped singing. Jacy felt the Gumbo King's shadow stop the sun.

"You're that Charlane girl, aren't you?" a voice boomed from up where birds flew. "Jacy, is it?"

Excuse me, Mister King, but two little girls are disappeared and please sir you would Highness your help . . .

Jacy felt the rehearsed words crash together in

her mouth. She closed her eyes to hide. The Gumbo King rapped the top of Jacy's head with a knuckle.

"Knock, knock, girl. I know you're in there. I command you to speak to the Gumbo King."

Jacy pressed her palms against her eyes. She felt the sun return to her shoulders and when she opened her eyes the Gumbo King was walking away, singing again.

". . . So if you're aching and empty and don't know what to do,
call the Gumbo King and he'll see you through."

Jacy felt like crying, ashamed she was too scared to talk to a king. She ran home and closed herself in her room, thinking to herself . . .

Who steals little girls? What do they do with them?

2

Detective Carson Ryder traced his latex-gloved finger slowly over the mattress, as if reading in Braille. His eyes were closed, his head canted in concentration, intensifying the impression of a blind man searching for messages. After a few moments he sighed and pushed black hair from his forehead, opening his eyes to survey the small, dank-smelling room.

Like most in the neighborhood, the cramped apartment was furnished on poverty's budget: bare bulb in the ceiling, three-legged chair in a corner, torn paper curtains at the windows. The bed was a mattress on the floor, sheet pulled aside, amoebic shapes staining its surface.

A battered chest of drawers flanked the mattress, the red leg of a pair of tights drooping from a drawer like a wind sock on an airless day. Atop the chest sat a photograph in a listing frame, a black girl, eight or nine, whimsical twigs of hair poking from her head. She had laughing eyes and a smile one tooth shy of perfection.

"My baby, you've got to find my baby," a woman wailed from outside the bedroom, her voice rising toward hysteria.

"Where were you last night, Ms Shearing?" a policewoman questioned. "What time did you get in? When did you last see LaShelle?"

The woman replied with a sound like a keening gull. Ryder closed the door. Another minute and the woman would be screaming.

"Is it blood?" Ryder asked the bespectacled, rope-skinny black man crouched beside the mattress, his tie flung over his shoulder.

"Old blood," deputy chief of Forensics Wayne Hembree said, lifting a mattress button and studying its underside with a penlight. "Hell, Carson, this mattress has probably been around since the Battle of Mobile Bay. Nosebleeds. Menses. God knows what."

Ryder let his eyes drift to the window, morning sun backlighting brick tenements across the street. A sultry day promised and being delivered, continuing a late-September heatwave as hot and fetid as lions' breath. Right on schedule the woman started screaming. Hembree winced and turned his moon-round face to Ryder.

"You see the kitchen window, the grating torn away?"

Ryder nodded.

"Think this is another one, Carson?" Hembree asked. "Abduction?"

Yes, Ryder thought. But didn't allow the word

5

to reach his lips. He opened the door to the hall outside the small apartment. It was quiet, the woman escorted away. He turned and shot a final glance at the mattress. Sunlight beamed through the window, lighting dust motes in the air. They drifted to the bedding like pinpoint flares.

"You leaving, Carson?" Hembree asked.

Ryder froze. "Is that a loaded question, Bree?"

The tech's eyes narrowed behind thick eyeglass lenses. "It's been a crazy couple of months. But it'll all settle out for the best. Forget the politics and do your job."

"Squill's back and in charge of the department," Ryder said, walking out the door. "And what the hell is my job any more?"

Every morning at daybreak the Gumbo King whisked white flour into hot oil to create roux, the heart of gumbo, the stew-thick concoction of meats, seafood, vegetables and spices that was the gustatory equivalent of a religious experience in South Louisianans. There was light roux the color of *café au lait* to let the delicate sea-taste of shrimp and crab shine through. For the middle roux, he let the flour touch the color of pecan skin, best for chicken. And finally, his favorite, the dark roux. The color of chicory coffee with a teaspoon of cream dribbled in, the dark roux needed sturdy counterpoint: andouille sausage, tasso ham. Shrimp and crab were nearly overwhelmed by the dark roux, but left hints against the gravy-thick sauce, playing their notes.

Gumbo was a matter of balance and harmony. Nothing more. But nothing less, either.

Behind the roux skillets, shrimp heads, chicken carcasses and vegetables bubbled in large pots. When the broths reduced to essences, the Gumbo King orchestrated the day's gumbos, his wooden spoon a maestro's baton on a four-count beat – stir, spice, taste, frown. When the frown turned to a smile the gumbo was ready.

The first bowls appeared in the server's window shortly after eleven a.m., and the steaming parade of gumbo – plus brown bags of carryout – continued until early evening. After the last diners drifted out, the Gumbo King swept and mopped the sixteen-table dining room. He poured leftover gumbo into plastic tubs and drove six blocks to a soup kitchen, Charity's Hand Mission, where the gumbo joined other donations in feeding the neighborhood's destitute.

On his fourth trip, a year back, he'd watched in horror as Father Tim, the adolescent-faced Jesuit who shepherded the mission, poured three different gumbos together before closing them in the refrigerator.

"You can't treat gumbo that way," the Gumbo King snarled. "It's discordant."

"It's simply gumbo," the priest said.

"Hash is simple, gumbo is art."

"Mixing saves time; there's less to clean," Father Tim reasoned.

"Then pour everything, gumbo, bread, crackers,

Jell-O, juice, coffee, into a tub and ladle it into cups. Think of all the time that would save."

Before Father Tim could concoct a suitably Jesuitical response, the Gumbo King went for the priest's belly.

"Have you tried my gumbo?" he asked innocently.

"They're all incredible," Father Tim said. "Though my favorite is –"

"So you grab yours before they're slopped together?"

While the priest considered how much of a corner he'd backed into, the Gumbo King folded his arms, closed his eyes, and waited.

"You're right," Father Tim decided. "No mixing."

"Amen," said the Gumbo King.

3

Ryder left the apartment to Hembree and the techs from Forensics. He passed a fingerprint technician dusting the door frame.

"Uh, Carson," the tech said. "About Harry. I just want to say again how sorry we all are, and how much . . ."

Ryder waved the words away, *not now*. The man understood and resumed his task. Ryder opened the front door of the building to find the sun had lit the sky to crystalline blue. He walked on to the stoop with the tech's words echoing in his head, wishing Harry Nautilus was with him, that the pair could sit on Ryder's deck, watch the gulf waves, and get deep under the hood of these horrific abductions.

But there was no Harry Nautilus. The loss of his long-time partner was devastating. When added to the reappearance of Terrence Squill as acting chief of police . . .

"You, Mr Po-liceman!"

An angry voice pulled Ryder from the dark tumble of his thoughts.

"You, Mr Po-liceman. Yes, you. A third black child disappeared into nowhere, right?"

Ryder halted on the stoop, sun-blind, blinking toward the source of the artificially loud voice.

"Third child?" he asked, locating the voice: Reverend Damon Turnbull in the bed of a blue pickup, bullhorn in hand. A news van pulled to the curb. A crowd began forming around the diminutive black preacher in the cream-colored suit.

"Mr Po-liceman don't even know how many girls been stolen," Turnbull sneered to the crowd. He aimed the bullhorn back toward Ryder. "Let me help you remember. One year ago little Darla Dumont, eleven years old, disappeared and nothin' was ever found of her. A week back Maya Ledbetter was stole right off the street. Then last night LaShelle Shearing was slipped right out of this here apartment."

Ryder winced. He'd been so absorbed in the two recent abductions he'd not included Darla Dumont in his count. Her investigation was ongoing, and her case was naturally being compared to the latest abductions, but his omission of Darla in the tally made him look foolish.

"I know about Darla. It's just that we've been concentr—"

Turnbull wasn't interested. He turned to the crowd.

"Someone snuck another black child away. What happens to the mother? Stuck in a po-lice car and hauled off like a criminal."

Ryder stared across the flood of faces, puzzled by how everyone seemed to have materialized from nowhere. There'd been no over-the-air communications; the woman had called in the missing child from a public phone. Ryder had been a block away in the cruiser of uniformed Sergeant Roland Zemain, discussing a recent domestic homicide. Notice of the potential abduction arrived via the computer in Zemain's cruiser and the pair had run silent to the address. Only the recent arrival of the crime-scene van gave indication of a problem. A few cops and techs knew. The mayor had probably been notified. That ought to have been it.

How'd Turnbull and the media get here so fast? Ryder wondered.

"Where's your voice, Mister Detective?" Turnbull called above the crowd, a gold-ringed finger pointing like an accusation. "And where's that little girl's mama?"

The mother had been taken to headquarters for further questioning, her answers incomplete and evasive, soaked in the guilt of someone who'd spent the night elsewhere, leaving her child alone.

Ryder said, "She's been taken in for questioning. It's routine."

Turnbull spun to the people on the street, his face smeared with indignation. "You think they take white mamas to the police station to ask *them*

11

questions? You think that's what white folks think is *routine?*"

The crowd growled the negative.

"We need more information," Ryder said, embarrassed by his voice, no match for the preacher's resonant baritone, a voice larger than the man himself.

Turnbull waved his arms high, commanding silence.

"A white baby girl disappears, how many police they put on the trail of that child?"

"A hundred," yelled a voice from the crowd.

"Ever' damn one of 'em," said another.

"We're investigating," Ryder called out, trying to keep his rising confusion from his words. "We're looking into everything."

Sergeant Zemain appeared at Ryder's side. "I called for backup, Carson. Maybe we should haul ass while the street's still copasetic. If they got no one for Turnbull to aim them at, things'll chill. Otherwise . . ." Zemain nodded at the far end of the block, men stepping from doorways, old women hobbling their way.

"Save our babies," Turnbull chanted. "Save our . . ." The crowd picked it up, fists pounding the beat against the air. Angry men pushed to the front, a dozen feet from the cops and closing. Ryder debated unholstering his weapon.

"Stop!"

The preacher's voice cut the air. The crowd slowed, eyes skimming between Ryder and Turnbull.

12

"People! Stop where you are. I said stop, y'all! We've said our piece for now. Stand back, let them by."

Distant sirens grew louder.

"Easy does it, Carson," Zemain whispered. The pair walked forward as the crowd grudgingly parted. A man with arms like fire hoses spat at Ryder's feet. A woman so old her face seemed mummified stared as though Ryder was the source of all trouble in the world. A professorial black man studied Zemain and said, "Looking snowy white today, Uncle Tom."

Three cruisers screeched on to the sidewalk, cops with batons pushing toward Ryder and Zemain.

"Stay calm, people," Turnbull ordered. "Don't start no trouble cuz it'll just fall back on us. Let's don't start hurting ourselves."

Cordoned by uniforms, Ryder slipped into a cruiser beside an overweight fifty-ish patrolman known as Weez. Weez chuckled. "Nice crowd, Ryder. You passin' out free ribs or something?"

They pulled away through a barrage of curses. Ryder turned to see the crowd slowly dispersing, angry, mistrustful eyes on both sides.

It wasn't how Harry Nautilus would have handled it, Ryder thought.

". . . ninety-goddamn-eight, ninety-goddamn-nine, one-fucking-hundred."

Rose finished his standing curls, bent his knees and returned fifty pounds of barbell to the floor.

He plucked a towel from the weight bench and sopped sweat from his armpits before wiping his face. He undid the lifting belt and let it drop, kicking it into a corner cluttered with clothes and nutrition-bar wrappers. His thumbs slipped beneath the band of his jockstrap and stretched it open to ventilate his matted genitals.

Rose looked out the window at a rising sun backlighting live oaks hung with Spanish moss. Feeding Time. He slipped on gray sweats and went to the kitchen to make peanut-butter-and-jelly sandwiches, pushing aside a stack of *Powerlifter Monthly*. He tried to avoid touching the peanut butter; it was oily with fat and he was afraid it would somehow creep under his flesh. Though Rose was five-eleven and weighed two hundred and thirty-five pounds, he had the body fat of a competition whippet.

The sandwiches completed, he poured two cans of Vita-Pro Energizing Power Shake into a Tupperware pitcher and whisked in three raw eggs. Healthy food grew healthy bodies. The sandwiches went into a paper sack with the drink mixture.

Rose walked out the back door of the wooden bungalow, squinting in the sunlight. Though he lived in an ageing subdivision, the planning haphazard and dictated by surrounding wetland, Rose's house stood alone, the nearest neighbor thirty yards distant and separated by a thicket of pines and water oaks. His yard was plank-fenced to six feet.

14

A chevron of pelicans passed overhead as Rose went to a barrel-wide shaft, hatched and secured by a heavy marine lock. The shaft descended to a submerged steel tank resembling a dwarf submarine, ten feet long, five wide, six tall. It was a hurricane shelter, a place to ride out a storm in an emergency.

Rose descended steel rungs to a chamber lit by a solitary 40-watt bulb. Two girls huddled like kittens on a cot at the far end of the cylinder. Maya Ledbetter, the one who'd been there a week, was mewing softly, LaShelle Shearing, the one picked up late last night, tried to burrow beneath the wadded blankets. The girls were restrained with lengths of clothesline knotted to the cot, the cot bolted to the floor.

"Mister Breakfast's here," Rose sang in a wispy falsetto. "He's got goodies for your bellies . . ."

He crept forward. Maya's eyes filled with fright. She retreated to the farthest corner of the cot. Rose set the sandwiches on a TV tray.

"Come out, come out wherever you are, LaShelle," he prompted the crying girl. "It's peanut butter and jelly. Everybody likes PB&J, right?"

The girl burrowed deeper beneath the covers.

Rose traded the full pitcher of shake mix for the empty one in the cooler beside the bed, then bagged the leavings in the travel toilet and replaced the liner. He turned to leave, liner bag and empty pitcher in hand. Before ascending he turned to study the terrified girls.

15

He wanted to stay and talk. But he'd been ordered to perform his tasks and get out. Rose willed himself to ascend the rungs. He returned to the house and set the full toilet bag on the floor in the shower, ignoring it through three sets of curls and two hundred crunches.

Then he was back in the bathroom, peering into the bag, fascinated by all things female.

4

Four in the afternoon and seven cops plus Ryder surrounded the long table in the administrative conference room: Terrence Squill, the acting chief of police, Deputy Chief Carl Bidwell, and captains Roy Grady and Bobby Harlan.

Lieutenant Tom Mason, Ryder's immediate supervisor, was there, as was Roland Zemain. Coal black and the approximate build of a Humvee, Zemain had been the ranking uniform on the scene and his street sense was unquestioned. For years the department had tried to move him into plain-clothes or administration and he'd been as unyielding as titanium rebar.

"The street beats on me one day, kisses me the next," Zemain had once explained to Ryder. "It's a love-hate thing, and when the hate steps in front, I'll get out."

The seat beside Squill went to Commander Ainsley Duckworth, who didn't sit on the chair as much as absorb it, a man who looked fat from a block away, imposing at a half-block, with the last twenty feet making people wish they'd chosen the other side of the street. Part of it was the eyes, small and hard and tucked beneath a ponderous sheet of brow. Another was his mouth; too small to enclose his teeth, they seemed permanently bared.

Beside Duckworth was Bobby Myers from Internal Affairs. Ryder figured the whippy, rat-faced Myers was there to run errands for Squill or Duckworth, taking orders being Myers's sole talent. Myers was gnawing on his fingernails as if something tasty was stuck beneath them.

When everyone was settled, coffee, pens and notepads on the table, Squill stopped studying his nails and trained eyes as blue as acetone flames on Ryder.

"So, Ryder, when were you made spokesman for the department? I forget."

"I was hoping to calm the crowd. Explain that we were working on the abductions."

"I can tell how well they believed you. Especially with Turnbull making you sound like some mealy-mouth crossing guard."

"What gets me is, where did they come from?" Ryder said. "Turnbull, the crowd?"

"What are you talking about?"

Zemain cleared his throat. "Detective Ryder was in my cruiser, Chief. I was giving him street skinny on that domestic last week – wife spread hubby's brains across the kitchen with the skillet? The call

18

about the gone girl came over the computer. We ran silent, didn't park directly out front."

Ryder leaned forward. "No one was nearby on the sidewalk, Chief, nobody in the hall. If the mother told the neighbors, you couldn't tell. I was under the impression she came home from a night of partying, found the empty bed, and called 911."

Squill rubbed the short salt-and-pepper hair at his temples and glared.

"So the hell what?"

Ryder said, "How'd Turnbull find out? The mother seemed too disoriented to think about calling a preacher; it doesn't fit."

Squill's cold voice sank to sub-zero. "What does it matter? It happened. I'll tell you what matters – a half-hour ago I had to report to the goddamn mayor. You ever have to stand in front of that sanctimonious bitch and explain not only why three girls are missing without a trace, but why our own detectives are creating – what's the word she used? – 'discord' in the black community?"

"No, sir," Ryder said, thinking, *How come all the assholes fall up?*

"Of course not; that's my job. Your job is creating confrontations."

"It wasn't a confrontation, Chief," Zemain said. "It was a difference of opinion with a couple rough edges."

Squill speared Zemain with a glance. "Guess what, Sergeant? It's my ass that gets used to sand them down."

Ryder said, "I'm still trying to figure how Turnbull got there so fast."

"Christ, Ryder," Squill said, shaking his head, "are you a detective or a parrot? Give it a rest."

The room fell silent. Squill said, "OK. Let's move on to some real police work. Anybody have anything new? Somebody tell me yes."

Deputy Chief Bidwell, head of the uniformed division, sighed. "We've got guys rousting peds and working snitches, but nothing so far."

"Anything from Forensics? ME's office?"

Grady from Investigative cleared his throat and leaned forward. "The perp entered though the alley-side kitchen window, no easy job."

"Why?" Squill said.

"The window was grated but the grate was popped off. The bars were stuck in concrete. Forensics says it probably took a heavy prybar and a lot of strength."

"A mechanical device? Hydraulic jack?" Squill asked.

"There weren't any scratch marks where it would have been anchored, but that doesn't rule it out."

"Wouldn't it have made a racket coming off?"

Zemain said, "The apartment's next to the Zanzibar Lounge. Jukebox always cranked to the max. You could fire a cannon in the alley and no one'd hear it."

Squill rolled his eyes. "I've got what . . . a hundred years' experience in this room? And what's

20

this team of giants brought me? A prybar theory."

Grady said, "Something's got to break soon, Chief. We're going to –"

Squill cut him off with an upraised palm. "Here's the way it is, Captain. The blacks are pissing on the mayor's shoes, the mayor's pissing on my shoes. Guess whose shoes I'm getting ready to piss on?"

When no one volunteered an answer, Squill stood, making no attempt to conceal his disgust. "That's it, gentlemen; dismissed. How about you get out there and try some police work?"

Pure Squill, Ryder thought as he watched the cops file out, *police work as urination.* In the two months Squill had been acting chief, Ryder had yet to hear him utter a single encouragement, a solitary *well done.* He led through intimidation and innuendo, put-downs and politics. *"I don't walk past Squill,"* the generally fearless Zemain once confessed, *"without some Kevlar over my back."*

Will I be able to survive? Ryder wondered.

5

Truman Desmond fought to keep from smacking the kid upside the head. The boy was crossing his eyes and sticking out his tongue as Truman tried to focus his camera.

"That's funny," Truman said. "I can't wait until your mama sees your school picture."

That did the trick, Truman noted in his eyepiece, the little monster sucking in his tongue and blinking moronically into the lens. Truman pressed the shutter release and the flash popped.

"I think my eyes was closed," the kid protested.

"They were open," Truman said. "You're done."

"They felt closed."

Truman looked toward the teacher, a portly woman with thick glasses. She was at the door on the far side of the room and looking down the hall.

"Git," Truman spat at the kid, who grudgingly slid from the stool and joined the others lining the outside hall. "That's it," Truman called to the teacher. "I'm finished with your class."

"Wait," the teacher said. Truman heard running footsteps and a tiny, slender girl ran into the room, her arms stacked with books.

"I was at the library," the girl said. "I forgot the time."

Truman stared at the girl. The recognition was instant, like a bolt of clear lightning.

She was a Keeper.

Truman rolled his camera in his hands, pretending to study something. He pushed stringy blond hair from his forehead and looked at the teacher with apology in his eyes.

"Doggone. I've got to recharge. How about I send her back when I'm done? Just take a sec."

"She knows the way," the teacher said, and led the class from the small locker room hastily designated as photo studio.

"Have a seat, little miss," Truman said. "Do you need help getting up? The stool's kind of high."

"I can get it." The girl clambered up on the stool set before the dappled background.

"What's your name, dear?" Truman said, eyes moving between his camera and subject. *You could fall into that smile, and those eyes are so huge.*

"Jacy. Jacy Charlane."

23

"How old are you, Jacy Charlane?"

"Nine. Almost."

Truman held the camera at waist level and clicked off two shots without flash.

"I didn't get ready," the girl said.

"I'm not taking pictures, dear. This is part of recharging the camera."

"Oh. Sorry."

Truman knelt on the floor and took two more up-angling pictures.

"Still recharging?" Jacy asked.

Truman smiled and stood. He slipped the camera into the tripod.

"Say cheese, Miss Jacy Charlane."

"Everybody says cheese. Can I say something different?"

"I don't know, sweetie. It says in the rule book everyone's supposed to say cheese. I don't want to get in trouble."

"No one will know but you and me."

Truman studied Jacy and tapped his chin. "I think you're too much to one side. Tilt your head just the tiniest bit, dear. No, more. Wait, too much. Let me help."

Truman walked over and tilted Jacy's head a few degrees. He leaned back and checked, then smoothed her hair, his fingers grazing her neck.

Jacy said, "I'm telling."

Truman felt his throat tighten. "What did you say, dear?" he rasped.

24

"I said I'm gonna tell everybody."

"Tell everybody . . . what?"

Jacy giggled. "That you're the best Picture Man ever. The old one was a sourpuss."

Truman closed his eyes and let out a deep breath. He looked out the door. No one there. He drew the door shut and jogged to his camera.

"That's a pretty dress, Jacy. Pull it up a teensy bit more and show those pretty knees. Maybe put your feet on the top rung."

"Isn't it just faces in the pictures?"

"It helps me focus. Do you always ask so many questions?" Truman zoomed the lens and snapped shots as he spoke.

"Aunt Nike says question everything. I live with her."

"A smart woman. And with an interesting name, too. Is she named after –"

"Everybody thinks she's named after shoes. She's named after a famous lady from a long time ago. Her name came from her papa, who drew pictures they make houses from. It means something like 'always a winner'."

"Too cool. Do you live with Aunt Nike in a house or an apartment? Wait. Don't move. These are practice shots."

"An apartment."

Truman said, "I don't know if I'd feel as safe in an apartment as a house. Are you ever alone there? Like at night?"

"Sometimes Aunt Nike has to be out. But she

built cages over the windows and has big locks on the door. A board to jam it shut, too."

"Good for her. What kind of work does Aunt Nike do?"

"She paints pictures when she feels good. Sometimes she's . . . sick and can't paint."

"I'm sorry to hear that. Does Aunt Nike work at home? That would be nice for you guys."

"When she works she's always at home. In the room with her paint stuff."

"My mama used to work at home. Sometimes I wanted to get off and be all alone. Do you like to be alone now and then, Jacy?"

"Sometimes I go to a special place."

Truman heard the squeak of sneakers and clickety-click of hard shoes, the next class walking down the hall.

"Tell me about your special place, Jacy. And straighten your skirt. Hurry."

"The little park at the end of my street. There's a bench in the shade and I like to read books there after school."

"A park bench in the afternoon? Cool."

The door opened to an ancient woman with a face like a prune, blue photography forms in her hand. She looked at Truman like he was a bug.

"Room 130," the woman snapped. "You're ready for us, right?"

Truman bent over his camera and turned on the flash. "One more shot. Here it comes, Miss Jacy. Say cheese."

"Pickle!"

Jacy giggled and winked at Truman before jumping from the stool and skipping away into the hall. Truman giggled as well, but deep inside himself, where the prune-faced bitch couldn't hear.

6

Returning from a food delivery to Charity's Hand Mission, the Gumbo King drove slowly through the streets, sipping a beer and watching people emerge from bars and apartments. Night was almost in charge, the western sky a pale and fading orange. Heat rose from the concrete with no breeze to move it away, the air syrupy thick. Though heat clung to his face like a mask, the Gumbo King drove with windows down, letting the sounds in and feeling the vibes from the street.

He stopped at a light and saw Nike Charlane walking the street a half-block distant, moving away. She stumbled on broken pavement, then passed two males holding liquor bottles cloaked in brown bags. One man squeezed his genitals and jerked his hips at her. The other man laughed. Nike passed by as if in another dimension.

The Gumbo King shook his head. He'd known Nike for years: she'd beat the dope for three or four months, then stumble hard for a couple weeks.

But even when consumed by the demons, she looked good – just like now, trim in her red velvet jacket and white blouse, long legs scissoring the black slacks. Though she was thirty-four, he admired how she'd kept the loose-limbed strut of a teenager.

Nike turned down a slender alley shortcutting to her street. The light changed and he started to drive. Something made him glance in the mirror. The two men moved toward the alley, glancing over their shoulders. The Gumbo King cut the wheels hard on his pickup and jabbed the accelerator, the truck reversing in the intersection. Horns blared.

The Gumbo King pulled up on the sidewalk, slid the short-barreled .32 from the ankle holster and crept down the littered alley. A yellow streetlamp flickered and he saw three people in a shadowed recess behind a building, Nike in a corner, the younger man tight against her while the older one scrabbled through her purse. Sandhill pulled the small pistol against his palm to hide it and moved soundlessly until a few steps away.

"Put the wallet back in the purse and the purse on the ground."

The men jerked around. Nike leaned against the building and he saw her blouse pushed up where the guy'd been pawing at her. The men waited for him to ID himself as a cop. When he didn't, the fear in their eyes turned to confusion, then to hard amusement.

"Get outta here, silly muthafucka," the younger of them said, eighteen maybe, tight cornrows coiling over his head, a gold tooth gleaming in his mouth. He wore knee-length shorts of some material resembling oiled silk, a white tee hanging down. The other man was taller, broader, and a decade older. He wore long, ballooning pants and a tight muscle shirt, and watched silently through dry, dead eyes.

The Gumbo King kept the weapon cupped and hidden. "Come on, Nike. I'll give you a ride home."

"You know this bitch?" Gold Tooth said. "Tell you what, cracker boy, you pass over fifty bucks and she all yours."

"Fifty bucks? For what?"

Gold Tooth leered and rubbed his crotch. "For getting her engine all warmed up for you."

"Fuck you," Nike slurred, trying to push away from the wall. The silent man inched closer to the Gumbo King.

"Yeah," the Gumbo King said. "I got to agree with the lady."

The smile fell from Gold Tooth's lips. "Now you disrespecting me."

The Gumbo King said, "You want my respect? Maybe. But first tell me what you've done to earn it."

Nike started laughing. "He's got you there, nigga."

Gold Tooth's eyes slitted like bunkers. "You a smart-ass muthafucka, ain't you," he hissed, starting to bob his shoulders, using motion as a distraction. The silent man crept still closer, finger-tips sliding into a pocket. The Gumbo King shifted his weight to his rear leg, measuring the distance to the silent man. He saw Gold Tooth's eyes flick and knew the pair had reached an agreement.

The second man's hand slid from the pocket to reveal a filleting knife. He fell into a crouch, his eyes alive now, electric. The Gumbo King debated revealing the pistol, kept it palmed, settling into his own crouch, weight on his rear leg. He pointed down the alley, past the knife wielder.

"Martians!" he bellowed.

The silent man's eyes couldn't help flicking that way. By the time they flicked back, the Gumbo King's boot was through the man's testicles and moving upward, slowing against cartilage. The knife skittered away as he crumbled to the pavement, clutching himself and grunting out small wet sounds.

Gold Tooth found himself staring into the Gumbo King's revolver. He lifted his hands and held them palms out, as if the Gumbo King were a nightmare he could push away.

"Wait, man . . ."

"Back up," the Gumbo King ordered.

"Oh shit, man; look, that was his play," Gold Tooth said, his voice a register higher, quivering. "I wasn't doing nothin'."

"Back up. Get out of the light." The Gumbo King lowered the revolver to chest height and jabbed the man backwards until his shoulder blades pressed the building.

"Don't hurt me, man. I'm sorry. I didn't mean nothin'."

Though against the wall, the man kept backpedaling, as though he could slip between the bricks. The Gumbo King raised the revolver until it pointed at the man's throat. "You were about to tell me why I should respect you."

"Oh man, that was jus' talk."

The Gumbo King thumbed back the hammer. "You don't understand. If I don't hear something in ten seconds, you're dead."

"Lord almighty, mister. Please don't shoot me."

"Hollow-points at this distance isn't shooting, it's spattering."

"Oh Jesus. No man, please. Oh please, Jesus."

"Prayer is a good idea, though perhaps ineffective. Eight seconds."

"Oh no, man. No."

"Tell me why should I respect you. Seven."

"I can't think. I can't think of nothing. Please . . ."

"A reason for respect. Six."

The man closed his eyes and shook his head. "I ain't done nothin' for respect, mister. I'm a fuck-up, man. A total fuck-up." Tears sluiced down the man's face.

The Gumbo King said, "Five seconds." His hand tightened around the taped grip.

"I'm not evil, mister. Just a fuck-up. I ain't lying.

Please, I don't want to die. My mama'd go crazy. I'm the only one she got left. She love me."

"Four seconds."

The Gumbo King sighted down the barrel. Nike Charlane looked at him as though awakening from a dream.

"Don't," she whispered. "Stop."

The Gumbo King said, "Two seconds."

The man squeezed his eyes shut, whimpering.

"Don't do this," Nike pleaded. "Please."

The Gumbo King paused and regarded the man curiously for a long moment.

"Did you mention something about your mama actually liking you?"

The man wailed and sank to his knees. "She love me and I don't know why."

The Gumbo King lowered to a crouch. "Luck is on your side today, partner; I'm letting you live. Not because I respect you, but because I respect your mother. Anyone loving you must have vast reserves of love and patience. But I need a promise from you . . . what is your name?"

"T-Tee-TeeShawn. TeeShawn Green."

The Gumbo King put his fingers under the man's chin and lifted his head until their eyes met. "I need, TeeShawn Green, for you to assure me you will perform a deed worthy of respect. Not my respect, but your mother's."

"I will. I pro-pro-promise."

"Do you understand why you'll do this, TeeShawn?"

"Yes – I mean, no. N-Nossir, not really."

"Because your mother's love saved your life tonight, TeeShawn. Do you understand that?"

The man's head bobbed. The Gumbo King uncocked the gun and released Green's chin. He tumbled forward, weeping, wiping snot and tears from his face with the back of his hand. Across the alley the groin-kicked man made the sound of air escaping from a wet valve. The Gumbo King sheathed the revolver and stood slowly, framed in streetlight.

"You were really gonna kill that boy?" Nike asked softly, clutching her jacket as if it had turned to winter in the alley. The Gumbo King retrieved the fallen knife, wedged its blade between the building and a drainpipe, and with one swift motion cracked the blade off at the grip.

"That the king can do no wrong is a necessary and fundamental principle of the English constitution," he said, as if pronouncing an edict. He smiled broadly and winked at Nike Charlane.

"Blackstone," he added.

7

Truman Desmond retrieved the external hard drive from beneath the wooden flooring of his photo studio. He retreated to his cramped office behind the studio's anteroom and plugged it into his computer.

The day's shoot had provided several possibilities for his collection, lilies fresh from the field. Added to selections from other schools, it made a bouquet of seven little American beauties.

Truman smiled approvingly as he transferred Jacy Charlane's photos to the drive. The low-angle shots first, then the mid-range ones as she studied the camera with thoughtful eyes. Next came the portrait photo, her smile wide and radiant.

Finally, he loaded sound effects. Viewers could, if they wished, study Desmond's offerings to a tinkly music-box version of "Thank Heaven for Little Girls".

Truman scooped a handful of Cheezos from the bag beside the computer, washing them down with a Mountain Dew. He studied the screen. The Charlane girl was a magnificent find, and he figured her portfolio would create quite a stir when piped to his roster of specialists.

For years, Truman had obtained his photos from playgrounds and public beaches and hanging at the mall with an up-angled camera hidden in a shopping bag. By trading and selling and doing custom work, he'd learned to identify a specific clientele: wealthy bulwarks of business and society who could never act on their desires. Truman had stumbled into the school-photographer job. His photography studio had been suffering the down economy, plus he'd had to back off on his secret business when the cops got heavy into net monitoring. Noting a solicitation for school-photography bids in the *Mobile Register*, he immediately saw the potential for combining his hidden business with a legitimate income. It had been a stroke of genius and would, correctly plotted and cautiously paced, make him a millionaire.

Footsteps at the door; Truman Desmond froze as the doorknob shook violently. He jabbed in panic at the keyboard. The computer locked up with Jacy Charlane on the screen.

The door banged open.

"Company's coming," called a laughing voice. "Zip up your pants."

Truman Desmond closed his eyes and his head slumped forward, his heart jackhammering his ribs.

36

The idiot simply wouldn't follow the procedure: three fast buzzes, pause, then a final long buzz.

Truman rolled his chair back to look through his doorway. His brother Roosevelt stood in the anteroom riffling through the day's mail, a carob-coated nutrition bar clenched in his teeth like a cigar.

"You didn't use the code, Rose!" Truman railed.

Rose grunted at bills and flyers. "Anyone can buzz like that. I'm the only one with my voice."

"We've got to be careful, you outsized idiot. It's not a game."

Rose scowled and looked up. When his eyes saw the image on the computer screen, he threw the mail over his shoulder.

"Hey man, who's that?"

Truman was hunched over the keyboard, trying to shut off the screen when Rose's sausage-thick fingers surrounded his hand.

"Leggo, Rose," he whined.

"C'mon Tru, who's the chickie? Move over, goddammit. Lemme see."

"Come on, Rose. I got work to do."

"Move the hell out of the way, Truman."

Truman cursed and rolled back. If Roosevelt wanted him out of the way he'd simply pick him up and move him, the advantage of spending twelve of twenty-four years lifting weights.

"Hurry up and look," Truman pouted. "Then find something to do."

Rose Desmond put his face to the screen. "What's baby's name?"

37

"Lorelei."

Rose said, "Not her made-up name, asshole. Her real name."

"How do you know it's not her real name?"

"Vitriana. Kittinia. Lorelei. Every name you make up for the website sounds like a fucking Caribbean island. You're so predictable, Tru. Now, what's pretty baby's name?"

"Jacy. Come on, Rose, I've got to get done and get the drive stashed. Somebody's got to do the work around here."

Rose turned from the screen, the veins in his neck visibly pulsing. "Don't you give me that shit like I don't do anything. You're not around them every day. Taking them food. Smelling their smells. Sometimes I wish I could –"

"They're product, Rose," Truman snapped. "No interaction. We've discussed it. As soon as we're done we'll get away, have some fun. Hell, between Vitriana and Kittinia and Nalique –"

"Darla, Maya and LaShelle. Use real names so I can follow."

"No matter what you call them we have a shit-load of money, Rose. With lots more to come."

Rose snorted and pulled another power bar from his pocket, tore an end from the silver package and let it fall to the floor. He balled the remaining package and flicked it into the trash drum across the room, whispering "two points" when it dropped.

Truman said, "This will all be over soon, Rose. We'll get away for a while, anywhere we want."

"When?"

"The buyer's picking up Kittinia – Maya, to you – at the farmhouse in a couple weeks. The buyer and I are negotiating the delivery schedule for LaShelle. How about letting me get back to work?"

Rose Desmond spun his brother back to the computer and stalked away. Truman finished the website work and returned the hard drive to its hidey-hole beneath the floorboards. He found Rose sitting in the studio and reading *Pex*, a magazine devoted to pectoral muscles.

"You leaving soon?" Truman asked.

Rose didn't look up. "Finish this article and I'm a goner."

"You gonna check the product tonight, Rose?"

"Yeah. Go too long without emptying the crapper and it gets rank down there."

Tru walked to his brother and kissed him on the mouth. Practice-kissing, they called it, and it wasn't faggy because they didn't use tongues. Tru straightened and said, "We'll get business over with and find something just for us, brother. A celebration."

The door closed and Rose heard the locks slide into place. He gave Truman ten minutes before he pulled the drive from the floorboards. He wanted to see the new girl again.

The girl was rigid with fear as Rose climbed the storm-shelter rungs with her over his shoulder. "I like you a lot, Jacy," he said, lifting her outside the hatch, clutching her hand as he followed. The night was cloudless and steamy, the stars smudged with haze. "I'm going to teach you to dance. You like to dance?"

"My name's not Jacy," the girl said, quivering, eyes wet with tears. "It's LaShelle. Why did you take me from my house? Why am I in that place down there?"

"You're very pretty, LaShelle. You have nice eyes."

"Please, mister. I want my mama. I want to go home. Please don't hurt me."

"I've got music inside." Rose swiveled his hips, snapped his fingers and smiled. "I'll teach you to dance. It's good exercise."

"Please, mister. I don't want to learn no dancing." Tears ran down her cheeks.

Rose guided LaShelle Shearing into the house. He shut the door and slid the deadbolts.

It was ten p.m. when Ryder stopped at the morgue. He knew Clair Peltier would be working late, trying to make a dent in her paperwork. The guard buzzed him through the building's main entrance, gilt writing on the door proclaiming Dr Clair Peltier as Chief Medical Examiner, Alabama Bureau of Forensics, Mobile Branch. He waved to the guard and stepped lightly down the hall to Dr Peltier's office, hoping to catch her by surprise.

She was at her desk, eyes down, reading glasses poised on her delicate nose as she penned notes on a stack of forms. Her shoulder-length hair was as black as wet coal. Ryder studied the ubiquitous vase on the desk, overflowing with bright flowers from her garden. The floral scents turned the air into a sweet oasis amidst the astringent morgue smells.

"Don't be thinking you're sly, Ryder," Peltier said without looking up. "I heard your footsteps all the way down the hall, tiptoe or not."

"You're a difficult woman to sneak up on, Doctor," Ryder said. "But then, you're a difficult woman, period."

Clair Peltier looked up from her writing. "I'm not sure I should be alone with you, Ryder. Is anyone near?"

Ryder leaned out the door and looked up and down the hall: empty. "The closest person is the guard. He's half-napping in the foyer."

When Ryder turned back, Clair Peltier was in front of him. Their lips met, brief and chaste and, for a shadow of a moment, something more. Over the years their relationship started acidic, sweetened into a year as lovers, finally reaching today's point, an understanding each would always be there for the other, occasionally physically, always emotionally.

Ryder stepped back and looked into the blue eyes that struck lightning into his soul.

"You're really leaving, Clair?"

"I have to go. You know that."

"Doesn't mean I have to believe it."

Peltier brushed an errant lock of dark hair from

41

Ryder's forehead. "Come with me then, Carson. You'll believe it when we're sitting on the lanai and watching the waves. I know you could use the vacation. Come on, accompany a girl to a symposium in Hawaii."

"I can't leave. My cases will fall down the same rat hole as everything else."

"Departmental politics are still that ugly?"

"It's like Squill dropped the MPD into a blender. Everything's torn apart, mixed up."

Peltier shook her head. "It seemed to happen overnight."

"The king changed and his pawns own the board. Squill's in control, I'm at his mercy."

Clair Peltier stepped back and leaned against her desk, arms crossed. "I know you hate to talk about the situation, Carson, so I try not to ask too much. But can you give me a few more details about how Squill got back in charge after three years? Demoted from Investigative to Public Relations after screwing up the case here in the morgue, right? I thought he was finished as a player."

Ryder stepped to the door and took another check of the hall, no such thing as being too careful when discussing Squill. The bastard's sycophantic spies were everywhere. He turned back to Peltier, his voice quieter.

"Putting Squill in charge of PR gave him the two things a political monster covets: access and information. You saw how he turned it into a position in Internal Affairs, which gave him even more access and information. The heavy-duty kind. Rumor and innuendo, half-truths and half-lies, not necessarily the same thing. He's used his years in IA to quietly elevate those on his side, kneecap those in his way."

"Like former Chief Plackett?"

"When Plackett sent off his résumé for that chief's position in Tampa – a feeler, like people do every day – Squill found out, then used his public-relations links to make it seem Plackett had accepted the job. Squill burned Plackett's bridges for him, and before the poor naïve idiot knew it, he was history. Pity the job in Tampa never came through."

Clair Peltier shook her head. "Is everyone in the department unhappy?"

"If Squill likes you – meaning you're one of his yes-men robots – you've got it made. If he's doesn't like you, you're screwed."

"You and Harry never got along with Squill, right? You have a bad history there?"

"He hates me," Ryder said. "Given all that's happened in the last few weeks, maybe I should start looking for another job."

"Don't, Carson. No. It scares me when you talk like that."

"I've got to be realistic, Clair."

"Things change. People, events, police depart-ments. Just keep pushing ahead. I'll only be gone for a couple of weeks. Hold on, for now at least.

We can talk about it more when I get back, right?"

Ryder leaned back and studied the ceiling, like some form of answer was painted there.

"Carson?" Peltier prompted.

He nodded. "No decisions until you get back."

They started to embrace, but broke off at the sound of approaching footsteps; the guard on his rounds. Peltier blew Ryder a kiss through lips bright as roses. Ryder left, buoyed by a few minutes in his girlfriend's presence.

But a minute later, crossing the night-dark parking lot and waving mosquitoes from his face, the buoyancy was replaced by a strange, breath-stealing feeling in his gut, as if something venomous was paralleling his path, operating just past the edge of his vision.

8

Truman said, "She's gone, you dumb fuck."

Rose stared up at the ceiling. He was lying on the floor in the same semi-fetal position Truman had found him, ten minutes after the midnight phone call.

"Tru? Could you come over here? I think something's wrong."

"You touched one, didn't you? DIDN'T YOU?"

"I was teaching her to dance, Tru. That's all. She started yelling out the window. I put my hand over her mouth. Maybe I squeezed too much . . ."

"Out the window? You took her out of the shelter?"

"She stopped yelling, but she got real still. I wasn't doing anything nasty, Tru. I swear."

Truman looked toward the sheet-covered form on the carpeted floor. He'd seen enough crime dramas to know the rug would be covered with the girl's hair and fingernails and spit and god-knows-what other stuff the cops could find.

"We've got to get rid of her. Now. The rug too."

"I'll do it, Tru. I know exactly how."

"There can't be any traces of us. You know what I mean?"

"I know a condemned house not too far away. It's like kindling."

"Jesus, Rose. LaShelle was going to the guy that bought Darla last year. I'm working on a repeat-business concept here."

"I'll take care of everything. I promise."

"You just goddamn better. We have obligations. We're businessmen."

Truman went to sit on the dark back porch. Seconds later he heard a ripping sound as Rose yanked carpet from the bedroom floor.

Ryder watched Mayor Norma Philips enter the briefing room, silencing it suddenly and completely. Stormin' Norma, she was often called, with other printable appellations ranging from tree hugger to naïf to bull in a china shop. The unprintables were more extensive. A councilwoman and former community organizer, Philips had improbably – and to everyone's utter astonishment including her own – somersaulted Mobile's established political network to become interim mayor some months before.

A tall and loose-limbed brunette in her mid-forties, Philips had the strength of features proponents called handsome and detractors labeled horsy. She wore simple, inexpensive suits and eschewed any form of ornamentation save for a thirty-dollar Timex currently on its third band.

Ryder found her abrasive, impolitic, and incapable of crossing a room without stepping on every toe there. He also felt she could be a first-rate mayor if she somehow survived the upcoming election.

It was a measure of either her naïveté or bullheadedness that she stood before them now, Ryder thought, watching the sullen discomfort of Squill. A politically attuned mayor would have dealt with Squill alone, but the grassroots-trained Philips felt the way to get anything done started with soldiers, not generals. She nodded to Bidwell, who stood uneasily beside Squill.

Fit looking, if on the portly side, with jowls beginning to measure gravity, the fifty-four-year-old Bidwell had risen through the ranks on a tripoded ladder of caution, committed noncommittal, and a sincere, media-friendly visage. Ryder suspected Squill had summoned Bidwell because his uniformed presence would add a policely look amidst all the plainclothes.

"This is everyone working the investigations, *Acting* Chief?" Philips asked, studying a dozen sitting detectives. Ryder was in the third of four rows. No one sat in the front row but Duckworth, who chewed a toothpick and smirked at the mayor when her back was turned.

"Everyone associated with the abductions, like you asked, Mayor," Squill said. "They've all been briefed on the body in the fire. It could be a coincidence. We're still not sure if –"

"Three missing girls between eight and twelve years old? Black? A body found in a fire in a condemned house not –" she looked at her watch – four hours ago? A blaze the Fire Marshall calls blatant arson? Now the ME's telling me it's the body of an African-American female seven to ten years old? What's your definition of 'coincidence,' *Acting* Chief?"

Ryder saw Squill flinch each time the mayor punched the word *acting*. No one in the department dared use any title other than the unmodified *Chief*.

She said, "The black community's going to get hot when it's out that the girl's dead. They think the lack of information means you're not doing jackshit. Got any leads you're not telling the media about, stuff you're holding?"

"No, Mayor." Squill looked like he was chewing shingles. Philips threw a mournful glance over the assembled cops, a vegan scanning the buffet at a roadkill restaurant.

"Anyone else besides Homicide and Missing Persons have usable experience? Anyone in Vice?"

Squill shook his head. "We're using Vice for leads on peds and molesters. Nothing there yet."

Philips sighed heavily. "OK, how about former detectives? Retireds? Any experienced eyes out there could come take a look?"

"A couple we could ask, Mayor," Squill said,

barely controlling his fury at being questioned about his handling of the cases. "Braden, DeWitt. I'll give them a call."

Bidwell cleared his throat. "Excuse me, Chief, but Braden's in Hawaii and DeWitt's so crippled up with emphysema he can barely stand. We got a guy on sick leave, but his doctor barred him from working."

Philips turned her back to Squill and faced the men in the room. "Anyone here have an idea? A little electricity in the gray matter?"

The room was as silent as the bottom of the sea. Everyone looked at someone else. Philips scanned each face in turn.

"Come on, boys. Don't be shy. Speak up."

Ryder watched Zemain's hand lift and return to the desktop three times before his fingertips scratched the air. "Excuse me, Mayor?"

"What is it, Sergeant Zemain?"

Zemain cleared his throat. Ryder saw sweat on the back of his neck.

"Uh, we had one guy who might be a consideration . . . This guy, he, uh, came at cases his own way, sort of out of the box . . ."

Squill narrowed his eyes at the stuttering Zemain.

"The guy got almost weird about cases, Mayor . . . real tightly focused; obsessive, some people said, working days without sleeping. Living at the department. Kept a cot in the basement . . ."

"Oh, for chrissakes, Zemain," Squill spat.

49

"I know what you're thinking. No way. No stinking way."

"Will you let me conduct my own meeting, Acting Chief?" Philips said. "Go on, Sergeant."

"All of a sudden he'd get this look and you knew he had it figured –"

"You're trying to get Sandhill in here, aren't you, Zemain?" Squill snarled. "You're pimping for *Sandhill*."

"He had the highest case-clearance rate three years running."

Bidwell frowned. "You sure, Roland? I thought it was four." He winced when he realized he'd made a contribution.

"Sandhill's been gone for years." Squill looked ready to vault the front row of chairs for Zemain's throat. "Out of here. Good-damned-riddance." Squill turned to Philips. "Mayor, Sandhill's not anyone you'd want to have messing in this case. Trust me on this."

"This Sandhill, he still around here?" Philips asked.

Squill shook his head in disgust. "It's not an option, Mayor. Sandhill's not a cop any more – he's a goddamn fry cook."

"He's not a fry cook, Chief," Zemain corrected. "He's the Gumbo King."

9

The head was wrapped in white from crown to above the eyebrows, resembling a mummy in progress. An IV-tubed hand emerged from beneath a thin blanket, reached to the head, and pushed at the heavy swathing. The hand clenched in frustration, then opened toward Ryder, fingers flicking the *gimme* motion.

"Hand me that fork, Carson."

"I just see a spoon."

"Gimme that, then."

Ryder slapped a teaspoon into the outstretched palm as if he were handing a surgeon a scalpel. The hand jammed the spoon beneath the edge of the bandages and stirred from side to side.

"Oh lawd, the motion is the potion. Nothing worse than an itch you can't scratch."

Harry Nautilus handed the spoon back to Ryder. "I'll be damn glad when they unwrap this cock-eyed turban." His voice was a thin rasp. "It's hair growing back that causes the damn itching."

"How long you gonna be gone, brother?" Ryder asked.

Nautilus rolled his eyes. "Answer's the same as last time, Carson. The docs got me barred from any sort of duty for at least two more months."

The room smelled of inactivity and disinfectant. There were various medications on the bedside table. Nautilus wore scarlet pajamas with outsize paisley swirls. Three months ago, before the attack, he weighed two hundred and forty pounds. He was now a hundred and ninety, the bones of his square face sharp and prominent. Even the brushy hyphen of his mustache looked emaciated.

"How about your memory, Harry? Anything new there?"

Nautilus held his hands in the air, balling them into fists and flicking them open. He repeated the action several times.

"Are you supposed to exercise your hands?" Ryder asked, perplexed. "Does it help something?"

"I'm counting all the times you asked that question. If I remember anything, you'll damn well be the first to hear."

Ryder knew his partner was angry at more than the memory loss. It rankled to have been blindsided. Nautilus had been walking in his neighborhood at ten at night when someone had crept up from behind and slammed his head with a pipe or other blunt instrument. His wallet had been taken, along with his watch. Only a dog walker coming by minutes later prevented Harry Nautilus from succumbing to a hemorrhage in his brain. He remembered nothing of the incident. It was black coated with black and buried in a pile of shadows.

"Try, Harry."

"There's nothing else there yet, Carson," Nautilus rumbled. "I remember going out for a walk. The next thing I remember is waking up with half a hospital hooked to me, plus your ugly face beside the bed."

Nautilus's aunt, Sophie Hopewright, bustled through the door. Fifty-eight and more administrator than nurse these days, she managed a hospital's nurse-training program. But the moment she'd heard of her nephew's injury, she'd turned a room in her home into a convalescent center, overseeing Nautilus's recovery with the demeanor of a dyspeptic drill sergeant. Ryder thought of her as Attila the Nurse.

"Move your skinny butt to the side, Ryder," she commanded, brandishing a thermometer in his face. He retreated to a corner and watched the tall woman with short, steel-gray hair dispatch her tasks.

"Don't you tire him out," she admonished, a scowl promising dire retribution if he disobeyed.

"Fifteen minutes, max, Soph," Ryder pledged, hand in the air.

"Five," she said, no room for a counter-offer. Ryder hugged the wall to keep from getting sucked into the woman's slipstream as she thundered from the room. He edged back to bedside.

53

"Months until you come back to the department, Harry? What if you do real good, ace all your tests or whatever? Could you come back sooner?"

Nautilus sighed. "We can talk about that later. Fill me in on the latest at work."

"You saw the news about this morning's fire, the young girl's body?"

"I figured it was your vic."

"The black community thinks we're sitting on our thumbs. There's nothing to go on so far. Forensics is combing the ashes, but . . ."

"Something'll break, Carson. Most of Investigative's working the case, right?"

"There's no focus, just Squill's endless run-in-circles meetings."

Nautilus nodded. "With Squill giving orders but keeping a delegator's distance, I'll bet."

"Squill's letting Duckworth make command decisions," Ryder moaned. "It's insane."

"It's completely logical," Nautilus corrected. "Duckworth's as driven and amoral as Squill, but content to whisper in Caesar's ear, not be Caesar."

Ryder paused. "All this time, before you're allowed back . . ." His voice rose with hope. "You're sure that's set in stone?"

Nautilus didn't seem to hear. He reached for a plastic cup of melting ice, sipped noisily through a bent straw, set the cup down.

"Hey, Carson, you ever dig into that stack of cold cases Tom laid on my desk a few days before I got jumped?"

Changing the subject, Ryder noted. It was hardly likely Harry had given the cases a moment's thought. The unit's overseer, Lieutenant Tom Mason, routinely handed out unsolved cases to the detective teams, hoping fresh eyes might find something.

"Are you kidding, Harry? When you got bonked, I sent the cases back to Property. I never had the time to even open the files."

Ryder looked out the window. The Fairhope water tower loomed in the dark sky, feeding water to the town like a floating metal heart. Ryder watched red lights pulse on the tower before turning back to his partner.

"A strange thing happened at a meeting today, Harry. Mayor Philips came by. She wanted to know if there were any retired or inactive dicks that might help work the cases, shed some light."

Nautilus nodded. "She's got to be feeling heat, especially from the black community. Nothing strange about that."

"Here's where the weird comes in. Zemain mentioned Conner Sandhill. I vaguely remember him, big guy, kept to himself. He left the force a little after I made detective. Odd guy, from what little I recall. No one seemed to talk about Sandhill after that. You never have."

Nautilus grunted.

"What?" Ryder asked.

"Nothing. Keep going."

"I remember Sandhill working sex crimes and

cold cases. Then he just disappeared. When Zemain floated Sandhill's name, Squill sank it with cannon fire. I hear he runs that restaurant on Parlor Street. The one you never want to go to, right?"

Nautilus looked away to refill his drinking glass. "I got other places I like better."

"What happened with Sandhill, Harry?"

"I don't like talking from rumors. Things get scrambled."

"What kind of ru—"

Sophie stampeded through the door, tapping her watch crystal with a fingernail. "That's it. Time's up, Ryder. You take your ten o'clock meds, Harry?"

"Uh . . ."

"I knew it. Get them pills in your mouth before I do. You keep forgetting and I'll have the pharmacist mix 'em in suppository form. Then I'm gonna buy me a hammer. Get my drift, Harry Nautilus?"

Ryder winced and tiptoed from the room.

Heading back across the bay, Ryder was troubled that his partner didn't want to discuss when he'd return to work, immediately changing the subject. The avoidance was puzzling. He was on the causeway when a thought hit him so hard it kicked the breath from his lungs and he had to pull off the road.

Heart pounding in his chest, Ryder did the math . . .

Harry was forty-six years old. He joined the force when he was twenty-two. Twenty-four years

56

in, and the sick time kicked it right up to a full-pension twenty-five.

Harry Nautilus didn't need to come back. He could retire with full benefits if he wished.

Ryder closed his eyes and listened to breaking waves until his lost breath returned. He drove home slowly, crossing the bridge to Dauphin Island near midnight. Entering his stilt-standing beachfront home, he noted a single call on his answering machine, the screen blinking the number of Harry's cellphone.

Ryder stood in the dark and punched play. The voice of Harry Nautilus filled the room.

"Carson, no one would be better for taking a look at the abduction cases than Sandhill . . ."

A long empty hiss followed, like his partner had something he needed to add. Ryder pictured Harry Nautilus in his bed, phone in hand, frowning, trying to give Ryder some form of explanation, or enlightenment. Anything beyond sixteen words.

Nothing seemed to come. Nautilus hung up.

10

At ten a.m. Sandhill finished wiping the last letter of his neon sign, the G in king. He tucked the rag in the back pocket of his jeans and debated turning the sign on. Though the restaurant was an hour from opening, Sandhill loved the sizzle and crackle as his sign flickered into life.

After Hurricane Katrina destroyed the New Orleans restaurant where he'd been the head chef, Sandhill tried a couple other places as an assistant, didn't like perverting his craft – *powdered garlic? Factory-made andouille? Blasphemy!* – and a year back had returned to Mobile, toying with the thought of opening his own restaurant. Ninety-nine per cent of him dismissed the idea as pure lunacy. One morning, however, while the rational ninety-nine per cent was still in bed, a subversive one per cent smuggled him to the sign shop to put a hefty down payment on the creation of a neon-red THE GUMBO KING, a bright yellow crown flashing at a rakish angle above the cursive letters.

Thus invested in a magnificent work of signage, he'd felt logically compelled to follow through, and eleven weeks later the doors of the restaurant opened.

Sandhill heard a knock at the locked door. He opened it, ready to recite the hours, when Nike Charlane walked wordlessly past, swung a crocheted purse the size of a grocery bag on to the nearest table, and sat. She wore impenetrably dark sunglasses, a blue ball cap, and a white tee with the logo of the Mobile Art Museum and Exploreum. Paint-speckled canvas pants fell to outsized flip-flops. Sandhill sat and stared into the void of her Ray-Bans.

Nike took a deep breath. "Listen, Conner, about the other night in the alley, I wanted to say –"

"Wait," Sandhill said. He reached across the table and gently removed Nike's sunglasses. Her outsized eyes were laced with red.

"Aha, there you are."

She blinked. "I wanted to say thanks for the other night."

"It was no problem."

"Uh, Conner, I'm a little fuzzy on details, but you had a gun to that boy's head. You wouldn't have –"

"An act. At least with that damned misaligned kid. I would have enjoyed shooting the other one."

"I was afraid you were going to when he pulled the knife."

"If the kick had missed, it was my next choice. I preferred avoiding that route, thus avoiding unnecessary contact with the constabulary.

There's some of them don't love me, strange as it seems."

Nike shook her head. "I shouldn't have gone down the alley."

"You weren't thinking straight."

"I'm better now."

"For how long?"

She started to speak, then stood and swept her purse from the table. "Thanks again. I have to go."

"Stay for coffee."

"I don't need lectures, Conner."

"Bad things are happening, Nike. You've got to keep that little girl safe. Jacy's not safe when you're on a binge."

She stared through him. But, at the corners of her eyes, he saw fear.

"You're making more out of it than it is, Conner. Most of the time I'm fine."

"That's denial. Most of the time won't cut it. Try all of the time."

Nike feigned a look at her watch. "Aren't you late for your self-righteousness class? I'd hate for them to start without you; they'd miss so much." She slung the purse over her shoulder and started away.

"Nike."

She closed her eyes, sucked in a breath and turned. "I've got things to do, Conner. What is it?"

"How's your painting going?"

The anger in her face softened. "It's . . . good. Thanks for asking."

Sandhill smiled. "That's great to hear. How about the next time you go off on a toot you paint a target on Jacy's back? Maybe a few words under it, something like, 'Come and get me.'"

Nike's eyes widened until there seemed no more face for them, and she walked away on legs as stiff as posts.

Ryder was at his desk, rethinking his time with Harry Nautilus and wondering if anything else could go wrong in his life. The phone rang. It was Commander Ainsley Duckworth, Squill's majordomo.

"Hey, Ryder, the chief needs to see you."

Acting chief, Ryder thought, hearing Mayor Philips in his head. "What's he want, Ducks?"

"The name's Duckworth, Ryder. *Commander* Duckworth to you. Here's your first command of the day: How about you hustle your worthless ass over here, pronto. The chief's got a chore for you."

11

Ryder drove by the restaurant three times before parking, like if he kept circling the block, the restaurant might disappear. When it didn't, he parked in front of a neon window sign screaming THE GUMBO KING.

He stood on the sidewalk, lifted his sunglasses, and studied the neighborhood. A half mile from the heart of the city, it was working class, more black than white, sixty–forty maybe. This particular block was zoned for business: restaurant, dry cleaner, beauty parlor, a storefront grocery with a table of fresh fruit and vegetables displayed outside the door. A small park occupied half of the next block, green space reclaimed after a warehouse had burned to the ground. It had been then-councilwoman Norma Philips who'd spearheaded the project, Ryder recalled.

He dropped the shades in his pocket, turned to the restaurant, and went inside.

Ryder was surprised at how neat the place was, light and airy, with glittering strands of Mardi Gras beads strung from pine walls polished to a buttery glow. Here and there hung festival masks either frightening or comical. The air was perfumed with thyme and garlic and cayenne. Clifton Chenier played the "Zydeco Cha Cha" over the sound system. There were no customers, but it was just past eleven a.m., the place open maybe five minutes.

Before he'd even pulled out his chair, a big-bosomed black woman with an electric smile banged through the doors from the kitchen, a pot of coffee in one hand, white ceramic mug in the other.

"You look like a man needin' caffeine," she said, filling the mug and setting it on the table.

"Actually, I need to see Conner Sandhill."

The woman's smile flattened into tight-eyed scrutiny. Her toe tapped the floor.

"You're a cop, right?"

"I've been getting conflicting opinions. But I think so."

The waitress returned to the kitchen. Ryder heard a female whisper followed by a deep male groan. Sandhill arrived a minute later. He was a big, barrel-chested guy wearing a felt crown and a vest fronted with purple sequins. Sequins were missing and the blank areas had been filled in with purple dots of paint. Sandhill sat – nimbly for such a moose, Ryder noted, feeling Sandhill give him the once-over with large eyes, his bushy mustache twitching as if he were checking Ryder's scent.

"I remember seeing you a time or two, Ryder. Years ago. You go after the psychos these days, right? Is that why you're here? Has someone reported me as psychotic?"

"I was ordered here by the acting chief of police, Mr Sandhill. He wanted me to talk to you."

Sandhill slammed his fist on the table.

"CORNBREAD!"

The waitress pushed through the kitchen doors seconds later. She slid a plate on to the table, four steaming squares of cornbread, butter and honey to the side.

"I'm not hungry," Ryder said, not wanting to break bread with the guy.

"I'd advise it," Sandhill said. "Stress has put you off your feed lately, right, Detective? People getting on you about losing weight?"

Ryder stared, nonplussed. A half dozen people, Nautilus included, had asked if he was on a diet. Just yesterday Clair Peltier had given him her third Your-Body-Needs-Sleep-and-Fuel lecture in two weeks.

"Uh, how did you know that?"

Sandhill nodded at Ryder's waist. "Your belt's buckled to a new hole. More tongue's showing on the far side."

Ryder had pulled the belt two notches tighter the preceding week. He looked down and saw the old indentation in the leather from years in the same position. The leather beside the current hole was unmarred. One glance and Sandhill had scoped it out and added it up.

Jesus, Ryder thought.

"Eat," Sandhill said.

Driven by the glorious aroma, Ryder couldn't help himself, wolfing down two pieces of the yellow manna.

"Now that you've had a bit of a repast," Sandhill said, buttering his own piece of cornbread, "might I ask what the ever-talented Terrence Squill wants of me?"

"We've got a problem, Mr Sandhill." Ryder dabbed crumbs from his mouth with a napkin. "The missing girls. Nothing's coming together. We need fresh eyes. Plus we found one of the abducted girls, LaShelle Shearing. Dead."

"The body in the fire." Sandhill nodded. "You guys aren't doing real good, PR-wise."

"A girl abducted a year ago, then two girls taken in under two weeks. No evidence, nothing. No one's seen anything, heard anything."

Sandhill pushed the platter to Ryder. One square of cornbread left. Ryder grabbed it.

"Who's leading the investigations?" Sandhill asked.

"I did at first, by default. Like you noted, I'm a member of the PSIT, which stands for –"

"The Psychopathological and Sociopathological Investigative Team," Sandhill completed, staring Ryder in the eye. "You and Harry Nautilus. For two guys, you've had big results. The morgue killer, the serial-killer-memorabilia freaks, the family of millionaire psychos that weirdness in New York, that preacher case . . . I'd think you'd be a natural on the abduction, Ryder. You've got an interesting history with psychopaths."

Maybe because my brother's crazy, Ryder

considered saying. *A man accused of killing five women.* Or perhaps because I grew up in a house where any wrong word or glance or sound could turn my father from a respected engineer into a violent, raging whirlwind of hate. My brother Jeremy killed my father, was institutionalized for years, escaping months ago, slipping from my hands in New York. I watched my mother die a horrific death, refusing medicine, hoping her pain purchased her way into a Heaven she feared she'd lost by not better protecting my brother and me. I dropped a Masters in psychology to become a cop . . . after years of studying the worst psychopaths and sociopaths in the penal system.

How about that for history, Sandhill?

Instead, Ryder sighed and shook his head. "Squill doesn't care about experience, just payback. He installed Meyers as lead, supposedly. But Meyers is run by Duckworth, who happens to be –"

"A wholly owned subsidiary of Squill," Sandhill said. "Nothing changes, does it? Who had the great fucking idea of putting Squill into Internal Affairs, giving him a springboard back into the action? Probably that dolt, Bidwell. Now Bidwell's taking orders from Squill. It's ironic, but what Bidwell deserves, of course."

Ryder found it interesting that a guy gone from the department for several years was so well informed.

"I've got a favor to ask, Mr Sandhill."

Sandhill held the plate to the side of the table and brushed crumbs on to it with the side of his hand.

"My answer is no."

"Just see if anyone missed anything. Stop by the department and take a look."

"The department and I don't get along."

Ryder sighed. "I don't care about your past, Sandhill. We're in trouble here."

"The department has shit on its shoes. I'm fine. And you're either lying or misled; no way Squill wants me within a thousand miles of the MPD."

"The mayor ordered Squill to contact you."

"Bullshit, Ryder. The woman doesn't know me from Adam's poodle."

"She asked Squill about former cops who might help. Zemain ran your name up the flagpole, but others kept it flying. Even Bidwell, for crying out loud."

Sandhill crossed his arms on the table, leaned forward. "So if our new little lady mayor wants me, and Squill is required to act on the request, how is it, Detective Ryder, that you got the dirty job of asking?"

Ryder felt his jaw clench. "Squill's hated me for years. If I don't convince you to give the department a few hours to mollify the mayor, Squill will spin it to look like I failed, not him."

Sandhill leaned back in his chair. He slipped the crown from his head, dusted it with his palm, returned it to his head.

"You've got to understand, Detective, I'm gone from the game; I've got a new life now. I like it."

"What you're saying is, no way?"

"What I'm saying is, if MPD wants my services on a consultation basis, it might be arranged."

"You mean you'll charge."

Sandhill winked. "Nothing gets by you, Detective Ryder. You're a pro."

"What sort of, uh, payment you thinking about, Sandhill?"

The Gumbo King pursed his lips, eyes flicking horizontally as if balancing weights on a scale.

"An official apology, both verbal and written; reinstatement of my pension vestment with accrued interest . . ."

"Come on, Sandhill, they'll never –"

"And two hundred bucks an hour for my consultation time."

"You're crazy."

The Gumbo King crossed his arms high on his chest.

"So have I spoken, so let it be writ."

Ryder stood and walked to the door without looking back, wondering what Squill's next move would be. *Shooting the messenger?* He stepped outside and headed to the departmental Crown Victoria.

"Ryder!" Sandhill bellowed.

Ryder turned to see the restaurateur filling the open doorway, his face expressionless beneath the crown.

"Harry Nautilus," Sandhill said. "How's he doing?"

"He's struggling and it'll take a while. But he's on the upswing."

The door closed without comment.

12

The first official visitor Sandhill saw was the fire inspector, Gillard; a *spontaneous incendiary inspection*, Gillard termed the visit, the first Sandhill had heard of the term. Though Gillard had been through twice before and found wires, conduits, oven placement, ventilation and fire extinguishers all in checkmark order, something had changed.

"Out of compliance in these areas –" Gillard snapped a sheet from a carbon-insert form and presented it to Sandhill. "The place is a three-alarmer waiting to happen."

"How long to comply?" Sandhill asked.

"One week."

"Then?"

Gillard tapped the door as he left, enjoying himself. "We nail this fucker shut."

Sandhill stared at the closed door, thinking, *Here it comes . . .*

The second visitor was Wentz from the Health Department, who took an hour to scratch up three violations. Sandhill listened calmly as the inspector, a fortyish guy with a whiskey nose, recited arcane statutes, some of them on the books for over a century. Sandhill knew the only restaurant in the city that could pass all codes would be a place that blossomed afresh nightly, a new and perfect restaurant every sunrise.

The inspection ended on a discordant note, Sandhill's patience wearing out when Wentz made a reference to cockroaches. Sandhill grabbed Wentz by the shirtfront and held the inspector's nose an inch from the heat-shimmering oven door, threatening to roast the man's face.

"I just do what I'm told," Wentz howled, eyes closed against the heat, urine dribbling down his leg and across the floor, probably another code violation.

Two days after his first meeting with Sandhill, Ryder pushed through the door a second time. He'd called earlier, requested a meeting. Sandhill had grunted something vaguely like assent and hung up.

Sandhill sat at the table below the sign, shuffling through mail, not acknowledging his visitor. Ryder pulled out a chair, watching Sandhill arrange the mail in precise stacks. The tallest stack was bills. Ryder figured running a small restaurant was like walking a tightrope.

"They're putting heat on me, Ryder," Sandhill said without looking up. "Sending inspectors. You didn't have anything to do with this, I hope."

Ryder felt a flush of anger. "Did you expect anything else from Squill? He's desperate. The mayor keeps asking if he's gotten you to come in."

"What a pair, an interim mayor and an acting chief of police. Must be like working in a madhouse."

"Actually, Sandhill, I think the mayor's pretty good."

Sandhill rolled his eyes. Ryder said, "Take a look at things, Sandhill. Read the reports. That's all. Jesus, the guy from the Health Department says you tried to jam his face into an oven."

"Only because my deep-fryer wasn't on."

"He could have filed a complaint, had you arrested."

Sandhill snorted. "Wentz has been dirty from payoffs for years. He'd overlook botulism for a roll of nickels. He won't do anything to call attention to himself. Besides, he's just an automaton."

Ryder pulled a photo from his pocket and slid it across the table, picture side down. Sandhill looked from the white square to Ryder.

"What's that?"

"Turn it over."

Sandhill picked up the photo, winced. "Don't do this to me, Ryder. Don't you fucking dare."

Ryder scraped his chair forward and put his elbows on the table. "Maya Ledbetter, disappeared two weeks ago while walking to her grandmother's."

Sandhill jumped up and began pacing like an angry lion in a tight cage.

"I am not a cop any more. Check the sign on the window: The Gumbo King. I like my life, Ryder – it's peaceful and I *feed* people."

Ryder produced a second photo, the one he'd pulled from the frame in the room with the stained mattress. He held it high.

"LaShelle Shearing. Someone pried the bars from her window . . ."

"You're sandbagging me, you bastard."

". . . found burned beyond recognition in an abandoned house –"

Sandhill grabbed a napkin dispenser and fired it over Ryder's head into the wall, napkins spilling across the floor. Ryder pulled a third photo from his jacket and held it high.

"Darla Dumont, disappeared one year ago without a tra—"

A timer bell rang from the kitchen. Sandhill said, "That means it's time for you to leave, Ryder." Sandhill strode to the kitchen and the swinging doors closed behind him.

When they didn't re-open, Ryder sighed, tucked the photos in his pocket, and left.

13

Walter Hutchinson Mattoon stood at the prow of the *Petite Angel* and watched the sun rise over the glassy morning sea, the sparse clouds bright as hammered copper. The only sounds were a low rumble of the ship's engine and the hull cleaving water five stories below. Though his suit was dark and the day equatorially hot, Mattoon showed no sign of sweating. He ran a hand over his spear-pointed widow's peak, patted down a wind-blown lock of black hair, and clasped his hands behind his slender back.

He heard a muffled *ahem* a dozen paces behind and turned to a diminutive man in a captain's suit. The man pulled his five-foot-two toward five-three and snapped a crisp salute.

"Yes, Captain Sampanong?" Mattoon enquired.

"I think we have solved a mystery, Mr Mattoon."

Mattoon followed Captain Trili Sampanong into the body of the ship and down two flights of stairs, finding a tucked-away space between two towering containers. An overturned wooden chair was on the floor, beside it several pornographic magazines and an upended ashtray.

Mattoon looked to the corner to find his steward, Pierre Valvane, in a crumpled heap, his mouth a smear of blood. The man was moaning. Above the steward stood a tall man with a shaved head, shirtless, his muscles like iron cords and his rotten-tooth mouth a festering parody of a grin.

Most of the crew had been drawn to the commotion, and Mattoon saw the world in his employees' faces: Asian, European, Slavic, African, Middle Eastern. All were silent and impassive, more curious than anything.

"What is this?" Mattoon said.

"I find him in here drinking," the bald man said, jabbing a finger toward the steward at his feet.

Mattoon raised a dark eyebrow. "Drinking is not prohibited, Tenzel. Not if done on the first shift of a double shift off duty."

"I find him drinking this."

The bald man reached beneath the steward and produced an empty bottle of Mattoon's Château d'Yquem, part of a case that an inventory had revealed either missing or miscounted.

The steward moaned again. The bald man kicked him in the knee.

"Steady, Tenzel," Mattoon said. "Don't render him useless."

Mattoon stepped closer and considered the situation. On the one hand, he hated thievery and could not in any way countenance its appearance on his ship; on the other hand, he employed thieves. Mattoon approached the steward, setting the toes of his sleek black loafers a meter from the man's nose.

"Mr Valvane, do you hear me?"

"*Oui*, yes," the man said, his voice breaking. "I'm sorry, it won't hap—"

The bald man stepped on to the steward's ankle. "You don't talk. You listen."

"Tenzel, please."

The bald man reluctantly stepped from the steward's leg. Mattoon lowered to a crouch. "Are you upset with me, Mr Valvane? Do you not find the accommodations pleasing? The working conditions satisfactory? Has the food not been to your liking?"

"I make a terrible mistake. I'm sorry."

"It's good that you recognize your error, Mr Valvane. Redemptive. Am I to understand that it won't happen again?"

"*Oui*. I mean, *non*."

Mattoon patted the man's shoulder. "Very good. You are to return to your cabin, and I expect you to remain confined there for two weeks. Your meals will be supplied and you will be expected to shower daily. Stand him up, Tenzel."

With an upward swoop of a rippling arm, the

bald man seemed to levitate the steward to his feet by little more than will. The steward trembled on wobbly knees.

"M-May I return to my cabin by myself, Mr Mattoon?"

Mattoon considered the request, then shook his head as if saddened by his upcoming words.

"No, Mr Valvane. I want Tenzel to accompany you."

The steward's eyes widened in fear. Mattoon saw the front of the steward's pants darken with urine.

"P-Please. I can –"

"Shhhh. Go with Tenzel, Mr Valvane."

"Please, Mr Mattoon, sir. I beg you –"

Mattoon turned his back. The steward began weeping. The bald man, his grin incandescent, led the bawling man away.

"To your stations, gentlemen," Mattoon said to the captain and circling crew. Tenzel Atwan's visit to Valvane's room would result in a blinding dose of pain, but no structural damage. Mattoon glanced at their faces. He saw no anger, only acceptance of the rules. They filed away.

It had to de done. The rules of the ship were spare and easy to remember: Hard work, no thievery, no telling tales when off the ship, and absolute obedience to Mattoon. In return, the pay was quadruple the going rate, the crew quarters furnished with the comforts and amenities of a four-star hotel. The meals were prepared by a Cordon Bleu-trained chef. Prostitutes were procured in every port at ship's expense.

Turnover was almost non-existent, lessened further in that all crewmen were fugitives from somewhere. Mattoon had bought his master steam-fitter and oiler, both smugglers, out of life sentences in Rwanda for five thousand dollars each. The chef had ducked his *gros bonnet* out of Paris just ahead of an Interpol drug investigation. Scotland Yard wanted his communications officer for black-mail, his electrician for forgery. The only man not wanted by name was Tenzel Atwan, and only because his crimes left no accusatory fingers pointing.

Mattoon took the stairs back to the weather-deck, the main deck. It was bare of cargo, the two up-thrusting crane posts resembling vestigial masts. The decks of most container ships held hundreds of metal boxes stacked high, hundreds more in the holds. The *Petite Angel*, diminutive at a length of 91 meters, currently carried only sixty-seven containers, all below, all loaded in Montevideo.

Making a profit didn't matter with the *Petite Angel*; Mattoon owned a fleet of huge container ships, the rail lines of the shipping lanes, and they ran full, hard, and ceaselessly. The *Petite Angel*, a bulk carrier converted to containers, was Mattoon's sole residence, a home that traversed oceans. Still, a businessman makes money, and *Angel* always carried freight to pay the bills. Within days her cargo would be offloaded at the Mobile docks, with the ship taking on containers for the return trip.

In addition, Mattoon would pick up one more item in Mobile – much smaller, though infinitely more valuable.

He checked his watch and a horizontal smile touched his lips. Dear would be waking up and getting ready for her day. His steps gained speed as he returned to his quarters.

Mattoon occupied the entire level beneath the bridge, the space as much museum as lodging, the gray of the ship transformed into teak walls and blood-red carpet. The main room was three-fourths of the living area, heavy maroon drapes covering the windows, four overlooking the weatherdeck, two on each side of the door. Full-length mirrors with gilded baroque frames stood between the windows. Furniture held one corner, an L of couch sections facing twin chairs across a low table, leather and mahogany the dominant materials. In the opposite corner was a waist-high map cabinet with a roseate marble top.

The visual center of the room was a burled walnut desk spanning three meters in length, two in width. Though it seemed a Dickens'-era piece that might have graced the offices of Lloyd's, it had been crafted five years prior at the cost of seventeen thousand British pounds. The desktop held only a hard leather writing pad, a multi-buttoned communications station, and an antique ship's clock of gleaming brass, its spring-driven mechanism replaced with electronics.

The room would have been dark but for track-mounted spots pinpointing glass cabinets of yellowed scrimshaw. Wall-hung shadow boxes displayed antique navigational equipment, astrolabes, sextants, compasses; Walter Mattoon was a collector of small objects of beauty, utility, or both.

Mattoon sat in the leather chair behind his desk and opened the top drawer to display a panel of switches. He touched one and the curtains retreated from the windows, the boundless horizon revealed. He touched another and low music fell from hidden speakers, Scarlatti.

"Dear?" he called toward a curtained doorway at the rear of the main room. "Are you awake yet? Have you dressed?"

A young black girl stepped into the room. She wore a flowing designer gown, mauve, the décolletage high and demure over the modest swell of her breasts. A red silk orchid floated behind an ear. Mattoon rose in acknowledgement.

"Shall we take the morning breeze, Dear?" Mattoon said, sliding a slender arm behind her and guiding her toward the door. Though he knew Dear had gone by the name of Darla Dumont for the eleven years of her life in Mobile, he never used it, the name part of a life that no longer existed. She was Dear. They were always Dear.

The girl's eyes looked through Mattoon, out a window, across the sea and beyond. She walked as if in a gray and meaningless dream. Her look troubled him and he stopped. "Dear? Are you all right?"

She continued staring out the window. Mattoon regarded her with sad eyes; knowing from experience she had started dissolving. His love could do that, Mattoon knew. None of his glorious Dears had endured even a year before dissolving into nothingness.

"Love is such sweet pain," Mattoon whispered. "But we are blessed to receive it."

The girl had slumped forward. Mattoon sighed and sent her back to her room. He went to his desk calendar and, for the third time that morning, counted the days until the ship reached Mobile.

The next morning Sandhill pushed his key into the restaurant door when he felt a tug behind the knees of his jeans. He turned and looked down. A little girl, lean as a twig, dressed in pink jeans and a white tee, some current cartoon animal on the shirt.

"Jacy Charlane?"

Jacy stared mutely at her sky-blue sneakers.

Sandhill frowned. "Well, what is it?"

She shuffled her feet, wrung her hands. Sandhill tapped a finger on Jacy's head. "Talk, girl. I know you're in there. The Gumbo King's got chores to do, vittles to cook. What do you want?"

Still studying her shoes, she held her hand up and finger-waved him closer. He sighed and lowered to a knee. Jacy cupped her hands and encircled Sandhill's ear.

"I have to tell you a secret, your highness."

Her breath was warm on his ear. He hoped she wasn't carrying a cold or some childhood affliction.

"One quick secret, then I have to get busy. Is today your birthday? Did I guess it?"

"My birthday's not for three weeks," she whispered. "It's a bad secret."

"Did you lose something? A toy? I'll bet if you retraced your steps – went back where you –"

"Someone is stealing little girls, Mr King."

Sandhill froze. He took a deep breath and nodded slowly. "I've, uh, heard about that. It's a sad thing. Listen, Jacy, I wouldn't worry too much about –"

"One was in a burned-down house. On the TV they told her name was LaShelle."

"Jacy, uh, maybe your aunt could explain –"

"Did LaShelle feel the burning, Mr King?"

Sandhill put his hand on her shoulder and felt her shaking like her breath should be visible in the air. "Jacy, I don't really know anything about that."

She said, "I touched my hand on a hot pan once . . . I picked it up and it hurt terrible . . ." She put her hands to her eyes and started crying.

Sandhill scanned the street. Ted Spikes's grocery was half a block away. "Would you like an ice cream, Jacy? We could head to Teddy's. Does that sound good?"

Tears poured down her cheeks. "Why would someone steal little girls and burn them? Did they feel the . . ."

Sandhill swooped her into his arms and stood. "Ssssh. Don't cry," he said, wondering what the hell to do. Jacy tucked her face under Sandhill's chin and wept softly, kitten sounds, her tears dropping hot on his neck. He pushed open the door of the restaurant and stepped inside, cool and dark and perfumed with spices.

"It'll be fine, Jacy," he crooned. "I talked to a policeman yesterday and he said they're doing real good in finding the bad person."

"Then how come the little girl got burned up?"

Sandhill paused, closed his eyes; *good question*. "They'll do better soon. It takes time to learn things."

"You could help look for the little girls. You could do that."

"There's nothing I can do, Jacy. Only the police are allowed to investigate. It's the rule."

Jacy squeezed Sandhill's neck. "You don't have rules. You can do anything you want. You're a king."

She started sobbing. Sandhill carried her around the room for several minutes. He noted the time.

"Hey Jacy, you ever turn on the lights in a restaurant?"

She kept her face buried in his shoulder, shook her head.

"Let's go over here to the switches," he said.

"You can make the place come alive. Is that cool or what?"

She nodded, sniffling, wiping away tears with her wrist. Sandhill held her to the wall switches. "Flip 'em all up. Don't be afraid."

She looked at him instead of the switches. "Can you help find the girls, Mr King? Please?"

Sandhill closed his eyes.

"I'll see what I can do, Jacy. No promises, though."

She reached out and snapped the switches. The fluorescent lights in the ceiling sputtered awake. The sign hissed. Hummed. Flickered.

Paused as if gathering force . . .

The Gumbo King wrote itself large and red against the sky.

Photos from the fire were spread across Ryder's desk, companions to those tacked to the gray divider beside him. The pictures showed charred joists. Seared floors. Carbonized walls. Several shots centered on a small object that resembled a . . . Ryder didn't want to think what it resembled; he had no words for it.

Pressed against his desk was Harry Nautilus's desk, its surface empty and desolate. Ryder looked away as his phone rang. Bertie Wagnall, the phone jockey, burped: "You got a call on four, Ryder. Some guy says he's Henry the Fifth. The fifth what?"

Ryder's heart dropped a beat. "I got it, Bertie."

"Ryder, you got the weirdest friggin' snitches."

Ryder punched the line and snatched the phone. Sandhill said, "It's me, Detective Ryder. I'll come by and look at the files late this morning. Pro bono."

Ryder's shoulders slumped in relief.

"Thanks, Sandhill."

"I've got one condition, Detective."

"Which is?"

"I don't want to see anyone above the rank of sergeant. Got that?"

14

Sandhill stood in his apartment tying his tie for the third time, scowling at the mirror, trying to get the wide end longer than the skinny end. He hated leaving the simmering gumbos, fearful they'd suffer in his absence. Each was an act of precision balance, the fulcrum shifting daily and dependent on such factors as whether the shrimp were from the bay or the bluewater, the freshness of the thyme and heat of the cayenne, the pungency of the onions. Gumbo, that sensory explosion of sight and smell and gustatory overload, was, at heart, one of the subtlest of the kitchen's creations, a struggle for harmony.

He cursed and went at the tie a fourth time, grateful the gumbos would be under the watchful eyes of Marie Belfontaine. Fifty-two, dark as chocolate, able to set one-hundred-fifty pounds into motions that still pulled whistles from street corners, Marie was his kitchen confidante, his whisper-hoarder, his Richelieu. She'd appeared three weeks before opening, sawdust on the floor, wires dangling from the ceiling, Sandhill wondering if the idea of opening a gumbo joint was divine inspiration or one of his darker urges gone hideously awry.

"You can tear this up," she'd said, handing him the HELP WANTED sign from the door.

"Actually, I'll probably need a few more people," Sandhill said, a scarlet handkerchief wrapping the thumb he'd mistaken for a nail minutes earlier.

"You already thinking of expanding?" Marie said, looking at the space destined to become his dining area. "Your gumbo that good?"

"I'm planning sixteen four tops. To wait on them I'll probably need –"

"To find me more work to do, if that's all the piddling number of folks you gonna put in here."

"I might need kitchen help, too," Sandhill said, not really knowing what he was looking for, never having hired anyone before.

Marie narrowed an eye. "Cook?"

"Prep help, maybe. Pot-watching if I make a shopping run. But I do the main cooking."

Marie smiled at Sandhill like he'd cleared a high-set hurdle. "Good. You gonna make gumbo, you got to have one cook. Gumbo may look like committee food, but good God Almighty it surely ain't. Let me tell you . . ."

Marie's five-minute discourse on gumbo was less science than theology and when she'd finished

86

Sandhill was uncertain whether to hire her or propose.

Sandhill tied his tie for the fifth time. Though the new windows were triple-paned for insulation, he heard voices from the street drifting up to his second-story digs. He lived above the restaurant in a failed dance studio, a box sixty feet long, thirty wide, fourteen high. The former dressing room was subdivided into a small bedroom and large bathroom. Cabinets and a counter, hanging implement rack and appliances turned a corner into a kitchen.

Before moving in, Sandhill had painted everything white: floor, walls, ceiling, trim. Then, like arranging thoughts in a clarified mind, he'd added furniture and decorated. His major furnishings were blond maple. The back wall held five twelve-foot-long bookshelves, sixty running feet with few inches to spare. A large Oriental carpet beneath a table and six chairs suggested the dining area. Posters from local events hung on the walls, the controlled chaos of a Jackson Pollock reproduction hovered above the sofa. Six ceiling fans, a legacy of the dance studio, spun lazily overhead. The only sense of disarray came from books and magazines scattered throughout the apartment, some open, some closed, most cluttered with bookmarks.

"Finally," Sandhill growled, pulling the tie tight, it having acquiesced to near-evenness. He stepped back to put his head-to-toe image in the bathroom mirror – the dark brown suit needing pressing he had neither the time nor skill for, white shirt, dark tie. His basic uniform for years. It felt tight and uncomfortable, an inch or two of gumbo new to his waist.

He sat on his bed to put on his shoes, instinctively reaching for the ankle-holstered .32 on the nightstand. The small Colt didn't offer much firepower, but it was light and, when he wore floppy jeans, invisible to the ordinary citizen.

The holster had been two hundred bucks, but the leather was molded glove-tight to the revolver and the strap was lined with sheepskin for comfort. Sandhill had made only one modification, carefully peeling a small section of the sheepskin from the cowhide strap, creating a small pocket, like the coin pocket in a pair of jeans. The pocket held a simple wire lockpick. Two years back a state cop had been blindsided by a canny felon and restrained with his own cuffs until being shot to death. Sandhill modified his holster the next day.

He bent to Velcro-strap the holster to his ankle, caught himself. *I'm going to a cop shop, for crying out loud.* He slipped the weapon back in the nightstand, locked up the apartment, and stopped into the restaurant. Marie was in the kitchen with a stirring-spoon in one hand, romance novel in the other.

"I'm outta here for a few hours, Marie. We need anything from the market?"

She studied Sandhill and wrinkled her nose. "You going in dressed like that?"

"I thought about nudity, but clothes seemed more appropriate."

"You look like a po-liceman."

"I was, remember? They give you these clothes with your detective's shield and you wear them for life. When you die they strip you and give the clothes to a new-made detective."

"You not a cop any more."

"And?"

"Look at you. Going to that place and you somebody different."

"They're just clothes, Marie."

She *hmphed* and turned away.

Sandhill said, "Marie? Hello?"

She kept her back to him. "They owning you again and you not out the door of your own place."

"Come on, Marie. Aren't you being a bit sensitive? I mean –"

Marie spun and gaveled the spoon against the pot. "You ain't no cop no more, Conner Sandhill. You the Gumbo King, right? Like you all the time preaching at everybody else: To thine own self . . ."

She let the words hang in the air.

"Be true," Sandhill completed, stripping the tie from his neck.

"Late in the year for Mardi Gras, ain't it, Carson?" Detective Roy Trent said, looking from a window to the parking lot.

"What are you talking about?" Ryder said.

"You won't believe what fell off a float and's heading this way," Trent said, a grin bridging his outsized ears from lobe to lobe.

A minute later Sandhill strode into the room wearing a purple vest trimmed in gold brocade. His felt crown was high and crisply ironed. He wore a black tee shirt and jeans with black Converse hightops slapping the floor.

Mouths fell open. Ryder muttered, steering Sandhill away from the looks and down the hall to the meeting room.

"Is there a reason for the get-up?"

"Makes me feel regal."

"I was hoping we might pull this off without fanfare."

Sandhill said, "Ever read Castaneda?"

Ryder paused; raised an eyebrow. He opened the door to the meeting room. "It's been years. Why?"

"Remember the sorcerer's concept of controlled folly? Folly with a purpose?"

Ryder was about to make a flip comment but saw Sandhill's face was deadly serious. Ryder displayed the IN USE sign on the door and closed it behind them.

"Would you like me to hang up your vest and crown?"

"I'll wait until the brass has been and gone," Sandhill said, wiggling chairs until finding one without a squeak. He sat and pulled close the pile of reports.

"I told them your condition," Ryder said. "That they weren't supposed to be here."

"Precisely why they will be," Sandhill said, picking up a file and starting to read.

Ryder sat quietly as Sandhill absorbed data, often grunting, occasionally asking questions. Some questions seemed penetrating, some childishly basic, others made no sense at all.

The door opened without a knock and Ryder glanced up in irritation. Bidwell pushed through just ahead of Squill. Ainsley Duckworth was in the acting chief's wake, the wet marbles of the commander's eyes peering from under the heavy brow. He showed Ryder his teeth. Zemain brought up the rear, embarrassment written across his face.

"Oh shit," Squill said, counterbalancing feigned surprise with a smirk. "We didn't know anyone was in here."

"Hi, Roland," Sandhill said to Zemain.

Ryder said, "Uh, we're looking through some things here, Chief . . ."

Squill ignored Ryder and looked at Sandhill as if he'd suddenly materialized.

"Nice hat, Sandhill. Get it at a Halloween store?"

"It's a crown," Sandhill said. "I got it at Kings'R'Us."

Zemain deftly turned a chuckle into a throat-clearing sound. Bidwell blanked his face and looked out the window.

"That's right," Squill said. "I heard you were

king of the fry cooks or something. How's being a fry cook compare with being a detective?"

Sandhill thought a moment. "A cook only has to be there when the food goes in."

Squill's smile melted. "How long you planning on being here, Sandhill?"

"I can leave right now if you want." Sandhill stood.

Bidwell, ever the arbiter, jumped in, patting Sandhill's shoulder, easing him back to the chair. "Sit, Conner. Take all the time you need." Bidwell shot Squill a sidelong glance saying, *We got him, let's use him.*

Squill turned away, muscles working in his clenched jaw. Sandhill picked up a photo, and began studying it.

"Sure would be nice to have a little privacy," he said.

After three hours of studying every scrap of paper and photo associated with the girls' disappearances and asking Ryder a stream of questions, Sandhill began jamming material into a manila folio.

"It's a jumble. I've got some ideas, but I want to think a little more. I'll take some stuff with me."

Ryder raised a dark eyebrow. "I'll have to clear it. I'm pretty sure you're not supposed to take things home."

"Never ask, Detective Ryder. Just do. You get a lot more accomplished that way."

"The world according to Conner Sandhill?"

"It's a kingly principle, Detective. Ever read *The Golden Bough*? Frazer asserts that a monarchy can develop much faster than a democracy. Picture a group of hunters on a hill deciding which direction to go. In a democracy everyone has an opinion to be argued and dissected and voted on. In a monarchy the king points his finger and says, 'We're going there.'"

"For better or worse."

"It depends on the king. If he moves from reason and the proper accumulation of kingly wisdom, the journey stands a solid chance of success."

"And if he doesn't?"

Sandhill tied the folio shut, walked to the door. "At least it's motion. Henry Moore bores me, but I purely love Calder."

Sandhill was at the back entrance when Squill slipped from a side hall, eyes slitted at the folio under Sandhill's arm.

"You're leaving everything right here, Sandhill. I figured you'd try and take something on the sly. That's a habit of yours, isn't it?"

"I don't work well from memory, Terrence."

Squill bristled at the use of his first name. "Case information is for cops only. It stays."

Sandhill threw the folio in the air and Squill made a clumsy catch. "It's all yours, Terrence. I was going to look a little more, but if you don't want me to, that's fine. Our deal's done. I expect to find my doorway clear of inspectors when I get back."

"Inspectors?" Squill said, a smile ghosting his thin lips. "What inspectors?"

"You're bush league, Terrence. Harassing me with pissant bureaucrats is as bush as it gets."

"You dishonored the badge, Sandhill. You owe us."

"You dream that in your sleep, too?"

"Listen to me, you smug bastard –"

"I don't have to any more, Terrence. And I like the quiet."

Sandhill started to the door, but stopped as pictures in his mind began aligning. He watched the pictures for a moment, then turned to Squill.

"Just one thing, Terrence. I don't think LaShelle Shearing was killed in the house that burned. I think she was murdered somewhere else and taken there."

Squill's face froze for an instant, then resumed its sneer.

"None of the Forensics techs said that. What makes you so sure?"

Sandhill nodded at the files in Squill's hand. "It's right there, Terrence. You figure it out."

Sandhill stepped through the door. It was raining but he was focused on the pictures in his head and didn't notice.

15

Four p.m. and the restaurant was empty of customers. Marie was at the market, Sandhill at a table struggling with bookkeeping when the health inspector, Wentz, slunk through the door carrying a thick brown envelope. Wentz raised his hand like a white flag and nodded at the envelope.

"Easy, Sandhill. I'm just here to bring you this."

"A running record of my infractions?"

Holding the envelope in front of him, Wentz edged closer, a man trying to feed a grizzly while keeping his arm. "I don't know what the hell it is. I was over by Seven Hills when I got a call saying drive all the way back in town, pick it up, deliver it to you. Like I ain't got enough to do, I got to be messenger boy for the goddamn –"

Sandhill snatched the envelope. He looked inside and saw copies of the files on the abductions.

"Is this everything?"

"No," Wentz said, retreating to the door.

"I'm supposed to tell you that taking the folder buys probation on the inspections."

Sandhill stared at the door after it closed, then pushed aside his pencils and calculator and tapped the package slowly with his forefinger. That Wentz himself had been detailed to deliver the files and message was a diplomatic maneuver, a small gesture of truce. But the inspections had been suspended, not stopped, keeping alive the threat of being closed down.

Sandhill figured the handshake was from Bidwell and a couple other brass hats, the squeeze at the end coming from Squill.

"Hey, Sophie," Ryder said into his desk phone, "I can't get Harry on his cell. All I get is his voice-mail. Could you tell him to call me?"

"Harry's back at the hospital."

"My God. Is he –"

"Easy, Ryder. His temperature went up to 103° last night. An infection, not uncommon. It's safer to hospitalize him for a day or two. He'll receive high doses of antibiotics, be monitored around the clock."

"Are you sure he's –"

"Harry was fretting and moaning all the way there. Asked if he could leave his head at the desk and they could mail it to him when they got everything fixed. That tell you anything?"

Ryder exhaled. If Harry was well enough to bitch, he wasn't at death's door.

"I'll run over to the hospital."

"Don't you dare. Harry needs medicine and quiet, emphasis on the quiet. You got that?"

"I hear you loud and clear, Soph."

Which was the truth; Ryder's phone volume was set on high, the signal crisp and sharp.

The trip to the hospital took fifteen minutes. Finagling Harry's room number from a pretty young nurse took thirty seconds. He slipped up a back stairwell to avoid the nurses' station on Harry's floor. It was suppertime and food carts were being wheeled from room to room. He waited until the hall was free of staff, then fast-walked to room 307.

Ryder took a deep breath and stepped through the open door. The air tasted cold and sharp, like it had been rinsed in alcohol. Harry Nautilus was flat on his back, appearing to be asleep. His eyes blinked open at Ryder's footsteps.

Nautilus chuckled. "Ain't no hiding from you, is there?"

"I thought I was going to have to get my dog to track you down."

"How's that fifty-species mutt doing?"

Ryder smiled. "Mr Mix-up's at camp, basically. My neighbour is watching him for a couple of weeks, until things settle down."

"The animal shelter lady?"

"Yep. Mix-up gets fed and walked and spends the day playing with kindred spirits." Ryder's face went serious. "You OK, bro?"

"They're bombing me with industrial-strength antibiotics. It's strong shit; my ass is flat wore out."

"I stopped by to ask a couple questions. I'm outta here in two minutes, I swear."

"I admire your persistence, Cars, but I still haven't remembered anything about the attack. Sometimes it feels like something's there – like I can hear words – but when I try and listen closer, they disappear. I'm trying."

Ryder shot a glance outside the door; no one coming to haul him away. He pulled a chair to the bedside and sat.

"I'm not here about that. I need to know more about Sandhill."

Nautilus sighed and rolled his eyes. "Six foot three or four, maybe two-forty pounds, brown eyes and brown –"

"Come on, what did he do, Harry? Insubordination, right? I figure this Sandhill as the type of guy who'd walk right up and spit in –"

"Committed his resignation."

"What?"

"Here's all I know, Carson: Sandhill was there one day, gone the next. The brass sent out a one-paragraph memo saying Sandhill had 'committed his resignation'."

"Instead of 'submitted his resignation'? A Freudian slip? Maybe meaning he'd committed something illegal?"

"I figure whoever dashed out the memo – Squill, I'd guess – was in too much of a hurry to proofread."

Ryder leaned back into the chair and mulled it

over. Sandhill'd been thirty-seven or so at the time, a sex crimes and cold-case hotshot. Didn't seem a time to resign from the department.

"Sandhill was forced out, maybe? Pissing too many people off?"

Nautilus shook his head. "You want to push a guy off the force, you re-assign him to work he hates, or a subordinate position. But if you cut him loose, he'll come swinging back with a police-union lawyer. Neither happened with Sandhill."

"So Sandhill really did resign?"

"Or knew it was the best offer he'd get."

Ryder leaned forward in the chair and lowered his voice. "What was the scuttlebutt, Harry? There's always scuttlebutt."

Nautilus yawned and settled his head into the pillow. "I heard a dozen theories. I'm gonna let you work with him, decide for yourself."

"Come on, Harry. Give me just a little somethi—"

"Sorry," Nautilus yawned again. "Sandhill's all yours, Carson."

Ryder nodded and stood. His partner was falling asleep. Ryder scooted the chair against the wall.

"Anything else you can add, bro?"

Nautilus pursed his lips and stared at the inside of his eyelids, finally nodding to himself. "Watch Sandhill, Carson," he said, his voice whispering toward sleep. "Watch him real close."

16

Sandhill stood at the threshold of Nike Charlane's second-floor apartment and absorbed the sensory barrage of compacted living. Televisions dueled with stereos. A couple argued behind a door two apartments down. Running feet thundered on the floor above his head. Babies cried. Cabbage cooked. Dogs barked.

Though wanting to turn and run, Sandhill willed his knuckles to rap the steel door. He centered himself so Nike could see him through the peephole. She'd called a half-hour before, wanting to talk, but not saying what about. He'd walked over, two blocks.

The door opened. Nike stayed behind it and all he saw was her hand gesturing him in. It was a corner apartment, quieter than most. She went to the living room, crooking her finger for him to follow. The scent of fresh cookies sweetened the air.

Paintings were everywhere: on the walls, on the floor, tucked behind the couch. Most were portraits, faces of electric color clear-glazed so heavily they appeared to be floating under sun-bright water. Sandhill found them beautiful and unsettling, like hummingbirds preserved in amber.

Nike pointed to the couch, worn but not thread-bare. "Have a seat, Conner."

"I've only got a few minutes."

"So spend them sitting."

He sat slowly and leaned forward, elbows on his knees, not committing himself to comfort. Nike took a chair, a low glass table gleaming between them like a field of ice.

Sandhill said, "I want to apologize. For the other morning."

"Don't. You were right."

"My comment about painting the target was in lousy taste."

"True. But that's you, Conner."

"My overall theme still stands, Nike. I think –"

Nike cut Sandhill off with a wave. She stood and began pacing. "I'm going into treatment, Conner. I talked to the center yesterday."

"That's tremendous, Nike. Where you were last time?"

"That one didn't take too well, did it? No. A program in Birmingham. More intensive and isolated. More focused on the psychology of . . . addiction. All I do is work on the job at hand."

"If there's anything I can do to help . . ."

"There is. I want you to take care of Jacy while I'm away."

Sandhill looked liked he'd stepped waist deep into frigid water. It took several seconds to thaw his voice.

"I can't do that. She's a little girl."

"You said I wasn't keeping her safe. You're right. When I'm . . . when I'm sick, I'm useless. I turn into a ghost."

"You've got to have friends who can do a better job than me. I don't even – I guess I like Jacy and all – but I'm not big on . . ."

"You don't understand children because you've never been around them."

"No offense, but I don't care to be; I'm not sure I liked kids when I was one. But that's not the –"

"There's no one I trust to keep her as safe as you can."

Sandhill shook his head. "Nike, it's out of the question. Men in their forties do not have eight-year-old girls running around their apartments."

"Yes they do, Conner. They're called fathers."

"I don't want to be anyone's father."

Nike stared at Sandhill. An ambulance charged down the street, siren howling. The siren disappeared in the distance before Nike spoke.

"But you could have been, Conner. A few months' difference and . . ."

Sandhill studied the carpet. "I don't want to go there, Nike. It was forever ago."

"Funny, it doesn't seem that long to me."

Sandhill said nothing. Nike leaned against the

wall, arms crossed, eyes hard on Sandhill. "You ever grieve for Thena, Conner? You weren't at the funeral. You were close by though, right?"

He stood and glanced at his watch. "I've got to go, Nike; things to do at the restaurant."

"You were outside, maybe. On the street?"

Sandhill took a step toward the door. Nike said, "You're running away. Don't run from this, Conner. Sit down."

He turned, sighed, and sat as gingerly as a man with damaged knees.

Nike said, "I'll be in treatment for three weeks. It won't be hard to take care of Jacy. She sleeps eight hours. Most days she's at school another eight. You'll hardly have to look at her."

"It's not that I don't want to look at her, it's –"

"Shush. She'll have one suitcase and a bag of books. I doubt you have any Frosty-O's for her breakfast, so I'll supply that. She loves gumbo so supper's taken care of, maybe a toasted cheese sandwich now and then. With dill pickles. Don't burn the bread but make sure the cheese melts through."

"No, Nike. It's impossible."

"She'll be shy at first, but pretty soon she'll wear your ear out. You'll be amazed how bright she is . . ."

"Nike."

"She does her homework directly after school, then she can play. Bedtime is nine thirty and you have to read her a story. I'll have everything written down."

"Nike, I didn't say I'd do this."

Nike sat beside Sandhill. "Please, Conner. I can't go away if I'm afraid for Jacy. You're the only one I trust to protect her."

"I just don't think I'm qualified to –"

She picked up his hand, squeezing it as if her need went past words and only a signal transmitted through bones and flesh could express it.

"I know I'm asking a lot. But please, do it for me." She paused. "No, Conner, not for me, do it for Thena."

Sandhill closed his eyes. The pounding of his heart was so loud he barely heard himself speak.

"When does this experience start?"

"Thanks, Conner. I'll bring Jacy by tonight." Nike kissed Sandhill's cheek. "Now I know she'll be safe."

A bored Roosevelt wandered back toward Truman's office, pausing to unwrap a power bar, drop the torn-off end on the floor, ball up the remaining package and arc it into the trash can, whispering *two points* when it dropped.

Truman sat at the computer, the only light coming from the screen. The secret, external drive was in place. He stopped his cutting and pasting of a web-page template and wrinkled his nose.

"Jeez, Rose. Do you have to eat those damned things in here? They stink."

"It's just carob, Tru."

Truman jabbed his finger toward the back of his

throat and made a gagging sound. Rose curled his arm and pointed to a mountainous bicep. "Here's mine. Let's see yours, junk-food junkie."

Truman mouthed *up yours* and looked back to the screen. Rose watched as Truman stacked empty rectangles on a field of crimson.

"What are you doing, Tru?"

"Changing the site. Then I'm writing the buyer to tell him there was some trouble with his selection."

"You telling him what the trouble was?"

Truman pecked at the keys. "Don't be a moron, Rose."

"What'll you do?"

"Make another offer, give him another choice."

Rose said, "You've got a bunch more in the gallery."

Truman closed his eyes and shook his head. "He's seen the whole gallery, Rose. He picked LaShelle. I can't offer him products he's already rejected. 'Oh, excuse me, my brother killed your first selection, what's your second choice?' It's not good business, Rose; I'm trying to build a reputation for service and quality."

Rose rolled his eyes, then leaned in and studied the screen as his brother jockeyed photos and background colors on the computer screen.

"Who are you showing?"

Truman said, "Ones he hasn't seen before. Shots taken in the last couple weeks."

"You're putting the new pictures up tonight?"

Truman shook his head. "No. Tonight I'll send an apology. Tomorrow will be the showing. I'm hoping one'll set him off."

"Which ones are they?" Rose asked, his brow furrowing in concern.

Truman leaned back, slowly enumerating on his fingers. "Let's see. There's Dawn and, uh, Teena."

"That's two. You said four."

"I can count, asswipe, I'm thinking. Uh, Berri."

"Three."

"And . . . oh shit, I can't remember her name. The one that said pickle instead of cheese. Jacy, that's it."

Rose frowned. "Jacy?"

"Is there an echo in here?"

"Which do you think he'll pick?" Rose whispered.

"Look at my hands, Rose. You see a crystal ball?"

Four time zones to the east, the *Petite Angel* bore westward at twelve knots, its bow knifing swells of a sudden storm. Lightning flashed pictures of the storm's tumult: White-capped waves, gray spray lathering the bow, roiling bottoms of black clouds. When the storm had been a distant blossom on the radar, Captain Sampanong had flooded the bilges and now the ship rode steady and solid. Within Mattoon's quarters a slow roll and muted thunder were lone hints of the slashing weather.

Mattoon sat at his desk sipping claret from a

106

balloon glass. He'd checked Dear and found her in her usual position, curled tight beneath the bed. He'd furnished her room with a canopy bed sheeted with silk and curtained with velvet, but she chose to sleep in the tight space beneath it.

But not for long, Matton thought, rolling the glass between his palms. The universe was about to shift, and new love would soon be entering his life.

An explosion of thunder drew him to open the window. Between the flashes of lightning Mattoon studied his reflection as if watching a man outside looking in, a man with an angular face topped with ink-black hair and a widow's peak so severe and pointed it resembled a honed mohawk.

Mattoon lifted his glass in salute to the man in the storm, saw him return the salutation. He went to the map cabinet and retrieved a large satellite photo of upper Mobile Bay, studying a land parcel just below Mobile, acreage on which he had quietly taken options, though not under the name of Mattoon Maritime. That information would be revealed in the most propitious manner possible. Money could enter regions quietly, or with great clamor, Mattoon knew; he preferred clamor, but at the hour of his choosing.

Mattoon had long ago learned that, when large and sudden investment entered an area, a small percentage had to be parceled off to local fixers and politicians. Bribes, graft, mordita . . . whatever, it was all just business, an investment in getting zoning codes changed, environmental requirements waived, inspections amended.

The few that knew of his Mobile aspirations were already at his door with their hands out. By paying them, he made them complicit. And with complicity came their protection.

The ship's clock chimed above low rumbles of disappearing thunder; Mattoon quickly replaced the map in the cabinet. He returned to the desk, flipped a switch. Heralded by a soft whir, a flat monitor rose from within the desk. Mattoon slid a microwave keyboard and mouse from a drawer. There was a particular site he wanted to view, transient, appearing five minutes a day.

Mattoon sent passwords and ID, fingers playing keys as tenderly as coaxing a lullaby from a piano.

"Thank heaven . . ." The words sang through his head as the three corresponding tones signaled connection. The screen stayed black. Mattoon keyed in a final set of numbers.

". . . for little girls," the notes concluded, and the screen lit with smiling faces of schoolgirls. A flashing light in the corner signaled a direct communication, perhaps more information about the location and time of the exchange. A year ago, during the acquisition of Dear, the transference had gone flawlessly – a meeting on a nighttime dock, a quivering body hustled between vehicles. The package had been transferred to the ship and opened in safe and distant waters.

In a very short time the exchange would operate again.

Mattoon touched the cursor to the blinking light and clicked. The dark of the screen was replaced with a virtual notepad. The message was brief:

We regret to inform you that problems with your selection (Nalique) cancel our ability to make delivery. We apologize. The problems are not a threat to our business or to yourself. We wish to assure you of our continued devotion to service and satisfaction and will give alternatives ASAP.

Thank you for your continued patronage.

Mattoon stared at the screen for a full minute, then printed the message, just so he could rip the page to pieces.

17

It was closing on nine a.m. when Ryder pushed through the door of the Forensics department. The temperature outside was already in the humid mid eighties and the low-set air conditioning felt good. He checked in and wandered back to the main lab, seeing Wayne Hembree twiddling with a microscope. Hembree looked up at the approaching footsteps.

"Howdy, Carson. Did I hear you right on the phone? Sandhill's actually coming in?"

"I told him nine, for whatever's that's worth."

Hembree eyeballed the clock: 8.59 a.m. "Never knew him to be late. Never knew him to be early. Never saw him coming, he just appeared. The lab was one of his favorite haunts. He'd slip over here on slow days just to ask questions and paw through stuff. Kind of like someone else I know."

Ryder found it odd that Hembree hadn't mentioned Sandhill's "troubles", and actually seemed buoyed by a visit from the tainted ex-detective.

"How's the Gumbo King doing?" Hembree asked.

Ryder shrugged. "I really wouldn't know, Bree. Keeping busy, I guess. The restaurant and all."

"My wife and I ate there a few weeks back. Five p.m. Saturday and the wait line was out the door. Sandhill in the back singing, the waitress laughing and being in three places at the same time. Great food. Sandhill didn't see me until we were ready to leave. Wouldn't take my money and sent us out with a quart of gumbo for the freezer, besides."

"Because if your ass got any skinnier it'd slip between the cracks in a park bench," Sandhill said, suddenly in the room. "What you got for me to look at, Bree?"

Hembree's eyes shot challenge over the tops of his outsize glasses. "Huh-uh, Conner. First you have to show me yours. Word has it you think the girl was brought to the house instead of being killed there. I can't find anything tells me one way or the other."

Sandhill produced a scrap of notepaper from the pocket of his paisley vest and studied his scrawls.

"Could you get me scene photos P-138-43 through 49?"

Hembree dialed an internal line and made the request. A minute later a woman criminalist brought the seven photos. Sandhill queued the 8 x 10s on the tabletop and tapped one as Hembree and Ryder leaned in.

"Check this out, gentlemen."

"Looks like burnt carpet," Ryder said.

Hembree nodded. "It's what's left of the cheap-ass acrylic carpet from the floor in the living room."

"What'd you get from it, Bree?" Sandhill asked.

"Almost nothing. We've been trying to raise bloodstains, make protein checks. The fire pretty much toasted it."

"Look closer." Sandhill tapped another photo in the rank, a close-up of a corner of the melted fabric. Hembree put a loupe to his eye and leaned over the photo. Several dark and slightly curled projections angled from the rug like thorns.

"Carpet tacks," Hembree said. "So what? It's a carpet. The fire charred away the pine flooring and the tacks became visible."

"Look at the tip of the tack. It's bent. Just a tad."

The Forensics tech frowned through the lens. "And?"

"That's what happens when you pull carpet off a floor," Sandhill said. "The points of carpet tacks are thin and easily bent. Unless you pull the carpet straight up, they curl."

Ryder ran it through his head. Saw the light. "The carpet was already up."

"May change things," Sandhill said.

Hembree leaned over the loupe and studied the tacks for a full minute.

"Beautiful. How the hell'd you figure that out, Conner?"

"I yanked out a roomful of raggedy-ass carpet when fixing up the restaurant. I was on a spit-and-bandage budget and thought I'd put the tacks in a jar and use them again. To get carpet up you lean back for leverage and start yanking. The tacks always bent. Only a careful vertical pull kept them straight, and not always, either."

Ryder pictured Sandhill removing the carpet in the restaurant, turning it into an experiment. Pull. Study. Yank. Study.

He said, "It's not conclusive of anything."

"No," Sandhill said. "But it is *suggestive* that the girl *might* have been killed elsewhere and her body rolled in the carpet and taken to the house, the fire then set. Maybe LaShelle was being kept with Maya." He raised a dark eyebrow.

"Jesus," Hembree said. "Maybe Maya's still alive."

Sandhill crossed his arms. "Your turn to show me yours, Bree."

Hembree riffled through the papers, selected one and studied it.

"The body was burned deeply – too much heat, by the way, to determine if sexual activity had occurred. But the stomach was intact. We've been doing contents analysis."

Sandhill nodded, waiting.

"Peanut butter was the prime finding. Relatively undigested and probably consumed within an hour of her death. Gluten and other starches indicate bread. Components from the breakdown of fructose indicate –"

"Jelly," Ryder said quietly. "Peanut-butter-and-jelly sandwiches."

Hembree nodded approvingly. "Jam, actually. Probably grape."

He slipped another report from the pile and handed it to Ryder. There was a graph attached resembling a spiky drawing of mountains. Ryder studied the report and began mumbling.

"Manganese, calcium, phosphorus, dicalcium phosphate, folic acid . . ."

Hembree separated another report from the stack, lines at varying heights, and handed it to Sandhill. He began reading aloud.

"Magnesium, zinc, chromium . . ."

"Lecithin, albumin, choline bitartrate," Ryder said. "Plus protease, cellulose, lipase."

Sandhill said, "Selenium, copper, molybdenum."

"Amylase," Ryder said.

"Potassium," Sandhill countered, snapping a nail against the report. "Plus Vitamins A through K."

Ryder frowned at the forensics specialist. "My God, Bree. This little girl was given the mother of all One-a-Day vitamins."

"I didn't find any binders that indicate pills," Hembree said. "I think she had one of those energy drinks. Like athletes and weightlifters use. And consider the albumin in the test. It wasn't processed."

"An energy drink with fresh egg in it," Ryder said.

Hembree said, "It's the best guess so far."

Sandhill lofted an eyebrow. "The perp making a conscious effort to ensure the girls get good nutrition?"

Ryder said, "Maybe. But is he mixing it for them, or sharing his?"

"If you're not into this kind of stuff, it probably wouldn't occur to you to use it. He's sharing. It's a good bet our boy's into health: heavy-duty exercise, strength training, distance running, something like that."

Ryder shook his head. "Why feed your captives a nutrition drink when you're planning on killing them in a week?"

Sandhill said, "Exactly. Take it the next step."

"He wasn't planning on a death, you think?"

"The fire was an addendum, maybe. A cover-up for a mistake."

"It works," Ryder said. "If something went wrong."

Sandhill nodded. "Why go through all the trouble and risk of pulling a kid from her house or taking her from a well-traveled street? If all you crave is sex, why not pluck a lone kid from a back street or playground?"

Hembree closed his eyes. "That's cold, Conner."

"It's how the savages think, Bree. This time there's maybe another scenario. Like the perp's concerned with the physical well-being of the girls."

"Keeping them healthy for longer, uh, usage?" Hembree grimaced.

"Maybe," Sandhill said. "But it suggests Maya

115

could be alive, at least until whatever's happening plays out. Maybe even Darla; hell, that kid in Missouri was found after four years. And keeping the girls nourished reinforces the idea the girls are carefully targeted, maybe know the perp. How's that sit with you, Ryder?"

Ryder felt his pulse quicken. For the first time, the case had a direction.

"Tight and right," he said.

18

It was ten a.m. when Mattoon summoned Sampanong from the bridge. Mattoon had slept poorly, kept awake by his anger at those who'd reneged on their deal. But, as often when anger rose in him, he transformed energy into action, focusing on his plans for Mobile. He gestured across charts, maps and satellite photos on his desk, bright in the track spot light from above.

"What do you think, Captain?"

Sampanong leaned over the materials. "It seems ideally located, Mr Mattoon. Highway 65, Highway 10. The Intercoastal Waterway intersecting the bay. Spurs to major rail lines."

"The dockage itself?" Mattoon asked.

The captain scanned the water depth, tapping the map with a nut-brown finger. "Dredged to fifty feet, huge turning basin; navigating the facility will be like parking an automobile."

"I'm planning the installation of two cranes to begin with, fixed and mobile. Ample warehousing.

Cold storage. You too must tell no one, Captain. No scuttlebutt when communicating with others."

Sampanong looked mortified. "Mr Mattoon, I would never, ever –"

"Infusing tens of millions of dollars into a local economy is a powerful tool, Captain, and I hope to wield it with maximum leverage."

"Of course, Mr Mattoon. I understand."

Mattoon looked at the clock and nodded, a sign the conversation was over. Sampanong didn't quite conceal his relief as he scurried out the door. Mattoon's mouth flattened into a smile, sure Sampanong was as close-lipped as a corpse, but it never hurt to remind his men that secrecy was sacrosanct on the *Petite Angel*.

Mattoon activated his computer. While the secret website only appeared for five minutes daily, communiqués from the site's owner could arrive anytime, and Mattoon had checked hourly since the wretched news about Nalique last evening.

A light flashed on his screen, indicating a communication. Mattoon ran the encrypted information through a decrypt program and a page appeared. He scanned the worthless, simpering message and his mind registered the words " . . . *for your approval . . .*"

He scrolled down to find a sextet of faces against a neutral background " . . . *hope to replace your original selection with an alternate offering in the same . . .*"

Mattoon studied the faces in sequence. Dross.

Common as rocks in a quarry. No face could compare with the beauty of Nalique. What had happened to her? Had someone else taken her? With growing anger Mattoon leaned over the last photo . . .

And forgot how to breathe.

The name beneath the photo was Lorelei. A blinking star atop the photo indicated more pictures were available. He clicked the cursor over the star and a montage of Loreleis unfolded.

Mattoon leaned close and studied each photo in the montage as if it were a secret message for him alone. His anger dissolved and he realized the replacement of Nalique with Lorelei was the universe's way of rewarding him for the purity of his life.

"I knew it!" Truman exulted, leaping from the computer chair and launching fists clenched in victory. Rose was supine on the floor, sucking a power bar and squeezing hard rubber balls in both fists. The veins in his forearms stood out like mole-burrows.

"What?" Rose grunted.

"Our customer went crazy for Lorelei. Listen to his note: 'With Lorelei you have outdone my expectations. I accept the substitution. But this selection ABSOLUTELY MUST NOT fall through. I INSIST on your fulfillment of this obligation. I am several days from arrival in your city and will soon make contact to establish payment and trans-feral procedures.'"

Truman heard the balls bounce dully on the floor. Rose slipped to the computer, staring at the faces on the monitor.

"Which one's Lorelei?" Rose whispered.

Truman looked curiously at Rose. "What's wrong with your voice?"

Rose closed his eyes and took a deep breath. "I asked, which one's Lorelei?"

"Her," Truman said, tapping the brightest smile on the screen. "Jacy Charlane."

Marie wiped the table to a gloss, then slid the salt and pepper and condiments back to its center. Sandhill sat two tables away in a chamois vest and crown. He'd stashed produce in the coolers, rotated the inventory, and was currently itemizing needs, scratching on a yellow pad with a failing ballpoint pen. Every few seconds he'd curse and bang the pen against the edge of the table. The restaurant was empty save for three anglers lingering over beers and lies.

"You like having that little girl around, don't you?" Marie said.

"What?" Sandhill grunted, not looking up. Marie tucked the towel into her apron strap and sashayed to Sandhill's side.

"Jacy. You like having her around. Already you not acting half as crazy as usual; all calm-down quiet and, I swear, even polite a time or two."

Sandhill smacked the pen against the table and

scowled darkly. "What are you babbling about, Marie? Have you been at the wine?"

"Taking her to the movies. Fixin' ice creams. She said you been telling her stories every night 'fore bed. What kind of story did you tell her about a ball of string and a cave?"

"Theseus and the Minotaur, from Greek myth. Theseus went into the Minotaur's labyrinth to slay it and –"

"Whoa . . . what's a Mina, mino . . ."

"Minotaur. A beast with the head and shoulders of a bull, the torso and legs of a man. Theseus unwound a ball of string to keep from getting lost in the labyrinth."

"Jacy thinks that story is the coolest thing she ever heard, Conner."

Sandhill growled and threw the pen across the room. "I'm just doing what Nike wants, Marie, trying to keep the kid entertained. I'm probably boring her senseless."

"Ha! You that girl's hero. She follow you around like you carrying a sack of gumdrops with a hole in it."

"I am a guy who fixes her two meals a day. Nothing more and nothing less."

"You got starry eyes for her, too, don't you?"

Sandhill pulled a fresh pen from his pocket and reconvened scratching at the pad. "I'm working here, Marie."

Marie stepped close and clapped her hand over Sandhill's wristwatch. "Tell me what time it is."

"That does it. I'm hiding the sherry."

"Come on, Conner Sandhill. What time is it?"

Sandhill sighed as if indulging a madwoman. "Three-fifteen or so."

Marie lifted her hand, checked the time, and laughed.

Sandhill said, "Why are you braying?"

"Last week you'd been lucky to know what hour it was. Now you almost exact on the minute."

"I know I'm going to love your theory on this."

"Jacy gonna walk in here prompt at three thirty. You counting down the minutes. That little girl done stole your heart."

Sandhill's neck reddened. "Could you bring me the phone book, Marie? I want to call the Mental Health Hotline. You need help."

Marie kissed the tip of her finger and pressed it to Sandhill's forehead. "You cute when embarrassed, you know that?" She spun, clapped her hands and sashayed to the kitchen. For a moment the anglers forgot their fish. Sandhill rolled his eyes and returned to his list. He wrote for several seconds before glancing at his watch.

"What time is it now, Gumbo King?" Marie called through the server's window, giggling like a schoolgirl.

Truman Desmond slid the white van down the alley toward the inner-city park. He pulled his wide-brimmed straw hat over his sunglassed eyes and sank lower in the seat.

The park was surrounded on the sides and back with an eight-foot cyclone fence. There was a sitting area of benches, the area studded with shade trees. The playground and basketball court was a hundred feet away. Truman idled down the alley, moving his eyes between the slender alley and the park. He saw a small figure perched cross-legged on a bench.

Jacy Charlane.

She had a book in her lap, her eyes intent on the pages. Truman's heart jumped into race mode, almost palpitating. If the fence wasn't there he could have driven right up to Jacy Charlane, put on his best concerned smile.

"Hi, Jacy, want to help me find a lost puppy?"

No, that line would never work on her. Too bright, too cautious, probably turned wary by some oldster's warnings. He'd already checked her address. She lived on the second floor, front, which ruled out a window entry. A shame; it had worked perfectly with LaShelle Shearing.

During the photo session Truman discovered the Shearing girl's mama spent a lot of nights out, daddy long gone. He'd also found out her windows were grated. But Rose prybarred the grating from the window in seconds, and in went Truman.

Shearing had been a cakewalk, a muscle job. Maya had been snatched from the sidewalk at night. Jacy's abduction would be a bit more difficult – having to come off in broad daylight – and perhaps necessitating a mixture of guile and muscle.

Desmond stopped the van a hundred feet away. He slipped a pen and notepad from his pocket and started sketching a map. The main problems, he could see, were the heavy chain-link fence and, of course, making sure no one saw a thing. There were no windows on the buildings siding the park, and the bench was tucked back in the bushes, far from the activity on the playground and basketball court.

The heavy fence? Desmond allowed himself a brief smile; when you have a brother with arms like phone poles, you simply give him a boltcutter and a dozen seconds.

Truman tugged the hat even lower and pulled past Jacy and into the street. Rose could cut the fence that night. Get everything ready for The Acquisition.

19

"All this crap and an election year, too."

Mayor Philips turned from the center window of her office. The protestors below took her back as an insult and chanted louder, thrusting their signs like battle pikes. FIND OUR CHILDREN, read one; another said, PHILIPS = SELLOUT! A third proclaimed, FIGHT THE POLICE.

Philips shook her head at the angry sounds bleeding into her office, the third day of demonstrations organized by Reverend Turnbull. The deep-voiced, bantam-built minister stood at the point of the crowd – restrained by a sawhorse barricade – waving his fist and leading chants through his bullhorn. Philips leaned against the front of her desk while Squill took his turn at the window, gritting his teeth at the spectacle.

"I could have that bastard with the fight-the-cops sign arrested for incitement to mayhem."

"Good idea. When that's done you can shoot flares into a refinery."

"It's an insult to me and to every cop on the force."

"It's a First Amendment right. You remember the First Amendment? Free speech and all that?"

Squill started to argue, but checked himself. Philips crossed her arms. "Let's talk about the abductions. What happened with that ex-detective looking at the files?"

"Sandhill. He produced what I said he would. Nothing. Zero. A waste of time."

"Have the rest of you found out anything? Please tell me yes."

"The girl in the house wasn't killed there. Chances are she was killed somewhere else. Since no other bodies have turned up . . ."

Philips's eyes widened. "The other girls might be alive?"

Squill shrugged.

"Something to pray for," the mayor said. "What else?"

"The medical examiner's office found evidence suggesting abduction by someone who's into athletics or strength training. We're checking peds known to be into sports and weightlifting. We're also working closer with Mississippi and Florida."

Philips arched an eyebrow. "Sounds like a bit of headway. None of this came from that guy you had in to look at the cases?"

Squill prickled. "I told you, he was a waste of time."

Thomas Clay, the mayor's assistant, knocked

and entered, looking harried as usual, his wispy comb-over bouncing as he crossed the room. He held a sheaf of computer printouts under his arm and a dozen pieces of mail in his hand. He tossed the letters into the inbox on the mayor's desk.

Philips nodded at the mail. "Anything need fast attention, Tom?"

"Usual speaking invites. A certificate of appreciation from the Sierra Club. Two pieces of hate mail quoting scripture, knew you'd enjoy them. Notice of a mayors' meeting in Montgomery next month – you should go; I'll keep you updated. I round-filed the rest, the usual junk."

"Thanks, Tom."

Clay moved to the window. "I've been watching from my office. It's getting heated out there. Turnbull's whipping them into a frenzy."

"I can deal with Turnbull," Squill said. "Chill his black ass in jail a few days."

Philips's gray eyes blazed at Squill. "You'll do nothing of the sort."

"He's close to inciting to riot. Like yesterday's rally in Bienville Square. He's right on the edge."

"Leave him alone."

Squill's lips creased into a flat smile. "You're telling me to overlook illegal behavior? Can I get that in writing, Mayor?"

"He's done nothing illegal."

"Not quite. But if he does, it's my call how to deal with it, not yours." Squill's eyes smirked. "Is that all you wanted to talk about, Mayor?"

"For now."

Squill wheeled and departed, ramrod straight, almost strutting. Clay pressed the door shut. "There goes a cottonmouth with a badge," he said, unbuttoning his pale suit and sitting in the wing-back chair facing Philips's desk. She sighed and nodded at the papers in her assistant's lap.

"The latest figures?"

Clay's manicured nails tapped the printouts. "Fresh from the pollsters' prediction mill."

"What's the word?"

He unfolded several sheets, studied them. "You lead Runion by three points. With a –"

Philips managed a weary smile. "Margin of error of about four points. I know."

"Right now I think you'd clinch it . . ."

"I hear that 'but' sound in your voice, Tom. But what?"

"There's a wild card in the deck."

"Which is?"

"The flint-edge conservatives'll never vote for you, the la-la liberals always will. There's a big middle distance, Norma. And in that wide, fence-sitting middle are folks who think the mayor's responsible when a stray dog shits in their yard."

"And?"

"No matter what happens or who starts it, it's your fault."

Philips skirted the window and studied the hardest face in the crowd, the dark-suited, clerical-collared man waving his hands and brandishing a

128

bullhorn, gold rings lighting his fingers. Reverend Turnbull saw her and pointed at the window, screaming, "Traitor!"

She said, "So if even a paltry few of the black community get cranked up enough to bust some windows –"

"The hard-cores will spit and sputter and say, 'We told y'all so; let a fe-male in office and this is what you gonna get.' Some of those folks on the fence will listen."

"And my election's cooked."

Clay jabbed the air with an invisible implement. "Stick a fork in it, Norma; it's done."

"I hate politics," she sighed. "How did I ever get to be mayor?"

Clay re-folded the printouts. "That's the easy part: old Mayor Dobbins got caught with his hand in the till and you got appointed. The tough part starts with staying mayor." He paused and stared sympathetically at Philips. "If that's what you really want."

Norma Philips's eyes were lost out the window again.

"More than anything," she said. "God forgive me for it."

Half past eight in the evening. The Gumbo King restaurant had a CLOSED sign in the window. Sandhill popped the caps from a pair of beers and brought them to the table where Ryder was leaning back and staring at the ceiling.

"You look a little lost, Detective Ryder."

Ryder sat forward and took the beer. "I was thinking about a woman. She's in Hawaii right now. At a symposium."

"You wish you were there, right? Wearing a lei and playing ukelele to your lady friend." Sandhill made a strumming motion.

Ryder sighed. "I was thinking more about pineapples."

Sandhill started to ask one question, let it slide, shifted to another. "So how goes the investigation?"

"I dropped by to say you were right, Sandhill."

"I'm not surprised. What was I right about?"

"Hembree Fed-Ex'd carpet and tack samples to the FBI lab. The carpet had been pulled from somewhere."

Sandhill leaned back and tented his fingers against his lips. "Two girls stolen a week apart, only one shows up in the fire. If the purpose was to burn the body beyond recovery of any evidence, DNA, a perp's prints, and both girls were dead –"

"We've been there. Likely they'd both have gone in the fire, but Maya Ledbetter's still out there somewhere."

"So where is Maya? How is she being used?"

"Used?" Ryder said. "That's a grim way to put it."

"It's the way we have to think. What else is there? Ransom? From what I get, neither of the girls' families could scrape together more than twelve bucks and a fistful of food stamps. You guys manage anything else?"

"We're certain that Maya Ledbetter was snatched from Bix Street between Oak and Clary. A record store clerk at Bix and Oak was pretty sure he saw her the night she disappeared. You know the story . . ."

Sandhill said, "Yeah. Mama hits Story's Lounge on buck-a-beer Tuesday and drinks till she pisses herself. Maya always walks over to granny's on Tuesday nights. Granny lives on Clary."

"So now we know the girl made it as far as Oak."

"Why'd the clerk wait to tell the story?"

Ryder said, "Didn't hear about the abduction. Been at a fish camp up the Tensaw."

Sandhill scanned the area in his head. "So instead of seven blocks to look at, it's down to three. I know the area. It's OK until you get to –"

"The last block before Clary. An old warehouse. But still, the traffic's steady on that stretch. Someone pulling a yelling kid off the street would have been noticed, unless she got in willingly, meaning she probably knew the perp. Or he knew the perfect place for the grab."

"Or both." Sandhill was up, scrabbling through his pockets for his keys. "Let's us go a-surveying, Detective Ryder."

They were walking into the street when Sandhill abruptly went back inside. He re-emerged a minute later carrying two plastic tubs of gumbo and wearing his crown.

20

Sandhill and Ryder walked the route Maya Ledbetter had taken. A fast-fading sun bronzed a final corner of sky as night air lay hot and thick, sticky to the touch. Though a few people were on the street, most hunkered in bars, safe behind the neon windows. Sandhill's crown gathered looks but, because wary eyes picked up cop vibes, no remarks.

The pair walked past the two bar-lit blocks to a darker one occupied by a two-story redbrick warehouse, a FOR SALE OR LEASE sign faded almost white.

"Think she walked this side of the street, Detective Ryder?"

"The other side would have been out of her way."

They crunched across broken glass, the night darkening with distance from the corner street-lamp. Cars hissed by like so many anonymous boxes. Ryder pointed ahead.

"The grandmother's apartment is on the next corner. Which means the best place for her abductor to wait would have been right here."

Sandhill stopped at the tight recess of a loading bay and slipped a small Maglite from his pocket. He walked back fifty feet to the dock itself, covered with rotting skids and scattered newspapers, his light reflecting from dead bottles of Thunderbird and Gallo port, here and there a bottle of gut-rip whiskey. The bay stunk of urine and feces and vomit.

"Wino lair," Ryder said. "Place to sleep it off. The recess is deep enough to avoid overt notice by the cops, plus the loading dock's wood, easier sleeping than concrete. Not a bad crash, altogether. If you can get used to the smell."

A sound from the sidewalk. In an eye-blink Ryder had his back to the wall. He tiptoed over broken glass and garbage, then sprang, flinging an arm around the corner.

He reeled in a skinny, wild-haired white guy dressed in Salvation Army motley: camo pants belted with clothesline, a stained white dress shirt, mismatched running shoes, an outsized black rain-coat nearly reaching the pavement. Ryder pulled the protesting man into the bay by his shirtfront, Sandhill aiming the flashlight into red-threaded eyes huge with fear.

"I know this guy," Sandhill said. "Hey there, brother Franklin."

"Who's talking at me?" the man said.

Sandhill turned the flashlight on his face. The wino broke into a gap-toothed grin. Ryder released his shirt.

"Yo, Gumbo King. What you doing back here?"

"I'm checking into the disappearance of that little girl that lived a couple blocks from here, on Franklin."

The man frowned. "I heard 'bout that ugliness."

"What else you hear?"

"I don't tune in too hard to the news, you know what I mean."

"What were you doing around the corner, Franklin?"

"Heard y'all back here rootin' around. Just was listening."

"We in your living room?"

"Here? Too damn stinkin'. I crib a couple blocks over. Got me a prime hidey-hole ahind a printing place. Got these big old bins of paper I can make my nest."

"You know anyone cribs here?"

"Not regular."

"Any cops ask you if you'd seen or heard anything about the girl's disappearance?"

"Hunh-uh. I see cops, my feet turn around."

"I figured. See you later, Franklin."

Sandhill slapped palms with the wino. The man turned to go, hesitated. "Gumbo King? You got a buck for a man with sad luck?"

Sandhill flipped through his wallet, popped out

a five and some ones. The bills disappeared in a swoosh of outsized sleeve.

"You're gonna get some food with that, aren't you, Franklin?"

"Uh, yeah, sure . . ."

Sandhill sighed. "Come on with us, brother. Lemme buy you supper."

When they reached Sandhill's truck he filled a foam cup with crab gumbo and handed it to the wino. He two-handed the cup of gumbo to purple lips with shaking fingers, thick drops of sauce dribbling down his chin as his tongue licked into the cup, getting every drop.

Finished, he belched and dropped the cup on the sidewalk.

"FOR CHRISSAKES, FRANKLIN!" the Gumbo King roared.

Ryder froze. The wino's eyes widened in terror. "What? *What?*"

Sandhill jabbed his finger at a trash receptacle twenty feet distant. "Don't litter. Use a trash can."

The man looked mortified, almost diving to retrieve the cup. When they drove away Ryder watched the man jam the cup deep into the wastebasket, pushing it deeper with his foot, making sure the cup wouldn't escape.

"How you know that rummy, Sandhill?" Ryder asked.

"He's a semi-regular at the soup kitchen we're headed to now. You guys check street people like Franklin?"

135

"As much as we could. It's hard to get a fix; they float around, aimless."

Sandhill shook his head. "No, Ryder. They rarely wander aimlessly. When your life revolves around getting drunk and finding a safe place to sleep it off, you develop a finely honed regimen. You find what works and keep doing it."

Ryder filed the information away, wondering what else he would learn from the strange ex-cop.

Ryder had passed by the mission a hundred times but had never been inside: two stories of whitewashed mason block with one big window downstairs, CHARITY'S HAND MISSION painted on the glass in gold. The paint was flaking and from a distance read H IT AND MISS. Sandhill retrieved the tubs of gumbo and the pair pushed through the door.

Ryder saw a dozen banquet-style tables surrounded by metal folding chairs. Over two dozen of the chairs were claimed by bodies, all looking like they'd gone through a wringer, some more times than others. The room smelled of coffee and sweat, sour breath and unwashed clothes. A large crucifix centered the front wall, Christ's head turned away, as if He Himself had tired of the nightly parade of wretches. A serving table held limp sandwiches and spotted bananas. Several men broke into grins when they saw Sandhill.

"Looky there, it's his highness."

"Hey Gumbo King, what'd you bring?"

There were swinging wood doors to the side; a

kitchen, Ryder noted, aluminum pots and pans visible through round windows. The doors burst open for a man in his late twenties, carrying a bowl of slaw, which he set beside the sandwiches. He was slender, blond, and dressed like any younger guy on Casual Friday: brown loafers, blue jeans, tee shirt. Instead of touting a brand of sportswear, the shirt said, *God Knows This Place Needs More Work.* The man looked up, saw Sandhill, brightened.

"I was wondering if I'd see you tonight, Conner."

Sandhill set the tubs of gumbo on the table. "Not too much left over today, Tim. A quart of crab, a couple quarts chicken and sausage. This is Detective Carson Ryder. And this, Ryder, is Saint Timothy of the Downtrodden."

Ryder smiled and extended his hand. "Never met a saint, Padre. Thought you'd glow."

"Call me Tim," the priest grinned. "And the glow, like everything else, is snarled in red tape somewhere."

Sandhill nodded at the crowd. "Not a bad house tonight, Tim."

"We're running near capacity most nights lately. It's the abductions. My folks don't know the details, just that there's something dark on the streets. Fear registers, and they've been more inclined to sleep in here than out there."

"That's what I'd like to ask your folks about, if I may."

137

Father Tim lifted a puzzled eyebrow. "You're with the police again, Conner? But I thought –"

"A purely temporary arrangement, Tim. Too depressing to talk about."

Sandhill walked to the front of the room and clapped his hands. "Listen up, folks. I need three minutes of your time. There's been two little black girls abducted in the past three weeks. These girls are seven and eight years old. One was taken over by Braxton. One was taken just blocks from here, down by Clary. She was found dead in a house fire, arson."

A mumble of voices, anger and fear.

"I know no one here's involved in anything like that. But someone might know something and don't know that they know. I'm particularly interested in outsiders who might have been seen around the warehouse in the twelve-hundred block of Clary."

Murmurings as the information was digested.

"Anything?" Sandhill asked. "Anyone?"

An Appalachian-accented voice twanged from one of the near tables.

"Just maybe I know something about that."

Ryder leaned against the wall and studied the speaker. Mid-twenties. White. Average height with wide shoulders. Long dirty-blond hair with the accent on dirty. A cocky grin. A sleeveless red shirt displaying jailhouse tattoos on arms that retained definition. Ryder figured the guy for a biker who'd drank and drugged away the bike and most everything else; on the downhill slide, but hadn't lost the biceps or the attitude yet.

Sandhill said, "Talk to me."

The man batted his eyes at the ceiling. "Say please."

"Please talk to me."

The man spoke slowly, enjoying being the center of attention.

"I been sleeping there. Ain't much of nothing but a place to lay. Had another place over behind the parts store, but some muthafucks done run me off. Took four of 'em, though. I started up sleeping at the truck dock. No big deal."

"How about it . . . you see anyone different hanging around there a couple weeks back?"

"Might have."

"I'm not talking ordinary. I'm talking about maybe a person didn't fit in with the street crowd."

The man milked the moment like he was thinking hard, whisking his chin with his fingers.

"Coulda been."

Sandhill said, "How about telling me about it."

"Say please."

"Please tell me about it."

The man cupped a hand behind his ear. "I didn't hear you."

Sandhill upped the volume. "Please tell me about it."

The man leaned back, laced his fingers behind his head, and grinned.

"I dunno, partner. Anything in it for me?"

Sandhill crossed the floor in a half-heartbeat, seized the man by his hair and the back of his pants, half-dragging and half throwing him into the kitchen, the doors swinging shut behind them. A long angry howl was followed by a clamor of pots and final stentorian *bong*.

Father Tim shot Ryder an anxious glance.

Ryder crossed his arms, not moving from the wall. "All I can tell you is it's a good thing the guy wasn't littering, Father."

"His name is Lee Ray Harland," Sandhill said as they drove away. "Hits the mission once a week for a shower and three-four times for chow. Like he said, he's been cooping at the dock now and then."

Sandhill flicked on the AC. Cool air hissed into the cab. He angled a vent over his face, sighed, and continued.

"A week or so ago – most of these guys have no concept of time – Harland went to the dock for a pint of gin he'd stuck behind the skids. He said it was getting dark, so that puts it around seven thirty. Two guys pulled up in a cream or white van. A guy got out and ran Harland off; said he owned the warehouse and it was private property I checked. The owner's eighty-six, lives in Florida."

"Harland have a description of the guy who ran him off?"

Sandhill shook his head. "The visitors arrived

after Harland put down most of the gin. He's hazy on detail. He thinks the guy was young, maybe had blond hair under a light-colored Stetson-style hat, straw. He remembers the guy keeping the brim pulled low over his eyes. Wore shades, too."

"Late in the day for sunglasses," Ryder noted. "Unless you're hiding behind them."

"You got it. But mostly Harland recalls a Chihuahua."

"The guy had a dog?" Ryder said.

"No. Harlan kept saying the guy reminded him of a Chihuahua: small and loud."

"Great. We don't need a police artist, we need a Kennel Club registry." Ryder thought a moment. "How come a biker-boy like Harland didn't just whup the yappy guy's ass?"

"Because of the man in the van. Harland had a canine description for him, too."

Ryder raised an eyebrow. "Which was?"

"Bulldog. Huge fucking bulldog."

21

Truman leaned out the window of his van. "I've been looking for you, Jacy. I thought you might be in the park. I want to show you something. Can you come here? Over to the van?"

"Aunt Nike says never go up to people I don't know."

"You know me, Jacy."

"Just from school. Not through and through."

"I want to show you something. You won't believe how cool it is."

"What?"

"Your school pictures. Hurry and I'll let you see."

"The pictures don't come to school like always?"

"All the ordinary pictures go to school. I was bringing you yours because it's super special."

"Special how?"

"It won a contest . . ."

*   *   *

Norma Philips turned from her office window.

"Quieter out there this afternoon, Tom."

A dozen protesters walked on the pavement below, a few chanting half-heartedly, most talking among themselves. Tom Clay sat in the high-backed chair in front of Philips's desk, a legal pad and PDA in his lap.

"Turnbull's not there to fire them up. It's the fifteenth of the month, payday for some folks. He's out counting rent money."

"Doing what?"

Clay produced a pocket aerosol of breath freshener and spritzed his tonsils. "Turnbull's a slumlord, Norma. You think he buys silk suits and gold rings by passing the plate at an inner-city church?"

"A slumlord preacher?"

Clay flicked lint from his tie. "If he didn't preach he'd just be one more mouth feasting on the poor. This way, he's a businessman who got the calling. Plus being a community rabble-rouser keeps the code-enforcement team from coming down too hard on his ratbucket properties. If they do, he howls that he's being persecuted for being a black organizer."

"And people believe him?"

Clay grinned mischievously and pressed his hands together as if in prayer. "He's a man of the cloth."

"Y'know, Tom, sometimes I feel pretty naïve."

"You're a great community organizer, Norma, a red-hot wire. You've saved greenspace and wetlands, fought for that new park, the clinic, but you're still a babe in the woods, politically. However, I have no doubt you'll be a quick learner . . ." Clay winked, "given another term."

"And on that subject, what's my event today?"

Clay consulted his PDA. "Supper at the Morningview A.M.E. church. Unfortunately, Runion's attending a Chamber of Commerce dance. Guess who'll pick up more campaign money?"

"It's not about money, Tom."

"It's all about money, Norma. And image. If you're seen as a person who can get things done, you're halfway there. The other half is buying ads saying you can get things done. Runion's got five times the war chest you have."

She shrugged. "What can I do?"

"It'd help if the cops nailed the bastard taking the girls," Clay said.

"How's that boost me in the public eye?"

"As mayor, you get to talk up the great work of the police, administrative teamwork, government in action, all that feel-good bullpuckey. You get a halo just from standing beside the angels. Plus, the protests will stop. They remind people there's something bad happening, which unfairly comes to rest on your shoulders."

"I don't have much control over –"

Clay smiled wryly. "Keep pushing Squill to solve this case now; stay in his face. Be a shrill and relentless harpy; it's what you've always been best at."

Philips tucked a stray strand of hair behind her ear. "Squill does what he wants, Tom. God knows what it is, though. He seems to be trying to find the person taking the girls, or at least the rank-and-file is. They've got a couple new leads, but . . ." She held her hands out, empty.

Clay said, "Can you at least tell the public what the leads are? It might give them some hope and settle things down a bit."

"I won't risk jeopardizing the investigation just to grab a few quick points in the polls."

Clay grinned. "Just testing."

She shook her head. "Say the killer is caught. I do the brothers-in-arms bit with the police. Am I the one who benefits most?"

"No. That'd be Squill. He'll grab the big headlines. But you get to bask in reflected glory."

"But what if the case isn't solved? The protests get worse, even violent, and I lose the election. Who will Runion push as chief of police?"

"Squill. They're two peas in a pod."

"So no matter what happens, Squill comes out on top."

"This is politics, Norma. Cream sinks, shit rises."

Philips smiled sadly. "How many years you been watching the rise and fall, Tom? Fifteen or so?"

"I've been a city employee for . . ." Clay looked at the ceiling, counted silently. "Sixteen years, Norma. Parks department, police oversight board and so forth. Just another brick in the wall, until you."

"You know how things work. I don't. And some-body's got to keep me honest."

Her smile dropped away and she tapped an unpolished nail on her watch. "I suppose I should work on my speech for tonight."

Clay left. Philips began jotting notes for her speech. She wasn't looking forward to the event. The audience would be polite but insistent on information regarding the missing girls. What answers did she have for them? Squill was full of assurances that his department was doing everything possible, but what did that mean? Despite the personality of a slime-eel, the man projected confidence and ability, but in twenty years of community activism, she'd found that packages didn't always reflect content.

And what happened to the ex-cop who was supposed to be such a firebrand? Squill said the guy didn't find anything new. But suddenly comes word the department's looking at athletic types. Where'd that come from?

She reached for her phone. Her assistant answered halfway through the first ring.

"What you need, Norma?"

"Quick question, Tom. You ever hear of an ex-cop named Thornhill or something like that?"

Clay's line clicked dead.

"What kind of contest did my picture win?" Jacy asked.

"A special contest for the best school picture in

the whole state of Alabama. The winner goes to Montgomery and gets on TV and in the papers. It's like the Junior Miss Pageant."

"Can you show me the picture?"

"We're too far apart for you to see it."

"You could bring it to the fence."

"I sprained my ankle yesterday and can't walk. I'll mail it. Unless you can come over here."

"The fence is in the way."

"There's a hole in the fence, Jacy. Like a door. Right over there. You can push through."

Jacy walked to the cut in the fence. She pushed the fencing to and fro, testing the opening by pressing a foot against the mesh.

"The Junior Miss Pageant? For sure?"

22

Clay rushed through Philips's door without knocking. He slid the door shut, making sure the latch clicked.

"Thornhill? Did you mean Sandhill, Norma?"

"Something-hill; I guess that was it. Why?"

"Where'd you hear about Sandhill?" Clay asked.

"A meeting with the police department a couple weeks back. There was this detective – former detective, I guess – and some cops wanted him to study the abductions, see if he could contribute anything."

"*Squill* wanted Sandhill to look at the cases?"

"Squill about had a hissy-fit. It was other people at the meeting. That Zemain fellow, for one. Even Bidwell seemed for it."

"That makes more sense. Did Sandhill take this look?"

Philips nodded. "He did, but nothing came of it, according to Squill. Who's Sandhill?"

Clay clasped his hands behind his back and

wandered to the window. Philips watched him study a storm-ready sky, as if answers were scribed in the thickening cumulus. After a silent minute, he turned, leaned against the wall and crossed his arms.

"Let me spin you a tale about one John Conner Sandhill, Norma."

"What kind of tale? Good? Bad?"

"No one's quite sure," Clay said.

Sandhill had his monthly meeting with his accountant and it was 4.15 before he returned to the restaurant. Every seat sat bare, but in an hour people would be standing in line for a table. Marie was at the door when he entered.

"Sorry I'm late, but the news is good: We don't have to live under a bridge this week. Where's Jacy?" He held up a bag. "I thought we'd take a break from gumbo tonight and I brought po-boys." He yelled to the kitchen. "Hey, Jacy, you back there? Get out here, girl." Sandhill looked at Marie. "I hope you guys didn't wait ice cream on me."

"I thought Jacy was with you, Conner," she whispered. "I hoped you'd picked her up at the park and gone off somewhere together."

Sandhill's brow tightened. "She's not here?"

"I ain't seen her," Marie said, her voice starting to tremble. "And she always here by now."

Sandhill looked at his watch. Jacy was forty-five minutes past her usual entrance.

"Call the school, see if she's there. I'll check outside."

Sandhill hit the door at a run. He was at the park in a minute, jogging it end to end, looking into bushes, behind trees. Two black men in their mid-twenties were playing one-on-one. Sandhill strode on to the court.

"Yo, man, we got a game here," said one of the players, heavyset, his shirt soaked with sweat.

"You see a little girl in the park this afternoon?" Sandhill said. "Eight years old. Blue dress."

"I playin' ball, man. I see the hoop."

The heavy man turned away from Sandhill, ignoring him to sight from free-throw stance. When he bent his knees for the shot, Sandhill slapped the ball away.

"Hey, crazy muthafucker . . ."

Sandhill said, "You didn't see a kid, maybe back there on that bench?"

"Said I wasn't lookin'."

The man glared at Sandhill and bent to grab the basketball. Sandhill set his foot on the ball, held it tight against the asphalt.

"Yo, Jack, chill," the other player yelled to Sandhill. The man trotted over, tall and lanky and wearing a Little Richard mustache.

"This kid you talkin' about. Black girl about this high? Always got her nose in a book?"

"That's her."

"She here all the time. Almost every day."

"Today?" Sandhill asked.

The man nodded. "Sure 'nough. 'Til maybe a half-hour ago."

"You see her leave?"

"Hunh-uh. She here, then I look over and she gone. Something wrong, man? You lookin' sick."

23

A half-drowned ghost walked through night rain falling in plumb-straight lines, rain sizzling over black pavement, rain roaring down the drain grates. Neon bar light shone over sheeting water, the ghost's feet splashing through reflections, slogging, shoes squishing with every step. The sodden apparition pushed through the bar-room door and stood dripping in the middle of the floor. Voices stopped. The click of pool balls halted. Cigarettes hung in mid-air.

"I'm looking for a little girl," the ghost said, the fiftieth time in five hours. "Black. Eight years old. Probably taken from the park on the 1400 block of Ardmore. Was anyone around there at that time?"

"You po-lice done been here two times axin' that," a woman's voice said. "Nobody saw nothing."

The ghost studied the faces; no averted eyes, no looks of lying, several faces stunned sober by the moment, struck with concern and sympathy.

Conner Sandhill turned and ghosted back into the night. The rain was so loud and Sandhill so deep in his thoughts he didn't hear the heavy black SUV slip up behind him. The light from the 500,000-candlepower spotlight seared his eyes and blinded him. He threw his hands between the light and his face.

Doors slammed and hard hands gripped his arms. He spun from the grip on his right into the person holding him at the left and brought his elbow up hard, feeling it connect with a jaw, hearing a pained grunt. Someone put a chokehold on him from behind, a thick arm wrapping his neck like a python. Sandhill gripped the arm, held it tight and went limp, two-hundred-forty pounds pulling his attacker with him as he fell to the pavement. He rolled as he hit, flipping his attacker over and breaking his grip. He drove rigid fingers into the soft tissue at the base of the man's throat, pushed to his feet . . .

And heard a round jacked into a chamber.

"Freeze your ass, Sandhill!" a voice yelled. "Get your hands up where I can see them – now!"

Half blind from the beam, Sandhill turned to the voice and saw only a dark shape against the light. He glared at it and kept his hands open and wide.

"Screw you, Ducky."

His two attackers struggled to their feet. Sandhill saw Bobby Tandy and Corly Watkins, two pencil dicks from Internal Affairs and longtime enlistees in Squill's sycophantic army. Sandhill was happy to see Tandy with hand to throat, gasping for air.

"You're under arrest, Sandhill. Stay cool."

Commander Ainsley Duckworth stood three paces distant, rain sluicing from his hat brim to the wide shoulders of a brown raincoat, his nine-millimeter service weapon aimed at the center of Sandhill's chest. Sandhill moved his hands away from his body.

"Arrest. What the hell for?"

"We've been following you an hour. You've been interfering with police business . . ."

"You've been following *me*? An eight-year-old girl snatched off the street and you people are following me, you sick fuck?"

". . . and maybe impersonating a police officer."

Sandhill swiped wet hair from his eyes and glared at Duckworth. "How's it feel, Ducks? Is it like being back in Internal Affairs again? I'm surprised you're here; you always did your best work from a distance."

"In IA I went after piece-of-shit cops. You're just a piece-of-shit civilian." Duckworth gestured with the muzzle. "Get in the car, whorehill. But first lose the ankle piece."

"The only place I'm going is home."

Tandy and Watkins were snarl-faced and circling Sandhill, but not moving into range. Duckworth said, "Don't add to your worries. Pass over the iron and get in the car. Chief Squill wants to talk to you."

154

"This is going to come back and haunt, you, Ducky," Sandhill said.

"Not a chance. Pass over the iron, scumhill."

Sandhill bent, lifted his pant leg. He wanted to keep the holster on; having the illegal lockpick drop out could complicate matters.

"Don't get your undies in a wad, Ducks. I'm pulling the piece and handing it over."

He two-fingered the .32 to Duckworth's wide palm and they headed downtown.

"All that's going on and you're following me?" Sandhill said from the back seat. "You're absolutely frigging useless, Ducks."

"*I'm* useless, Sandhill?" Duckworth's grin was palpable in the dark of the car. "Which one of us was supposed to be watching the Charlane girl?"

Rain beat against the starboard windows of Mattoon's quarters, a line of squalls coming in from the east as the ship nosed higher into the Caribbean. A dozen white tapers burned from sconces secured to the bulkheads of the main room.

Mattoon sat at his keyboard, a crystal tumbler of absinthe beside him, the shimmering green liqueur poured from a Belle Époque bottle of Pernod Fils, one of a dozen he'd purchased at four thousand dollars a bottle. He allowed himself a journey with the hypnotic distillation of wormwood every few weeks, the drug seeming to heighten and focus his senses.

His fingers danced over the keyboard as he entered a code he could recite in his sleep. His heart pulsed in his throat.

The screen flickered. It lit to a photo of Lorelei in a pink blouse and blue jeans. She slept on a double bed, head cocked to one side, her wrists and pink-socked feet loosely bound with clothesline. The photo appeared to have been taken in the dark by flash. His heart soaring, Mattoon read the accompanying communiqué.

Your product has been secured (encrypted photo file enclosed) and is in excellent condition. We will use the same transfer method as last year unless advised otherwise. The 50% upfront fee should be directed to the following account number . . .

Mattoon felt the absinthe rise in his mind like an icy wind. He made the financial transaction from his keyboard, then walked to the window and looked across the storm-dazzled night. The rain seemed to strike the ship in rhythmic sheets, a symphony of water. He started dancing, a jittering tiptoe shuffle, shoulders bouncing, hands held high. The rain beat harder against the windows. Mattoon removed his shirt and continued dancing, elbows above his shoulders, hands clawing at the air.

He removed his pants. In Mattoon's mind the rain became a sonic river of harmonies, shifting and iridescent. Mattoon danced naked through the river, feeling it sweep and flow and surge toward flood. He threw the door wide and danced on to the walkway. The rain drove his eyes shut, beat his hair flat. Mattoon grabbed the rail and screamed his name at the sky until the lighting answered. He screamed again and again, until his voice broke like glass against the wind.

Mattoon cried, and as he wept, he laughed. His hands grabbed for rain, pulled it close, wiped it across his face, down his body, rinsing himself clean with rain and tears and thunder. He stumbled back into the room. Water fell from his skin, from his eyes, spurted from within him; it was all glorious water. He slid to the floor with unfocused eyes.

His grin was all teeth as he lay spent and gasping, the carpet behind him as wet and glistening as if tracked by a legion of snails.

24

The booking room smelled of fear and anger and wet bodies. Sandhill sat for half an hour, watching the dismal parade of wife-beaters and drunks, bar-fighters and car-boosters, pickpockets and dope peddlers.

Squill finally arrived, grinning like a man who'd just discovered a hundred forgotten dollars in a pair of pants.

"You bought yourself some real trouble, Sandhill. Assaulting an officer."

"Won't work, Terrence. Your piss-monkeys were too fired up to ID themselves before crawling over me."

"I was thinking more along the lines of impersonating a cop."

"You mean in the bars? I never ID'd myself as a cop; I'm not that stupid."

"You didn't do much to correct the notion, did you?"

"I can't be responsible for the misconceptions

of others when I've done nothing to contribute to those beliefs. People occasionally mistake you for a cop, Terrence. It's not your fault."

Squill put a mirror-bright black wingtip on the bench beside Sandhill and bent low.

"You can't piss me off, Sandhill, so don't wear yourself out trying. I know how shitty you must feel, having fucked up your babysitting job so royally. But if I ever hear of you interfering in police business again – and you and I both know that's exactly what you were doing tonight – I'm gonna slam-dunk your ass in jail. Then I'll make sure your cell-buddies know you're an ex-cop. You might be able to boot around Tandy and Watkins; let's see how you do in a concrete box full of blacks and bikers."

Sandhill's knuckles whitened. He whispered, "Are we done here?"

Squill pushed off the bench. "That's up to you. Stay where you belong, slinging hash, and it's over. Mess in the case and it's just started."

Sandhill stood until his eyes were level with Squill's. "Your investigation is foundering, Terrence. This isn't your usual drooling sicko out there – it's got a different feel. I can help; you know it, I know it. But this isn't about the girls, is it? It's because I dropped the dime on your little sideline security business way back when. Get past it, Terrence, for the sake of the –"

"Get out," Squill hissed through clenched teeth. "Get out while you can."

"I can pick up my gun, Terrence? Since no charges seem to be being filed in this little, uh, misunderstanding?"

Squill spun on a heel and retreated into the station. Sandhill retrieved his weapon from a desk sergeant who wouldn't meet his eyes. Outside, the rain had been replaced by a sprinkling of stars. He heard a horn, followed by Ryder squealing to the curb in a battered gray pickup.

"Jacy?" Sandhill asked, climbing inside.

Ryder shook his head. "Nothing yet."

"Take me to Brill Street. I've got some places to check."

"There's nothing you can do, Sandhill. I'm dropping you at your truck."

Sandhill's voice bristled. "Jacy's out there, Ryder."

"So are about a hundred cops. Plus the state and county boys. We've got BOLOs stretching from Florida to Louisiana."

"Be On the Look-Out for what?" Sandhill said, voice rising with anger. "You have no description of the perp, car, anything. What the hell they going to do? Stand in the fucking street with a sign saying, 'Honk if you've got Jacy?'"

"Crank it back a notch, Sandhill. You'll need the energy soon enough."

"What the hell for?"

"For the girl's mother," Ryder said gently. "She's back at the restaurant. Waiting."

* * *

160

Turn Left at BP Station, go 2.4 miles to sign for Terry's Fish Camp . . .

Wallace Wainwright Benson III, fifty-six years of age, sat on the boards of a major bank, a stock brokerage, an old-line insurance firm. Politicians sought his benediction. His wife having divorced him twelve years previously, he ate daily at one of three exclusive clubs. He enjoyed golf, but not slinging the clubs into the car, so he'd purchased a small estate bordering the fourth fairway of one of the three finest golf courses in Ohio. Twice named "Mr Charitable Giving" in the *Columbus Dispatch*, Benson's company had recently endowed a chair at Ohio State University's College of Business and Finance.

But tonight he was just a terrified man in a Mercedes-Benz, fourteen aching hours south of home. Though his AC was set to the highest register, he was sweating like a roofer in July, stopping every few minutes to consult instructions on a sheet of paper.

Turn right, proceed 1.6 miles . . .

He'd driven like a scared old woman on his way south, until he realized it was the drive north that demanded utmost care.

See old boat on blocks. Go 0.2 past, turn left on dirt road . . .

Before leaving he'd transferred a down payment of one hundred and twenty-five thousand dollars to a Caribbean bank. It was no big deal, his guest-house cost twice that. And he never had guests.

Road dead ends. Turn right down dirt path to old farmhouse. Stop and wait.

He pulled up to a gray wooden house in the last stages of rot. Spanish moss ghosted the live oak above his car. He turned down the AC so he might hear any motion in the night, but heard only burring crickets and the jackhammer of his heart.

A heart that nearly stopped when headlamps from a white van tucked back in the trees flicked on, then off. He heard doors creaking open. The sound of feet lifted high to trample through weeds. Two men in dark clothing and stocking masks appeared in front of his car. One was a rail, the other large as two men, at least across the chest and arms.

"Cut the lights," a voice hissed. Then, dark, the only light from wheeling stars in a sky of ink. Footsteps drew closer. Light from a flashlight struck his eyes, blinding him.

"Christ, not in his face," the skinny man said.

"You fucking hold it next time," the big one said. Then, "Let me see the trunk. Did you make a good nest?"

"A wh-what?"

"Get out and open the fucking trunk," the huge man commanded.

Benson complied with trembling fingers. The man scowled at the mish-mash of blankets and pillows. He yanked them out and hung them over Benson's quivering shoulders, then carefully replaced them one by one, crafting smooth layers, tucking, folding, giving the trunk interior a soft evenness. He removed the two pillows, fluffed them, set them back inside.

"Air?" he grunted.

"It's ventilated," Benson said, his voice cracking. The big man said nothing. He clomped into the woods, returning a minute later carrying a slumping cylindrical bundle, which he lowered into the trunk as gingerly as if it were antique porcelain.

"Come and see your dreams," the skinny man said.

Benson shook so much he could barely walk. The small man's hand peeled back a flap of black cloth. Two incredibly beautiful eyes stared back at him. The mouth was covered with thick courses of tape. The eyes were wet and terrified.

"Kittinia," Benson whispered, breathless.

The skinny man smiled. "Her real name's Maya. Or whatever you want to name her. You can do that, you know. She's all yours."

Wallace Wainwright Benson III, a man who joked easily with senators, uttered a dry squeak.

"She was fed an hour ago," the man continued. "Don't open the trunk until you're where it's safe. You understand?"

Benson nodded and the huge man flicked the trunk closed with a fingertip. The man stared at Benson for a long time, then followed his skinny partner into the trees. Twenty seconds later the van was gone.

Benson waited for the wild beating of his heart to subside, then retraced his tracks until he saw the lights of Interstate 10. Joining the anonymous eastbound traffic, his night exploded into blossoms of black flowers, the décor of a world where every wish was granted.

"Where's Nike, Marie?" Sandhill asked, standing in the dining room and smelling of rain and sweat and anger. It was past midnight. The sign and most of the lights were off, a single bank of rear fluorescents casting long shadows across the dining room.

Marie stopped pacing. She shut her eyes and shook her head. "After the po-lice axed all their questions, that poor girl walked back and forth two hours, quiet as death and shaking like a scared lamb. I say, 'Nike, sit down, get some rest 'til Conner come in.' Then 'bout a half-hour back she said she needed to go out. I told her it wasn't the way, but I couldn't keep her in here, Conner, Lord knows I tried." Marie dabbed her eyes with a tissue. "If she gets messed up, it's gonna tear her apart when she come out of it. For a long time after that, too."

"She can't help it, Marie; it's a disease."

"I told her it was my fault, but she didn't hear. I tried to say –"

Sandhill shook his head. "No, goddammit, Marie. I'm the one Nike left in charge."

". . . how I wasn't thinking, how I shoulda axed

164

you to pick her up at school or gone myself. I shoulda −"

"Marie . . ."

"I've got two grandbabies, Conner. I watch them like a mama hawk. But I wasn't watching over Jacy like I shoulda been."

Sandhill picked up a chair, banged its legs on the floor. "Dammit. How many times do I have to say I don't want to hear it, Marie."

Marie's eyes flared. "Don't you be telling me what to −"

The chair banged down again, a leg splintered off.

"Enough!"

Marie started to yell back, caught herself. Sandhill sat and looked away. Marie closed her eyes and shook her head, then walked to Sandhill. She sat and put her hand on his forearm.

"I got my right to feel bad too, Conner. Nike talked to me before she picked you to watch Jacy. She picked you for more reasons than you know."

Sandhill closed his eyes. "One of the reasons was that you'd be around to help out."

Marie nodded. "She knew you ain't big on kids and wouldn't be easy with the idea of keeping Jacy, but you'd be able to ax me things if you needed."

Sandhill took a deep breath, released it slowly. Marie watched, started to talk, checked herself. He walked to the window and stood behind his sign, looking through the dark tubes of chargeless neon.

"Another reason was that you and Nike believed in me, Marie; as an ex-cop I could protect Jacy from horror."

Marie walked to the window, turned Sandhill to her, pulled him tight and laid her head against his chest. "It wasn't that you was a cop, Conner. Nike and I both believed there was a special light acrost you. Evil would pass us over if you was around."

Marie and Sandhill stood by the window looking like lovers frozen in a slow dance. Outside on the street a taxi rounded the corner and glided toward the restaurant. It slid by, but a hundred feet down the block it made a sharp U-turn, cut its lights, and returned to park in the shadows across the street.

25

Marie's hand flew to her mouth. "Conner, there's someone outside!"

Sandhill spun to the window. A slender black man stared through the glass. He pointed to the entrance. Sandhill flung the door open.

"We're closed."

"I know, man. I want to talk to you."

"What about?"

The man fanned his face with his hand. "It hot out here, man. Share some AC."

Sandhill stepped aside and the man scooted by low and fast. He was young, late teens or early twenties, with a gold stud in his right lobe, black jeans and a blue uniform shirt with *Ace Taxi* embroidered on a pocket.

"I know you from somewhere," Sandhill said.

The man smiled hesitantly and a gold tooth gleamed between his lips.

"About two weeks back you was gonna shoot me."

Sandhill stared, nodded. "Devon Green, that the name?"

"TeeShawn Green."

"We got some stuff going down here, Green. Speak your piece."

"I heard about it, mister. I'm sorry. About the little girl, I mean. But what I'm here for, man, is about that lady . . . the girl's mama?"

Sandhill stepped forward, eyes narrowed. "What do you know about –"

Green held his hands up defensively. "I driving a cab, now, mister. Doing it almos' a week. After that stuff in the alley, I started . . . thinking 'bout how all I could say after nineteen years was what a fuck-up I was. It shamed me. I know the city good, so I got a job humpin' a hack. I figure if I keep at it and get a good work record –"

"Save the soliloquy, Green. Tell me about Nike."

Green walked to the window and glanced across the street at the cab. "I was driving by earlier on and that woman Nike waved me down and wanted me to carry her to a place on Brevard near Twentieth. It ain't nowhere a decent woman wants to be."

"You talking about the Full House?" Sandhill said. "After-hours club?"

Green nodded. "A *nasty* place. Lotsa bad shit to get into."

"She's there now?" Sandhill asked, resignation in his voice.

"No, man. She across the street in my taxi.

When I saw she the one lost that little girl, I told her I wasn't carrying her no place like the Full House. I told dispatch I was taking my break and took her out the causeway. I parked where she could look at the water, like I do when I'm sad. I got outta the taxi and walked forty, fifty feet, but could still hear her crying. When I went back she said she wanted to come here."

"She high?"

"She didn't fix or smoke or drink or nothing I saw. She in bad shape though, man, sick with the grief, hurting all the way through."

Sandhill started through the door, then stopped to pull out his wallet. Without a thought he yanked all the bills out – tens, twenties, a fifty – and thrust them at the cabdriver. Green looked them over and carefully plucked out a ten and four ones.

"This pays the taxi company, man. I ain't taking nothing cuz I still owing . . . you know?"

Sandhill laid a hand over Green's shoulder, squeezed it, and followed him out the door. A minute later Nike slouched in a few steps ahead of Sandhill and walked to the center of the room, staring blankly at the walls. Sandhill tried to ease her to a chair.

"Don't touch me, Conner," she said, pushing his hands away. "You don't want to get your hands dirty."

Marie stepped forward. "No honey, don't do this."

"Do what, Marie? I'm scum . . . I promised

Thena I'd keep her daughter safe. But could I stay straight enough to take care of her even before all this madness started?"

Sandhill said, "Don't go that road, Nike. It was my –"

"Fault? Your fault I was in treatment? Your fault I can't honor a deathbed promise to my own sister? What you did, Conner, was everything I asked you to do."

Nike dropped into a chair, eyes on the floor. "You've worked on these kind of cases before, Conner. What are the statistics? What are the chances?"

"You can't ask me that, Nike. They're all different."

Nike slammed her open hand on the table, salt, pepper, condiments and sweeteners pitching to the floor.

"I said tell me the goddamn chances."

"The odds are pretty good, Nike. We just have to keep pressing the cops to –"

"You're a lousy liar, Conner. Jacy's going to die, isn't she?"

Sandhill closed his eyes. "Nike . . ."

"He's going to hurt her and kill her, throw her in a house and set it on fire, isn't he, Conner? Aren't those the odds?"

Marie stepped closer, opening her arms. "Baby . . ."

Nike turned away. A shiver took her body like a seizure. "What's happening to Jacy? Is she calling for me? Crying for me? Is she even . . . even . . ."

Her voice broke into wet shards and she stood violently, knocking over the table. She kicked it away, picked up a chair, and threw it at the window. Glass exploded outward. The shattered signage of THE GUMBO KING hung against the air for an instant, then crashed to the floor. Nike clutched her head in her hands, fell to her knees, and began screaming like her soul was in flames.

26

Morning had arrived clear and fresh. Mattoon and Dear walked the rails of the weatherdeck, sternward, his hand over the girl's bare shoulder. He'd asked her to wear the long gown, green as the morning sea, its hem gently swirling at her toes. Behind her ear was a rose of white silk.

"You look beautiful this morning, Dear," Mattoon said quietly. "Like a princess."

The girl looked away.

"Do you know what day this is?" Mattoon prodded. "Our anniversary. One year together. What do you say to that?"

The girl said nothing. Mattoon turned to the sound of a low whistle. Tenzel Atwan appeared from an internal staircase two dozen meters away.

"Wait right here, Dear. I'll return in a moment."

Mattoon went to the shirtless Atwan. The man was incapable of standing still, his muscles coiling like snakes under his oiled skin as he twitched and shifted weight from foot to foot.

"Yes, Tenzel?"

"Radar say no ships in area. Closest behind us is four hours to get here."

Mattoon considered the information and nodded. "Very well. Start dumping the garbage."

Atwan disappeared back into the stairway. Mattoon studied the turned-away girl for a long moment, as if fixing a portrait in his mind. He returned to her side and led her sternward until they ran out of ship. Mattoon leaned against the white rail. Five stories below the ship's turbulence roiled the water, sending vortices spinning from the stern like twisting sparks.

"We've enjoyed a wonderful year, Dear," Mattoon said. "You came to me as unformed clay and I molded a woman. Then, with the twin gifts of my mind and body, I saved that woman from her base nature and made her truly *live*. Remember how well you lived, Dear? Few get such chances in life, reap such rewards."

The girl stared away. Mattoon put his hand at the small of her back and coaxed her to the railing. "You've had a year that millions of women would trade their sorry little lives for."

The crew began jettisoning accumulated garbage and other detritus. Mattoon smelled rotting food, human waste, broken-down oil from the engine room. The churning wake glistened with flotsam and sewage.

The girl's face began to quiver and weep. Mattoon pulled her close. Lifted her face to his.

"It's a beautiful day, Dear. Isn't it? Let me hold you in my arms."

When he lifted her, the girl seemed as light as a sparrow, Mattoon noted. Or a kite, green against the sky for a moment, then fluttering end over end into the foaming water.

After Marie took Nike home, Sandhill covered the broken window with a sheet of plywood. He wrote *Closed Due to Family Emergency* on boxboard and taped it to the door. He put coffee in the machine for thirty cups and water for ten, then turned on his police-band scanner. He pulled out the case reports and began looking for anything he might have missed.

When the phone rang at eight a.m. he was expecting Ryder.

"Mr Sandhill, this is Thomas Clay from Mayor Philips's office. First, let me offer you my deepest sympathy; I understand the Charlane girl was under your care when the abduction occurred."

Sandhill said nothing.

"But that's not the full reason for my call, sir. The mayor would appreciate it if you could drop by to see her this morning."

"Why?"

"She doesn't discuss everything with me, Mr Sandhill. Can you come over, say about ten?"

Sandhill looked at his watch and sighed. "I suppose. Listen, Clay, I'm not into any politician's long-winded –"

"Neither is Mayor Philips, sir. She'll expect you in two hours."

Sandhill tossed the phone back in the cradle and cursed bureaucratic madness. Ten-to-one this was one of Squill's gambits; it had been the mayor who'd sparked Sandhill's fleeting return to the MPD, now Squill was probably using her to make sure Sandhill kept his nose out of things. Under some proper political guise of condolences, no doubt. He muttered darkly beneath his breath and began sifting through the cases again.

Something in there was bothering him, but what?

It surprised the manager of Security Devices, Inc. to find a customer waiting at the door at eight a.m., a monster of a man, bull-chested, arms like a normal man's thighs. The manager, a slender bespectacled Hispanic man in his early thirties, pulled out his keys.

"I don't usually find people waiting. What is it, an emergency?"

Rose said, "I need one of those small cameras. One I can hook up to my TV." He followed the manager inside, where it was cool and quiet and smelled of carpet cleaner.

"Color or black and white? Color's a few hundred more."

"I want the best picture I can get."

"High-res color. Step over here and I'll show you what I've got."

Rose inspected several systems as the manager explained their differences, then chose a remote-zoom model. The man rang up the purchases and looked Rose over.

"Damn, man. Wish I had a build like that. What's your chest . . . fifty-two, fifty-four?"

Rose sucked in a deep breath, said, "Fifty-five and a half, last I checked."

"Women go for that super-ripped look, do they?"

Rose grinned and Elvis-Presleyed his hips. "Drives them wild, buddy. Like animals."

27

"Have a seat, Mr Sandhill," Norma Philips said from behind her desk, pushing aside a stack of official papers.

Sandhill stood motionless, arms crossing his faded denim shirt, studying Norma Philips as if uncertain of her species.

She said, "Fine. You can stand if you want."

"I don't have time for whatever Squill put you up to. In case you haven't heard –"

"Acting Chief Squill put me up to nothing. And you have my deepest sympathy."

"I don't want your deepest anything. What I want is out of here."

"And what I want is fifteen minutes of your time."

Sandhill adjusted his watch. "You get five. When it beeps, I'm gone. Talk."

Philips slipped on reading glasses. She pulled a manila folder from her desk drawer, licked her fingertip, and opened it.

Lifting a slender eyebrow, Philips said, "You've quite the interesting resumé, John Conner Sandhill."

"I can die content. Is that all you wanted to say?"

Philips ignored Sandhill and began thumbing through the sheets in the folder. "You went to law school. Tulane. Three years later you dropped out." She looked at him over the top of her glasses. "Was it too tough for you?"

"Reading and memorizing? Listen, lady, if I wanted to –"

She held up her hand to cut him off; it was Philips's turn to study Sandhill as if he were an exotic species. "No, it wasn't tough, was it? If anything it was too easy. Too pat. Maybe you needed more of a challenge. Maybe you wanted to work the front edge of the legal system, right out there on the streets. Was that it?"

"You want payment for this analysis, doctor?"

Her eyes returned to the file. "Helluva record. Top rank at the academy. Three years as a patrol officer, then detective: Crimes Against Property, Vice, ending up in Sex Crimes division and working cold cases at the same time. Around here that's a rocket-fueled career. Easy to see why: You had a knack for solving crimes. The tough ones."

Sandhill turned toward the door. "It's been great fun, Mayor, but I've got things to do."

Philips looked at her watch. "Stay, Mr Sandhill. I've got two minutes on the meter." She again lifted

178

the folder and read. "Commendations. Citations for excellence, citations for bravery. But despite your exceptional record, you were never Officer of the Year. May I ask why?"

Sandhill snorted. "It's a political recognition."

Philips slipped a page from the folder and gave it a glance. "Maybe another answer is in your performance reviews. No one could ever accuse you of being a team player. My, my . . . what does it say here? 'Detective Sandhill refuses to recognize that a chain of command is essential to the efficient operation of the department.'"

"A comment from a desk jockey who should have a chair bolted to his ass to save him time looking for one."

"Yet you continued to receive commendations. Then, four years back, like a car slamming a wall, your career's over. 'Self-initiated termination' is what it says in your records. A cryptic term I've never encountered before. Your pension is revoked, all benefits cut off. What's that about?"

Sandhill started to speak, changed his mind. Philips dropped the folder on her desk and stared into his eyes, gray into brown. The alarm on Sandhill's watch beeped.

"It's been a picnic, Mayor. Let's do it again next year." He turned and walked to the door. When his hand closed around the knob Philips spoke, almost in a whisper.

"Mr Sandhill, there's something else I know about you."

Sandhill rolled his eyes again. "My hat size?"

"No," she said. "You're a thief."

Sophie gave Ryder a dark eye, then wheeled from the front door and hustled wordlessly into the kitchen. He hoped she was too involved in some cooking task to monitor his time with Harry. Tiptoeing to Harry's room, he considered asking a point-blank question about retirement, but wasn't ready for the wrong answer.

Nautilus was cranked to half sitting in the rental bed, the white wires of an iPod headset running to his ears. He saw Ryder and thumbed off the music, tossed the earpiece to the bed.

"Hey, bro," Ryder said. "How's the head machinery?"

"Infection's cleared, no big deal. I'm feeling pretty damn good, actually."

"So how's the old memory? They fix it so you can recall –"

Sophie appeared, a small sand-filled timer in her hand. She brandished it in Ryder's face.

"Man's just out of the hospital, Ryder. You can talk 'til the last grain of sand rolls down that egg timer. Then you're seeing the welcome mat from upside-down."

Ryder frowned at the mini-hourglass. "How long do your eggs take?"

"Three minutes."

She inverted the timer on the bedside table, shot Ryder a glare and left the room. Ryder reached to

180

turn the timer, grab a couple extra minutes. "Don't you dare," Sophie called from two rooms away. Ryder drew his hand back as if it had been slapped.

Nautilus shrugged, then tapped his temple, "I hear a voice in my head, Carson. Maybe it's just a dream. It's hardly there, like an echo."

Ryder pulled up a chair and sat.

"And this voice is saying?"

"The voice says, 'Details, details, details.'"

Ryder frowned. "Details?"

"I feel the voice more than hear it, like it's coming from inside my head. Does that make sense?"

"If the guy was crouched over you, whispering into your ear, maybe."

Nautilus stared out the window, teeth gritting as he fought to clear the wisps. He turned to Ryder, puzzlement on his face. "Another thing about the voice. The tone is angry. Or scared. Or both. There's more, but it's a jumble."

"Try."

"It sounds like the voice is saying, 'Why . . .'" Nautilus closed his eyes and Ryder leaned forward, watching his partner strain for the memory. "'Why . . . can't you people leave . . . all this shit alone?'"

Nautilus opened his eyes. His head fell back to the pillow.

"Details, details, details," Ryder repeated. "Why can't you people leave all this shit alone?"

Nautilus shrugged. "Or maybe my dented head's making it all up."

The last grain tumbled through the neck of the timer. Ryder started to ask another question but Sophie appeared at the door in full glare.

"Your egg's cooked," she said.

28

Sandhill's hand froze on the knob. Philips said, "You were caught red-handed stealing from the evidence room."

"That's not in the file."

The flint in Philips's stare negated her thin smile. "Oh, I know, Mr Sandhill. It's not in any file anywhere. As we both know, some information is too sensitive to be collected."

Sandhill turned to the mayor, met her eyes. "Where did you get this . . . story?"

"Not relevant. Officially, you were brought up on Conduct Unbecoming an Officer. But one week later you quit the department. Or were fired. Or a combination. Nothing was spelled out in detail. It's truly strange."

"It's ancient history, Mayor," Sandhill said. "Leave it be."

"Rumor has it your ego outgrew your brains. You were afraid of someone else solving the murders and stealing your thunder. By hoarding the evidence you hoped to find something others had missed and raise your chances of making the bust. The great Conner Sandhill solves another case, his biggest yet. You'd use the brownie points to move up the ladder, make the jump to administration . . ."

"Administration?" Sandhill spat the word as if it were an insect in his mouth. "I'd sooner have terminal hemorrhoids. What a load of bullshit."

"Set me straight."

He walked to the window. The clouds had darkened and opening ticks of rain measured the glass.

"The first dead girl was Sally Harkness," he said, watching the protesters break ranks and run for cover, umbrellas appearing like toadstools. "A prostitute. Twenty-three years old when she was beaten to death. A body blow lacerated her liver. She bled to death inside herself."

"This was when?"

"Six years ago. Her body was dumped in an alley. The case is still unsolved."

"What was it to you?"

"I couldn't stop thinking about it, the brutality, the sense of vengeance. And the guy was hands-on, a puncher. That makes it personal. A couple months later, another young woman's body showed up in a park. Tami Zelinger, a twenty-year-old hooker with a face beaten into putty. Again, no leads. Like with Harkness, the slim pickings of evidence were finally put into storage."

The rain started drumming hard against the

glass. Lightning flared in the distance, thunder running three beats behind.

Sandhill said, "Another year passed and another woman was found dead. Jiliana Simpkins. She'd been attacked so savagely I knew it was related to the Harkness and Zelinger cases. Another tie was the hair. Two were natural redheads, another always worked in a bright red wig."

Philips said, "The red-hair angle – I don't recall it."

"Wasn't publicized. The media'd inevitably label them 'The Redhead Murders', like a Sherlock Holmes story. Plus we needed to weed out the pathetic geeks who confess to every murder of a woman."

Philips shook her head. "Sick."

Sandhill continued. "I went back to check the evidence, hoping to find a pattern besides the savagery and hair. Plus DNA identification had improved. Less of a sample needed. Mitochondrial advances." Sandhill paused. "I failed. Evidence in the earlier cases was missing. I checked it against the log."

"A bookkeeping error?"

"I knew the dicks who logged the stuff in. One, Norbert Bayle, is so anal-retentive he'd log in an ant crossing the floor; the other, Harry Nautilus, is just damn good with details, doesn't make mistakes. Nautilus probably cross-checks his cross-checking."

"You figured someone got to the evidence. Is that it?"

"Theft isn't unknown in property rooms. Guns, knives, watches, jewelry. But this was clothing, hairs, a cast of a footprint. I figured someone was damaging the cases. I decided to take some of the evidence home and keep it safe."

"But told no one. Why?"

"I trusted no one, Mayor. At that point, I couldn't."

"But you got nailed in the act, right?"

Sandhill snorted. "I'm a lousy thief. I thought I'd skirted all the security cameras, but missed seeing one. It didn't miss seeing me, standing in the shelves jamming evidence bags into my pants and jacket."

Philips pursed her lips and tapped her fingertips together. "Mr Sandhill, I can't tell if you're feeding me hamburgers or horseshit."

Sandhill shrugged. "The menu doesn't matter; given the videotape, I had no defense. I was allowed to resign without prosecution – also sans pension and benefits – the matter hushed up lest the department get a black eye."

"No one listened to your side?"

"Several people believed me. Not the few that counted."

"Chief Hoskins?"

"Didn't matter. The tier below him ran the department."

186

"Squill?"

"The major player. He was a deputy chief back then. We'd had dust-ups over the years, never gotten along. When he saw a chance to comb me out of his hair, he came up with all that crap about my grandstanding, sold it to a couple other tin-hat fools and I was history."

"Deputy Chief Bidwell?"

"A captain back then. I like Carl as a person, but he's a natural doormat, hates the sound of rocking boats. He scurried off and hid from the whole ugly discussion. That left the thumb-up or thumb-down to Emperor Squill. The lions roared and I got eaten."

"But you didn't depart without leaving an arrow in Squill's chest, did you?" Philips wasn't consulting the file any more; she was running on information supplied by Tom Clay.

A wisp of smile crossed Sandhill's face. "More like a dart. I'd discovered Squill owned a quiet interest in a security business. Part of his sales pitch was suggesting increased police patrols around businesses contracting with the firm. I made it known, and Terrence got a little shit on his britches."

Philips nodded, understanding. "Enough that the commission gave him the temporary 'acting' designation when Plackett left, not the full jump to chief. Is that how I should read it?"

Sandhill nodded. "Until after the elections, when a new group might make a decision one way or another. You know how politicians love to pass the buck."

She ignored the barb. "One more thing, Mr Sandhill. Who do you think took the evidence?"

"That's the sad bullshit of it. There are only ten guys working shifts in the property room, stuck away with the roaches. Guys getting old, or injured in the line of duty, who can't stand to be anywhere but in a cop station. I'd trust most of those guys with anything I own. Or thought I could." Sandhill looked at his watch. "I gotta get running. Things to do."

"Like what?"

"That's my business."

Philips rose from her chair, put her hands on her desk, leaned forward.

"Listen, Mr Sandhill, I'm very sorry about the Charlane girl; I hope she's found safe, and soon. But I remind you that you're a civilian. You have to stay away from the case or face arrest for interfering with police business."

"That was why you wanted me here? To tell me that?"

Philips studied Sandhill. "I wanted to hear about your dismissal."

Sandhill grabbed the doorknob. "You heard. So long, Mayor."

"Stay out of the cases, Mr Sandhill."

Sandhill pulled the door open. Lightning exploded nearby and the lights flickered for an instant.

"Mr Sandhill, did you hear me?" Philips said.

"I know the rules, Mayor."

Sandhill stepped into the hall and pulled the door shut behind him. Philips continued to stare at the closed door as if Sandhill's picture were etched across it with acid.

"But will you play by them, Mr Sandhill?" she whispered.

Seconds after Sandhill left the mayor's office, Tom Clay slipped in. He tossed the day's mail in her inbox and took a seat.

"How'd it go, Norma?"

Philips sat at her desk drumming a pencil across her palm. "He's an interesting man with a strange story."

"You believe his tale?"

"Reply hazy, ask again later."

Clay raised a thin eyebrow. "Did you tell him that a mayor can discretionarily reinstate officers pending a new hearing?"

"No, I didn't, Tom. I want to think about that option a bit more."

"You think he'll stick his nose into things?"

"I'm counting on it. Maybe he'll find something we can buy into."

Clay raised an eyebrow. "And if he gets his ass in the blades?"

"We have no involvement; I specifically told him to keep his distance from the case."

Clay leaned back and tented his fingers. "You're

getting better at politics, Norma, covering your ass. How you feel about that?"

Philips flipped the pencil on to her desk. "Nauseated."

Clay nodded somberly.

"Good," he said.

29

Sandhill went to his apartment, stripped off his tie, flung it across the room, and called Marie. She reported that Nike had locked herself in her apartment and wanted to be left alone. Marie added, "The po-lice stopped one more time to ax questions. There was two of them: a guy name Duck-something and I can't remember the other."

"Ainsley Duckworth and Wade Meyers."

She hesitated. Sandhill knew that Marie, in light of his former occupation, was cautious in her criticism of cops.

"Uh-huh, yeah, that's them. They any good, Conner?"

Sandhill hated Squill's lap Dobermans. But now was the time for truth, not grudges. "I don't think Meyers could find his ass with a bloodhound. But Duckworth, foul and unhappy as he is, knows the ropes and somewhere underneath all that pissed-off-bubba crap is intelligence."

"If you say so, Conner. I don't like either of

them a wink. Specially Duck-whatever. He got cruel in his eyes, a man picks wings off bugs. Something in him ain't right, Conner."

"Neither is what you would call attuned to human emotions, Marie."

"That's your way of talking, Conner. Me, I say they a pair of grade-A cracker assholes."

"There's that aspect, too."

Marie hesitated. "I got what you wanted from Nike. The uh . . . you know. I dropped it by the restaurant early on. You find it?"

Sandhill looked across the table at the brown 8 x 10 envelope. He hadn't touched it and didn't want to.

"I got it, Marie. Thanks."

After hanging up, Sandhill's hand lingered on the phone, wanting to call Nike, but knowing there was nothing to say. Not now. The best thing to do was what he did best: work the case, Squill be damned, Norma Philips be damned. Something in the materials was bothering him, no, *calling* to him. It was something subtle, like a soft fragrance in a distant room, touching at the edge of his senses.

But now he had to deal with the envelope. He opened it gingerly and shook it over the table. A 5 x 7 color photograph of Jacy slid out. He turned it face side down, not yet ready to look.

Next, he shuffled through photos of the other girls: Darla Dumont, eleven, gone a year; Maya Ledbetter and LaShelle Shearing, both taken within the past two weeks.

Their families had supplied several photos of each, and Sandhill selected headshots with the best lighting. He placed Darla, Maya and LaShelle before him. He turned Jacy's picture over and saw her smiling into his eyes like she'd done a hundred times in the past six days.

The world shimmered, then swam. Sandhill stood quickly, wiping his arm across his eyes and breathing deeply. He went to the sink and splashed cold water across his face. Toweled it off roughly. He looked in the mirror and saw wet strands of hair falling into eyes puffed with lack of sleep.

When he returned, he slid Jacy's photo into the row with the others. He studied the photos carefully, noting the large, symmetric features and bright, outgoing smiles; Sandhill felt touched by their innocence and the foreshadowing of the beauty adulthood could bring.

He walked circles around the table, studying, thinking. Three headshots. All heads slightly canted. All faces smiling. All eyes directly into the camera. All backgrounds neutral. All slightly sidelit.

"School pictures," he whispered, knowing what had been pricking at the edges of his mind. And that it wasn't a revelation; in fact, it probably meant exactly nothing.

Still, Sandhill was up and fumbling his tie back on. He started out the door, paused. He pulled his phone and called Carson Ryder. They spoke a few minutes, Ryder promising to check into things.

Ryder called back two hours later. "I went through the school interviews, Sandhill. No mention of a school photographer in any of them. It's one of those things no one thinks of."

"Damn," Sandhill said. "You think it's important?"

"I checked schools, just got back from the school Darla Dumont attended last year. When she disappeared."

"And?" Sandhill's voice was laced with expectation.

"Different photographers. Guy named Philbee was Darla's photographer. Retired last year. A man named Desmond took the pics at the schools attended by the other girls."

"Shit," Sandhill grunted. "No connection."

Ryder said, "Still, I'm heading over to Desmond Photography now, just to look at the bird. Somebody has to clear him."

"What's the address, Ryder? I'll meet you there."

"Uh, Sandhill, this is police business . . ."

"Of course it is," Sandhill said. "I just need to get my passport photo re-done."

A long pause was followed by Ryder's weary sigh.

"I'll pick you up in ten minutes."

The broom made angry swooshing sounds as Truman swept dust and debris across the wooden slats of his studio floor. A dozen wrapper ends from Rose's power bars lay in the pile; his brother was a pig. Truman was brushing the pile toward the trash canister when the buzzer sounded. Not Rose; he'd have simply let himself in. There was no pickup scheduled. A salesman, maybe? Or sometimes people wandered in without appointments.

Three raps struck the door like hammer blows. "Police."

Truman closed his eyes. It was them. Finally, inevitably. He set the broom aside and walked softly to the door. He peeked through the peephole, seeing two men through the distortion of the fisheye lens, one close, one in the background. A badge floated a few inches from the lens.

"Police. Open up, please."

Truman pushed the tails of his white shirt deeper in his Dockers, licked his palms, and brushed his hair back. The trick was to remain calm and professional. If he kept his cool, this was as close as they would ever get. The delivery of Maya Ledbetter had been flawless the other night; by now she'd be hidden away somewhere in Ohio. Only the Charlane girl remained. After her delivery he'd flood the hurricane shelter to wash away any evidence. Then he and Rose would go into hibernation again until another wealthy customer surfaced.

Affecting bemusement, he opened the door to a slender man about six feet tall, a white linen jacket over jeans, boat shoes. His hair looked like it had fought the comb and won. Truman allowed himself an inner grin; the guy looked like a twit. The other man was a big guy, slouching like an ape.

"Mr Desmond?" the twit asked.

Truman continued the look of surprised concern perfected in front of the mirror. "Yes, that's me. What can I do for you?"

"I'm Detective Carson Ryder, MPD."

Beside the badge in the fold-open wallet was a photo ID. Desmond leaned close, smiled and shook his head.

"Something wrong?" Ryder-twit asked.

"Not a very flattering shot, Detective Ryder. Do you think I could get the photo franchise for police IDs? I promise a better result."

The big ape gurgled and dug inside a rumpled jacket. "Lemme show you my ID. I look like I should be hanging off the Empire State Building swatting planes."

The twit looked irritated and put his hand on the ape's arm to stop all the scrabbling.

"Mr Desmond, this is –"

"Conner," the ape said. He grinned, tapped his gut, and burped into his palm. Truman opened the door quickly and widely, demonstrating his willingness to be of service in any police matter. The twit seemed to be the guy in charge, which – given that the ape seemed to have the brains of a sandwich – made sense.

The twit said, "We understand you take the school pictures for the Banks and Washington schools."

Truman widened his eyes in confusion. "All the elementaries, actually, Detective Ryder. Could I ask what this is in reference to?"

"We want to ask a few questions about the girls who were abducted. We're interviewing everyone who's been in their schools."

Truman let his face droop into sadness. "What can I say? It's a terrible thing. How can I help?"

"A few questions. A few minutes of your time."

"There's more room in the studio, gentlemen. Follow me."

Truman led them through the anteroom to his worktable at the front of the studio. He snapped on a single photoflood above the table, bathing it in crisp white light. The rest of the window-less studio stayed shadowy gray. He leaned against the table, picked up his can of Mountain Dew and took a drink before slapping his forehead.

"Excuse my poor manners. Could I get you gentlemen a drink? There's Dew and red pop and maybe some . . ."

The twit said, "We're fine, Mr Desmond, thanks."

Truman picked up a half-bag of Cheezo chips, shook it at his visitors, and was again declined. The twit cop was very polite, almost apologetic. He reached in his jacket pocket and produced four photos, spreading them on the table.

Vitriana, Kittinia, Nalique, Lorelei. Darlene, Maya, LaShelle, Jacy.

197

"Are these your work, Mr Desmond?" the twit asked.

"Three are. I can tell by the lighting and backdrop."

"Which one isn't?"

Truman studied the photo the cop was holding – a school picture, which, though he hadn't taken it, pleased Truman with its irony. It was Darla Dumont, the girl from last year, the chance meeting that had led to Truman's new and lucrative enterprise.

Truman had been sticking Desmond Photography handbills under car wipers at the Winn-Dixie when Darla rode up on her bicycle and asked what he was doing. She was a tawny and impressive little peach, bright, chatty, eager. Truman immediately recalled a message in one of the secret chatrooms: the poster had implied, with utmost tact and shading, an interest beyond photos, a desire for a "corporeal entity".

Truman had looked up the word "corporeal" – *material*, *bodily* – and he knew what the man wanted. Thus commenced a delicate interchange, Truman determining the man might pay as much as a quarter-million dollars to own the correct "entity".

Truman enlisted Darla to place handbills, all the while questioning her about school, family, places she went to be alone. He gave her twenty dollars and pledged her to secrecy.

"Don't tell anyone, and I'll let you help me do this again."

198

He'd had a camera in his car and snapped several shots of Darla, posting them to his correspondent that evening. After a week of feeling one another out, a deal was sealed. He met Darla two days later, as arranged. Rose sprang from the van, and everything ticked like clockwork, the buyer retrieving his product at the Mobile docks a few days later and wiring the fee to a Caymans bank account. When the school-photography job opened, Truman had jumped, slowly and carefully building his bank of selected photos and making his offer known to his select and slender roster.

I can get you more than pictures . . .

Truman tapped Darla/Vitriana. "I didn't take this picture." It was true.

"You sure?"

"I don't have a backdrop like that."

While the ape looked around like he'd never seen a photo studio before, the twit cop scribbled in a cheap notebook. "How long have you been working with the schools?" the twit asked, looking bored.

"This is my first year. I've specialized in family portraiture since starting in business eight years ago, plus some advertising and PR work. Weddings. Bar Mitzvahs. A few passport photos. But this year I thought I'd give school photography a shot. The paperwork's a hassle, but next year I'm going to hire an assistant."

"You process the photos yourself?"

Truman shook his head. "I contract with a bulk

199

processor. They print them on sheets, handle the orders."

"Do you have much interaction with the students?"

Truman chuckled. "It's an assembly line. Sit, say cheese, sit, say cheese, sit . . ."

The twit smiled at Truman's wit. Dealing with these yokels was *fun*.

"How about access to personal family information?" the twit asked.

"The parent or guardian fills out a form for records and billing purposes."

"Is a home address on that form?"

Truman took a sip of soda. "Um, yes. But I never use it. It's for the schools."

"You keep the forms?"

Truman popped a Cheezo in his mouth, crunching as he spoke. "If I left them with the schools they'd disappear. I hang on to the info until the photos are delivered, then shred and dump it."

"No one else works here with you?"

Truman slapped bright orange Cheezo powder from his palms. "I'm a one-man show, unfortunately."

"Bookkeeper?"

"I keep my own books. Sure you don't want a pop or a snack?"

"No thanks."

An interrogator's voice rumbled from behind Truman. "Which do you like best, Mr Desmond, little girls or little boys?"

200

Truman's heart jammed in his throat. He blanked his face, and turned to the ape, shocked to see it had wandered completely across the studio and was in the far corner, standing near the removable flooring above the external drive.

Truman fought to keep his voice even. "I'm sorry, Detective Conner. What?"

The ape scratched its head, stifled a yawn, stretched like it was ready for bed. "You know, like who's easiest to take pictures of? I figure the boys for a pain in the ass. I was."

Desmond relaxed and offered a knowing smile. "You're right, Detective Conner, the girls. The boys are always showing off for each other, crossing their eyes or sticking out their tongues."

The ape made a gurgling sound Tru assumed was a giggle, and said, "Hell, I still do."

The twit shook his head slowly, as if saying, *Look what I'm burdened with.*

There were a few more meaningless questions before the cops left, the twit in the lead, the ape slouching behind. Truman knew he should have felt secure when the door closed, but a warning light was blinking in his head. Sometime during the interview, the ape had moved away. How could it move so softly on the creaky wood floors? What had the ape been doing? Looking at?

Should I worry? Did I do something wrong?

No, because there was nothing the ape could have found. The only incriminating object in the studio was the external drive, and it was safe.

The ape's simple-minded question about boys and girls almost made Truman fill his drawers. But he hadn't flinched, had he? Instead, he'd delivered an Academy Award performance, sliding past the question like a greased eel.

Truman shrugged the worry from his shoulders. The way he'd handled those yokels was brilliant; he could have pissed in their mouths and they'd have thanked him for the lemonade. Still, he was glad they had gone; something about that big ape gave him chills.

He picked up the broom and resumed sweeping the dust and crumbs and torn edges of Rose's power-bar wrappers.

30

Sandhill and Ryder drove two blocks and parked in the rear of a Popeye's restaurant. The smell of fried chicken poured into Sandhill's truck like hot fog. Ryder watched a stray dog feast on chicken scraps at the edge of the asphalt.

Sandhill said, "So what'd you take from the guy?"

"He seems like a typical photographer, but something's hinky. Probably has nothing to do with the abductions, but he's got a worm somewhere in his gut. He was jumpier than he looked."

Sandhill nodded. "Smug little bastard thought he was leading us around like carnival ponies."

"What was in the back cabinets?" Ryder asked.

"One held tripods, conduit, switch boxes, reflector stands. The other was a snack stash: three industrial-size cases of Cheezos from one of those discount joints. Plus paper towels and cleaning supplies."

"I saw you snatch something from the floor."

Sandhill used the nails of his thumb and forefinger to extract several pieces of silver paper from his pocket. A car behind them pulled out and Ryder waited until it was gone before leaning close.

"What is it?"

Sandhill shook his head, staring at the paper. "No idea. I saw a bunch of them in a pile of sweepings. I was just thinking, the way you tear something like this off . . ." Sandhill mimed ripping the end from a package.

"Yeah, perfect for thumb and forefinger prints. I'll take it to the lab tonight," Ryder said.

"How about you drop me at Nike's? I want to check on her."

There was a long pause; Ryder contemplating a question he'd had for a couple of days. "Can I ask you a question, Sandhill? Something I've been wondering about?"

Sandhill raised an eyebrow. "And the subject?"

"How Jacy came to be with Nike Charlane . . ."

Sandhill looked away, out the window. "Jacy's real mother died. Ovarian cancer. The kid was three. Nike's the girl's aunt and she –"

"Not that. I know you and Nike Charlane are friends, but I'm feeling something more between you two, something deep and complex. Were you two ever lovers?"

Sandhill sighed. "Not Nike . . . Thena. Thena and I were lovers."

"Thena?"

"Nike's older sister, Athena – Jacy's mother.

It ended years ago. Almost a decade. We were together less than a year. Then Thena split for someone more her style, I guess."

"Were they much alike, Nike and Thena?"

"Nike is pragmatic. Thena was metaphysical. New Age-y spiritual: Tarot cards, crystals, whatever."

Ryder raised an eyebrow. "What kind of work did she do?"

"Made jewelry from precious metals and polished stones. We'd be walking in a park and she'd reach down and grab some dusty chunk of rock. Two days later it would be set in silver and shining like a rainbow."

"Where'd you meet her?"

"The Church Street Cemetery, behind the library. I'd taken out some books and headed to the grave-yard to read. Thena waltzed into the cemetery wearing a rainbow skirt, brocaded vest, hoop earrings, silver bells tinkling from a bracelet. Hair a mane of wild curls. She was happy as a kid at the circus, smiling, touching gravestones like old friends. I thought . . ."

– *that woman's crazy. Or on something. But wow . . .*

"A good-looking woman, I take it?"

"The regal bones of Nike with larger, gentler eyes. I couldn't keep my eyes off her. A few minutes later she jangled by a few feet away."

– *What cloud are you on, lady?*

"She moved like snow, floating. I went back

into the library to exchange one book for another. When I came out she was cross-legged on the hood of my truck holding a deck of Tarot cards."

– *Excuse me, lady. My truck has an appointment and wants me to drive it there.*

– *Here, hold these cards. Come on, they won't bite. No, tighter. That's it. Now pass them back. My, your hand is cool for such a warm day. Take three cards from the deck . . .*

– *I don't have time for games, lady.*

– *Are you scared? A big man like you?*

– *One, two, three. Three cards. Now what?*

– *Lay them face up in front of me.*

– *Whatever you want, lady. Here's a guy in a crown, an old bum in rags, and a woman with a set of scales. We done here?*

– *Oh my.*

– *Oh my what? Look, lady, I've got to be –*

– *The King of Cups, the Hermit, and the card of Justice. That's very . . . unusual.*

– *Could you stop staring at me? And maybe tell me how long you're going to be squatting on my hood?*

– *I'm not sure. How many notes are in a song?*

"She sounds like an original," Ryder said.

"Somehow we ended up ended up having supper at that seafood joint on the causeway. She was vegetarian, sat there smiling over her salad watching me chow down on snapper and filet until I felt – Jesus – guilty."

– *Two hours and I don't know your name.*

– Is it important? Athena Diana Charlane. From mythology; my father loved the stories. Friends call me Thena.

– Athena is the goddess of war, isn't she?

– Of many things, including handicrafts – more to my taste. And Diana is generally regarded as the goddess –

– of the hunt. What do you hunt, Thena?

– The heart of the matter. Or hearts.

Ryder said, "I have a hard time visualizing you with someone so . . . different."

"We were fire and water. Or earth and sky. Pick any opposites you want. By all rational rights we should have run from one another the second our eyes met. But I was . . . enchanted."

– What are you feeling, Conner?

"She drove me nuts at times, Ryder, always asking, 'What are you feeling, Conner?' I'd say, 'I'm not *feeling* anything, Thena, I'm thinking.' She'd get that damned elusive smile on her lips and say, 'So how do you feel about what you're thinking?'"

"How did it fall apart?" Ryder's voice was a whisper.

"One day Thena said she'd been called to a mission and would have to go away for a while."

"Mission? You didn't try to –"

"It was her life, not mine. My thinking was she happened on another guy like she'd happened on me. Someone more touchy-feely. Jacy was born a year after she bailed, as I later discovered from

207

Nike. Thena'd found what she'd been hunting. Or who."

"Was it love between you and Thena?"

Sandhill looked away, said, "Let's git."

Ryder cranked on the engine, put the truck in gear, and pulled from the lot. They were fifteen blocks from Popeye's before Sandhill spoke again.

"It was good, Ryder. I've never felt that good since."

31

"We can't stay closed through this, Conner," Marie scolded.

Sandhill had returned to the restaurant to find the CLOSED sign replaced by OPEN 4 P.M. TO-DAY.

"I don't have time to deal with the place, Marie."

"I'll handle everything today; tomorrow I got Dora coming in. I talked to her about working full time for a while and she said she'd do anything."

"Marie, I don't want you to –"

"I need to do something, Conner. If I sit around I just shake and cry. And we need the money, you know we do."

She was right, as usual, Sandhill admitted, heading to the kitchen to check the gumbos. He'd been in the kitchen a half-hour when the phone rang.

"Conner?"

It was Nike, her voice weary, but not so ragged.

"Nike. How are you? Can I –"

"That damned Turnbull's over here wanting to hold a candle-fucking-light vigil or something. There must be fifty people in the street. Why would anyone hold a freaking candlelight vigil in broad daylight?"

Sandhill's watch confirmed his opinion: 4 p.m. "To get it on the five o'clock news."

"I don't want that bastard using me like that, using Jacy like that."

"If it's peaceful there's nothing you can do."

"He's got a bullhorn and he's yelling 'Save our babies' over and over. I don't think I can take this, Conner."

Nike fell silent and Sandhill heard amplified ranting in the background. "Do you want to come over here? Or go to Marie's?"

"I'd feel better at your place, Conner. Please come get me. I can't deal with this kind of craziness now."

"I'll call Ryder. He and Roland Zemain can walk you out. I don't think a heavy police presence would be good."

"Hurry, Conner. Please hurry."

Sandhill called Ryder, who'd already gotten word.

"The brass is still discussing what to do, Sandhill. On one hand those people have the right to peaceful assembly; on the other –"

"Screw the brass. Nike wants out of there. Can you do it? I want to scope out the crowd; the abductor may be drawn to the action."

Ryder said, "Squill send me? Not a chance."

"I'll have Nike call and say she wants to leave. But only with you."

Ryder said, "Squill'll be bad pissed."

Sandhill noted Ryder sounded elevated by the prospect. "Squill was born pissed. Can you take Nike to my place?"

"Done. By the way, there were latents on that silver wrapper. A full thumb and index and a partial middle. They didn't belong to Truman Desmond."

"Desmond's got prints in the system? For what?"

"Anyone doing business with the schools gets printed. Desmond's clean, no record. Not even a parking ticket. And whoever left the prints is just as immaculate."

"Shit. I was hoping photo-boy'd have some type of sexo beef – weenie wagging or something. Give you a chance to toss his place."

"Can't do it," Ryder lamented. "Desmond's clean as a new whistle."

Walter Mattoon's various in-port dealings often required local phone directories and he'd collected nearly thirty of them. He checked his watch, made the time corrections, and figured it was just past noon in Mobile. He had the communications engineer make the satellite connection, then sat back at his desk and listened as connections fell into place, tapping the small ad in the Mobile Yellow Pages.

A leisurely drawl danced through the phone. "Bridgett's Bridal Fashions."

"I need to speak to someone in charge," Mattoon said.

The woman said, "That would be me. Bridgett Boistellier, the owner."

"My name is Ernest Martel. I'm with Angel Productions, an independent film company currently shooting a commercial in the Mobile area."

"Yes sir. How can I help you?"

"Let me give you the scenario. A little girl is dreaming of the day she gets married. But time is mixed up and she dreams herself in a wedding dress while still youthful. We have a dress that was made for her, but I don't think it's right. It's far, far too contemporary."

"Clean, straight lines? No lace or ruffles?"

"I don't want strict traditional, but a more formalized elegance."

"Full veil, sleeves, lace at the bodice, a layering effect from the waist down . . ."

"Exactly. No veil, though. I – the camera needs to see her face."

"I can do that. I'll need the girl in for a fitting, of course."

"No can do. She's being flown in from Tallahassee just the day of the filming. I can call back with her exact dimensions . . . uh, measurements."

"If that's the only way."

"There's one other little thing, a slight time constraint."

"When will you need it, Mr Martel?"

"Four days from now."

"I'm sorry, Mr Martel. Four days is way too little time to –"

"How much do you normally charge? A general range."

"We're probably talking about twelve to fifteen hundred dollars, but like I said about the time –"

"Have it ready in three days and I'll pay you ten thousand dollars. We can send your bank a down payment within minutes. Now, Miss Boistellier, how does that sound?"

A throaty chuckle. "Like I'm going to be working nights."

Seconds after Truman sat, a black waitress waltzed by with a tray of full gumbo bowls in one hand, a pitcher of tea in the other, yet somehow managed to set a blue paper menu in front of him. She looked tired.

"I'll be right back to get your order, hon."

Truman felt a thrill as he looked past the menu at the restaurant. According to the news, it was owned by some guy supposedly watching Jacy Charlane when she was taken. The girl's mother was out of town visiting relatives, went the reports. Now that Truman had beaten the cops, he felt safe to do as he pleased, and it pleased him to eat at *The Gumbo King*. He wondered if the man was in the kitchen. He also wondered why the front window had been replaced with a sheet of plywood.

The waitress returned. "Now then, hon, what'll you have?"

He ordered crab gumbo, salad, and sweet tea, angling his chair for a better look at the kitchen area. The waitress disappeared through the swinging doors but he saw no one else but customers, a third of the tables taken by diners, a mix of ages, races and genders. Truman was disappointed; he'd seen the mothers and one father of the other girls on television, but he'd never personally seen anyone affected by his actions. He thought it would be exciting, and had told Rose to meet him at the restaurant. Truman checked his watch; the idiot was always late.

His salad appeared before him: romaine, endive, and bibb lettuces studded with gleaming tomatoes, chunks of feta cheese, and pepperoncini. He picked the peppers up by their stems and, when no one was looking, tossed them beneath the table. He flooded the salad with Italian dressing, emptied two packets of sugar over it, and began eating.

As he chewed, he considered how well his business was going. The secret was specialization. Every possible taste lurked in the cyberwilderness where he once traded in playground photos, but it was the specialists who pulled the top dollars. Truman decided to specialize in young, exceptionally lovely black girls, offered not as photos, but as ownable merchandise. His list of potential buyers was small, those who made enquiries even smaller, the buyers' list smaller still.

But the money was so big.

He was also planning on repeat business. Hadn't it happened already – the buyer for the Charlane girl the same man who'd purchased Darla Dumont, the test girl, last year? A very wary man, demanding double encryption, sending Tru the key, taking days to nail down the details of the purchase. Last year, before wiring the down payment, he'd demanded proof the operation wasn't a scam, and Tru had sent copies of news stories about the abduction along with photos of the bound and waiting product.

The transfer had taken place on the Mobile River, a dark pier above the State Docks, and had worked flawlessly.

The waitress reappeared at Truman's shoulder. "I'm sorry, hon, we don't have crab today, it's shrimp gumbo. We didn't make as much gumbo as usual and –"

Truman picked up the single-sheet menu and poked at it with his fork. "It says right here, 'crab gumbo'."

"Like I said, I didn't get a chance to –"

Truman leaned back and rolled his eyes. "What kind of place is this? Promise one thing then not deliver."

"I'm sorry. Today we just have shrimp, chicken and andouille, shrimp and andouille, and okra. We have seafood etouffeé; it has fresh crab in it."

"Yeah, gimme that."

She chugged away. Truman looked up to see Rose pushing through the door in split-sided denim shorts and a sleeveless white sweatshirt. A slender wreath of gold chains encircled his massive pink neck. Several customers watched Rose discreetly, one woman at a corner table nudging her female companion and pointing with her eyes as Rose crossed the room. Truman studied the women; they were pretty, with shining hair and suntanned legs crossed beneath the table. Truman detested the looks Rose's muscles generated, but felt visceral gratification at being seen with him.

If you girlies knew what I know . . .

He knew that Rose – who drew steady and unashamed stares from women and flickering, unsettled glances from men – was terrified by any woman past adolescence. Tru had set Rose up with women in the past only to watch the slab-bodied behemoth blush and stutter, sweating like there was a lawn sprinkler beneath his clothes.

Rose bent his knees and lowered to the chair as if readying for a clean-and-jerk. "Isn't this the place where –"

"Yes."

Rose looked around and laughed. "Too cool."

The nearest other patrons were two tables away. Truman leaned toward Rose as he sat. "How's our last piece of product?"

Rose said, "I fed her and she went to sleep."

"The buyer posted a message. He wants us to

216

get her measurements. Like how tall she is and how long her legs are and things. A shitload of measurements. He wants them by this afternoon."

"What the hell for, Tru?"

"I didn't ask, Rose. A man pays quarter-million bucks for a product, I'll measure anything he wants. That's the way a service business works." Truman speared a forkful of salad. "Hey, you been watching the kid on your new TV and milking the mongoose?"

Rose colored and looked away. "No. Fuck you."

Truman smiled slyly. "I thought that's why you spent all that money on the camera hookup to the shelter."

Rose started to stand. "Fuck you again. You want to eat alone?"

"Sit down. Get a sense of humor, Rose. Jeez."

The waitress spun by, moving fast. "I'll be with you in a minute, hon," she said, unable to hide the microsecond double take at Rose.

"Don't order the crab gumbo; the menu's a lie," Truman said, making sure it was loud enough for the waitress to hear as she bounced her fat tits past the table.

"When's . . . little princess get picked up?" Rose asked over the top of the menu.

"Three days. Or four. I get the feeling that the buyer's on some kind of schedule. Like maybe a business trip or something. It was like this last year, remember? The waiting, then all of a sudden the phone call and –"

Truman paused and cocked his head.

"What?" Rose asked.

Truman spun toward the kitchen and looked at the swinging doors and the server's window. "A voice from back there. It reminded me of . . ."

Sandhill burst through the doors.

"Christ!" Truman spat, jerking his head toward the wall, trying to hide his face by pretending to scratch it.

"What is it?" Rose asked.

"Get up and stand between me and that guy over there – don't look at him! – quick, like you're showing me something in your wallet. Do it!"

Rose positioned himself between his brother and the big man in the floppy crown, pulling from his wallet the first thing he touched, a photo of himself oiled up and posing. He bent and pretended to explain some aspect of it to Truman.

"What the hell's going on, Tru?"

"Shhh!"

From the corner of his eye Truman watched the crowned ape stride to the beverage station where the waitress was filling drink cups. The ape and waitress whispered back and forth, then the ape shot out the door.

"He's gone, let's go," Truman whispered.

"Who was that, Tru? What's wrong?"

Truman stood and pulled a five from his wallet. He grabbed Marie's hand as she passed and jammed the bill into it. "We're out of here. I think

I got food poisoning from that rotten fucking salad."

Truman pulled the van from the curb, his hands tight on the wheel. "That guy in the restaurant. He was one of the cops that came by today. The ones I told you about."

"He's a *cop*?"

"He said he was. No, wait . . ." Truman replayed the afternoon's events in his head. "He didn't say he was. And he didn't show me ID, either. I think he faked me out."

"What's going on, Tru?" Rose's voice was up a register, like speaking through helium.

Truman thought through the scenario. "It means the cops were bringing the big guy around hoping he'd see someone he knew, someone the cops were trying to identify."

"What does that mean?"

Truman's face slowly lit in a grin. "It means I passed inspection, brother, just like I said I would. How's about giving me a high five?"

32

Sandhill parked at the end of Nike's block and strode to a restless crowd surrounding Reverend Damon Turnbull. High in the bed of a pickup with a bullhorn to his lips, he was condemning a white power structure treating black children as throwaways. The words were inflammatory and, at least as far as Sandhill had seen in his career, untrue. He muttered under his breath. A black man sucking from a brown paper bag looked over the top of his sunglasses.

"What you say?"

"Talking to myself," Sandhill said, passing by.

"White muthafucker," the man spat at Sandhill's back.

Sandhill felt ugliness in the hot air, a smog of hatred and anger. He saw Ryder on the high stoop outside the entrance to Nike's apartment building. Beside him was Roland Zemain, his uniform traded for paint-stained sweat pants and a tee shirt proclaiming, ROLL TIDE. Zemain had

brought two fellow street cops, black guys taut
with energy beneath street clothes. They were
doing a decent job of looking unobtrusive,
homies hanging on the stoop, listening to
Turnbull.

Sandhill checked the far end of the block. He
knew there'd be cruisers positioned around the
corner, waiting for trouble. He hoped they stayed
out of sight; gasoline on coals if they showed up.
A potential nightmare.

Ryder glanced at Nike. She was sitting on the
couch, her eyes rimmed with red, fingertips
shaking. He looked away, thinking his problems
were petty in comparison.

She said, "Thanks for coming, Detective Ryder;
I can't take this right now."

"We'll go to Sandhill's place. He says Marie'll
be finished at seven. You ready?"

Ryder gave Nike his hand as she stood. She felt
weightless, Ryder thought, a woman stripped of
everything but breath. She walked to the window
and looked down at the crowd.

"Look at the anger and betrayal in their eyes,
Detective Ryder, and how skilled Turnbull is at
feeding that anger."

"Non sequiturs glued together with misconceptions," Ryder said. He watched the minister stop
chanting to pluck a cellphone from the jacket of
his black suit. Turnbull listened without speaking,
concern clouding his face. He dropped the phone

in his pocket and begin climbing from the bed of the pickup.

Ryder turned to Nike. "We'll just walk to the car. It'll be a noisy walk, but don't pay anyone any mind."

"Is Conner coming?"

"He's checking if anyone in the crowd looks suspicious. Sometimes . . . the people who do these things, they like to . . ."

"To watch. To feed off of pain. I know." Nike Charlane stood and took a deep breath. "Let's go."

When they opened the door to the street, the crowd went quiet. "Trouble," Ryder said.

"What?" Zemain asked from behind.

"Turnbull's gone."

A Channel 5 news van now stood in place of Turnbull's truck. A videographer stood on the roof of the van, his camera a glass eye studying Ryder. A half-dozen women wearing nametags proclaiming *New Morning A.M.E.* Church stepped to the top of the stoop.

"We're on your side, Miz Charlane," said an elderly woman in a floral bonnet. "We want to make the police go find your Jacy."

Nike spoke quietly. "Thank you for your concern. But please, just go home."

The crowd drew tighter, listening. A woman from the church handed Nike a candle. "For your baby. We're praying for your little girl." The woman spun to Ryder. "Why don't you find this poor woman's baby, Mr Po-liceman? Why you not doing anything but axin' peoples the same questions over and over?"

Ryder kept his voice low. "The chief explained all this, ma'am. He's been on TV, radio. We're doing our best. Now please stand aside."

"Your best just ain't muthafuckin' good enough, is it now?" a man yelled from below on the pavement. He seemed drunk, eyes wet, words slushy at the edges. He waved a paper-bagged bottle as punctuation. The churchwoman's eyebrows lifted slightly, as if the man had spoken her true words.

Ryder said, "Clear a path. We're coming through."

The man waved a fist. "I said your best ain't good enough. What you say to that?"

Ryder ignored him. Another man, his arms bulging like a dockworker's, pointed to Nike Charlane and yelled, "Where you taking her?"

Nike herself wheeled to face the man, her eyes hard. "He's taking me to a friend's house. Leave us alone."

"You trusting the po-lice? You crazy, girl."

Nike threw the candle and it bounced off the man's chest. "Go away, dammit!" The man's eyes filled with embarrassment and he retreated into a crowd growing thicker and tighter with each passing second.

"Excuse me, excuse me, ladies and gennulmens, let me through, please and thank you, sirs . . ."

A black man in his sixties with pewter hair and a wiry body shouldered through the crowd.

223

He hobbled up the steps, blocking Nike's path. He turned to the angry faces.

"Come on, ladies and gennulmens, please let these folks go where they need to get. Give this po-liceman some respect. He just doing what he told, that's all."

"Who you? Rodney King?" a voice taunted from the crowd, sparking calls of derision.

"Sir –" Ryder said.

"Let these folks through," the old man called to the crowd. "This woman is sad an' these police-mens just doin' they job."

"Get your ass on home, ol' man," a voice yelled. The crowd jeered and hooted at the man's intercession.

"Sir, it's you that's in our way," Ryder said. "Would you please go back down the steps and –"

The man turned to Ryder with his hands high and open. "Them folks is just angry and got nowhere to go with it, sirs. If I could get them to listen –"

The man was cut off by a sudden scream of sirens as four cruisers whipped around the corner, tires screeching, engines roaring.

"What the hell?" Ryder said.

"Shit," Zemain said. "Not now."

Ryder ducked his head and started down the stairs. He felt a jolt at his shoulder and lifted his head to see their gray-haired defender tumble from the side of the stoop, arms flailing. He bumped a heavy woman, sending her spinning, then slammed the pavement face-first.

Ryder stared open-mouthed as the man pushed his head up, thick strands of blood stitching his mouth to the sidewalk. For a split second, everyone went silent. Even the sirens seemed to fade into the distance.

"You see that?" the first voice from the silence yelled. "Cop shoved that old man off the step."

"An old man and they tried to kill him."

"Muthafucka cops."

"Get the bastards!"

A paper-bagged bottle exploded against the wall of the apartment building. "Go!" Zemain yelled, pushing Ryder and Nike ahead. The crowd surged forward. Curses filled the air. Cops spilled from the cruisers, the batons like exclamation marks in their upraised hands.

33

Ryder said, "I don't remember even touching the old guy. The crowd was belly to belly and we were trying to get to the vehicle."

He stared at the faces around him; half the police brass, a captain from Internal affairs, Duckworth and Meyers, Zemain. Bidwell was at a conference in Montgomery. Ryder had sped Nike Charlane to the restaurant, then immediately burned rubber to headquarters for the meeting demanded by Squill. He suspected the meeting was going to be what was called a "barbecue", and he was the one trussed for the spit.

Squill said, "The old man hit the ground like a goddamn pumpkin. Everyone saw it. More importantly, the cameras saw it."

"It was an accident."

Acting Chief Squill dry-washed his face in his hands, nodded to the DVD. "You seen the news, Ryder?"

The video flickered on to the screen. A guy selling campers finished his pitch and an anchor-woman appeared. The scene switched to Ryder walking from the apartment, Nike beside him, Zemain in the rear.

The on-scene reporter's voice: *". . . a crowd was gathering at the front of the building when members of MPD exited with the girl's mother . . ."*

The camera opened to a wide shot of the crowd.

". . . crowd growing unruly when an elderly man attempted to defuse the situation . . ."

All eyes went to the video: The black guy hobbling up the stoop and facing the crowd to make his plea, then turning to Ryder, hands up, submissive.

"Here it is," Squill said.

Ryder ducked and pushed forward, the guy suddenly tumbling from the steps like a dropped scarecrow, legs and arms flapping loose, slamming the woman before smacking the pavement.

Someone in the room said, "Ouch."

Ryder said, "Maybe I tripped him."

A close-up followed, the man helped to his feet as he wiped blood from his face and staggered against the stoop to brace himself. The reporter's voice-over: *"The man who fell, asking to not be identified, was in town visiting relatives when he says he found himself in the middle of the disturbance."*

The screen cut to a shot of the man, dazed and bloody. *". . . and I saw that the people was getting, you know, upset, and I thought I'd try and help, maybe put some calm in things, but . . ."*

"*But what happened next, sir?*"

"*That po-liceman ran at me like a football player and next thing I know I'm laying on the ground. I don't know why he want to hurt me, I was just trying to help.*"

"What happened to the injured guy?" Myers asked.

Zemain said, "We sent people to check on him, but he'd gone. Told people he wanted to get back to Huntsville where it was safe."

"He just disappeared?" someone asked.

"Until we hear from his lawyer," Squill said. He turned to Ryder. "Not bad, Ryder. You start out escorting a woman from her apartment and end up inciting a riot. You didn't finish what you started last week, had to go get it right?"

Zemain said, "We were cool until the cars rolled. The crowd blew up and we had to push our way out. That's when the old guy went over." He looked at the faces around the table. "And for the record, I think the guy tripped on his own shoelaces."

Squill sneered. "I don't care if he stepped on his dick, Sergeant. The perception is that Ryder didn't like the guy in his face and gave him the heave-ho."

"I didn't try to hurt him. I barely touched him."

Squill stood. "Detective Ryder, you are officially off this investigation. In fact, until I decide what to do with you, you're suspended."

"Sir, I respectfully ask that you review –"

"Get out, Ryder. I'm sick of looking at you."

Nike lay on Sandhill's couch, staring at the white of his ceiling. Sandhill had pulled a chair beside her and was holding her hand.

"Jacy's alive, Conner. I know it. I don't know how I do, but I can feel it."

Sandhill closed his eyes. All he could feel was Nike's hand in his own.

Still, he said, "I feel she is too, Nike. Alive."

"But that little girl in the house, the one that burned, what happened with –"

"I don't know. I think something went wrong. Maybe she was . . . maybe we shouldn't discuss this now, Nike."

Nike plucked a tissue from a box on the table, wiped her face. "Let's talk about it, Conner. I'm scared numb and my insides feel like ice, but I need to talk."

Talking would probably do her good, Sandhill thought. Since Jacy's abduction, Nike had been running on fear and guilt and the dark voice behind the heart that ceaselessly whispers, *The worst is yet to come.*

He said, "You did an incredible job yesterday, staying away from the bad things."

"It wasn't me that kept me straight, it was the cab driver. I wanted to fall into that dark hole and hide. He wouldn't take me where I wanted to go."

"You could have gotten out and taken another

cab, right? But you didn't. TeeShawn Green got you past the moment of craving and you kept yourself safe. That took strength and resolve."

"I don't have much left, Conner."

"Strength isn't a limited resource, it's self-renewing. You use it, you get more."

"I have to know, Conner – are the cops really doing everything? Turnbull's got me thinking that maybe –"

"Forget that yappy bastard, Nike. Turnbull's a media junkie, Sharpton Lite. Whoever's taking the girls is methodical, a planner, someone who selects his targets, then waits for the perfect moment. That's what's kept him ahead of us."

"What makes these people start, Conner? What makes an adult have fantasies about children?"

Sandhill's eyes tightened with controlled anger. "A mindscape from hell. A shrink might call it some form of psychological stunting, a huge displacement of sexual focus. Most sexual abusers of children were abused themselves."

Nike shook her head sadly. "Passing on the sickness. It's . . . it's like vampires."

Sandhill thought a long moment.

"Vampires? Yes, Nike. As close as we truly come to them, I think."

There was a gentle knock at the door and Marie entered, her face heavy with fear and concern. When she saw Nike standing and talking, Marie managed a smile.

"Nike, you ready to come to my place, get some sleep tonight, child?"

Nike nodded to Marie, then turned to Sandhill. "You planning on getting some rest yourself, Conner?"

"Sure," Sandhill lied. In a little over an hour he and Ryder were going to the property and records annex to root through the physical evidence on Darla Dumont, the girl abducted last year. Groping at straws.

The women walked to the threshold when Nike paused and turned to Sandhill. Her eyes seemed elsewhere in time, lost in a distant moment.

"Listen, Conner, there's something I've been wanting to say . . ."

Marie seemed to hold her breath, looking between Sandhill and Nike. Sandhill furrowed his brow.

"What?"

Nike's eyes suddenly looked no more than simply weary. "No. It's nothing. We'll talk about it later." She turned away and started down the steps, wiping away a tear. Sandhill looked at Marie and raised an eyebrow.

Marie said, "It's Jacy's birthday next week, Conner. She going to be nine years old."

Sandhill nodded; Jacy had spoken about it a couple of times.

"That little girl's birthday coming up next week," Marie repeated, then turned to catch up with Nike.

Sandhill closed the door, his brow knit in confusion, feeling as if a huge and indefinable presence had entered the room and licked the back of his neck, disappearing just as he turned.

34

Sandhill said, "You sure you want to do this, Ryder?"

"No. Which is why we've got to do it right now, before I think about it any more." Ryder took the corner fast, tires squealing.

"You're on suspension, right?"

"Squill blames the riot on me. Says I pushed the old guy off the stoop." Ryder squeezed through a yellow light. "Maybe I did. But it was an accident."

"If you get found out, it'll be . . ." Sandhill let his words hang in the air.

"Squill's not going to send out a memo on my suspension. The news'll take a while to filter down."

Ryder whipped the truck into the parking lot beside the MPD property room. The near-deserted lot was desolate under yellow lamplight. Sandhill stared at the building and made no move to leave the car. Ryder got out, closed the door, bent to look in the window.

"Something wrong?" Ryder asked.

"I haven't been here since the night I snuck in for the evidence. When I was tracking the guy killing the redheads. Trying to find that one detail, that one little arrow pointing the way."

Ryder looked between the building and Sandhill. "Given what happened that night, afterward . . . If you had it to do all over again, would you still do things the same?"

Sandhill reluctantly pushed himself from the car. He stuck his hands in his pockets and stared at the property building with a dark light in his eyes.

"I wouldn't."

"You'd have stayed away?"

"No," Sandhill said, walking toward the building. "This time I'd make goddamn sure I knew *exactly* where every camera was."

They stopped at the door. Ryder pressed the buzzer and looked at the video lens set into the brick, letting the night-duty clerk see who was outside. He checked his watch. "Almost midnight. I expect Squill and his robocops are in beddy-bye, dreaming of hot lights and rubber hoses."

Ryder thumbed the buzzer a second time. The lock disengaged. Ryder pressed through the door with Sandhill on his heels. The property annex had a green-walled front section where a clerk sat behind a counter. Beneath the counter were file cabinets, and to the clerk's left were security monitors. At the back of the small room, through a large door with red-lettered signs screaming NO

234

UNAUTHORIZED ADMITTANCE and NO SMOKING, was a rabbit-warren of shelves and boxes holding the detritus of crimes collected over decades.

There were two points of ingress: the front entrance, and a locked steel door in the back, now with a much better lock than the one Sandhill had picked. The smell was the same as ever, he noted: a musty mix of tobacco smoke, burnt coffee and cleaning solutions.

The eleven p.m. to seven a.m. shift was manned by a single clerk instead of two. Ryder muttered "shit" when he saw Leland Royce, a sixty-ish former street cop with a heavy dose of attitude. Ryder noted Royce hastily eject a videotape from the master surveillance console as they entered, sliding the tape beneath the counter.

Ryder filed the motion under *curious*.

Royce looked up, a stump of cigar in a wet, outsized mouth, his nose a webwork of veins. Fleshy half-moons bagged beneath rheumy eyes. Perched on the high stool behind the counter, Royce resembled a balding pear ripening into dissolution.

"Lord, looky here – it's Conner Sandhill. Somebody lock the place down."

"How you keeping, Lee?" Ryder said.

Royce shifted his corpulence to break wind and looked past Ryder. "What's Sandhill doing here, Ryder? He forget to steal something?"

"Can it, Lee," Ryder said. "He and I were hanging out when I remembered I needed to look at a case before tomorrow. We're going back into the file room for a few minutes."

"No, Ryder. Not tonight."

The door buzzer sounded. Royce padded back to his work area and checked the monitor before releasing the lock. A man in a green uniform carried in a cardboard box with a surgical mask on it. He set the box on the floor and left, returning a minute later with a six-foot stepladder and a sheaf of brown paper bags.

Royce slapped a pudgy hand on the counter. "You can come back at six in the morning, Ryder. Alone."

The uniformed man opened the box and removed several canisters resembling miniature fire extinguishers. Sandhill noted the logo embroidered on the man's shirt: *PestPro Industrial Pest Control.* They watched him tuck the paper bags in his belt, then walk into the warehouse section, setting his ladder beneath a surveillance camera.

Ryder nodded at the newcomer. "What's happening, Lee?"

"We get roaches in here, silverfish. Bigger critters, too, not that the fuckin' roaches aren't the size of shoes. Mice, sometimes a rat. Got to knock 'em back before they eat the joint up. This guy'll set off some insect bombs and other stuff. Fills the property room with smog until it looks like LA. Works for six months and we do it again."

"You breathe in that stuff, Lee?" Ryder said. "The bug crap?"

"Hell no. Shit poisons your brain. That's why the back'll get closed off."

Ryder stepped to the counter and watched the exterminator climb the ladder, a bag in his hand and a roll of tape at his hip. The exterminator popped a bag open and peeled strips of tape from the roll.

Ryder furrowed his brow. "What's he doing now?"

"They gotta put bags over the cameras. So the chemicals don't fog the lenses."

Ryder watched the exterminator slip a bag over the camera and tape it tight.

"What do you do while the chemicals work, Lee – drink coffee? Nap?"

Royce slitted his eyes and jutted his jaw. "Fuck you. I do bookkeeping. Filing. Catching up. I think it's time I saw your sorry ass leaving out that door. And I think the chief's gonna be wondering what you and Sandhill were doing here when I mention it come morning."

Sandhill shot Ryder a *You're sunk* look and walked to the door. Ryder turned to follow, stopped. He looked at Royce's work area behind the counter where his hand had been busy when they entered. The ejected videotape was tucked beneath a sheaf of papers. Ryder leaned across the counter and snatched the tape.

"Hey, gimme that," Royce said, grabbing for the cassette and missing. Ryder studied the video jacket; several young men in various stages of arousal cavorting in a pink-themed hotel room.

"*Tight Buns Party Boys Crazy in Vegas*? This yours, Lee?"

Royce turned the color of a ripe tomato. "That's . . . a piece of evidence," he stammered. "I just hadn't got to logging it in yet."

"Sure, of course, that's what I figured."

Ryder put the tape back on Royce's desk and replaced the papers over it, like tucking it into history, maybe never mentioned to anyone.

"We're heading out, Lee," Ryder said. "But could you answer me a couple questions first?"

The clerk champed his dead cigar and studied the floor. "What you want to know?"

"Didn't you once tell me the cameras were never off? And that Property was never unattended?"

"Four, maybe five hours twice a year? Never thought about it. What's it to you?"

Ryder frowned. "Same time during the year, or does it vary?"

"You could set your calendar by them. What? You got rats in your fancy-ass place out on Dauphin Island?"

Ryder didn't hear Royce's question; he and Sandhill watched the exterminator move his ladder to the next camera and prepare to blind it.

By two a.m. Sandhill was home, slumped on the couch, nodding off in fitful bursts. With each awakening he paced the room, dark, lit only by a streetlamp through the window. At three a.m. he drifted into a dream edged with broken glass. He eased past the ragged shards and was in the central room of a shadowy cave. Tunnels ran in all directions, spokes from the hub of a wheel. When he walked toward one of the tunnels, the whole system moved with him; no matter how fast he walked he remained in the exact center of the room, the radiating tunnels neither an inch nearer nor an inch farther.

He heard a small voice calling from a great distance.

"Mr King, Mr King . . ."

On the rock floor of the cave lay a huge wooden mallet, beside it an oaken spike. He drove the spike into the rock until its head was flush with the floor. He tossed the mallet aside and took a few tentative steps. The system didn't follow him any more. It was pinioned in place, secured to something just below the surface.

"Mr King, Mr King . . ."

He put his ear to the opening of each tunnel in turn, trying to discern the correct path, somehow knowing the choice he made was the only choice he'd get. He heard echoes within echoes, sonic palimpsests.

"Mr Ring . . ."

The floor began to tremble, the rock chafing at the spike. Sandhill picked a tunnel and began running to the voice. The walls shivered and oily dust fell from above. Then, a light in the distance, a shimmering point of white. But he could no longer run, the floor now rippling like waves. He began crawling to the light, the voice.

"Mr Ring . . . Ring . . . Ring . . ."

A roar at his back, wood shattering like thunder, rock screaming. The cave tore loose and exploded in a fury of stone and glass.

Ring.

Sandhill opened his eyes and pushed wearily from the couch, his clothes soaked with icy sweat.

Ring.

The phone. It was in its usual place, the étagère by the window. The night outside was dead still, parked vehicles shining under streetlight. A car below had its sunroof partially open, poor judgment. Sandhill picked up the phone.

"This is Sandhill."

The line was alive, but no voice responded. "Is anyone there?" he growled.

Through the phone, Sandhill heard a cold click of metal, like the safety of a gun snapped off. He suddenly understood and spun from the window the instant a yellow chrysanthemum of rifle flame bloomed from the open sunroof. He felt his heart explode.

Sandhill dreamed he was back in the cave, but this time there was no light in the distance, only a black wave raging toward his fallen body. It roared over him like a storm, and washed the world away.

35

Rose descended the steps into the hurricane shelter, green flip-flops at the end of skinny legs with calves like grapefruit. He wore a scarlet Speedo and a sleeveless black sweatshirt. Rose studied the form on the cot.

"I know you're awake, Jacy. I put the camera in, remember? You were up and looking around a minute ago."

Jacy put her hands over her eyes and turned her head away.

Rose said, "I've brought food, Jacy. And something to drink. Aren't you going to talk to me?"

Her hands pushed tighter. "I know what you are."

"What am I?"

"A Minute Hour. Like in the Gumbo King's story. I'm in your place underground."

"I'm a what? I'm your friend, Jacy. Come on, let me see that pretty face. Talk to me."

"I don't have nothing to say to a Minute Hour. I want to go home."

"Come on, Jacy. Talk to me, please. You can even ask questions if you want."

One of Jacy's eyes showed between her fingers. "Why did you burn that girl up in the fire?"

Rose froze. "What?"

"You're the one taking the girls. You and the Picture Man from school. I heard the one girl burned in a fire."

Rose was unable to look at Jacy. "I – I think you're just letting your imagination get away from you . . ."

"Why did you burn that girl? You took her and you burned her."

"I just said I didn't."

"People are supposed to take care of each other. Didn't you know that? People help people, they don't let bad things happen to them. They're supposed to save them from bad things."

A voice in Rose's head said, *Save me, Rosie.*

Rose gasped. He stood so quickly his head banged off the roof of the shelter. He clutched his head and keened in pain. The faraway voice grew louder.

Save me, Rosie . . . please

Rose retreated from the shelter, climbing the ladder so quickly his flip-flops fell off. He didn't stop to retrieve them.

Norma Philips glowered at the radio in the bookcase behind her desk, reading glasses unable to contain the anger in her eyes. Tom Clay sat in a chair tugging at his tie and fiddling with his starched collar.

"*This is the way to run a city?*" a male voice drawled from the radio, "*The blacks gone to tearing everything up and the mayor just smiling and saying how she understands. These people gotta be put in jail if they can't act right. The police are doing everything they can and it's not their fault some people let their kids run at all hours. Somebody tell the mayor to wake up.*"

Philips raised her eyebrows at Clay. He said, "It's talk radio, Norma. It's for people who won't write the newspaper because it wears their crayons down."

"Weren't you the one told me talk radio was people saying what really pisses them off? It's been like this all morning, people complaining about –"

She stopped, another caller on the radio.

"*Yeah, I'd like to say this is what happens when the bleeding hearts get control. I saw the mayor on TV last night saying how sorry she was that the . . . Africans . . . was frustrated and how they should go right out and riot.*"

Philips said, "Dammit, I do understand the black community's frustration. And said so. Three girls are missing, one's dead. Dead!"

Clay tented his fingers and pursed his lips. "I hate to second-guess, but maybe you could have been tougher on the mob mentality that took over."

"Tougher how? I said violence was absolutely the wrong way to accomplish anything, Tom."

"You also said people should speak out when they feel wronged. Some people thought you were endorsing the crowd's actions."

"Cranks hear what they're listening for. I rejected violence. I said peaceful protest is one of the cornerstones of a free society. *Peaceful*. If I used the word once I used it a dozen times."

Clay smiled sadly. "There are people who think the words 'protest' and 'peace' are code for godless seculi-femini-liberi-humanism."

"Godless libero sec . . . Lord have mercy, Tom, are we still there?"

"Most people aren't, some will always be because hate is all they have. Unfortunately, having little else to do with their lives, they tend to vote."

Philips aimed a wry smile at her assistant. "This sure didn't help me in the election, did it?"

Clay looked away. "I don't know that it'll be much of a factor."

"I may be tone-deaf to politics, but my nose still works, Tom. I smell bullshit. Tell me the truth."

Clay sighed. "I heard Runion about fell to his knees praising Jesus when he got wind of the violence. He's probably taping commercials making it sound like you led the charge against the cops."

"I'd expect nothing less from that sawed-off salamander."

"It's going to get rough," Clay said. "You positive you want to be mayor?"

"Don't say 'want to be', Tom. Say 'remain'. I'm here and I'm staying right here." Philips wheeled to the bookcase, snapped off the radio and, for good measure, yanked out the plug.

"Whatever it takes," she added, leaving no room for dissent.

36

The funeral procession wound slowly down the street to the cemetery. The grass was fresh-mown and wet from a recent rain, glittering when sun broke through. A large gray awning marked the gravesite. Cars began parking, somber faces moving toward the earth's open wound as if drawn by horizontal gravity.

Nike and Marie were first from the car, followed by Ryder and Father Tim. Nike was ashen and trembling, but had insisted on coming. The quartet marched slowly across the grass, Marie sniffling into a tissue, murmuring, "The world is gone crazy."

Rank upon rank of white plastic chairs sat beneath the awning, its scalloped edges wafting in the breeze. To the side were the news cameras, the videographers behind them almost vestigial, as if the cameras had recorded death so often they could now do it on their own. The four mourners positioned themselves to the side of the cameras, preferring to stand, as others were doing. Ryder moved closer to Nike and put his arm around her waist, feeling her tremble.

The casket rested beside the grave, dark wood with handles of gleaming brass. The minister, an elderly black man whose church was two blocks from Sandhill's restaurant, stepped forward and cleared his throat. The crowd fell silent and all that could be heard were birds singing from the branches.

"Dearly beloved," the minister began in a voice like rusted iron. "We know not why the world moves as it does. That is not ours to know. We know not why those taken from us before their time are taken. It is not for us to know . . ."

Ryder watched a tear slide down Nike's cheek. He closed his eyes.

"What we can know," the minister continued, "is the King of All Kings is God, and it is to His Kingdom where the soul of LaShelle Shearing now rests, or plays, or watches as we gather in solemn remembrance of her brief life . . ."

When the service concluded, Nike remained silent and walked ahead with Marie, Ryder and Father Tim a dozen paces behind. Ryder discerned several plainclothes colleagues scanning the crowd from its edges, hoping against hope that the perpetrator had come to gloat.

"How's Conner?" Tim asked. "I tried to see him this morning after I'd heard, but the cops wouldn't let me in his room."

"He got lucky. A ballistics tech said the heavy thermal glass he installed in the apartment, combined with the oblique angle of the shot, probably deflected the slug just enough. It helicoptered across his ribs instead of punching through his heart."

"Will he be . . ."

Ryder nodded. "He'll be moving slow for a while, Padre, but the machinery's fine. Or will be. He's a little fuzzy right now, but aware enough to tell us what had gone down."

"Do you have any idea who'd do such a thing?"

"The shooter phoned the apartment, watched the window until he saw Sandhill, then took the shot. No peel-out getaway, so no tire tracks on the street; no shell left behind, no cigarette butts or trash dropped out the car window . . ."

"You say Conner got a call. Can it be traced?"

"It was from a cellphone. We should know something later this morning."

When he entered the hospital room, Ryder knew Sandhill was better by the way the exiting nurse rolled her eyes, as if to say, *You want him, you got him.* Sandhill had the bed cranked to sitting position and was muttering about the soul of a hospital that didn't have gumbo on the menu. His left arm was in a sling, his side a patch of gauze and tape. He was wearing his crown.

Sandhill picked up a plastic bedside urinal and shook it. "Need to take a leak, Ryder? They make it real easy here."

"No thanks. Glad to see you're feeling regal again."

Sandhill tapped the crown. "Marie brought it by to cheer me up. When she started up with jokes about barbecued ribs I sent her packing."

"How's the side?"

"When the pills wear off it feels like I'm being attacked by woodpeckers."

Ryder pulled a chair close to the bedside and sat. "You got luckier than hell, Sandhill."

"Never underestimate the power of energy conservation; I'm real glad I decided to insulate."

"You remember anything new?"

"I recall the ride home from the property room, trying to get some sleep. Then I'm on the floor with the phone under me, dialing 911, feeling like everything I got is pouring out of my side. Next thing I know, I'm here and someone's shining a spotlight into my eyes."

"It was a penlight. And you tried to strangle the intern using it."

Sandhill leaned toward Ryder, keeping his voice low. "I've touched a wire somewhere. You don't get potshot because someone doesn't like your hush puppies."

Ryder scooted forward until his knees thumped the bed. "You've been crashing through the underbrush for two days, Sandhill. Who stands out?"

"Could have been someone at the mission. Or someone in one of the bars; everyone knew I was out for information and maybe someone got scared and wanted to take an insurance shot. Hell, for all I know, it was that jerk-off biker from the mission, though I doubt it. How about another run at photo-boy, Desmond? See if he –"

"I can't do squat. Squill put me on suspension, remember?"

"That shithead. Only Squill would pull one of his best dicks from a case out of pique." Sandhill shot Ryder a look. "You sure it was an accident? There were times I got so pissed off at do-goodie bystanders I wanted to—"

Ryder waved the conjecture away. "I don't even remembering touching him. But once the cruisers whipped around the corner, everything started happening at rocket speed."

"Any witnesses to your action with the old guy?"

Ryder looked grim. "A TV camera for starters. I think that's what boiled Squill's butt; not that the guy fell, but that it got caught on tape."

Sandhill studied the blank screen of the television at the far end of his room.

"I'd love to see this event. I'll bet you could hook a player to that TV."

Ryder was back in an hour, walking in with a DVD player under his arm, wires trailing the floor. "I had to yank my player off my set," he said. "That was the easy part."

"The hard part being . . .?"

"Making a copy of the newscast. Squill came

strutting past the conference-room door a couple times. If he'd walked in and found me . . ."

"You'd be in blue again. What if Squill finds you here?"

Ryder shrugged. "Life goes on."

"Keep that positive attitude. Squill's gonna walk through the door in about ten seconds."

"What?"

"Listen down the hall . . . those footsteps? Who else you know walks like a storm trooper on crank?"

Ryder quickly set the player on the credenza and tried to shove the disk behind it, but there was no room. He stepped in front of the machine.

"Well if this ain't a gathering of the faithful," Squill said as he strode in the door, Duckworth following at the distance of a pull toy. "What the hell are you doing here, Ryder?"

"I was . . . visiting my uncle. In the cardiac unit. I stopped in to see if . . . Sandhill needed anything."

Squill's thin lip warped into a sneer. "You better learn to pick better friends, Ryder." He turned the glare on Sandhill. "Have you been messing in the cases? Enough to piss somebody off? If you're with-holding –"

Sandhill rolled his eyes. "Dammit, Terrence, I'm not the problem here. The problem is that person or persons unknown is out there plucking young girls from the streets, and they're damned skillful at it. Let me come in and work with the depart-ment, give me some leeway –"

"You're not setting a foot inside again."

"That your final offer?"

"We're not dickering here, Sandhill. You're a thief. It was a measure of my charity that you were allowed to resign. I could have had you locked tight."

"Charity?" Sandhill spoke the word as if puzzled by its meaning. "Don't you mean you were just avoiding negative publicity?"

Squill looked at Duckworth. "Let's go, Commander." He turned to leave, but his eye caught the player behind Ryder. He narrowed an eye at the machine and the boxed disk atop it.

"What's that, Ryder?"

"It's a DVD machine, Terrence," Sandhill interjected. "It plays movies so I don't have to watch soap operas and people gargling with maggots." Sandhill looked at Ryder. "Like I was saying before we got interrupted, Detective, if you get to a video store, I'd like *Henry V*, the Branagh version, *Hamlet*, the Burton version, and *Die Hard*, the Olivier version."

Squill reached past Ryder and picked up the disk in its plastic case. "What's this?"

Sandhill yawned and laced his fingers behind his head. "A copy of *Deep Throat*, the Disney version. Seems there was an eighth dwarf named Lengthy . . ."

Squill pitched the disk back on to the credenza. "Listen hard, smartass. If I find your shooting has anything to do with digging into police business

252

– or that you're withholding an atom's worth of information – you'll be trading that gown for stripes. And you know I'd love doing it." He turned his eyes to Ryder. "And if there's just a sniff of you helping him, you'll be gone in an hour."

Squill wheeled and clicked away, Duckworth on his heels.

Mattoon was at his computer, a tumbler of absinthe on his desk. There were trade-offs to the potent liqueur: When he zeroed in on selected thoughts, others slipped into gray; it was as if Mattoon were an archer drawing an arrow – all he saw was the center ring, crisp, large, dominant. All other rings turned soft and indistinct.

Mattoon had used his sharpened focus to draft a letter detailing plans and timetable for the docking facility on Mobile Bay. It would be a shiny plum for the politician announcing Mobile's partnership with Mattoon Marine, Ltd, and he had already decided who would reap the reward. Mattoon didn't resent that politicians would claim credit for doing basically nothing; he knew their instincts were tuned to reciprocity: do for me, I do for you. The best part was the more they did for you, the more you owned them. Until you could eat their souls and they'd brush your teeth afterward.

Mattoon had only the final paragraph to write. He sat and tapped out the text:

In conclusion: all property optioned for the MML facility is now locked in. Announcement approaching but will be timed to your needs. Thank you for your most gracious assistance in local matters. I look forward to a solid and profitable future relationship.

Sincerely,
Walter Hutchinson Mattoon, CEO
Mattoon Maritime Limited

Mattoon folded the draft and pressed a button on his desk to summon the steward, Sajeem Ghobali. Mattoon studied his watch; six seconds until the knock on his door. Formerly the assistant steward, Ghobali had been elevated to Mattoon's personal steward after Valvane's theft of the wine. Mattoon pressed a second button and the door unlatched, Ghobali's signal to enter.

"Sir," Ghobali said, stopping two steps inside the room and snapping a salute.

"Only the captain salutes, Mr Ghobali."

Ghobali stammered an apology and bowed.

"There you go, Mr Ghobali. Well done." Mattoon walked to the doorway and held out the envelope. "Take this to Mr Henson. Tell him it's first priority and should be in ground mail in Mobile with all possible dispatch."

"Yessir," Ghobali said, simultaneously attempting to bow and close the door behind him.

Mattoon pictured the process. Henson, the

communications engineer, electronically transferring the text to Samuel Natch, Mattoon Maritime's shipping agent in Mobile. Natch would print the missive on creamy, embossed Mattoon Maritime stationery, sign it with an electronic facsimile signature, then send it registered mail. The recipient would be reading the letter within two days.

It was the most personal way to communicate, Mattoon thought; using the mail as if he were in Mobile and not hundreds of miles southeast. That, and electronic mail could so easily be seen by the wrong eyes.

His task out of the way, Mattoon sipped from the crystal. He felt a shifting of aspect in his brain, as though birds were winging across it. The phone buzzed, a hushed sound across the thick carpet. Mattoon went to it and pressed the speakerphone.

"Yes?"

"I'm sorry to bother you, sir . . ."

"Mr Henson. What can I do for you? Did you get the letter I sent with Ghobali?"

"Yes, sir, I did. To whom would you like it addressed, sir? And are there any special considerations?"

Mattoon shook his head; he'd spent two hours getting the text just right and forgotten to include the recipient; an effect of the absinthe, no doubt.

"My apologies, Mr Henson. The letter is to be sent by registered mail. Remind Mr Natch it is to be on company stationery. And that the letter is personal and confidential. Note that the phrase

'Personal and Confidential' should be in capital letters and underscored."

"Personal and confidential," Henson repeated. Mattoon heard the man taking notes. "And the recipient and address, Mr Mattoon?"

"It goes to the Honorable Norma S. Philips, Mayor of Mobile, Alabama. I've written her previously, so her address is on file. Thank you, Mr Henson."

37

"Lemme see it again," Sandhill said, the hospital TV on the table spanning the bed. Ryder worked the controls of the player, scanning back to the beginning and pressing PLAY. Sandhill stopped spinning the urinal on his finger and leaned closer to the screen.

Ryder said, "It's hard to watch that old guy flying over the edge like –"

"Stop. Rewind it to just before he goes over. Start just as the guy does the Wallenda."

Sandhill's nose was almost touching the TV. Ryder advanced the video a frame at a time. The color was too bright and the edges of the images were soft with blur, but details were visible.

"Stop!" Sandhill barked. He pointed to a frozen image, the old man listing at an angle, just before falling. "Tell me, Ryder, what do you feel when you're about to fall and can't do jackshit about it?"

"Panic."

Sandhill tapped the screen. "That guy look panicked to you?"

Ryder squinted at the monitor. "He looks pretty calm, considering."

Ryder cranked off several more frames, the man now in the air. Sandhill said, "Stop," and tapped the screen with the urinal.

"Doesn't he seem awfully far from the stoop for a guy falling? He should have dropped like Newton's apple, but look how his back is arched."

Ryder looked at Sandhill, gave him a confused shrug. Sandhill drummed his fingernails on the urinal. "It looks as if he pushed off, like a diver. Advance it."

The images jerked forward in time: the man pinwheeling his arms, tumbling into an obese woman in a fruit-basket hat, knocking her backward as he plunged to the pavement.

"That's why he pushed off," Sandhill said. "He made sure he hit the woman first. Check her size. Consider the kinetic energy she absorbed."

Ryder studied the screen. "You're saying it's a fake tumble?"

"The woman broke his fall. You can't see the guy hit the pavement from this angle, but I'll bet he unfolded across the ground instead of hitting it flat."

"He bled like a butchered pig, Sandhill."

"So did a lot of people in *Reservoir Dogs*. You think they're in the Hollywood Cemetery?"

Ryder stood and began pacing. "So that's why

he disappeared so fast. He knew he couldn't stand up to a close look."

"True, Ryder. Which means you've got to find Mr Stumbles."

"He's in the wind, gone."

Sandhill spun the urinal around his finger as he thought. "A guy that old who's that good? He's left tracks. We'll need stills of the guy's face, close-ups. Can you get them if you're suspended?"

"No problem; Hembree hates Squill as much as we do. He'll give the job rush status. I'll send the shots to police agencies in 'Bama, Mississippi and Florida."

"Don't bother. Send them to insurance agencies."

"Insurance age—?"

"Not Smilin' Stan down the street. The big carriers. Direct the photos to their investigative departments." Sandhill tapped the urinal against the image frozen on the screen. "They've dealt with this boy in the past."

Rose lay on the couch and stared at the monitor on the coffee table. His eyes were red and his fingertips quivered. Jacy's words echoed in his head.

"Why did you burn that girl up in the fire? . . . People aren't supposed to do that. They're supposed to save people . . ."

Rose pressed his hands over his ears but Jacy kept talking.

"People save people . . . save people . . . save people . . ."

Rose shut off the monitor.

"SAVE ME, ROSIE!" screamed a voice in his head. "SAVE ME, ROSIE!

Rose shut his eyes. It never helped.

"Save me, Rosie . . . Save me Rosie . . . SavemeRosie . . ."

Fourteen years ago at the farm: Rose's mother screaming as the attendants took her on the final ride to the hospital, five strong men in white, one at each limb, another trying to control her head, spitting, biting, cursing. *Hang on to her legs, dammit . . . Somebody get the goddamn restraints . . .* Rose's mama howling, pissing, grunting. *Goddamn, get 'em buckled . . .* The door on the white ambulance opening like a square mouth as they tried to feed his mama into it, bucking, kicking, writhing.

"SavemeRosieSavemeRosieSaveme . . ."

Then . . . the white ambulance retreats down the lane from the farmhouse and disappears in a cloud of red dust. The dust floats in the hot air. Somewhere far out on the highway the ambulance changes its mind and returns through still-unsettled dust.

Like magic. Like a dream.

But it's no longer an ambulance, it's a station wagon, black, pitted with rust and low over leaking shocks and busted springs. The white-dressed men have become chunky, straw-haired Aunt Junella

260

and tall, thin Uncle Toll. He's wearing Big Ben overalls, knees bagged, cuffs rolled high over mud-stained boots. Aunt Junella's in a tight yellow dress opened up so you can see most of her nay-nays. She squat-kneels in the dusty gravel, her eyes as black as oiled coal, and touches a finger to Rose's mouth.

"My, you're a pretty little fellow, Rosie. Ain't he pretty, Toll? Pretty as a dolly with a dolly's pretty lips . . . That older brother of yours around, Rosie? You boys be coming with us for now . . ."

Rose lay motionless for an hour, until the voices in his head subsided to a misty background hiss. He tried pumping iron to relax, but felt drained. He fell on to the couch. After twice picking up the camera switch and tossing it back on the floor, he finally flicked the camera on. Jacy was awake and sitting on the bed, staring into the air. She seemed so sad. Mama was sad like that. One time she sat in the same chair for a whole bunch of days and nights, not talking, just looking at the wall like it was a television. She made water in the chair. Pretty soon after that Mama went away and Uncle Toll and Aunt Junella were there.

They taught him Playtime.

Truman wasn't invited to Playtime; he was three years older and hair was starting under his arms and around his thing. Aunt Junella said it made Truman too old to play. It was just the three of them.

Rose looked at Jacy and wished she would smile. More than anything he needed to see her smile.

When Ryder rushed into the hospital room at eight a.m., Sandhill was sitting up and reading the *Mobile Register*. He looked pale, but his eyes were alert.

Ryder said, "Ten minutes ago I got a call from a Karen Pell, head Fradulent Claims investigator for Gibraltar Insurance. Guess what?"

Sandhill closed the paper and set it aside, wincing when he moved too fast.

"She ID'd the fall artist."

Ryder flipped a thumbs-up. "James T. James, known in the insurance biz as Gentleman Jimmy-Jim. Seems Mr James used to make his living getting hit by cars, slipping on wet floors in super-markets and falling in icy parking lots. Gibraltar settled three claims with James – under different names – before they caught on."

"What's with the 'Gentleman' moniker?"

"He was very polite, unctuous. He'd drag himself up from being thumped halfway across the street – seemingly – and start apologizing to everyone. By the time he finished his act the driver and witnesses would be on his side."

Sandhill nodded. "Made it easy to file big against the carrier. Age?"

"Sixty-two."

Sandhill raised his eyebrows. "Old for a leaper. But not as old as he looks."

"Tough life, maybe. Pell hadn't heard of him pulling anything for a few years, thinks something must have drawn James out of retirement."

Sandhill nodded slowly. "A good payday, perhaps."

"Pell said it wouldn't be a lawsuit against the city, James being too well known in the insurance industry to pull it off. I got the impression he's sort of a legend."

"I doubt Jimmy-Jim took this recent tumble just to polish his craft. Wonder what the scam was. Or is."

Ryder said, "And who's paying for the performance."

"You got an address on this moke?"

"He moves around. But when he feels like hanging out he stays with a sister in Montgomery. I have her address and number."

"Why the smile, Ryder? You got a canary in there?"

Ryder tapped the cellphone at his waist. "I called James's sister twice today. A woman answered at seven-fifteen. But at seven-forty a male voice answered. It was James. Couldn't mistake that voice."

"He suspicious of the calls?"

"I was a wrong number when I got Sis, a siding company when I got James. Gentleman Jimmy-Jim isn't real polite to telemarketers."

"No one should be. Good work, Ryder. There gas in your tank?"

"Why?"

"You've got to get to Montgomery, find out what Jimbo was jumping for. You have to get him alone and discuss events. Any way possible, you get my drift."

"He's seen my face from six inches away, Sandhill. Remember? I won't be able to get close."

Sandhill picked up the paper and snapped it open. "You have to do it, Ryder. Improvise. Get creative, for chrissakes."

He began reading as if Ryder were already gone.

The neighborhood was middle class with tree-lined streets and small trim yards abloom with bougainvillea and myrtle and azaleas. Ryder was parked beside a canebrake a half-block distant from the address, watching an elderly black woman in a pink dress water the front yard of the house where James had answered the phone three hours ago. She was soaking the crape myrtles, seemingly obsessed that some tiny area of root system might escape wetting. He'd been watching the woman water for twenty minutes and was surprised the yard hadn't turned into a swamp.

He hadn't known his ruse until two blocks away, when he'd stopped into the Food World for a bottle of juice and noted a contest they were running. But his plan was contingent on the sister being at work, and she was obviously retired, in her seventies. It was steaming in his car and he was desperate for an idea, anything to get him into the house.

Then, luck: the woman stopped drowning her yard, coiled the hose and disappeared into the house. She returned three minutes later and stood beside the white Lincoln town car in the drive, scrabbling through a huge floral purse. His heart beating out *leave now, leave now, leave now,* Ryder watched her climb into the Lincoln and back carefully from the driveway of the single-story ranch house, heading his direction at the pace of an arthritic tortoise. Her rear bumper exhorted followers to *Praise Jesus*.

He waited two minutes after she'd passed – eyes straight ahead, hands on the wheel at ten and two – before pulling into the driveway. He walked a flagstone path to a multi-paned front door with lace curtains. The doorbell tolled three somber notes. After a long minute a finger slipped aside the curtain and a cautious male eye stared out.

"What you want?"

Ryder's sunglasses were outsize wraparounds he'd bought at Food World. He'd also bought a cheap white ball cap. Angled down, the cap and the shades hid the upper part of his face. The bottom half he was disguising with sourball candies.

The candy ruse he'd learned from Harry Nautilus: actions are better disguises than garb. The one time James had seen Ryder, on the stoop outside Nike's apartment, he was in slacks and dark sport coat, his fresh-shaven jaw clenched tight with fear and resolve. Now it was dark with a two-day beard, loose and floppy as he rolled hard candies across his tongue, clicking them against his teeth.

He'd removed his suit coat and tie and wore a goofy grin above stooped shoulders. The front of his white shirt had been puffed out to resemble a nascent beer belly. He held up a white envelope found in his glove box and spoke in a high drawl poised at the edge of cartoonish, sucking candy as he spoke.

"Aft'noon, suh. Is Miz Arnett in?"

"She out. What you want with her?"

"I'm Harold Carson, suh. Assistant day man'ger down't the Food World. Miz Arnett's this month's granprize winnuh."

"What the hell you talking about?"

"She put her name on a entry form for the box. Won a five-hunnut-dollar shoppin' spree. Anything she wants. I got her citif'cate right here."

Some of the wariness in the eye was replaced with interest. "Beer and wine too?"

"Anythin' up to five hunnut dollars."

The latch clicked and a hand snaked out. "I'm her brother, I'll see she gets it."

"I'm s'posed give the citif'cate to the winnuh."

The fingers wiggled. "I said I'll see she gets it. She ain't coming back for hours."

Ryder let out a loud breath and clicked the candies across his teeth, having a tough time making a decision.

"Tell you what, suh, how about you sign for it?

266

Maybe show a drivin' license or something. That'll take me off the hook with my boss."

"Yeah, shit, I can do that. Come in while I hunt it down."

The door opened and Ryder stepped inside, shutting the door behind him. It was an old woman's home: Nick-nacks and photos covering every horizontal surface, doilies under lamps, a plaster cast of Dürer's *Praying Hands* on an end table, psalms and inspirational phrases crocheted into throw pillows on the overstuffed couch. There was a scent of liniment in the cool air.

James said, "You wait here while I go and –"

Ryder blew the candies into James's face like small sugar torpedoes.

"What the hell –" James sputtered as Ryder threw an arm over the man's silk shirtfront, jammed a leg behind him, and flipped him face-up on the couch. He straddled the man, and pushed his head into the couch cushions with a throw pillow embroidered with the Twenty-third psalm.

"I want to talk about a stunt you pulled in Mobile."

He lifted the pillow. James's eyes were wide with surprise and anger. "What you talking about, I ain't been to Mobile in years."

Ryder stripped off the cap and shades. Gentleman Jimmy-Jim looked into Ryder's face.

Whispered, "Oh shit."

Ryder pushed the pillow over James's face again, harder. Put his mouth beside the man's ear.

"Mr James, I have no time to play games. I'm looking for two kidnapped girls and I think you have something to do with it."

Ryder pulled the pillow away, the anger and confusion in the man's eyes replaced with fear. "Them stolen girls? I had nothing to do with that. That's sick shit, man. I don't know nothing about them girls."

"Tell me about Mobile. Why'd you do it? Who paid you?" Ryder hovered the pillow over James's face.

"I don't know. That's the truth, man. I got a phone call a few days before my . . . act. Said if I could come outta retirement and do a bit I'd come out five grand ahead plus expenses. I held out for eight. Plus expenses."

"What was the bit?"

"Man on the phone said I had to make you guys – the cops – look bad, like po-lice brutality. Didn't care how I did it long's there was a crowd and TV cameras. Piece of cake, man, that little stoop and that fat ol' mama to drop on."

"Fake blood, too."

"Blood bags under my tongue. One bite and I'm gushing. Looks ugly as hell. But I didn't have nothing to do with no little girls."

"Who hired you?"

"I was only close to him twice, for the down payment and the final payoff. And I didn't see him; it was night."

Ryder tossed the pillow to the floor and stood

slowly, tacitly signaling belief in the story. If James continued to be truthful, Ryder would allow him the dignity of speaking without coercion.

"Tell me about meeting the bag man."

James narrowed a suspicious eye. "What gonna happen to me?"

"Depends on how I like what I hear."

"Man paid me from a car. Like I said, it was dark and I didn't barely see him. He pull up, flip me an envelope, I counted and got gone. Same the night after the action."

"You just fall off the turnip truck, James? You got some kind of read on the guy, didn't you? He white or black, young or old, ignorant or educated?"

James sighed, looked at the ceiling. "White guy. Kind of a round face. Over forty, but prob'ly not fifty. Not no high-falutin' professor kind of talk, but not ignorant. Asked if there was anything special I needed. Told me I might have to sit in Mobile a few days, wait out the right time."

"But you got lucky."

"Got me a call saying there was this preacher going over to stir things up at some apartment – and the timing might be right, y'know?"

"Tell me more about the pay. Man give you a number to call him at?"

"No number. But he knew about me. Said my age was pretty good, but it be better if I looked older. So I talcumed my hair to give it more age.

Bent over some and walked creaky, talked older, put a little Tom in it. I can do that stuff."

"You fooled me. What else?"

"I told the guy I couldn't do anything that brought in a lawsuit cuz I was on the hot list at all the big insurance carriers. He said it wasn't anything like that. I had to come to town, wait for the moment, stick it to the cops, and haul ass. I wasn't supposed to hang around and let the po-lice start in with questions."

"What kind of car the guy drive?"

"Kinda big, long. Square, not that air-ee-o-dynamic kind of thing. Dark, like black but maybe dark blue or purple or something. Nothing fancy like a Benz."

"What else?"

The man looked down and to the right, body language for lying.

"Nothing."

Ryder bent and picked up the pillow. James held up his hands and began backstepping. "You a cop. I can't tell no cop 'bout what I think."

"Here's how it is, Jimmy-Jim. I represent no police agency at the moment. Right now I want you to think of me as a concerned citizen." Ryder squeezed the pillow for emphasis.

"OK, Mister Concerned Citizen. It felt like the guy had some kind of in with the system, like the cops or something. Least that's what I figured."

"Why?"

"Way he talk. Like he knew how many cops

might show up at the scene, the way they be acting when they hit the ground. Said I could take some of my cues from the Rev, y'know; said the preacher-man love to hear hisself talk and I could maybe use his noise to play off."

"You get the feeling this preacher was clued to the action?"

James shrugged. "Can't say yes, can't say no."

Ryder turned toward the door. He paused and pulled out a business card, flipped it to James. "You come up with anything else, or hear from this guy, call this number. It'll be worth your while."

James studied the card, confusion in his eyes. "The Gumbo King? I'm supposed to call a mutha-fuckin' restaurant? Hey, come back here, man. What is this craziness?"

38

Jacy Charlane sat cross-legged on the cot with a book on her lap. There were books beside her on the bed, books on the floor. The Minute Hour had brought the books. He hadn't said a word, just set the books down near the steps that came from the World, then scampered up the ladder again.

Some of the books were baby books, picture books. But some were cool, with stories she could read. She didn't know why the Minute Hour had brought the books, but was happy he had. When she read the books it was like she wasn't there.

Sandhill floated blissfully in a cloudbank. It felt like a waterbed filled with warm custard; he wanted to lay in the clouds for ever.

"Mr Sandhill?"

Though he was in the clouds, the voice seemed to come from above. Sandhill reluctantly felt himself lift through the white layers. He fought to open his eyes. An angel was calling him, that's what it was. He sighted the angel between his feet, about a quarter-mile away, framed against a square of white as if guarding the portal to heaven.

The angel was psychically beaming him a recording of a conversation they'd had several years ago. *"It's Tylenol with codeine, Mr Sandhill. It'll make your side feel better. What's with the hat?"*

"It not a hat, Nurse Ratched, it a crown. I am the Kumbo Ging."

A load roar and the angel zoomed up to within feet. The roar trailed off to little more than a tingling in his temples.

"Mr Sandhill. Hello?"

It wasn't an angel; it was a woman. She was leaning against the credenza and backlit by the window. Each time she spoke she was louder.

"Mr Sandhill, I don't have much time."

He opened his eyes fully. "I hear you quite well, Mayor. You don't have to shout." The words came out slow and thick. Norma Philips moved closer and looked into his eyes dubiously.

"Are you tracking in there?"

He pointed at the table a few feet from his bed. "Water."

Sandhill fumbled for the bed control and raised himself to sitting position. Philips handed him the pitcher. He drank all the water, then rubbed ice over his face. The wall clock showed that he'd drifted off for three hours. Ryder would be back soon.

Philips gave Sandhill an arched eyebrow as water and ice splashed down the front of his gown. "Are you alright, Mr Sandhill? You sure you're coherent?"

"This is Oslo, 1956, right?"

"Don't screw around. I want to get gone before visitors arrive, but I want you fully rational before we talk."

Sandhill gave his face a second ice treatment, then dried it with the blanket. "OK, I'm rational. What's the hurry?"

Philips set a brown leather briefcase on the credenza and popped it open, removing a thick, rust-colored tome with splitting binding. On the binding, printed in gold leaf, were the words, *Alabama Legal Statutes and Enactments*.

"You were a law student for three years, Mr Sandhill. A good one, I suspect. Perhaps you'll be able to interpret this. Check section 32-A."

She handed him the opened book, her finger tapping the relevant paragraphs. Sandhill studied the heading. "Revised rights and privileges of the Mayor of Mobile, Alabama, enacted . . . February 4, 1923 . . . *1923*?"

"Read it."

It took less than a minute to read, his eyes widening with every sentence.

"Holy shit, Mayor. This was because of Prohibition, right?"

"I'd think so, given the date and newspaper accounts of the time. It seems there were some corrupt cops around, either bootlegging themselves or looking the other way. Good cops were booted from the force, probably because some of the brass were violating the Volstead Act. The mayor needed to reinstate cops he trusted, without permission of the police hierarchy."

Sandhill narrowed an eye at Philips. "This ordinance was never rescinded? It's still in effect?"

"A lot of old articles and ordinances are still on the books. You can't build a privy within eighty paces of a well. You can't tether a horse in front of a funeral parlor. They may be archaic, but they carry the full force of law."

"So you can reinstate me to the department?"

"All you need is an affidavit signed by the mayor," she said, pulling a single sheet of paper from her briefcase. "Just like this."

He studied the document: the date, two brief paragraphs and the mayor's signature. Philips said, "It'll keep you from getting busted for interfering with police business since, of course, you'll be a cop again, same rank."

Sandhill pictured himself holding up the sheet and yelling, "Stop thief."

"I'll need my shield."

"That I can't help you with." She paused, raised a questioning eyebrow. "Perhaps you might ask Acting Chief Squill."

"He's the last person I want to know about this."

"I suspect that's the right answer, Mr Sandhill."

Sandhill treated Philips to his best scowl. "Why are you doing this?"

"That's my business at present."

"Who else besides you knows about this?"

"No one."

"Can we keep it that way?"

Philips nodded. "I hoped we would."

Sandhill crossed his arms and looked Philips in the eye. "What exactly do you want me to do?"

"Investigate, Detective. Stick your nose into things. Find those girls."

She turned to leave. Sandhill cleared his throat. "I, ah, already have a couple of irons in the fire, your honor."

"Somehow, I expected that, Mr Sandhill," Philips said over her shoulder, the door closing in her wake.

"You did great with James, Ryder," Sandhill said, standing unsteadily in front of the mirror and buttoning his blue denim shirt for the second time. "Something strange is cooking, crazy gumbo, a porridge of the weird. I'm wondering if Gentleman Jimmy might be right about an MPD connection. But why would cops want to spark a riot? Politics? How's Philips rank with the boys in blue?"

Ryder thought for a moment, watching Sandhill wince as he bent to tie his shoes.

"Most cops didn't like her appointment, gut reaction to her community empowerment days. They figured she was another cop-hating lefty."

"Now?"

"She kicked that impression in the ass by immediately pushing for better equipment and training. Plus any cop can attend classes at University of South Alabama for a third of the cost, a federal grant she tracked down. She's also pushing to put more cops on the street. Most won't admit it, but the majority of the rank-and-file will vote for Philips come November."

"Aside from Terrence and his boys, what does the general brass think?"

"Pretty much the same, I imagine. Even if someone had it in for her, I can't see them taking a chance with a scammer like James. Too risky."

Sandhill snorted. "And they're not that creative."

"You think Squill could do it? He'd benefit most from a change of administration."

Sandhill stood and began filling a duffle with the hospital water pitcher, drinking cup, a packet of plastic dinnerware. He lifted the bedpan, studied it from all sides, then jammed it in the duffle.

"Terrence is so hot to be big chief I'm surprised he hasn't spontaneously combusted. But I always figured him as too lily-livered to risk his career by doing something starkly illegal. He'll slit your throat from behind, but he'll have all the right paperwork."

"You think?"

"I've been wrong before, Ryder. It's scarcer than snowmen in Morocco, but it's happened."

"So where from here?"

"Earlier I managed to walk down the hall and back without winding up on my belly. It's progress. I'm going to rest at home a couple hours then head back out."

Ryder knew arguing was futile. "I'll tag along. I got nothing else to do."

Sandhill lowered himself to the bed on rubbery knees. "Grab my crown over there, would you? Then let's blow this antiseptic hellhole and see about getting my shield back."

"It'll never happen."

"I can't do anything without my badge, Ryder. I might get my ass shot off if I can't wave it."

Ryder said, "Might be friendly fire, too."

Sandhill scowled at a dusty memory. "Squill adored the moment I handed over my shield."

"What'd he do with it?"

"Threw it in the top drawer of his desk and slammed it shut. He's changed desks a half-dozen times since then but I'd bet my badge is still in there, his biggest trophy. Terrence probably pulls it out every so often just to spit on it."

Ryder frowned at a thought in his head, like it was an unwelcome visitor. He dropped Sandhill at his apartment and drove away, the frown still clouding his face.

39

An hour passed. Sandhill answered the knock at his door in a purple bathrobe with a golden crown embroidered on the back. He liked it even though Marie said it made him look like a royal eggplant.

Ryder, his face wan, stood at Sandhill's threshold.

Sandhill said, "You look a little stressed, Ryder. Where'd you go?"

Ryder entered, jamming the badge wallet into Sandhill's hands as he passed. Sandhill's mouth dropped open and he studied the gold shield like it was the last piece of the true cross.

"Good old 1818. Ryder, you're amazing. Was it really in Squill's desk?"

Ryder walked to Sandhill's kitchen area, removed a bottle of Glenfiddich from a cabinet, and poured two fingers in a tumbler. His hands shook. So did his voice.

"Top drawer. In the back."

Sandhill said, "Was it tough to get?"

Ryder emptied the glass, poured another, banged down the liquor and brought the bottle to the couch. He sat heavily and put his palms over his eyes.

"Ryder?" Sandhill asked. "You OK?"

"I was rooting through Squill's drawer, pocketing the badge, when I heard his footsteps outside the door. I think I jumped over his desk."

Sandhill's eyes went wide. "He came in with you in his office?"

"I pretended I'd come to beg my way off suspension. He threw my ass out and said if he saw me anytime in the next month I'd spend my remaining career directing traffic."

"You're a warrior prince, Ryder. They'll build you a longhouse in Valhalla."

Ryder rubbed his gut. "Can you get ulcers in an afternoon, Sandhill?"

"There's antacid in the bathroom cabinet. You really jumped the desk?"

"Without touching it, I think." He paused. "I did get something interesting from Zemain; spoke with him outside HQ. Remember when the cruisers came around the corner by Nike's place and everything unraveled? Guess who told them to come running."

"Who?"

"No one knows. Someone got on the frequency screaming, 'Go, go, go . . . officers in trouble.' No one recognized the voice."

"Two-inch radio speakers aren't real accurate

for vocal quality. You get higher fidelity at a drive-through."

"No one's owned up to making the call. It's assumed someone saw the crowd tighten and thought we were in the soup."

"So either it was a panic call, or . . ."

"Or someone pouring gasoline on the flames."

"Curiouser and curiouser," Sandhill said, polishing his badge on his robe.

"There's something else, too. The phone company ID'd the cellphone used to call you. It belongs to Barney Sackwell."

Sandhill squinted at a recollection. "Name's familiar."

"He works in the City building, a traffic engineer. Not sure when he lost the phone. He was doing a traffic count on Airport Road when he noticed it was missing."

Sandhill nodded as the recollection pushed into the light.

"Sackwell the traffic geek. He was pushing to kill half the on-street parking on my block. I got the merchants together and we raised a stink. I don't think he likes me."

"It's no reason to shoot you, Conner. He'd used the phone on his way into work the day before yesterday, but later noticed it was gone."

"Not a smash and grab?"

"Sackwell said he found his passenger-side door unlocked. Also says he might have forgotten to lock it, but it'd be the first time; says he's real careful, even parking in the municipal garage."

"So if Sackwell did lock his door . . ."

"Someone used a key. Or maybe a slim-jim," Ryder said, referring to a metal strip used to disengage locking mechanisms.

"I'd vote for the slim-jim, easier to get. Who, outside of crooks, locksmiths and bartenders knows how to use one?"

"Repo men. Wrecker drivers. Parking attendants." Ryder paused. "And, of course . . ."

Sandhill nodded. "I know cops who can pop a door as fast as unzipping their pants."

Ryder held his hands out and studied them; the shaking had mostly subsided. "Where do we go next?"

Sandhill pulled his cellphone from his robe, index finger poised over the keypad.

"I think Gentleman Jimmy-Jim should pay me a visit. Got his number?"

40

At seven a.m. the door to the restaurant opened and James T. James walked to the table where Sandhill was scratching on a tablet. Sandhill's gaze started at green alligator loafers, ran up the sky-blue sharkskin slacks and over the pink silken shirt with a ruffled button line. It ended at wary eyes above a hard cosmetic smile.

Sandhill said, "You're one of the Temptations, right?"

James's grin disappeared and he angled his head to look down his nose. "You know who I is. Who you, man?"

"I'm the Gumbo King."

James raised an eyebrow at the spiky crown. "I hate to tell you this, King, but somebody been cutting on your fez."

Sandhill's boot pushed out the chair across from him. "Set a spell, Mr James."

James slowly lowered himself. "What you want

from me so muthafuckin' impo'tant I got to drive down here and look at you?"

"It's nice to see you, too." Sandhill nodded to the carafe and second cup on the table. "Coffee?"

James ignored the overture. "An' why you got that other crazy-ass guy using threats about tellin' stuff to my sister to get me here? She don't need to know nothing about what I did in Mo-bile. Bad on her heart. What you got against a nice old lady's heart?"

"I'll cut to the chase, Mr James. I need your observational skills."

James found his grin again. He reached for the coffee, poured a cup, sipped, then crossed his arms and leaned the chair back on its legs.

"You need me, huh? So what'm I getting paid for this gig, leasing you my skills?"

Sandhill pulled his badge wallet from his vest and flipped it open. He set it in front of James like a talisman.

"Your ass stays out of jail today, Gentleman Jim. How's that for a down payment?"

Jacy heard the door to the World open and the Minute Hour came down again. He had a little TV set and a short-leg table. She scooted back on the cot and watched silently as he set the TV on the table and plugged it in. Then he tied wires behind it and left. The television showed dancing sparkles. Jacy watched, thinking a show would come on.

284

When nothing happened, she began reading. The book was about the once-upon-a-time days when kings and knights were everywhere and saved m'ladies and people in trouble. It made her think of the Gumbo King. She wondered if he was looking for her, like Aunt Nike would be doing.

Or did he forget her?

No. The Gumbo King would be looking everywhere. It was his way. But could he see her deep under the ground, in a metal cave built by the Minute Hour?

She shivered and felt her eyes fill with water until caught by movement on the TV. The Minute Hour was sitting on a couch. He'd combed his hair and had on clothes like for church, a white shirt and those pants with edges.

The Minute Hour waved. Jacy didn't know what else to do, so she waved back.

Something seemed different.

Sandhill and James surveilled the morning shift change at MPD headquarters from a half-block distant, binoculars lifted as cops and support staff streamed through the doors. James scanned the crowd. "It's hard looking, man. They all crossing back and forth in front of one another. I be having cop nightmares for a month."

"Eyes see better when mouths are shut. Concentrate on the suits, not the uniforms."

After fifteen minutes, Sandhill hadn't seen Squill or Bidwell or several of the top honchos, and suspected they'd been summoned to an early-morning planning session. Still, bodies continued to trickle inside, and the pair focused on each face in turn, Jones grunting, *No . . . huh-uh . . . not the one . . . man, he a ugly mutha, ain't he . . . not him . . .*

The trickle dried up. "What you want me observatin' at now?" James said. "Them newspaper boxes over there?"

"Let's bag it," Sandhill said. "I knew this was too long a shot."

He saw an opening in the traffic, and squealed into the lane. Passing the building, James twisted 180 degrees in his seat. "Yo, that's sorta like the guy," James said. "Just coming 'round the corner, gray suit. *Ugly* gray suit."

Sandhill jabbed the brakes and heard a blast of air horn, a truck grille filling his rear-view. He was surrounded by traffic with nowhere to pull over.

James said, "He's almost inside. Whip it around, man."

Heart hammering, Sandhill turned at the next side street and doubled back, crawling past the station at five miles an hour, oblivious to the horns behind him.

"See him anywhere?" Sandhill said.

"Gone like dust in the rain, King. Must be inside."

Sandhill turned the corner by the parking lot and stopped. "What'd he look like?"

James studied a gray-suited figure a half-block away, pulling a paper from a *Mobile Press-Register* box. "Hey, there he is."

"It's the guy who paid you?" Sandhill asked.

"It was night. The guy looked kinda like that. I'm not full sure."

Sandhill aimed his binoculars at the distant figure. Grunted.

"You know the guy?" James said.

Sandhill lowered the glasses. "We've met a time or two."

Jacy grew tired with reading and set the books on the floor. The picture on the TV was showing the empty couch. Then, like knowing she was watching, the Minute Hour walked into the TV picture and sat. He was drinking from a straw in a big cup.

"Can you hear me, Jacy?"

Jacy looked at the camera eye, knowing it was how she looked at the Minute Hour. She nodded.

"I'm sorry I frightened you before, Jacy. I didn't mean to. Do you like the books I brought?"

"Some are for little kids. But I like . . ." Jacy held up her favorites and the Minute Hour nodded. His eyes looked away, then back.

"Jacy? You get scared when I come to visit, don't you?"

"Yes."

"I have to bring your food. And empty the toilet."

Jacy said, "It's when you look at me I get the most scared."

The Minute Hour made a sad face; Jacy was learning it had a bunch of them, like different colors of sad. He said, "Am I ugly? Do I look like a monster?"

"Aunt Nike says nobody's ugly. Everybody got somewhere pretty inside them. You got to look for it."

"Everybody has pretty in them? Your aunt says that?"

"She said she learned it from my mama."

"Where's your mama at, Jacy?"

"She got sick and the sick took her away to heaven."

"Do you miss your mama, Jacy?"

"Mostly not. Sometimes it's all I can think about. My Aunt Nike says Mama's always with me. Even if I can't see her, she's there to help me."

"Do you really believe that, Jacy? About your mama?"

"Through and through."

"How about your daddy?"

"I don't remember him at all, not even shadows."

"Do you get scared your mama isn't around to help you? Not now, but every day?"

"I have Aunt Nike and Miss Marie and the Gumbo King."

Jacy watched the Minute Hour set the cup on

the floor. He put his face in his hands and was quiet a long time before looking back at her.

"I'm scared all the time, Jacy. I'm scared to death."

"What are you scared about?"

The Minute Hour did another sad face; sad with its eyes closed. "I'm scared about me, Jacy. I'm scared I don't have any pretty place inside. Just ugly."

Jacy heard the sound of a door come through the TV. She watched as the Picture Man showed up in the TV. He was laughing.

"Having our little fantasy hour are we, Rose? Why the hell you dressed like that?"

"Shut up, Tru. Go away."

The Picture Man's face filled Jacy's TV screen. He said, "What's this doing here? What are you up to?"

The Minute Hour stood. "Leave that alone."

"Double cameras? Hah! That's funny. She watch you pull your peter?"

Jacy saw the Minute Hour jam the cup into the Picture Man's face, foamy white drink splashing all over. The Picture Man tried to slap at the Minute Hour but couldn't reach past his arms. Then they weren't on TV any more and there was a bunch of hollering and thumping. Jacy heard the Picture Man yell, "*Enjoy it while you can, asshole,*" and "*One more day,*" and the TV turned off.

One more day until I go home? Jacy wondered.

41

Ryder plucked a volume from Sandhill's shelf: *Advanced Forensic Techniques*. He opened it, saw a color plate of a body splayed open, and slid it back into place. He turned to Sandhill, sitting at the table in the apartment's dining area.

"So what does it mean, Sandhill? What James said?"

Sandhill scribbled on a legal pad, attempting to make connections between names. Lines were scratched out, redrawn, scratched out again. Sandhill threw the pad on the table.

"Maybe nothing. Maybe James was wrong. Still, he seemed pretty certain about the ID being the contact and payoff man."

Ryder frowned. "I'm not sure how much 'pretty certain' means from a scammer like James."

A knocking at the door, soft and hesitant. Sandhill rose and opened it. Nike stood outside. She looked past Sandhill to Ryder.

"I'm sorry, I didn't know you were here,

Detective Ryder. I didn't mean to bother you guys, I'll stop back later."

She turned to leave but Sandhill grabbed her arm. "Whoa, girl. Since when do me and Ryder scare you off?"

Ryder studied something in Nike Charlane's face and made a show of checking his watch and seeming surprised at the time.

"I was just leaving, Ms. Charlane. I'm overdue at a meeting."

"Overdue where?" Sandhill asked.

Ryder shot him a glance that said, *shut up*.

"Oh yeah," Sandhill said. "See you later."

Ryder descended the stairs. Nike drifted across the room to look out the window, as if preferring the damp heat to Sandhill's cool white spaces. "Jacy's ninth birthday is coming up soon, Conner."

"Marie mentioned it the other day. Jacy talked about it a time or two."

"Did you ever think about it? Her birthday?"

"I planned a party. Double chocolate cake, ice cream. I got her a kid's set of mythology books and a –"

"Not the festivities, Conner, the timing. Did you always think she was born in September?"

Sandhill's brow furrowed. "Come to think of it, I thought some years back you mentioned Jacy's birthday was around Christmas. But I guess a few months don't make a whole lot of dif—"

He froze. His eyes traced back and forth as if working equations on a mental blackboard. When he saw the sum chalked at the bottom, he turned to Nike, all color gone from his face.

"But that could mean . . ."

Nike looked in Sandhill's eyes. "The name Jacy comes from the letters J and C."

John Conner Sandhill stood abruptly and walked to the kitchen area, anger and confusion clouding his face. He put his hands on the counter-top and leaned slowly forward as if searching for balance in a shifted universe.

"Why the hell didn't Thena tell me? Why didn't you tell me?"

Nike said, "I swore I wouldn't and, contrary to Thena's wishes, I just did. I didn't agree with her decision to not tell you, Conner. But it was Thena's decision to make and mine to respect. Things are different now. And I think she'd want you to know."

"A baby. And all this time you've been telling me –"

"That Jacy was born in December. Thena said you weren't ready to know."

"But that's crazy, I –"

"Maybe you don't remember how you used to be, how little time you had for anything but yourself."

"For myself? *Myself*?"

"For your damned non-stop cases, then. Thena was going to tell you, at first. But she didn't see you for weeks. You were too busy being Mr Detective. You couldn't find a couple lousy hours to stop by, say, 'How you doin', Theen?' Maybe hear what she had to say, what was happening in her life?"

"I was working, that's all." The words weren't through Sandhill's lips before he knew they sounded shrill and defensive.

"You were living your work. There's a difference."

"I tried to be with her as often as –"

"'To thine own self be true' – isn't that one of your mantras? Think back, Conner, without rosy glasses. How much time did you really spend with Thena?"

Sandhill closed his eyes and tumbled through memories. Thena arriving as he was leaving; the "I'm-working-through-the-night" calls; missed meals; parties she'd attended expecting him to arrive, his only presence a late phone call expressing regret . . .

Nike said, "When Thena found out she was pregnant she was torn in half. It wasn't expected, and neither was the exhilaration she felt, the excitement. Thena interpreted her pregnancy as the most creative act imaginable, the creation of life. She believed such a creation demanded total involvement and nurturing."

"I was fully able to deal with whatever –"

Nike shut Sandhill off with a raised hand. "Exactly, Conner. Thena knew you wouldn't – couldn't – share her awe, her excitement, but she knew you'd deal with it. You'd regard it as a duty.

Thena didn't want dutiful, Conner. She needed to share in a joy and commitment you weren't ready for."

"So she left. She simply ran away."

Nike's eyes flared. "She wasn't running from, she was running *to*. To a life where she didn't have to parcel off her energy between her child and a part-time partner. Where she could devote everything to Jacy. Then, one day, when you'd changed, *if* you changed, she'd explain and . . ."

Sandhill walked slowly to the couch and sat. Nike sat beside him, bringing his hand to her lap and wrapping it in hers.

"You're different than you used to be, Conner. You started being different when you opened the restaurant. Started wearing those crazy vests, that goofy crown. I was standing in Spikes's grocery last year when you passed by, singing. Conner Sandhill singing! I know part of it was an act, just like being the iron-spined detecting machine was partly an act . . ."

"Act? What do you –"

"Both are part of you, but not all of you. I'm not saying you're another person; you're still a headstrong jackass and won't hear anyone else's opinion until all of yours are used up, but you're not so damned rigid any more." Nike paused, touched Sandhill's cheek. "I see how you've changed and I get sad Thena never got to."

Sandhill leaned his head back and stared into the white of the ceiling. "All this time I thought she'd found someone else. That she'd moved away to be with him."

Nike paused. "I was always surprised you let her go so easily. Thena was too. She was afraid you'd track her down, ask her to come back. She knew she'd be unable to resist."

"It wasn't that I didn't want her back; I thought she'd finally wised up. I never understood what she saw in me in the first place."

Nike's lips brushed Sandhill's fingertips and she laid her cheek softly against his hands. "She saw possibilities, the Conner Sandhill everyone else missed, the one you've become. Seeing possibilities was her gift, it was always . . . her . . ."

Nike's voice shook apart. Sandhill wrapped his arm around her shoulders. He watched the room begin to pitch and shimmer. Sandhill fought the tears knowing he would lose, having to fight them anyway, hating himself for it.

42

Sandhill's phone rang through spaces as silent as a closed book. "I'd better grab that," he said, squeezing Nike's shoulder. "It could be important."

Nike withdrew her arms from his neck and wiped her eyes with a tissue. Sandhill snatched the phone in mid-ring. Gentleman Jimmy James's voice hissed through the wires, fear heated with anger.

"What you trying to do to me?"

Sandhill said, "What do you mean, do to you?"

"You doggin' my ass. You got a guy on me; I made him soon's I pulled into my driveway. You said I was done."

Sandhill said, "Chill, James. What's going on?"

"There's a po-lice car out front, got that little antenna sticking up. You the only people know about me. What you got someone in my shadow for?"

"I don't. You recognize the guy in the car?"

"Might be that guy hired me. Coming to shut

me up. Permanent maybe. You got me found out, damn your white ass."

Sandhill's mind raced with pictures and probabilities. "No way, James. Whatever's going down was already in someone's plans. Your sister there?"

"She an' her church biddies went to some big prayin' meeting up in Memphis; be gone a week. Oh man, that car just pulled up the driveway. I think it's him, man."

Sandhill subconsciously lowered to a crouch, phone tight to his ear. "Listen, James. You got a back door? Where's it lead? OK; I want you to dial 911 and yell *Fire!* Call me when you're safe."

Sandhill hung up and stared at the phone for eight minutes. He picked it up halfway through the first ring. James said, "Shit, man, there's a whole buncha fire vee-hicles out front of the house, firemen staring at the place. Kinda funny, I think about it."

"Where you at, James?"

"Honeylee Blakee's place, next block over. I'm watching between the houses."

"Honey Lee . . .who's that?"

"Lady friend of mine, man. She old but she bold." Sandhill heard a woman's laughter in the background; it didn't sound that old.

"Where's the guy was in your driveway?"

"You tol' me scat, not stand and watch the show. But when the sirens started up in the distance, he burned his tires getting gone. Wherever he is, he not around here. Hope them firemen scared him off for good."

"Doubtful. Your lady friend let you stay a few days?"

"She like that idea fine, her husband have other thoughts. I got a couple guys in my poker-playin' crew let me rack with them a day or two."

"Do it. I'm going to deal with the situation down here."

"Gonna 'front the man in the gray suit?"

"Call me in two days, James. Things are about to change."

"That's what I comin' to like 'bout you, Mr Gumbo King," James chuckled. "You crazy as a foamin' dog, but you get shit done."

Sandhill tossed the phone back in the cradle and turned to Nike's questioning eyes. "Someone's watching James. Maybe to remind him to be quiet, or maybe to put him out of the game for keeps."

"James? That old man you said faked the fall?" Nike said. "Why?"

"James saw someone. Either they're having second thoughts about being seen, or this is the way they planned it all along."

"Who?"

Sandhill stood and pulled a black leather vest over his red tee shirt. He went to the table beside his bed and retrieved the holstered Colt, set it on the table. He jammed the badge wallet in the back pocket of his jeans.

"The person I'm going to talk to this afternoon. If I'm right, he'll be in Mobile in a couple hours.

It's time to jam a stick in the nest and see what comes slithering out."

Captain Sampanong made a final check of the radar and GPS readout as the *Petite Angel* entered the wide mouth of Mobile Bay, Fort Morgan to the east, Dauphin Island to the west. Satisfied with the new heading, Sampanong turned to his companion on the bridge. "We'll be berthed by five, Mr Mattoon, if we don't meet a lot of traffic in the river."

Mattoon surveyed the waters through binoculars. A gas platform lay a half-mile to portside. A dredging barge lumbered to starboard. Three hundred yards out, a charter fishing vessel crossed the *Petite Angel's* bow, its deck packed with beer-woozy anglers who'd paid eighty dollars apiece for a half-day of crossing lines and vomiting. A flat smile crept to his lips as he imagined crushing the boat beneath his bow, watching the flotsam emerge from the stern like shattered china.

Samapanong said, "You look pleased, Mr Mattoon. You plan to announce the new facility soon, I take it?"

"Not personally, Captain. I've hired whores to do it for me."

"Whores, sir?"

"Politicians. Puppets. Ones too proud to see the wires." He passed the binoculars to Sampanong. "Thank you, Captain. It's time for me to make several last-minute arrangements."

Back in the sanctuary of his cabin, Mattoon's fingers played across the computer keyboard and the screen lit with the image of Jacy Charlane bound on the cot. His palm stroked her pixilated face, and he removed from his desk the agenda for his evening. He picked up the phone and dialed the communications officer.

"Mr Henson? I need for you to connect me to Mobile. The mayor's office. You have the number in your log."

The call wouldn't take long, Mattoon reflected as he listened to connections clicking through the distance, his finger already tracking the next number on the list.

The number that brought Lorelei. By tomorrow she'd be his.

The dark car slid into the apartment building's lot and rumbled to the numbered slot under a listing carport riddled with dry rot. The apartments, twenty yards distant, were in similar disrepair; boxes built in the fifties, decomposing since the seventies – peeling paint, hanging gutters, cracked, weed-sprouting walkways, grass bleached a waterless yellow. The hot air smelled of rotting garbage.

Sandhill slipped from his truck and walked the fifty feet to the new arrival. A large man in a dark suit pushed from the vehicle, turned away as he reached back into the car to retrieve a battered black briefcase. Sandhill stopped a dozen feet behind the broad back.

"A detective commander living in white-trashville? They must not pay according to your talents, Ducky. Or maybe they do."

Ainsley Duckworth spun, startled, his eyes narrowing at the source of the question. He chewed a toothpick, his brick-like wedge of brow furrowed. Sandhill saw embarrassment. And an instant of fear, quickly covered.

"What the hell you doing here, Sandhill?"

"I wanted to ask how things were in Montgomery."

"Montgomery?"

"What were you going to do to James? Threats? Maybe a little rough stuff? Or were you planning a harder road? Must have been a surprise when the fire trucks rolled up."

Duckworth spat the toothpick to the ground. "What the fuck you talking about, Sandhill? Fire trucks? James who? Get out of here." Duckworth started toward his apartment, but Sandhill blocked the way.

"What's going on, Ducky? Why're you using a moke like Gentleman Jim to get the black community fired up?"

"Get outta my way, Sandhill. I think you're hallucinating. There fumes coming off that gumbo of yours?"

"Where's Terrence in all this, Ducks? You're not creative enough to pull something like this together on your own. And how do the abducted girls figure in?"

301

Duckworth set his briefcase on the tarmac. "You're one sick fuck, Sandhill. I'm looking for them, remember? I'm sorry that girl you were watching got snatched, but I wasn't the one supposed to be watching her. Don't take your failures out on me."

Sandhill stepped toward Duckworth, hands balled into fists. Duckworth's hand slipped beneath his jacket and unsnapped his holster.

"Hold up, whore breath. Another step and this action goes heavyweight. It's no secret you're shadowing these cases, getting weirder every day. I'll drop your ass and say you were babbling craziness, threatening me. You always pack that ankle piece, right? All I say is the crazy fuck went for it and I had no choice."

Sandhill stared at the grinning commander and realized he'd let anger and impatience spark a confrontation that was going nowhere. He'd learned nothing, lost any chance for shadowing Duckworth, if the man was the one James recognized. He'd tipped his hand; an asshole move. Sandhill turned and walked back toward his truck, followed by Duckworth's laughter.

"Get back to your kitchen, fry whore. I smell something burning."

43

"Go get her, Rose. It's time." Truman pulled a medicine vial from his pants pocket and tossed it to his brother. "Make sure she takes the sedative before we leave."

Rose stared at the vial in his hand, stricken.

"Come on, Rose, move it," Truman said. "I got the word an hour ago. We're meeting on the river, same place as last year."

"Why would he need another girl, Tru? He got one last year. What happened to Darla?"

"How the hell do I know? I don't send the buyers a questionnaire. Go get her."

Rose's eyes narrowed. "Don't order me around, Tru."

Truman looked at the television angled toward the couch, the small camera atop the TV. "Don't go getting all snippy because you're losing the audience for your playtime, Rose."

Rose stiffened and stared at his brother. "For my *what*?"

303

The smirk fell from Truman's face. "I didn't mean it like that, Rose, like back then. I meant . . ."

Rose spoke through clenched teeth. "You weren't called for playtime, Tru. Don't ever use that word again. Never. You don't know what it means."

"I said I'm sorry. I meant . . . Never mind what I meant. Just get her, brother." Truman pursed his lips. "But first, come kiss and make up, Rose; give me one."

Rose turned his face away. "I don't feel like it."

Truman patted his brother's back. "Things are tense now, it's that kind of business. But after tonight we'll have three-quarters of a million dollars in the bank." Truman pursed his lips again. "Come on, bro."

Rose leaned over, kissed Truman's lips and quickly pulled away.

"You and me, brother," Tru said as he mock-punched Rose's shoulder. "We'll let things cool off and start making withdrawals. I'll wash the money through the business and we'll live large. Plus we've still got more product on the site. I move four and that's another sweet mill. We'll live off the interest and never have to work."

Rose stared at the blank TV. "I don't want to do this any more, Tru. Steal girls."

"Come on, Rose. You get like this every time we make a delivery."

"It's different. I mean it this time."

"You get attached," Truman said, patting Rose's forearm. "It's sweet."

304

"No. Things are different. Jacy's . . . different."

"They're all different, Rose. Each a precious little gem. That's what makes them so valuable." Truman pursed his thin lips, wet them with a slip of tongue. "Come on, Rose, give me another."

They kissed again, Truman's hand slipping down Rose's back, gliding over his buttocks. "There we go, Rose. You and me. Now go get Lorelei."

Rose started away, then turned and glared over his shoulder. "It's Jacy, Tru. J-A-C-Y."

"Jacy then. Go get Jacy, Rose. Give her the pill. Hurry."

Ryder heard the outsize voice halfway up the stairs to Sandhill's apartment. He knocked and, when there was no answer, pushed open the door to see Sandhill side-arm a stack of papers from his dining-room table. Copies of the case files brought by the greasy inspector, Wentz, the pages scattered half the length of the room.

"It's here, it's goddamned here," Sandhill growled, oblivious to Ryder's presence. "Where is it?"

"Where's what?"

Sandhill didn't look happy to see Ryder. He didn't look happy about anything. "The piece, the goddamned key." He picked up a sheaf of photographs and threw them across the room.

"Key to what?"

"All this damned BULLSHIT!"

"Jeez, Sandhill, calm down."

"We've got nothing. It's all WORTHLESS!"

Sandhill kicked the table, upending it, sending reports, timelines, notes spilling all the way into the kitchen area. He punted the table again, sending a leg flying into the kitchen area.

Ryder grabbed Sandhill's arm. "Sandhill, listen –"

Sandhill yanked his arm away. "Let me be, Ryder. I'm working."

"You're not making sense. Stop and listen to me."

Ryder grabbed Sandhill's arm again. Sandhill spun, sending Ryder tripping forward over the stacks of papers. He caught himself on a chair piled with notepads and revised timelines, spilling them across the carpet.

"Dammit, Sandhill . . .' Ryder stormed back toward the red-faced restaurateur's back. Sandhill whirled, eyes blazing, fists tight and raised.

"Leave me alone, Ryder."

"Then stop acting like an asshole. Get your act together."

Sandhill waved a clenched fist under Ryder's nose. "I could knock your face through that window."

Ryder smacked the fist away. "Not a chance."

The two men circled one another, Sandhill quivering with anger, Ryder reflecting it right back.

A voice barked, "What in the hell is going on?"

The men turned to the open door. An aproned Marie stood framed in the doorway waving a ladle like a hatchet.

"Dora and me got fifty folks downstairs tryin' to

eat in peace an' all they hearing is the ceiling thumping like it's gonna crash down. If you silly-ass fools gonna try and kill yourselfs, do it somewhere else. Conner, you stop lookin' at me like that else I'll slap this ladle upside your head."

"You knew, didn't you, Marie? About Jacy?"

"Yes, I surely did, Conner."

He glared at her. "You didn't tell me. All the time we been together and you never told me."

"Wasn't mine to tell."

Ryder's head swiveled between Marie and Sandhill. "I'm missing something big here, right?"

Sandhill wavered for an instant, then sat heavily on the floor, his face contorted with misery. "Jacy's my daughter, Ryder. I found out an hour ago."

Ryder's jaw drooped. "Jesus," he whispered.

"My daughter, Thena's daughter. Ours."

"Jesus. *Jee-sus*."

"Yeah, it's been a three-Jesus day, Ryder. And it ain't even over."

Marie studied her boss. "If you think maybe you can behave without a head-whopping, I got customers to worry over."

Sandhill nodded his head. "I got it back together, Marie. Thanks."

Marie turned and walked downstairs to the restaurant. Ryder bent and began gathering papers. Sandhill remained on the floor.

"I screwed up, Ryder. I confronted Duckworth about James, got nothing for it but mud on my face. I had to slink off like a whipped puppy."

"Screw Duckworth. We've got to make sense of the case. Now. Tonight."

Sandhill stared at the upturned and broken table, the floor littered with reports, notepads and photographs. His eyes were red, his face dark with misery. "Nothing about this case makes sense. Nothing ties together. The events don't lead, they circle. It's all meaningless."

Ryder examined the room, awash in papers and documents, the careful stacks now tumbled together in chaos. "The facts are scrambled. We've got to be intuitive, find the invisible lines. You don't see them, you feel them."

Harry Nautilus had always felt events were connected with invisible lines that slowly began to show themselves until it was revealed that the detectives had been either missing or tripping over the lines at every turn. It was intuition, the ability to feel the lines – and instinctively know their importance – that made a great detective.

"Touchy-feely crap," Sandhill said. "Thena's type of thinking."

"We need it now, Sandhill. We need to start feeling for the lines."

Sandhill dropped his face into his hands and mumbled to the floor in a voice as soft as prayer.

Ryder said, "I'm sorry, I didn't hear you."

Sandhill looked up, his face a mask of bereavement. "I was wishing Thena was here, Ryder, like I've done a thousand times before. I want Thena to walk through the door and tell me what I'm supposed to do, what I'm supposed to connect. What I'm supposed to feel."

Ryder reached to Sandhill's shoulder and squeezed it. "We'll need coffee to keep working. I'll go downstairs and ask Marie to brew an extra strong pot."

Ryder closed the door behind him, starting down the steps. The stairway was quiet and he heard Sandhill's voice behind the door.

"How do I do this thing, Thena?" he pleaded, his voice ragged. "How do I do it, baby? Help me."

44

Rose descended the ladder with an armload of clothes. Jacy looked at him, her eyes suddenly allowing a moment of hope.

"Am I going home now?"

Rose opened his hand and showed Jacy a little white pill. "I'm supposed to give you this, Jacy. To make you sleep so you'll be quiet. But you'll wake up with a headache. Do you want that?"

"No. Am I –"

"Promise me on a cross-your-heart that you'll pretend to be asleep. I don't want you to have a headache, all right?"

"But am I –"

"Shhh. Where's that cross-your-heart?"

Jacy crossed her heart and zipped her lips. Rose turned his back while she changed into fresh clothes. Then he lifted her over his shoulder and carried her up the steps.

* * *

The old dock was a half-mile up-channel from the mouth of the Mobile River. Mattoon had bought the five-acre facility for storage until the shipping facility was complete. He had cut the main battery of security lights, the only illumination a pair of lamps a hundred feet away. He shifted uneasily in an ebony Mercedes tucked beside a green seatainer. The car had been offloaded from the *Petite Angel* immediately after the tugs had positioned the ship at the dock.

Downriver, lights twinkled across the light chop, a cool northeast wind blowing at a steady twelve knots, the heat of the day upended by the first true breath of fall. Mattoon buttoned his cashmere jacket and heard the sound of a vehicle turning off the main road. The lights stopped at the locked gate and blinked twice.

"She's here," he said, feeling his heart rise into his throat.

Atwan leapt from the vehicle and ran the hundred yards to the gate in sprinter's time. Mattoon watched him speak into the driver's window. As the white van passed through the gate, Atwan jumped on to the rear bumper with the agility of a cat.

Mattoon slid a stocking mask over his face before exiting the car. Disguise was crucial; after the announcement of his business intentions, his name and visage would dominate the media for days.

The van stopped a dozen feet away and killed

its lights. Mattoon felt giddy, unsteady, as if the air held intoxicants instead of the smell of brackish water glazed with fuel oil.

The doors of the van opened, and Mattoon stood face to face with the abductors, grotesquely mismatched bookends, one small and slight, the other huge. The small one smiled, cocky, just as he'd been the previous year. The other one, the bodybuilder, was new. His face held concern, but not fear. There was a sense of challenge behind his eyes.

Atwan began pacing in front of the bodybuilder as if Rose's size was a challenge, looking him up and down, sneering.

"Tenzel," Mattoon said, "I must talk to these gentlemen alone. Please wait by the automobile until I call for you."

Atwan spat beside the bodybuilder's feet and slipped to the near side of the Mercedes.

"What's bothering him?" the small man said.

"You must excuse my colleague. Land makes him nervous." Mattoon eyed the van. "She's inside?"

"Sleeping. A few milligrams of Demerol. She'll come around soon. You want to know her name?"

Mattoon had tracked events via computer link to the *Mobile Register's* website; Mattoon had tracked many things in the past weeks. "Her given name is Jacy Charlane. Though I admit a preference for Lorelei."

The bodybuilder stepped forward. "Her name's Jacy. If you call her Lorelei she'll get confused. It'll scare her."

"Rose," the smaller man cautioned.

"I have no intention of scaring her," Mattoon said politely, hiding anger at being told how to handle his woman.

"She likes to read, too. She needs lots of books. Get her some books."

Atwan strode into the group, his finger pointing at the big man's eyes. "You listen, not talk," he snarled.

"Tenzel! Be quiet and step aside!"

Atwan retreated several paces, his face smeared with disgust and anger, his eyes like fanned coals. The bodybuilder's protectiveness worried Mattoon.

"You haven't . . . touched her, have you?" he asked.

The small man said, "We are businesspeople. We deliver as promised."

Despite the tenseness of the exchange, Mattoon felt a flicker of joy. He nodded.

"Bring her to the car and we shall be finished. The balance will appear in your account tonight, as soon as I get back to . . . where I'm staying. Hurry; I have other business to conduct this evening."

45

Ryder had pushed the broken table aside and spread files and photos across the floor. Sandhill studied the papers as if walking a maze, occasionally picking one up, scanning it, and dropping it. "It's all shit," he whispered to himself. He'd taken a cold shower and his hair was wet and dripping.

Ryder walked counterpoint across the room, studying photos he saw in his dreams, reading words he'd read a hundred times before. He stopped at Sandhill's rumpled, cast-off crown, plucked it from the floor.

"Hey, Sandhill, catch."

Sandhill snatched the crown from the air, wadded it up and pushed it into his back pocket. Ryder's eyes fell on foil-shiny paper in a zippered plastic bag that had been beneath Sandhill's headpiece. He picked up the wrapper ends Sandhill had retrieved from Desmond's photography studio and bounced the bag in his hand.

"You ever figure out what these things are, Sandhill?"

Sandhill disgustedly threw a page of interviews to the floor, glanced at the silver scraps. "The ends of film packages, probably; there were a bunch of them. I wasn't thinking content, I was thinking what a nice surface it was for finger-prints. I forgot the scraps after Desmond came back negative."

Ryder poured the torn paper into his palm. With no need to handle the torn wrappers lightly, he tugged at one, tore it. "Not too strong. Cheap metallic paper." He lifted the bag to his nose and sniffed. He frowned and sniffed again.

Sandhill noticed the frown. "What?"

"Chocolate, sort of. Or maybe carob. There's a chemical smell in the background. It's a candy wrapper or something similar. Take a whiff."

"Why?"

"Smell it, dammit. I want your impression."

Sandhill sniffed the bag, shrugged. "Candy bars? Remember how Desmond was sucking down pop and chips? Candy fits his diet."

Ryder spread the half-dozen torn ends across the kitchen counter. "But what brand? You've spent as much time as me in the check-out aisle. All the candy bars are there for the kiddies to snatch up. You ever see a package this shiny?"

"Does it make a difference what was in it?"

Ryder scrutinized a scrap. "Here's one with the

bottoms of some lettering. Come on, Sandhill, wake up. What d'you think?"

Sandhill shot a hard eye at Ryder, then spun the letter to his viewpoint. "I'd say a C for sure, followed by an . . . I'd make it an A, lower-case."

"I'm with you. There's just a snatch of the third letter. It could be one of a dozen letters."

Ryder took another sniff from the bag. "I got a weird hunch, Sandhill. One that just flew in from far left field. Feel like a drive?"

"I could use some real air. Where we headed?"

"To a health-food joint. There's one over on LaPont."

"I don't like them, Tru," Rose whispered when the brothers were behind the van, Mattoon and Atwan out of earshot.

"This isn't a popularity contest," Truman hissed. "They're customers."

"I don't want Jacy with them, Tru. They're sick and nasty."

Mattoon's voice cut through the dark. "What are you two talking about? Hurry up."

Truman said, "Rose, don't fall apart."

"Why are you whispering? Is something wrong?"

Truman leaned out past the van. "Nothing's wrong, we'll be right there."

Mattoon said, "Tenzel, go help the gentlemen."

Atwan was at the back of the van in an eyeblink. "Move away, muscle man; I take girl."

He threw Jacy over his shoulder as if she were a rag doll. She started screaming, her voice piercing shadows and echoing between the buildings.

Atwan grabbed her jaw and clamped it tight. "Shut up, little girl."

The veins in Rose's neck pulsed like shocked worms. "What are you doing to her?"

Atwan sneered over his shoulder at Rose. "You shut up too, muscle man."

Rose strode over, grabbed Atwan's elbow. "What are you doing? You're scaring her."

Atwan leapt, spinning into the air, his foot connecting with Rose's head like a brick hitting a melon. Rose tottered, then fell face down on the concrete. Mattoon hissed, "Get in the car, Tenzel."

"Coming, Mr Mattoon."

Atwan opened the rear door and tossed Jacy inside before sliding into the driver's seat. Mattoon slid into the passenger's side. He stared at Atwan.

"You spoke my name, Tenzel."

"It was mistake."

Mattoon said, "Was it?"

Atwan's eyes glittered in the dark. "I can kill them."

Mattoon looked in the back seat, the frightened eyes, the tears. The beauty. He had no further need of the pair of pimps.

"Destroy them, Tenzel," Mattoon whispered.

Atwan grinned as he slipped a curved and

gleaming knife from beneath the seat. He gripped the handle hard to warm the tool to its task . . .

And disappeared out the window, feet kicking.

Truman spun the wheel and jammed the accelerator to the floor. The van fishtailed out the gate.

"Jesus, you killed the guy, Rose," Truman said, breathless. "You pulled the guy out of the car window and killed him."

They swerved on to the deserted frontage road. Rose turned to look into the dark behind them. "I squeezed him until he passed out, Tru. That's all. A lot you did to help."

"I was . . . making sure the other guy didn't do anything. I had your back, Rose."

"Oh sure. What was the other guy doing, Tru?"

"He just froze, scared shitless. I think he thought you were going to kill him, too."

"I didn't kill anyone, Tru. I just wanted them to go away."

"Guess what else is going away? A shitload of money. Guess what you just cost us?"

"You always said this was a partnership. That means I own half of her. I'll pay for your half from my money."

"We can't do business like this. The point is to anticipate client needs and then –"

"Screw your junior college bullshit."

Truman jammed on the brakes, the van skidding to a dusty halt. "How much money can we make from the girl business, Rose? How long

318

would it take you to make that working construction? You don't work most of the time, staying home and lifting those damned weights. You think I want to spend the rest of my life saying 'Smile' and 'Say cheese' and 'Watch the birdie'?"

Rose continued looking over his shoulder, studying a line of ships tethered in their slips. "Pull over there, Tru. Into the shadows."

Truman's voice lifted in hope. "You're going to take her back, make things right?"

"I want to see where those guys go. I bet they're from one of the ships. Pull behind that building."

"Haven't you done enough damage tonight?"

"They're sickos, Tru. You got to keep an eye on people like that."

It was ten when the brothers returned to Truman's studio. He tucked the van into the dark beside the metal dumpster serving the small strip center. Rose jumped out and walked to the driver's side. He yanked the door open.

"Get out of the van, Truman; I'm leaving."

"You're going home?"

"I'm going where it's quiet and I can think. All you do is make noise."

"You're going to the farm, aren't you? Every time you don't want to face something, you run to the farm."

"Get out, Truman."

"That ratty farm's not going to save you. Those days are gone, Rose."

"Out."

Truman reluctantly slipped to the pavement. "You saw where they were from – Pier B-2. It's not too late. If we take her back now –"

"I said I'm not doing that, Truman. Don't you ever listen?"

46

Eden's Garden grew in a foundered Dollar General store. The space overflowed with merchandise in racks and shelves. Cartons cluttered the floor. There were bins of nuts, barrels of beans, coolers packed with produce and juices. A sound system played whale calls punctuated by banjo.

Ryder leapt a crate of organic papayas and strode to the counter, where a dour purple-haired woman watched over the top of a paperback on chemical-free living. Her scowl said she judged the pair less than a hundred per cent pure and organic.

"We close at nine," she snipped. "That's in two minutes."

Ryder held up his badge and laid the pieces of wrapper on the counter. "You ever see anything like this?"

"It appears to be a badge."

"No, these –" Ryder tapped the wrapper shards. "That's quite evidently torn paper."

"Silvered outside, uncoated inside, blue lettering. You know anything might come wrapped in it? Any products?"

"Like I said, we're getting ready to –"

"Close up. You mentioned it. Concentrate on the wrapper, please."

The woman tweezed up a piece of wrapper with her fingernails, as though Ryder's touch had made it leprous. "Granola bar, maybe. Or a nutrition bar. We have dozens, something for everyone." The wrapper fluttered to the counter.

"Where are they?"

"I keep telling you, we close in –"

Ryder spun away, jogged the aisles until he located the nutrition products. Sandhill started checking at the far end of the shelves. They scanned the products, dug at boxes behind boxes.

"Here's a maybe," Ryder called, plucking a silver-wrapped bar from a rack proclaiming *Nature Made Right*. Sandhill ran over and compared the wrappers.

"Not the right shade. Not as metallicized either."

The woman appeared beside them, glaring, arms crossed, foot tapping beneath the hem of her tie-dyed skirt.

"We just closed. I insist that you leave this very –"

Ryder handed her a folded sheet of paper. She snapped it open and narrowed an eye at the curled amorphous shape in the copied photograph.

"What is this nonsense?"

"It was a young girl," Ryder said. "We're looking for her killer."

The woman turned still as stone. She quietly refolded the page and handed it to Ryder.

"What can I do?"

They searched for ten minutes, finding several silvered packets, none fitting the size or color of the pieces Sandhill had spirited from Desmond's studio.

"Damn," Ryder said. "It just felt right."

The woman frowned at a memory. "Hang on a sec." She disappeared into the rear of the store.

"Back here," she called after several seconds. The detectives ran to a storeroom, stocks of inventory on wooden shelves. The woman was tearing open a brown carton, a dozen more piled beside it.

"A delivery came this afternoon."

Sandhill and Ryder fell to their knees and began ripping at cartons.

"Shampoo," Sandhill said, peering into a box.

"I got bottles of vitamins here." Ryder grabbed another carton.

"Aloe creams," the woman said, throwing her opened box aside and reaching for another.

Ryder tore the top from a package. "Bags of kelp."

Sandhill paused in mid-rip. "Kelp? What in the hell do you –"

"How about these?" the woman said, holding aloft a silver-packaged bar, its wrapper showing an overdeveloped bicep above the words:

Ryder compared the bar to the largest scrap. "Listen to this: 'Carbosnackers are a potent combination of vitamins, minerals and carbohydrates created specifically for fast, high-energy needs. Perfect for runners, cyclists, climbers and weightlifters.'"

Sandhill studied the small print over the back of the package. "Magnesium, calcium, chromium, phosphorus, zinc, dicalcium phosphate, folic acid, lecithin, protease . . ." He raised his eyebrows. "Jesus, Ryder."

Ryder nodded. "Yeah. It's the same stuff found in the burned girl's stomach. Which makes it likely Desmond has an athletic buddy. Maybe big enough to look like a bulldog. Which makes little Truman . . ."

Sandhill stared at Ryder with amazement and admiration.

"Our chihuahua."

Truman paced the floor of his apartment and sucked from a can of Mountain Dew. The buyer had no idea who they were, right? They were nothing more than a website. The main man – Matune? Wasn't that what the bald fucker called him? – didn't even know they lived in Mobile, just the general area. The brothers were safe, if poorer: Rose's idiocy had tossed a quarter-million dollars down the crapper – and from a solid, repeat customer – but it could be made up. And he'd damn sure hold Rose to repaying.

Truman heard the phone ring downstairs in the studio. A wrong number, he figured, no one ever called much after business hours. It rang eight times.

He was opening the refrigerator to get another can of pop when the phone in his apartment rang. He closed the fridge and crossed the floor, thinking, *Rose, let it be Rose, let the bastard have changed his mind, it's not too late . . .*

"Rose?"

Truman heard an active emptiness, sensed the person at the end of the silent connection.

"Rose?" he repeated. "Is that you?"

Several seconds of silence were followed by a voice, a veneer of calm over a core of ice.

"Where is Lorelei?"

Truman's breath turned to stone in his throat. "Who?" he choked.

"Lorelei. Where is she?"

Truman lowered his voice a register and tried to sound black. "I'm sorry, I think you got the wrong number."

"Oh, I have your number all right, Mr Desmond. I've had it since our first exchanges last year. Did you know a knowledgeable computer type, given a little time and a lot of money, can –"

Truman slammed the phone down.

Four seconds later it rang again.

*   *   *

"Stay down on the floor, Jacy," Rose said. "Or you'll have to go in the back."

They were at a stoplight, the interior of the van red with the glow of the light. Jacy was crouched on the floor next to Rose. She looked up at him, her eyes expectant.

"Am I going home now?"

"First we're going to visit a farm. Do you like farms?"

"Are there cows and horses?"

"No."

"How can it be a farm?"

"It's more like a farm you live on. I used to live there."

"You lived there when you were a baby?"

"And when I was your age. And even older."

"Did you grow into a Minute Hour because your mama fed you farm food, like for bulls or horses?"

Rose laughed. "You're funny, Jacy. That's cute."

"Who lived with you?"

"My brother and my mama." Rose paused. "Then things changed."

"Is your mama there now?" Jacy asked.

The interior of the van turned green. Rose spun the wheel and turned into a lane thick with overhanging trees.

"She left a long time ago. But sometimes it feels like she's everywhere."

Truman piled clothes into his opened suitcase. He'd follow Rose to the weed-strangled, decaying acreage where they'd lived with Mama. Truman had tried to sell the land – half of it under water every spring – but Rose clung to the place like a drowning sailor clings to a bobbing spar, paying the paltry taxes, whining about how it was *where we lived with Mama, Tru.*

Mama the schizo nutcase, Truman thought, though he'd never tell Rose that. Truman would go to the farm and Rose be damned; they could lay low until the ship left Mobile, then figure out how to salvage some money from the situation. He could log on to the site and explain things to the man. Matune? Was that what the bald head-case called the client? Matune?

Matune. Truman froze with the suitcase in his hand. *He knew the man's name. That he had arrived in Mobile on a ship. Rose had discovered the ship's name and berth.*

Truman released a relieved breath. Secret knowledge was serious power. He'd tell the man to either accept a new girl or they'd dissolve the relationship. Maybe he'd make the guy a deal, ten grand off for his troubles. If Matune stayed pissy, all Truman had to do was play the name card.

"I've detailed our dealings, Mr Matune, all letters sent and received, everything. If anything happens to me, Mr Matune . . ."

Matune knew who Truman was, Truman knew who Matune was: A standoff. Truman slipped the curtain aside and peered out over the parking lot. Empty. Rose had the van, but Tru's little wagon was parked around back. He crept to the door hoping he'd remembered everything: Clothes, laptop, cologne, slippers . . .

Was that a sound outside? Truman slid his ear to the door. That was the problem with being next to the highway, the constant noise. He listened for a full minute, nothing. Truman was flicking off the light when the door exploded open and iron fingers encircled his throat.

"Hello, skinny man," Tenzel Atwan's voice whispered in his ear. "Where little girl? Where muscle man?"

"G-gone," Truman choked, the grip on his throat letting words out without letting air in.

"Gone to where?"

"Farm. Not . . . far."

"That a truth?

Truman's head nodded. "Tru-true," he choked.

"We find out fast, don't we?" the voice said with delight. The fingers tightened and the room began to spiral.

Just before he spun into darkness, Truman smelled something pungent. Oily.

47

"It's the police, Desmond. Open up."

Ryder hard-knuckled the door of Truman Desmond's apartment. It was an inch ajar and lights blazed inside. Sandhill stood behind, listening for a response. The only sound was traffic on the highway. Ryder pushed open the door and leaned across the threshold.

"I smell smoke."

"Meat burning?" Sandhill whispered. "Check the stove. Go slow."

"Desmond," Ryder called again, his weapon scanning the living room – cookie-cutter furniture, cheap television facing a recliner. On the TV table beside the chair were several books: *Marketing Principles*, *The Small Business Guide to the Future*, *Essentials of Entrepreneurship*.

Ryder followed his gun to the kitchen. The counter held a half-dozen boxes of sweetened cereal and a rolled-closed bag of Cheezos. An opened can of Mountain Dew sat beside a toaster. Ryder touched the can, still cold.

Sandhill stepped in, looked around, stopped dead. "Hear that?"

Ryder cocked his head. Shook it, *no*. Sandhill nodded to a shallow hallway behind the kitchen. "There it is again." His gun in his fist, he slipped beside a closed door and knocked hard.

"Desmond, it's the police."

"I hear it," Ryder whispered. "Coming from inside."

"High low," Sandhill said. "My break." Ryder nodded at the signal and lowered to a crouch. Sandhill whispered off the count.

"One . . . two . . . three . . ."

The door exploded under the impact of Sandhill's boot. Ryder swept in low, his weapon held two-handed and scanning. Sandhill stood by the doorframe, covering from above. The room stunk of seared flesh. Ryder's eyes were first to register the spectacle.

"Oh lord."

Desmond lay naked on the bed, his skin white as lard except for a patchwork of char black and angry red from his navel to his knees. A gray rectangle of tape covered his lips. His wrists were roped to the bedposts, ankles lashed to the frame. Ryder ran to the spread-eagled figure as Desmond's bowels voided.

"Mother of God. He's been burned, tortured. I think he's dying."

Ryder dialed for help as Sandhill severed Desmond's bindings, Ryder's eyes momentarily noting the precise, almost ornate knots holding Desmond to the bed. Sandhill knelt by the shivering figure and peeled tape from its mouth.

"Desmond, listen to me. You took Jacy, right? Or you know who did."

The figure sucked air, moaned as it exhaled. Its head lifted an inch, seemed to bob *yes*, fell back.

"Where is she?"

"Moo-on river . . . to be . . ."

"What? Come on, buddy, you can say it. Where's Jacy?"

"Moo-tune . . . to be . . . the river . . ."

Sandhill shook Truman's shoulders. "Why did you take the girls, Desmond?"

"Sell . . . girls. Rose fuh-fucked . . . up. B-buyer came back."

"Where's Jacy?"

"Moo-tune. To be . . ." Truman mumbled, froth spilling from his lips.

"I can't understand you, partner. Louder."

Truman's eyes fluttered closed. Sandhill felt for a pulse at his neck. "He's in shock. I can't find anything. His pulse is gone."

A wet breath rattled from Truman's throat. "Desmond, come back," Ryder yelled, slapping the photographer's face.

Truman's mouth opened and closed as if nursing, his fingers clawing Sandhill's forearm.

"D-d-damn . . . Rose."

Sandhill shook him like a rag doll. Truman Desmond's eyes widened as if seeing some hideous creature emerging from his chest. His scream drowned in his throat and his fingers slipped from Sandhill's arm. Truman's eyes rolled back in his head and a wet gasp fluttered through his lips.

"He's dying, Ryder."

Ryder grimaced, cleared Desmond's airway, then knelt beside the bed and attempted to revive him with rescue breathing. After three minutes with no effect, Ryder gave up.

"He's gone. Get out of here, Sandhill. Now."

"I'm not leaving you to take the heat when I caused –"

"You've got to stay outside and keep working. I can do more from inside, be there if more information turns up."

"Squill will nail your ass to the wall, Ryder."

"Squill needs me to fill in blanks. Get out. Find Jacy."

Sandhill moved to the door and paused. The sirens were closing fast. "Ryder, I'm damn sorry about getting you into all this."

Ryder's grin flashed beneath weary eyes. "Don't get maudlin, Sandhill. I opened the door to the china shop. All you did was wander in."

Tenzel Atwan jogged up the gangplank with the form over his shoulder. The guard on deck looked away, like the moment didn't exist. Atwan carried Jacy to an equipment room deep in the bowels of

332

the ship and set her on the floor, her eyes bright with tears.

"You, little girl, you wait here. Not talk. Touch nothing. You don't listen and I shoot you like I shoot muscle man."

Atwan closed the door. Jacy centered herself in the cone of light from a solitary yellow bulb, like it was the last light in the world.

Sandhill's tires squealed across the concrete. Things were clearing: photographer Desmond had access to elementary schoolchildren, had photos, home information. Desmond also had a helper who was athletic, perhaps appallingly powerful.

Sandhill's phone rang. He checked the incoming number: Ryder.

"What's up, Ryder? You still on the force?"

"Big news – fuel oil and kerosene were the flammables used on Truman, a strange combination. But the huge news is that Desmond has a brother, Roosevelt – "

"Rose," Sandhill whispered.

"You got it. This Roosevelt lives in a scruffy, isolated bungalow about three miles from Truman's studio. I'm at Rose Desmond's now."

"He's there?"

Ryder's voice dropped with disappointment. "Gone. But there's a shitload of weightlifting equipment. The guy's got pictures of himself in the bedroom; paint Roosevelt Desmond green and you got the Incredible Hulk. Listen to this: There's carpet missing in the living room, bent tacks in a corner."

"The carpet LaShelle was wrapped in when her body was burned."

"Whoops, hang on," Ryder said. Sandhill heard a muffle of excited voices, one of them Ryder. A minute later he was back.

"New info just in: coaxial cable running from a camera and TV in the living room to a hurricane shelter out back. Cots, heater, fridge, girls' clothing. That's all so far. Uh, Sandhill . . ."

"What?"

"I think I'm about to be unemployed. Squill's accusing us of running our own investigation. Duckworth's been keeping Squill on high boil, repeating how you'd humiliated Squill in the past, all that crap. Squill's so hot he says he's taking you down personally. I get the feeling he's dedicated to that proposition, so stay low and move fast."

48

Ryder stood in the middle of Rose Desmond's living room and clicked off the call to Sandhill. He saw Squill coming through the door and pushed his phone into his pocket. Techs and cops bustled through the small house. Drawers were on the floor, closets torn apart, furniture dismantled. Nothing indicated where Desmond might have fled. Squill strode to Ryder, almost standing on his toes. Duckworth and Bidwell followed.

"Where's Sandhill, Ryder?" Squill snarled.

"I don't know."

"He knows," Duckworth said. "Whatever game Sandhill's running, Ryder's in on it."

Ryder spun to Duckworth. "There's no fucking game, asshole. There's three girls missing. Sandhill's trying to find who took them."

"The brothers took the girls. Find Roosevelt Desmond, we solve the case."

Ryder shook his head. "It's not that easy. The Desmonds were brokering the girls. Something went haywire, or maybe the buyer's simply removing witnesses, and that means the Desmonds. The buyer tortured Truman and left him to die. He's done the same to Roosevelt or is trying to. If Rose Desmond is alive, he's holed up somewhere. The girl or girls might not be with him."

Squill leaned close, his shirt wrinkled, tie flapping outside his jacket. Ryder smelled hatred pouring from the man, a bitter odor.

"Sandhill knows more, doesn't he, Ryder? Tell the sonofabitch to come in. Tell us everything he knows. It's the only way he'll stay out of jail."

"He won't do it," Ryder said.

Duckworth stepped up. "We'll get Sandhill, Chief. And soon. But I've got to check on the roadblocks and see if the techs are uncovering anything. I'll call soon as I know something."

Duckworth jogged toward his vehicle, dialing his phone. He paused and shot a look at the scene; bathed in the blue-and-white lights of the official vehicles, the barely controlled confusion of too many people with too little to do. For a split second, Ryder thought he saw Duckworth grin, but wrote it off to the lights and shadows.

Ryder walked from the house to the yard. He slapped a mosquito from his cheek and stared into the black woods beside Desmond's house, spitting to remove Desmond's taste from his mouth, futile. He again ran the horrific scene through his head: Desmond burned, the stink of meat in the air,

Desmond splayed out like a sacrifice, knotted to the bed . . .

The knots.

Beautiful, symmetrical knots tied where a couple half-hitches would do. Tied by hands with knots ingrained in them, like a mariner, perhaps? And the accelerants: Fuel oil and kerosene. Ships ran on fuel oil, kerosene was used to cut grease.

Ryder shot a look over his back and slipped his phone from his pocket.

The roar of Sandhill's engine poured through the open windows. The moon was high and climbing, torn clouds tumbling across its face. He slid on to I-10, thinking *Moon. River. Tune. To be.*

"Or not to be?" he mumbled. Shakespeare, Hamlet? Didn't make sense. "Moon River" was an old song by Harold Arlen. No, Johnny Mercer. *River* made some sense. But which river? There was the Mobile, the Tensaw, the Dog, the Fish, the Magnolia and several smaller watercourses bridging the larger ones in the delta. Coastal Alabama was a webwork of rivers. He saw the lights of the eastern shore as he shifted lanes in the light traffic, wondering where to aim the truck.

Think!

Moon. River. Tune. To be. River. Be to. Be to, his mind repeated. Alphanumeric? What would it mean if it's 2-B or B-2?

His phone rang and he fumbled it from his pocket: Ryder again.

337

"What's up, Ryder?"

"Where are you? No, don't tell me. What'd you think about the knots holding Truman to the bed?"

"I missed Boy Scouts, Ryder. Knots are knots."

"Not these. I think they were tied by a seaman. And Desmond was burned by substances essential to a ship. Add it to the mix, Sandhill. Maybe the river Desmond was talking about is one with freighter access. That cuts it down to . . . oh shit."

"What?"

Sandhill heard a montage of loud voices, the phone fumbled, probably dropped, picked up. Ryder yelled something and another voice screamed back. Heavy breathing rasped on the other end of the connection.

"Ryder?" Sandhill whispered, his heart pounding. "Is that you?"

Squill's voice came from the phone, barely contained fury. "Your life is *over*, you meddling bastard. If you'd left it to us –"

"To you? You've been as effective as a cheese-cloth condom."

"Where you at, Sandhill? Make your life easier and come in right –"

Sandhill switched the phone off. He swept on to the off ramp, his apartment a few blocks distant. Squill disappeared from his head, replaced by the words *River. To be* or *2-B. Moon. Tune.*

To which he added, *mariner* and *ship*.

Sandhill blew through a red light, suddenly needing to check some things at his place before

Squill sent a team over. Or showed up himself. If it was already being reconnoitered, Squill wouldn't have called.

Sandhill passed the darkened restaurant and saw nothing resembling a stakeout. There was an unfamiliar car on the shadowed corner, but it was a white Acura, not a car the department used in surveillance.

He parked in the alley behind a dry cleaner's and sprinted to his quarters. He slammed drawers until he found his navigational charts of Mobile Bay. There were several places the big ships docked. He saw no 2-B's on Dog River or in the shipyard. He moved up the bay to the Mobile River.

There! A quarter-mile or so north of the bay, a series of piers, one to five A, two to four B, and so forth.

Two-B.

Sandhill phoned Information, dialed the number he was given.

"Mobile Bay Harbor Master's office," an older man's voice said, crisp and alert. "This is Driscoll speaking."

"This is Detective Conner Sandhill, Mobile Police, Mr Driscoll. I need info on who's berthed at Pier 2-B about a half-mile upriver."

A rustling of papers and Driscoll returned. "That's the *Petite Angel*. Docked at five twenty last night. South African registry. Container cargo, dropping some, taking some."

"Ownership?"

"MML. That's Mattoon Maritime Limited."

"Ma-tune?" *Moon-tune . . .muhntune . . . Matune.*

Driscoll spelled the name. "It's a medium-sized shipping line, but growing. Container ships, primarily. A few bulk carriers."

"That's all you know? Who's this Mattoon?"

"South African, originally. Mid-forties, maybe going on fifty. Building the line, getting into the terminal side, too, I heard. Sharp businessman, word has it. Maybe a little, uh, odd."

"Odd how, Mr Driscoll?"

Sandhill heard the metallic click of a Zippo-type lighter followed by a pipe drawing. Driscoll said, "This is a heavy-scuttlebutt business, officer; seamen love to talk. You would too, cooped aboard a ship for weeks at a time. Of course, a man learns to take the yap with a grain or two of salt . . ."

"I'll keep that in mind."

Driscoll took another tug at the pipe. "Rumors suggest Mattoon lives aboard one of his ships, maybe this *Petite Angel*. Hardly ever comes off. He supposedly hires lowlifes – thieves, contrabanders and worse – but pays top dollar and then some. I used to work with a guy who skippered South American routes. Said he'd heard Mattoon was investigated in Montevideo some years back, something to do with young girls . . ." Sandhill heard Driscoll's teeth champ on the pipe stem. "I'm not talking college age here, Detective."

Sandhill's hand went tight on the phone. He

took a deep breath and made himself focus on gathering facts.

"Crew size?"

"Ten to twelve normally."

"That's all?"

"How many people run a train? All a freighter needs is a captain to aim it, a few mechanical and electrical types to keep it healthy, and someone to cook the chow."

"Your info say when it's leaving?"

"Scheduled to disembark in two hours."

Sandhill thanked the man and hung up. He made sure the gun at his ankle was secure, then checked the street from the window: nothing resembling surveillance, yet. He'd put a couple miles under his tires, then phone Ryder, tell him about the call to Driscoll. He jogged to the door and opened it without thinking.

His world exploded into blue sparks and ball lightning.

49

The electrical storm drifted from Sandhill's head, leaving copper in his mouth and lead in his muscles. He shook wisps from his brain and found himself face down on his Oriental carpet, a field of violent color. He felt his wrists handcuffed behind him. He figured he'd been blasted with one of the new-generation stun guns. Knock an ox over, at least for a few seconds.

Sandhill heard the floor creak, someone standing above him. He'd pretty much figured who he'd see.

"That you, Terrence? Have you finally gone around the bend?"

Laughter. Not Squill's. Followed by a pleasant, casual voice.

"Nice to know even the great Conner Sandhill can get it wrong once in a while."

Sandhill struggled to roll on to his back. It took several seconds for the image to make sense in his brain.

"Tommy Clay?"

The mayor's assistant smiled down at Sandhill. He held a black device loosely at his side, the stun gun. Clay surveyed his surroundings. "Nice place, Mr Sandhill. Very organized, despite the image you project."

"Seems you're different than your image too, Clay."

Clay shrugged and walked to the kitchen area. A bottle of Scotch was on the counter. "Mind if I partake of your hospitality, Mr Sandhill?"

"Go for it, Tommy. I could use a few aspirin, myself. Top drawer on the counter."

"Of course." Clay filled a tumbler with ice and made a drink. He brought several aspirin, dropped them into Sandhill's mouth. Clay nodded to the couch. "Mind if I sit?"

"*Mi casa es tu casa.*"

Clay nodded politely and sat. "Thank you, Mr Sandhill. I hope the stun gun didn't cause much pain. I wasn't overly thrilled about having to deal with you. I'm basically nonviolent."

Sandhill narrowed an eye at Clay. "But you were sent to handle me because my old friend Terrence is otherwise occupied, is that it? He's busy looking important and issuing commands and you're running his errands. You're a natural-born gopher, Tommy. Subservience is in your blood."

Clay stiffened. He closed his eyes and let out a breath.

"I was warned that you like to get under people's

343

skins, Mr Sandhill. Keep them off balance. It won't work here, so you might as well make nice."

"All right, then. I'll be as docile as a kitten, with one request."

"Which is?"

"I'd like to know what the hell is happening."

Clay took a fastidious sip of Scotch, crossed his legs, and settled deep into the couch, a traveler fresh from abroad with wondrous stories to tell.

"A few months back the owner of a shipping line sent Mayor Philips an overview of plans to build commercial dockage facilities in Mobile Bay. Containerized shipping. Warehousing, railheads. First-phase expenditures between 180 and 200 million bucks, Mr Sandhill. Not a massive project, but for Mobile . . ."

Sandhill nodded. "For Mobile it's a big, juicy plum."

"New employment, good jobs, revitalization of the waterfront. And plenty of loose money floating around."

"I take it you and Mayor Philips figured how to soak up some of those bucks."

"Norma?" Clay laughed so hard he had to set his drink down.

Sandhill raised a perplexed eyebrow. "Didn't I hear you right, Tommy? Didn't you say the plans were communicated to Philips?"

Clay picked up his drink, his smile bright as a chandelier. "I open Norma's mail, Mr Sandhill;

344

hand her the wheat and shitcan the chaff. If I didn't, her mail would sit there until doomsday."

Sandhill stared at Clay until the light dawned.

"You never showed the letter to the mayor, Tommy. You responded on your own."

Clay's eyes glittered. "Sixteen years of toiling in the vineyards finally produced champagne. I contacted the sender and explained the situation: An iffy election, a mayor who'd stumbled into the position –"

"The mayor's a straight arrow, I take it?"

Clay rolled his eyes. "The woman's oblivious to practicalities. She'd have questioned the project . . . Is it right? What's the environmental impact? What control would the city have? All that obstructionist thinking. Don't get me wrong, Norma'd be a wonderful mayor in some dinky town in Oregon, hugging redwoods, scrubbing oil off birds . . . maybe even reinstating disgraced cops on the sly."

"You know about that?"

"I dug up that ancient statute, Mr Sandhill. Showed it to Norma. I wasn't sure she'd use it, but she's a trusting soul, right? She hid the reinstatment letter away in her desk, but . . ." Clay winked.

"But like with the mail, you spend a lot of time in her desk, right? Keeping tabs."

"It helps my cause to know what Norma's thinking and planning. And it was a wonderful boost to my plans to know she'd taken the responsibility of surreptitiously putting you back on the force. That responsibility will soon explode in her face. She'll never be electable anywhere."

"Our wannabe mayor, Runion, know much of this?"

"I told Runion's people of a major new industrial project planned for the region and said I might be able to delay its announcement a couple months . . ."

Sandhill filled in the thought. "Letting Runion deliver the news right before the election, like he had a role in the deal."

Clay flicked lint from his cuff. "And, of course, there's been all the recent unrest among our African-American citizenry."

Sandhill smiled sadly. "Not bad. You've gift-wrapped the election twelve different ways and set it down in Runion's lap. Little Tommy Clay finally squeezed his hand into the cookie jar."

Clay's eyes flared. "Screw you, Sandhill. I've been jerked around for sixteen years. Promised this, promised that. But always handed some shitpot position. I was parks director for three years, head of the police oversight board for six years, four in purchasing . . ." Clay twirled his finger in a circle. "Whoop-de-doodle."

"You're assistant to the mayor. That carries weight."

"Wouldn't you know? I finally get my foot in the door and Snow White's running the castle."

Sandhill said, "What you wangling for, Tommy?

Runion to appoint you somewhere you can suck graft? Code enforcement? Zoning?"

Clay walked to the kitchen and freshened his drink. "I'm leaving city government. I'm becoming MML's governmental liaison in Alabama."

"A lobbyist."

"This time the movers and shakers dance for me." Clay winked and snapped his fingers. "Doing that soft-money doe-see-doe."

Sandhill thought for a moment. "Where's Turnbull in all this? He kept the black community simmering until it finally boiled. What's Turnbull's prize?"

"Turnbull?" Clay wrinkled his nose. "He got to piss and moan about injustice, his forte."

Sandhill shook his head, uncomprehending.

Clay said, "I had a couple late-night meets with the Rev and suggested the investigation was getting short shrift because the victims were black. Turnbull bought his bullhorn the next day."

"Turnbull booked from the mob scene when he could have stayed and chilled things out. Why, if he wasn't clued into the plan?"

Clay mimed dialing a phone. "An anonymous call claiming one of the righteous Rev's roachy tenements was ablaze. His choice was hang with his people or scurry to his property. He scurried. Turnbull's nothing but hot air. I just maneuvered him so it blew to my advantage."

"Good puppeteering, Tommy. We always

347

wondered how Turnbull and the media made it to the scenes fast."

Clay did a thumbs-up. "As soon as a potential abduction was reported, the mayor's office was alerted. I'd make a few calls and presto: Instant demonstration."

Sandhill nodded grudging admiration. He had a hundred more questions, but one stood a thousand miles above the rest.

"Listen, Tommy. Your buddy, the shipping magnate . . . I take it you don't know about the girls?"

Clay frowned as if Sandhill was making bird sounds. "Did you say girls? What are you babbling about?"

"The guy's a pedophile, the one taking the girls, or at least one of them – Jacy Charlane."

Clay shook his head with amusement. "Nice try, Mr Sandhill. Resourceful use of current events."

"One of the kidnappers, Truman Desmond, got caught tonight. I was there. He fingered your man."

Clay's brow furrowed. "You don't mean that. It's not possible."

"It's more than possible, Tommy-boy. By the way, the guy's name is Walter Mattoon. Am I right?"

Sandhill watched a bead of sweat appear on Clay's forehead. His voice fell to a whisper.

"Details, Sandhill."

"Desmond used school pictures to offer the girls.

Over the web, I figure. He gave me Mattoon's name as a buyer, told me the ship's berth."

More sweat appeared on Clay's forehead. "Did you tell this to the cops?"

"Of course," Sandhill lied. "Mattoon is fried meat. There goes the old lobbying doe-see-doe."

Clay leapt from the couch and ran to the kitchen dialing his cellphone. "Call me as soon as you get a chance," he spat into the receiver.

Clay closed the clamshell phone and paced the small kitchen space, his eyes alight with fear.

The phone rang before a minute had passed. Clay whispered into it, a frenzy of hushed words.

His eyes shot toward Sandhill. More confused whispering. Then Clay's shoulders relaxed, as if an anvil had been lifted from them. He glared at Sandhill. Closed the phone.

"You lied, Sandhill. Whatever you know about Mr Mattoon, about anything . . . nothing's been communicated to the police. Everything's still safe."

Sandhill shrugged. It had been worth a shot.

She and the Minute Hour had been eating cookies in the house on the farm. He had been telling her the men by the water were very nasty men that never, ever had anywhere pretty inside them, just something like poison. He said even if they had put her on the boat, he would have saved her. It made him start crying and walking in circles.

But then the door smashed open and the terrible bald man was standing right in front of them. The

Minute Hour puffed himself up until he was even bigger and made a terrible loud roar – *Rrrrrrahhhhhhheeeeeee!* – and jumped at the bald man. The bald man aimed a big gun that made a loud click but no bang. The Minute Hour stuck his arms out in front of him and fell down with blood on his hand and pouring out of the middle of his head between his eyes.

Remembering made her cry harder. Her mind said to hide, but everywhere was filled with tools and pipes and rope and stuff. The metal-wall room smelled like the place Aunt Nike got her car fixed. There was a ball of string on the long table, like kite string, but brown and fuzzier. She touched the string. Picked an end loose from the grapefruit-sized ball.

Ball of string . . . ball of string . . .

"They-soos," she whispered. In her favorite story by the Gumbo King, They-soos unwrapped string in the caves of the Minute Hour.

Maybe the bald man was the real Minute Hour. He looked like a beast and he sure smelled like a beast.

Atwan pushed through the door. Jacy turned to run but was yanked over his shoulder, looking down his back at the table. She grabbed the ball as Atwan started walking. Her idea was to pull string off the ball. If she somehow got away she could follow it back to the tool room, which was by the bridge from the boat to the ground.

Her idea didn't work. The tail end of the string followed because she couldn't pull it off the ball fast enough. Then string got knotted up in her fingers. She started to cry again.

"Shut up," Atwan growled. He pulled Jacy tighter, squeezing the ball of twine from her hands. She watched it getting farther away and wondered why it was spinning instead of just laying there. Then she turned a corner into a huge room and didn't see the spinning ball any more.

The room was bigger than anywhere she'd ever been. It was open at the top and Jacy saw stars winking through her tears. The light in the room was yellow, and big metal boxes were like mountains. The nasty man put her in one of the boxes and closed the door.

Something was hurting her hand. She felt the end of the string caught in her fingers. She shook it away.

For the fourth time in ten minutes, Sandhill watched Clay check the window and his watch. After receiving the call about Mattoon, Clay had relaxed, the spring back in his step and a smile on his face. Clay walked to the wall mirror. He tightened his tie, flicked lint from his lapel.

"Got some business, Tommy?" Sandhill asked.

Clay produced a comb and neatened his hair. "I've got a late appearance at a cocktail affair with some of Norma's pathetic constituency. Then it's wait for the elections, express my deepest sorrow at her loss, and move upward and onward."

"A lobbyist," Sandhill said, "is hardly an upward motion."

351

Clay's face grew hard. He wheeled to Sandhill, but was distracted by the sound of a car outside. Clay spread the blinds and made an *all-clear* gesture. He stepped outside the door. Sandhill heard a buzz of conversation on the steps, the only clear word was Clay saying, "Later."

The downstairs door to the street closed and Sandhill heard stairs creak, hesitant footsteps at the now-open door.

"Come on in, friend," Sandhill said. "Join the party."

Terrence Squill crossed the threshold, a tight, ambiguous smile on his lips. He walked with caution, chin out, hands behind his back. He stopped at the edge of the carpet and studied Sandhill.

"What the hell have you done now, asshole?"

"Ah, the final link in the chain," Sandhill said. "Don't be shy, Terrence; have a seat and chat with me. Tell me all the dirty things you and Tommy Clay have been doing."

"I asked, what the hell have you started?"

"Got a gun behind your back?" Sandhill taunted. "You can show it to me, Terrence. Don't be scared, I'm tied tight."

Squill turned around. He wasn't holding a gun. His wrists were handcuffed together.

50

Commander Ainsley Duckworth followed Squill at several paces, pointing a nine-millimeter semi-automatic at the small of the acting chief's back. Duckworth kicked the door shut.

"You scared Tommy half to death with your lies, Sandhill. He really thought the department had been told some strange story about Mr Mattoon."

Squill turned to Duckworth. "Whatever's going on, Ainsley, you're digging your grave here."

Duckworth stifled a yawn and pointed the weapon at Squill's eyes. "Shut the fuck up and get into the bathroom."

Squill glared at Duckworth but obeyed. A minute later, Duckworth returned and stood over Sandhill.

"Hey, Ducky . . . were you as surprised as Tommy that your benefactor likes little girls?"

Duckworth dropped to his knees and closed his huge fist around Sandhill's windpipe. "I been waiting for this moment a long time, Sandhill. You and me and nothing between us. How's it feel, you meddling asshole?"

Sandhill gagged, reddened, no air reaching his lungs. Duckworth bent until whispering in Sandhill's ear.

"No breath, Sandhill? That's how I used to feel when you were around. Like I could never get a full breath."

Sandhill watched his world turn into a pinpoint of colorless light, Duckworth's voice like water rushing down a hole. And then the hand fell away and air rushed into his lungs, great sucking draughts of life. Vision sparkled back into Sandhill's eyes. Duckworth was standing above him.

"No, Sandhill. Not yet. But you were close. How'd it feel, scumbag, knowing there's no dodging the bullet this time around?"

Sandhill looked into Duckworth's eyes, saw a blistering hatred he couldn't comprehend. "It was you that shot me, Ducks. Right?"

"I been wanting to nail you a long time, Sandhill. Get you out of my life for ever."

"Why me? We had our dust-ups in the past, but so what, Ducky? You were in Internal Affairs. Everybody hated you, you hated everybody back. Why single me out? What did I do that stood out?"

Duckworth stared at Sandhill, as if deciding whether to confess some inner secret, let private moments escape into light. Sandhill watched a smile crawl across Duckworth's lips, a sparkle ignite behind his eyes, erotic in its intensity. Duckworth's tongue slipped from between his teeth like a serpent and licked circles around his mouth. His eyes went far away.

It's more than anger, Sandhill realized. He's insane.

"What is it Ducks? Tell me."

A clinking sound from the bathroom, Squill struggling with his handcuffs. Duckworth's eyes flashed toward Squill and the strange moment passed. He pointed the gun at Sandhill.

"Motorboat into the bathroom and join your buddy. Make one false move and it's over."

Sandhill leg-pushed himself across the floor on his back, trying to keep Duckworth talking, engaged. "How'd you hook up with Tommy Clay, Ducky? You're not a real likely pair."

"Tommy worked with the police oversight board some years back. We each saw in one another a certain ambition. So we stayed in touch, Tommy moving from shit job to shit job, fucked by the city like I got fucked by the department."

"You're a damned commander. What the hell are you talking about?"

"Life's finally gonna get good for me, Sandhill. No more living in shitsville. Did I mention I'll be head of security at the new facility? Big bucks."

Sandhill flashed back on the incongruity of Duckworth's living conditions, the roachy apartment complex with tumbled trash bins and beater vehicles in sagging carports.

"Come on, Sandhill," Duckworth growled, pointing at the bathroom. "Get in there."

Panting from the exertion, Sandhill pushed into the room. Squill was taped hand and foot in the corner, watching silently. Duckworth grabbed Sandhill's collar and pulled him so that he was sitting against the cream tiles of the wall.

Squill said, "You fucked up my investigation into the abductions, didn't you, Ainsley?"

Duckworth grinned. "I kept files shifting around, sent folks on wild-goose chases. Didn't let teams compare notes as much as they'd have liked. I just took the usual Terrence Squill cluster fuck and ramped it up ten per cent. It made a big political stink that did what it needed to do."

"Which was?"

"Keep the black community riled up." Duckworth grinned. "I don't know what the hell's going down with the stolen girls, and don't give a half-shit, but it couldn't have happened at a better time. Anyway, Chief, you better hope I do better at my next assignment."

"What the hell's that?"

Duckworth pulled a phone from his pocket. "I'm trying to track you down, Chief; seems you disappeared." He walked from the room dialing the phone.

Squill said, "What have you done, Sandhill? What did you dig up?"

"An ugly alliance, Terrence. High money and low politics. How'd Ducky get you here?"

Squill hung his head. "We left the scene to the techs, took off separately. He called and wanted to meet at that wrecking yard ten blocks west. Said one of his snitches saw you near there, I could nail your ass. Shit, everything seemed to be falling into place."

"Clay and Ducky played me, played you, played the whole damn city. Give me some info, Terrence. Ducky's a wacko. I need to figure what's cooking in his mind. How'd I buy top slot on his shit list?"

"What are you talking about?"

"He acts like I'm some kind of personal threat."

Squill frowned. "You haven't been around for years. You're paranoid, Sandhill."

"He admitted he took the shot at me. Paranoia?"

Squill absorbed the information, took a deep breath, let it out slowly. "It's not hard to get on Duckworth's bad side. He's got an angry streak in him most people don't see, he hides it good."

"Duckworth hide his anger? It's as blatant as a ten-buck toupee."

"I'm talking about a . . . a deeper kind of anger. A darkness. I don't know . . . it's my fault. I should never have let him . . ." Squill's words trailed off.

"Let him what? What are you hiding, Terrence?"

Squill turned away, his face suddenly red. "Nothing that means a goddamn thing, Sandhill.

We're in major fucking trouble here. Concentrate on that."

"Maybe if I knew why Duckworth hated me . . ."

The door opened and Sandhill fell quiet. Duckworth stepped in. He spun toilet tissue from the roll and laid it across his palm.

Sandhill said, "Ducks, you don't want to do this."

Duckworth reached into his pocket and produced Sandhill's .32.

"It's not worth it, Ducks," Sandhill said. "You'll never pull it off."

Squill looked at the unfolding scene, mute, a look between fear and confusion in his eyes. Duckworth cocked the weapon.

Sandhill yelled, "No, Ducks, don't!"

A flat crack. Terrence Squill convulsed, a bullet in his heart. His eyes went wild with terror for a count of three, by four they were turning to glass.

Smoke drizzled from Sandhill's .32. Duckworth touched the muzzle of the weapon between Sandhill's eyes. He laughed.

"Tommy and I were debating how to make you disappear, Sandhill. After what you said about him, I'm sure Mr Mattoon will provide a solution."

Duckworth tossed Sandhill's .32 behind the bathtub, then pinched out several strands of Sandhill's hair, laying the follicles across Squill's palm and closing the hand. Duckworth flushed the toilet paper, then pulled the stun gun from his pocket. He bent toward Sandhill with the device in his hand. Lightning danced between the prongs with the sound of electric laughter.

Mattoon was hanging up his phone when a knock came on the door. He disengaged the lock and Atwan entered, sweat glistening on his head.

"Girl in main hold. In container. She OK."

Mattoon nodded. "In these troublesome times it's best to keep her hidden until open sea." He paused. "She is sad, isn't she, Tenzel?"

Atwan knuckled his eye sockets. "Little girl cry, cry, cry."

"It is the final outpouring of her old life. The morning's ceremony will bind her to the future. Joy will surely follow. There's one more small item where I need your expertise, Tenzel. It seems a former policeman somehow pierced the edge of both the business operation and my personal life. The man is neutralized and requires fast and permanent removal. I have offered our services."

"What 'services' to mean?"

"That rusty container dropped from the crane in Kingston, we still have it, do we not?"

"Captain set on dock to sell to scrapyard."

"The policeman is arriving shortly. Secure him in the container and lift it back aboard. When we are beyond the reach of eyes . . ."

Atwan swung his arm like a crane boom and opened his hand. "Give him ride in submarine."

"I couldn't have said it better, Tenzel."

The front door of the farmhouse was open, the screen door kicked off its hinges by someone leaving with both arms occupied. A possum scrambled from the dense weeds, scurried beneath the white van and slipped up the steps to the door, rodent nose twitching, black eyes bright as sparks. It entered the house, the only illumination from a fallen lamp in the living room. The soft light filled the spaces with shadow.

The animal padded down the hall, following a wet and feral smell as strong as its own. It froze at a moaning sound, then crept forward, sniffing toward a mountainous shape blocking the hall . . .

Rose Desmond's arms were flung wide. One outflung arm was swollen, blood leaking from the palm of his hand and a wound below the bicep. In the center of his forehead, directly between his closed eyes, was a small dot of red, no larger than a dime, the spent blood pooling in his eye sockets.

The damaged arm struggled from a sticky pool of scarlet blood, the fingers quivering. Gravity pulled the arm slowly back to the floor. Rose lifted his head from the wooden slats.

"Jacy?" he whispered. "Where are you, Jacy?"

Rose moaned, a lung-shaking exhalation, and

his head dropped back into his arm spreading blood. His body convulsed twice and fell still. Eight feet away, the possum hissed and scampered back into the night.

Sandhill felt like he was in a drunken elevator, lurching and swaying as it rose. Small patches of light shone from a corner. He heard voices in the distance, and the diesel growl of heavy machinery.

Next, descent. His vision cleared. He was on his back in a semi-trailer sized metal container. The light came through small ragged holes in one side of the box, rust holes probably, with edges like torn paper. The air smelled of brine and fuel oil.

"Left, left," a voice echoed from somewhere below. Sandhill couldn't place the accent. Eastern Mediterranean? Slavic?

"Stop. Back. OK, down."

A jolting slam and everything was quiet save for the sound of disengaging metal latches. Sandhill rolled to a hole in the side of the box and looked into a huge room. It made sense now. He'd been boxed in a sea/land module and lifted by crane from the dock, then lowered into a ship's hold.

There was a harsh squeal as the container's door opened. Sandhill discerned the outline of a powerful-looking man, bald, backlit against the light in the hold. The man flicked on a flashlight and spotlit Sandhill's taped ankles.

"Roll," the voice commanded. "Want see hands."

"Where the hell am –"

A hard kick caught Sandhill in the thigh. He grunted with the pain.

"Roll now."

Sandhill rolled. The light played across his back as the man inspected Sandhill's handcuffed wrists and taped ankles. The container doors closed and footsteps echoed away.

51

Deputy Chief Carl Bidwell stared at the body of Terrence Squill, Bidwell's eyes unable to contain horror at the still-warm flesh slumped against the wall, arms and legs bound tight, the arterial blood bright and startling against the walls and floor.

"It's Sandhill's backup, right Detective Ryder? The .32?" Bidwell asked, holding the bagged weapon.

"It looks like it, but –"

"It's Sandhill's goddamn piece," Duckworth snapped. "Just like it's his hair in the chief's hand. We know it, Forensics will prove it."

"Why would he leave his gun?" Bidwell asked.

"It's rinky-dink. He grabbed more firepower before he took off."

Ryder studied the sprawling form on the floor. The sharp reek of blood stung his nostrils. "It wasn't Sandhill, Ducks. He wouldn't do this."

"Then who did, Detective Ryder?" Bidwell asked.

"I don't know. But I'll find out."

"Find out what?" Duckworth roared. "The chief is dead in Sandhill's bathroom in Sandhill's apartment above Sandhill's restaurant. How did the chief get here if Sandhill didn't bring him or lure him?"

Ryder glanced through the door at the living area: Drab-garbed detectives and blue uniforms milling and murmuring. Their faces were hard and anxious.

"I don't know."

Bidwell turned to Duckworth. "How *did* the chief get here, Commander? Last I saw was you two together at Roosevelt Desmond's house."

"Ryder was on the phone to Sandhill at Desmond's place. Chief Squill heard, grabbed the phone. The chief and Sandhill yelled back and forth, fighting."

Bidwell shot Ryder a raised eyebrow. Ryder said, "They argued. It wasn't much."

"Horseshit," Duckworth spat. "The chief told me Sandhill called him a hack and a loser. Typical Sandhill ego trip."

Ryder closed his eyes. He couldn't dispute Sandhill's style.

Bidwell said, "Christ. Chief Squill must have gone ballistic. What then?"

Duckworth shrugged. "The chief took off somewhere. I asked where he was going but he told me to mind my own business, said he'd see me at HQ. I almost got there. But when I couldn't raise the chief on the horn, I headed over here."

"Why come here?" Ryder asked. "Why not just go to HQ and wait for Squill?"

Duckworth's eyes flashed with anger, but he kept his voice even. "I got a bad feeling in my gut. I figure Sandhill went nuts when he screwed up and the Charlane girl got grabbed. He snapped his fucking crown."

Ryder said, "Sandhill hated Squill, but he wanted nothing to do with the man. None of this makes any sense."

"It all makes sense," Duckworth said. "The chief spearheaded the dump-Sandhill movement when he got caught thieving to advance his career."

"Sandhill was protecting evidence," Ryder said. "Something bad was happening, evidence being destroyed."

"THAT'S FUCKING RIDICULOUS!" Duckworth roared, his face squeezed tight in fury, his fists clenched. "WHY CAN'T YOU PEOPLE LEAVE ALL THIS SHIT ALONE?"

Ryder froze and stared at Duckworth. "What did you just say? What shit?"

Bidwell shot Duckworth a perplexed look. Duckworth frowned. His eyes darted from side to side. "All this . . . shit about Sandhill and evidence. That was years ago. What's happening now is one dead Chief of Police, killed by Ryder's buddy. I'll tell you something about Sandhill: He's slick, we might never find him. You'd like that, wouldn't you, Ryder, you little scuzzball?"

Ryder launched into Duckworth, grabbing the

man's shirtfront and jamming him against the wall.

"What's going on with you, Duckworth? What the hell's going on?"

"Detective Ryder!" Bidwell yelled. "Go outside to the street and wait. I'm sure we'll have more questions, so stay there, and that's an order."

Ryder backed away, his eyes never leaving Duckworth. The burly commander straightened his shirtfront, leering. "Assaulting a superior. I got the feeling this is your last day with us, Ryder."

Ryder strode from Sandhill's apartment. He went to the street and leaned against the restaurant, watching several cops wave a blue Prius toward a secured area halfway down the block. He saw a woman behind the wheel, Mayor Philips. Another car followed, a white Acura.

Ryder turned away, Duckworth's words echoing in his mind, turning his blood colder with each repetition.

I've got to get to Harry, he thought. *But how?*

The inside of Sandhill's container was dark save for pale light through the rust holes, enough to show the module had suffered misfortune at some point. It resembled the inside of a shoebox someone had sat on, then tried to reshape. Sandhill saw light through dime-sized punctures, rivet holes, the rivets that had once bound the corrugated skin to internal bracing.

Sandhill inventoried his assets: Clothing. Shoes

and shoelaces. A few coins jingling in his pockets. His badge wallet, ready for disposal along with its owner.

And his ankle holster, just above the dozen or so wrappings of silver tape. Duckworth had removed the .32, leaving Sandhill with useless leather strapped to his leg, or so he'd thought. But tucked behind the sheepskin liner was the small lockpick.

Could he reach it?

He wore the gun on the inside of his leg, the Velcro strap to the outside. If he could get the strap open, he could work on freeing the lockpick. Sandhill had more flexibility than most men his size, but hours of being bound had cramped his muscles, tightened them. He rolled on his side and arched his back, bent his legs, pulled his ankles upward. His ribs screamed with pain, stitches tearing.

He managed to grab his pants behind his knees and edge them above the holster, but when he reached for it – fingertips clawing centimeters away – his body shook convulsively and went no farther.

It wouldn't get better. His kicked thigh was swelling and stiffening. He needed something to snag the holster strap and peel it loose.

Light through a corroded section of the container's wall caught his eye, a hole the diameter of a softball. Sandhill wormed across the floor and positioned his feet against the hole. He pushed, and his heels cracked through the corroded edges.

Sandhill slowly withdrew his right foot, hoping the edge of the metal would snag the strap and free the holster.

It took a dozen tries before Sandhill felt the metal edge catch on the strap, heard Velcro sizzle. The holster fell to the floor.

Blinded by sweat, he writhed until his hands were over the holster. He fumbled the holster upside-down, rewarded a few seconds later by the tick of metal hitting the wood slats. He wriggled until his fingers located the lockpick.

Sandhill's numb digits dropped the pick a dozen times before he found the best position, the base of the pick steadied at the root of his thumb. As he struggled, he heard the rumble of a powerful engine, distant, but nearing. It didn't seem to be coming from within the ship, its own engines already a steady underlying shiver.

Several minutes later the click of the spring sounded and his hands were free. He peeled the tape from his legs. After massaging feeling back into his hands and shoulders, he crept to the door end of the trailer and ran his hands across its surface. The doors only opened from outside.

Sandhill went to the far end of the container. One metal panel was torn partway from the bracing. He leaned against it and felt it sway outward. Light poured in. He leaned harder and two damaged rivets popped out like gunfire.

Sandhill froze, listening for approaching foot-falls. The ship shuddered and the heavy throbbing of a powerful engine began echoing through the hold. Water drummed the hull.

The ship began moving sideways.

Sandhill speculated that a tug was against the hull, maneuvering the *Petite Angel* from the dock. He figured disembarking required the crew to man various stations and he might be alone for a while. Sandhill pitched himself against the damaged wall of the container like a battering ram.

More rivets popped. The panel waggled like a tent flap. Sandhill squeezed through. He saw at least fifty containers in the hold, a wall of semi-trailer-sized modules. He looked skyward through the huge opening. Stars drifted past. He was a speck in the hold of a ship he knew nothing about, looking for a smaller speck who might be God knows where.

He was unarmed. Moving out to sea. Cramped and crippled and wearing a headache the size of hell's back yard.

Think. Prioritize. First, find a weapon or weapons.

Sandhill heard footsteps and retreated between stacked containers. At the far side of the hold the bald man double-timed down metal steps, a dark-suited man following at a casual pace. Cursing under his breath, Sandhill squeezed back inside the container as the footfalls reached the floor and grew louder.

*   *   *

"Open up. Let me by."

Mayor Philips threaded through milling cops to the bathroom. The lapel of her tweed jacket still held the VOTE SMART, VOTE PHILIPS button from the fundraiser vacated minutes earlier. Behind her was Thomas Clay, pale and distressed, looking a heartbeat from fainting dead away. Philips pushed through the bathroom door, stared past Bidwell at the floor.

"My God. What happened?"

Bidwell said, "We're just starting to put the pieces . . ."

Duckworth out-volumed Bidwell. "An ex-dick, Mayor Philips. Conner Sandhill. Had a long-time blood grudge against the chief. Looks like it came to a head."

Thomas Clay took Philips's shoulders to turn her away. "Step over here, Norma. You don't need to see —"

She shrugged her assistant's hands away. "A grudge? That's why he did it?"

Duckworth said, "Sandhill'd been acting crazy, Mayor. He turned worse when that girl he was supposed to be watching got snatched. You warned him off, I heard. So did the chief. Sandhill wouldn't listen; acted like he thought he was still a cop."

"Oh shit," she said, covering her eyes with her hands.

Clay said, "What, Norma?"

She sighed. "He *is* a cop, Tom. I reinstated him with that old law you dug up. I thought maybe

370

he'd contribute to the investigation, a pair of experienced eyes working outside Squill's rigid confines."

Clay shot a glance at Bidwell and Duckworth and gently pushed the door half-closed, speaking in a whisper. "We'll keep it quiet, Norma. No one has to know. It'd be the kiss of death for your campaign. No one will say a thi—"

Duckworth said, "I won't tell, Mayor. Sandhill's slick, a bullshit salesman. He could convince anyone of anything."

Bidwell nodded his compliance, but Philips shook her head sadly. "Thank you, gentlemen. But it doesn't change a thing. I returned Sandhill's police powers. On my own and surreptitiously."

Clay said, "This might have happened anyway, Norma. You heard the commander, a long-simmering grudge. No one needs to know."

Philips pulled the campaign button from her jacket, looked at it, shook her head. She dropped the button in her pocket.

"Yes, they do, Tom. People need to know the whole story. That's how it's supposed to work."

Duckworth looked behind the backs of Philips and Bidwell. He stared at Clay and winked, as though blinking something from his eye.

52

The container door squealed open. Two men stood outlined in the soft amber light. The suited man was average in size and form, the other wide-shouldered, shirtless and seemingly constructed of various diameters of rope and cable.

"Ah, here's our new passenger, Tenzel," the suited man said, crisp and businesslike, a banker approving a loan. "Mr Sandhill, is it?"

The bald man slipped toward Sandhill, cat-stealthy, gun in one hand, flashlight in the other. He bent to check the ankle tape. Sandhill had quickly rewrapped his legs, hoping the silver façade would fool a cursory inspection. If he had to show his un-cuffed wrists, it was all over.

Sandhill mock-battled the tape, pounding his heels on the floor, gasping with effort. "You sons-abitches. Let me loose. People know where I am; the cavalry's on its way."

The suited man stepped forward. "I've been listening to the police bands. No one knows where you are, although every police agency from Florida to Mississippi seems desperate for your location. Some little contretemps which ended in the death of a police chief, perhaps?"

Sandhill squinted past the glare of the flashlight. "Where's Jacy?"

"Hurt him, Tenzel. Nothing major."

The bald man kicked Sandhill in the thigh. It was like being kicked by a mule. He couldn't stifle the gasp.

Mattoon said, "This is not merely a ship, sir; it is my sovereign nation. The privilege of questioning is mine alone. And my first question is, Why does the girl concern you so?"

"I'm a cop. What happened to the girls?"

Another kick stabbed into the nerve mass above Sandhill's knee. "One more time," Mattoon said, and a second kick arrived.

"The first kick was for the question. The second was for lying. You're no longer a policeman; you haven't been for years. When you were, you were a thief. What's a thief's interest with the girl?"

Sandhill spoke through clenched teeth. "She's the daughter of a friend."

"A good deed for a friend? Admirable, under ordinary rules. But a more refined set of rules holds here, sir. In my world you are an impediment."

"Impediment to what? Pederasty?"

The bald man's leg was a blur. Sandhill almost instinctively brought his hands around to grab at the pain in his leg. Instead he gritted his teeth and rocked side to side.

"An impediment to my happiness, Mr Sandhill. And nothing shall disturb my quest for joy." Mattoon nodded to Atwan. "Make sure he's restrained, then meet me on the bridge."

Atwan aimed his weapon at Sandhill and inscribed a circle with the muzzle. "Roll. I need see hands."

Mattoon reached the end of the trailer, hands clasped behind his back, stepping outside.

The bald man crouched into kick stance. "Roll now," he commanded.

"Mattoon," Sandhill called at the departing back. "Mattoon, I've got to tell you something."

Mattoon spoke over his shoulder without pausing. "I don't have time for your pleadings, Mr Sandhill, and strongly suggest that you heed Tenzel. Bon voyage."

"Mattoon! The girl; she's my –"

Atwan's kick felt like a bomb going off in his thigh. "Roll, fuck you dammit!"

"She's my daughter!" Sandhill screamed toward Mattoon. "Jacy Charlane is my daughter."

Mattoon stopped dead. He turned, his face quizzical, and stepped into the container.

"Say that again, Mr Sandhill."

"Jacy is my daughter. That's why I've been investigating."

Mattoon crouched over Sandhill's face as if whispering a secret to a corpse at a wake. "Tenzel likes pain more than he likes to eat, more than sex. Lie to me and he owns you. So think before you answer: You're truly the girl's father?"

"Who'd invent something like that?"

"You no question Mr Mattoon," the bald man snarled, but kept his distance. Mattoon straightened and walked to the door of the container. He looked through the hatch to the stars and studied them for a full minute.

"Father, daughter, suitor, all crossing the same sea," he whispered, his voice as soft as sand over glass. "Sharing the same voyage, the identical universal moment, the Now." Mattoon turned to study Sandhill. "What role have you been sent to play, Mr Sandhill?" he mused. "Why were you delivered to this moment?"

"Father give bride away, maybe," Atwan said. Mattoon turned his face sharply to Atwan, but checked his admonishment as a light came to his eyes.

"Bride?" Sandhill said. "*Bride?*"

Mattoon said, "Now I understand, Mr Sandhill. You've come bearing sanction."

Mattoon seemed to float from the container, leaving Atwan to close the doors. Sandhill's wrists went uninspected.

Ryder was outside the restaurant, leaning against the wall beside the shuttered window, glass shards still glittering on the sidewalk. The case seemed infected with madness. Part of the problem was not having Harry Nautilus at his side, the sanest man he knew. Or, in a strange inverse, he would have loved to consult his lost brother, Jeremy, a scholar of madness. But Jeremy had become no more than a phone call in the night, months sometimes going between calls. He wondered who his brother had become. What he had become.

A beeping interrupted his thoughts and Ryder watched the ambulance reverse toward the door to Sandhill's apartment, back doors wide for the body.

Mayor Philips exited the building, flanked by Bidwell and Duckworth. Bidwell shot Ryder a sad look, then climbed into a command vehicle, a dark SUV. Ryder figured that, as the department's public face, Bidwell had mountains of spin to create. Duckworth's eyes trained on Ryder like twin lasers. He patted the mayor on her shoulder – *wait a second* – then called to a pair of uniformed officers three dozen feet away.

"You, get over there and jam Detective Ryder's ass in the back of your cruiser. Shoot the fucker if he doesn't obey."

The officers exchanged nervous glances.

"I gave you a goddamn order," Duckworth repeated. "Do it."

Instead of waiting, Norma Philips had followed Duckworth, her eyes alert and scanning. She pointed to Ryder.

"That's the guy Sandhill was working with, right?"

"He and Sandhill were playing some angle. It's been a long time in coming, but Ryder's cooked."

Philips studied Ryder. "I want to talk to him. Alone."

"Not a good idea. Come over here and I'll get you a cup of –"

Philips ignored Duckworth and walked to Ryder. The two uniforms stopped in their tracks and looked uncertainly to Duckworth. "When those two are done talking, lock Ryder in that car. Got that?" he barked.

The men nodded. Duckworth shot Ryder and Philips a look of unconcealed anger, then turned his attention to the ambulance, its lights splashing the street with bursts of red and white.

Norma Philips bulled toward Ryder so fast he almost jumped from her path. Her eyes blazed into his. "I want some goddamn answers, Ryder. Lie to me and I'll do everything in my last weeks as mayor to nail your ass to a burning wall. Do you know where Sandhill is?"

"I have no idea."

"Everyone's telling me the sonuvabitch killed Squill."

"You've talked to Sandhill, Mayor. Did you get the impression he was a killer?"

"He impressed me as a man who did what he wanted, no matter what. His hatred of Squill was unconcealed."

Ryder spoke quietly. "Exactly, Mayor. If Sandhill wanted to kill Squill, the last thing he would have done was broadcast his hatred. And no one would ever find the body."

"You managed to keep Sandhill free of the cops, right? Filling him in, covering for him?"

"He was the best chance the cases had."

"You still believe that?"

"Completely."

Philips shot a glance toward Duckworth, now clearing bystanding cops from the doorway of Sandhill's apartment. The pair of cops assigned to hold Ryder watched attendants emerge with the bagged body.

Norma Philips dropped her voice to a whisper.

"You're not gambling with your job, Detective; you're gambling with your freedom, years of it. You've put all your chips on a man who wears purple vests and a floppy crown. Do you realize the potential consequences of believing in Sandhill?"

"Yes."

Philips sighed. "Jesus. Welcome to the club."

She stared at her Prius in the shadows down the block, then reached in her purse and produced a jangly clot of keys.

When the pair from hell closed the box, Sandhill waited until their footsteps evaporated before leaving the container. He limped into a corridor running toward the rear of the ship. A grimy foot-square box against a wall caught his eye, a red cross painted over it. He opened it, surprised to discover neat stacks of bandages, surgical tape, tubes of antiseptic cream . . .

And a big, beautiful bottle of aspirin.

Sandhill swallowed a dozen, hoping his body would stop screaming and he could think clearly. He continued down the hall, stopping once when his feet became entangled in baling twine, squatting to pull the twine from his ankles.

"I knew t'at goddamn line gonna bust like t'at . . ."

He heard voices approaching from a cross passage and flattened behind a thick vertical pipe. Two grimy crewman passed by. One was small and skinny. The other was large and slouch-shouldered, a blue-ribbon beer belly drooping over his belt.

"Put nudder collar on it," said the larger man in a Swedish-accented voice. "Wish t'damn hell sometime we fix t'ings down here. Got plenty money we spend on t'goddamn tiny girlfriends but none goddamn money come down to here."

"Sssssh," the smaller man cautioned. "Ain't bloody smart talkin' like that."

Sandhill pressed against the wall, ready to fight, but the men passed by. Sandhill heard a third voice, electronic. He crept to the cross corridor, leaned out, and saw the large man pull a walkie-talkie from his pocket.

"Yah, Captain, we on our way t'there now. Yes, sir. Fix up tight, ten minutes." The man jammed the transceiver back in his pocket. "Goddamn once I'd like to do t'job without t'goddamn captain ever' two minutes on t'radio, goddamn . . ."

The voices stopped somewhere near. Sandhill heard a clanging of metal, and the voices grew closer again. The pair walked by in the opposite direction, one shouldering a length of pipe, the other a huge wrench. They'd gone to a tool room, Sandhill figured.

When the men were distant Sandhill crept to the cross corridor. His feet again became ensnared. He growled at the ball of twine at his feet and kicked it aside.

Two dozen feet down the corridor was a mechanics substation. Sandhill saw two large tables, one a pipe-bending station, the other covered with sheet metal and duct tape. A work bench held balls of baling twine and the plastic strapping used in shipping.

Sandhill jammed a roll of duct tape in his pants, figuring it would be helpful in false-taping his wrists and ankles if necessary. The only tools were huge wrenches and hammers like sledges. A wheeled arc-welding station sat in a corner beside a bandsaw. Sandhill checked under the tables – more sheet metal. He lifted a sheet of metal and something small fell to the floor.

A knife. Short, flat wood handle and curved blade barely three inches long. But it was sharp, probably used to cut banding. As he dropped it in his pocket a shape in the dust of the tabletop pushed his heart into his throat: a tiny handprint.

Sandhill gently touched the print, the palm a soft crescent, tiny dots where fingers had rested. A dozen inches from the handprint, Sandhill noted a dustless shape on the tabletop, a spot where a small round object had recently sat, an object as large in diameter as a grapefruit.

Or one of the balls of twine.

"Tell me that part again, Mr King."

"What part, Jacy?"

"How They-soos undid the string in the cave of the Minute Hour. That's the coolest thing I ever heard of."

The engines increased in volume and Sandhill suspected the *Petite Angel* was heading for open sea. Knife in his pocket, tape in his pants, he slipped from the room. The aspirin was dulling the aches in his leg and side and head.

He returned to the ball of twine he'd kicked aside and traced the string across the greasy floor. He followed it around a corner, then another, staying low, moving as fast as possible.

"Goddamn the t'ings, never t'right goddamn size . . ."

The men were coming his way again. Sandhill dropped the string and looked wildly around – no pipes to tuck behind, just a long stretch of corridor behind him.

The steps grew closer. Sandhill saw a metal door to his right. He pulled it open and jumped inside, his heart racing. A bathroom. No, a *head*. There was a metal urinal against the gray wall and two stalls, one door closed, the other swinging wide.

Sandhill slipped into the open stall. He pushed the stall door shut and sat on the can. The door to the corridor opened. Footsteps crossed the floor to the urinal. A zipper fell and he heard liquid hitting metal.

Followed by a low grunt just inches away.

Sandhill looked beneath the divider and saw a foot in a blue canvas shoe, a sneaker. There was someone in the adjoining stall. The man in the stall grunted again, almost a moan. Sandhill hoped the guy was too busy with his unhappy bowels to want to talk. He heard the guy at the urinal finish up with a satisfied sigh, the pants rezipped.

The urinal user retreated from the room, pushed the door open. His footsteps paused. The man in the stall grunted again.

"Heinz?" The man at the door laughed. "T'at you in there, Heinz? I tol' you t'at goddamn sauer-kraut gonna kill you from t'inside out. Nex' time you goin' goddamn listen, eh?"

Another bark of laughter and the door closed. Sandhill flushed and escaped before the moaning man beside him started a conversation.

He picked up the string again, hand-over-handing along its path. It led back to the hold. He paused at the entrance to the cavernous area and listened; nothing but water against the hull and the basso grind of the ship's engines.

The string continued past dozens of stacked containers. It disappeared beneath the closed door of an orange container on the bottom row. Unlike the others, Sandhill saw no papers attached, customs forms or bills of lading or whatnot.

"Jacy?" he whispered in the slit between the doors. "Jacy."

Nothing.

He tapped the steel with his knuckles. "Jacy, it's Conner Sandhill."

A thumping from inside, like heels beating on floor.

53

"Jacy, you've got to be quiet," Sandhill said for the third time. "They'll hear you. Shhhh."

Jacy kept crying, a frenzy of terror and joy tumbling from her mouth, body shaking with the release, hands clutching at Sandhill as if trying to pull herself within his rib cage.

"Jacy, shush. Jacy. *Please.*"

She cried louder, the crying rolling downhill and getting faster and louder. Her cries seemed to fill the hold.

"Jacy, dammit. Shut up. They'll hear us. You've got to be . . ."

"I want my mama. I want my mama help me mama help me . . ."

"Jacy. Your mama's not here. She can't be. She sent me."

"I want my *mama*!"

"She's not here, Jacy. Please."

Jacy wailed. Sandhill pulled the girl tight to him. He rocked her on the floor of the echoing metal box.

"I WANT MY –"

Sandhill laid his hand over Jacy's mouth. Put his lips to her ear.

"I'm your daddy, Jacy. Listen to me. I'm your father."

A pause in the crying. "W-What?" she asked. "What did you say?"

"I'm your father, Jacy. I've come to take us home."

Harry Nautilus was snoring when Ryder shook his arm.

"Harry, wake up," Ryder whispered. "Come on."

"Carson? What are you –"

"Shhhhhh, dammit. She'll hear – Sophie."

Ryder saw his partner's dressing had been removed. The IV equipment had been taken away.

Nautilus checked the bedside clock. "It's past midnight. How'd you get in here?"

"Sophie needs a better lock on the back door. Listen, Squill's dead."

"Dead? What the hell hap—"

Ryder clamped his hand over Nautilus's mouth. "Shhhhh! He was found in Sandhill's apartment. All signs point to Sandhill, and everyone in law enforcement for five states around is looking for him."

Ryder lifted his hand from his partner's mouth. "And the girls?" Nautilus whispered, his eyes huge.

"We tracked down the guys taking the girls, two brothers. We found one in his apartment, tortured. He died a few minutes later; shock, I guess. The other brother's in the wind or dead. I'd bet on the latter. I think the girls have already been transferred, and the buyer's eliminating witnesses. There are still teams looking for the girls and the missing brother, but . . ." Ryder shook his head.

"Do you know where Sandhill is, Carson?"

Ryder walked toward the window. He looked into the night for several seconds, then turned back to Nautilus.

"Out there somewhere, trying to figure out what's happening. There's something else, bro, something troubling. Real troubling."

"What?"

"It was Duckworth that found Squill at Sandhill's place. Said he went there because he had a bad feeling in his gut."

"Duckworth? Intuition?"

"It gets weirder. Bidwell, Duckworth and I were at Sandhill's, Ducks and me at one another's throats, me defending Sandhill, Ducks calling him a thief. I made some remark about Sandhill protecting the evidence."

"And?"

"Ducks got this crazy look on his face and screamed, 'Why can't you people leave all this shit alone?'"

Nautilus froze.

Ryder said, "Those were your assailant's words, right, Harry? 'Details. details, details. Why can't you people leave all this shit alone?'"

"To the goddamn word," Nautilus whispered.

A motorcycle roared down the street, backfiring. Ryder winced. He waited for the bike to pass, stuck his head into the hall and listened for Sophie. Nothing. He tiptoed back to Nautilus, now sitting, his eyes alert, charged.

"Listen, Harry. You had some cases on your desk a few days before you got assaulted, right?"

"Cold cases. You were prepping for a trial, and I had a lighter-than-usual caseload. Tom Mason dropped off some old unsolved cases for me to look at."

"What were the cases about?"

"I never opened the jackets. They sat on my desk a few days and then I got taken down. Being cold, the files would have gone back to Property."

Ryder nodded. He stood and pulled Mayor Philips's keys from his pocket, shaking through them until he found the ignition key to the Prius.

Nautilus said, "If you're going where I think you're going, grab my shoes from the closet over there. I could use a shirt and pants, too."

Sandhill set his daughter down. "I'm going to leave now, Jacy."

"NO!"

He pressed his finger to her lips. "I won't be far, Jacy. I'm in a big box, too. About as far away as four cars end-to-end. Pretty close, right?"

She nodded, not pleased, but dealing with it.

Sandhill lifted her chin. "It's OK to be scared, but don't fall apart. You know the difference?"

"Falling apart is crying and screaming. Like I did before."

Sandhill stood, patted her shoulder in the near-dark. She had stopped trembling. "I'll be back in a while. Everything's gonna be fine. I promise."

"Are you going to take off what's holding my arms and legs?"

"If the bad people come back, it has to look like I haven't been here, right? That'll keep us both safe. I'm even going to have to put the tape back over your mouth."

"So it looks like you haven't been here."

"You got it, girl."

Sandhill gently reapplied the tape and kissed Jacy's forehead. He managed a smile, shot her a thumbs-up, then stood. Sandhill looked back as the light of the open door fell over Jacy. Her eyes were calm with trust. Leaving the trailer was the hardest thing he had ever done.

When Mattoon returned to Sandhill's container, he entered alone. Atwan remained at the opened doors, mistrustful, the weapon alert in his hands. The extent of Mattoon's psychosis Sandhill couldn't judge, but Sandhill had seen enough peds during his years with Sex Crimes to know Mattoon was a true pedophile as opposed to an "abductor" personality. The man was incapable of viewing his actions as harmful; in his mind he verged on saintly, beatified through his self-perceived adoration of young girls. There was no way to subvert the carcinomic delusion, only to harness it and ride.

Mattoon stood above Sandhill, arms crossed, feet planted.

"I am a wealthy man, Mr Sandhill. A man with much to give. Some would say – and I humbly submit they're correct – that a life with me would be one of boundless beauty. Travel, luxury, joy. I am by nature a gentle man, a romantic, a lover of beauty. Having so much I ask very little. Indeed, I have but one need."

"Jacy."

"I prefer to call her Dearest. Or will, after the consecration of the ceremony. For now she's Lorelei, her wandering name."

"What cere—" Sandhill caught himself, looked to Atwan, staring intently into the container. Mattoon nodded to the man. "It's all right, Tenzel, I'll briefly accept questions from Mr Sandhill."

"What ceremony?"

"The ceremony of combining, sir, conjoining. A celebration of joy times joy."

"Wedding."

"Similar, in your limited perspective, but far more meaningful. A ceremony cast in purity, chastity, untainted and expectant love. Tell me, what did you think when your daughter disappeared?"

"Jacy was dead. Or soon would be."

"But, as you see, not only is she alive, she's

preparing for a magical journey. Your fears have been transformed, night into day. Is that not correct?"

Mattoon looked to Sandhill expectantly, as if for validation.

"I know what you're thinking, Mr Sandhill, the base nature of your thoughts. Shame on you. Your culturally biased mind is dwelling on the physical nature of the union. Like so many others, you're haunted by misplaced anxieties. My motives are pure, my soul is pure. Women open like flowers, Mr Sandhill, far earlier than expected. Only the purest know and understand this, and none better than I. Which is why I have come to you with an offer."

Sandhill nodded, choosing his words carefully, playing to the needs of the man's delusion.

"You want me to somehow help in your . . . quest for purity?"

Mattoon crouched beside Sandhill. "Sanction the union. Give your daughter to me in the ceremony. Lift her to me and encourage her to enwrap me in her arms. Help in her crossing."

Sandhill affected a long moment of thought. "What of me? What do I get?"

"Gentle departure, Mr Sandhill. I had told Tenzel that, before you were sent to the bottom of the sea, he could savor several hours – days, perhaps – with you . . ."

Sandhill turned his head to Atwan, grinning at the end of the container, a malicious engine of sickness and depravity. Mattoon continued. "But if you give your daughter to me at my ceremony, I promise your death will be swift and without pain."

Sandhill closed his eyes. "All I can ask, I guess."

"It's more than you know, sir. Tenzel is a man of extreme appetites."

"What do you want me to do?"

Mattoon smiled and stood. "You will soon be called for. Your restraints removed. You'll receive a bath, fresh clothes. The captain will perform the ceremony. My manservant and Tenzel will gather as proper witnesses. The magical occasion will present itself, and I trust you will perform your half of the bargain admirably. Can I count on that?"

"I'll be ready," Sandhill promised.

Mattoon left the container. Atwan slammed the doors closed and followed. When the pair were climbing from the hold, Mattoon said, "Have Mr Ghobali find decent garments for our guest, Tenzel. He's about the size of Borsky in the engine room. Make Sandhill clean and presentable. Have him ready in an hour."

"Policeman say he give away girl?"

"He has agreed, much to my delight."

"After he give her, what?"

Mattoon turned and patted Atwan's shoulder.

"He's yours, Tenzel. My gift to you on this beautiful day."

54

After the meeting with Mattoon, Sandhill studied the encounter from all sides. Purity, innocence, chastity . . . Jacy was an emblem, a flower of purity in Mattoon's perverse concept of reality.

Could he tear that flower away before Mattoon's hands closed around it?

Guards, crew, whatever, owned the topside of the ship, the decks. He had seen them through the huge hatch, hustling through their tasks, occasionally staring down into the tight nest of containers where Sandhill crouched. Their constant presence had quashed his initial thought: grab Jacy, make for a lifeboat, get into the sea.

Until he imagined the noise such a project would make — tarps flapping in the wind, racheting chains, a hull slapping water. And did he have any idea how to lower a lifeboat?

None.

Think.

He'd considered radioing for help, but that

took a radio. There seemed no such devices below save for the crew's short range hand-helds. He'd shot glances through the hatch to the ship's superstructure, bristling with antennae. Chances were the radio operator's lair was up there as well, in the open, a tower he did not dare climb.

Think!

He had one weapon, an almost laughable semblance of a knife. But the short blade could wreck an eye or sever an artery. Could he conceal it beneath the pad of gauze on his ribs? Sandhill felt hope's adrenalin sparkle through his veins until Mattoon's words echoed in his head.

You'll receive a bath, fresh clothes . . .

And thus stripped, will get a full-body search. The hard-muscled man was an insane robot, but he was efficient and wary. Mattoon said there would be four from the ship at the ceremony: Mattoon, Captain, manservant, and the monster named Tenzel.

Terrible odds. Sandhill stared at the knife in his palm. There was no way to get the implement to the bridge.

He closed his eyes against the sweat ticking into his eyes.

Think, goddammit.

Five minutes later, Sandhill pushed from the container and crept to Jacy's metal prison. He stretched out beside her.

"I'm pretty sure of what's going to happen, Jacy. Some of it. I have a plan. It'll take both of us."

"I can do anything now. With you here."

"I'm going to need you to be very brave, like Theseus. You think you can do that?"

"I'll be brave."

Sandhill took a deep breath and pictured events as he hoped to shape them.

"OK. Here's what I need for you to do . . ."

Ryder and Nautilus stood at the entry of the building housing the MPD's property room. They stared into the security camera above the door and listened to the tinny voice of Leland Royce through the intercom.

"Ryder? What the hell are you doing here? Is that Harry Nautilus? Harry, I thought you were still recup—"

"Open sesame, Royce," Ryder said, banging the door. "Let us in."

"I don't think I should."

Harry Nautilus glared at the camera above the entry. "Open the damned door, Leland. Right now."

A pause. "Sure, Harry."

The lock buzzed open and the pair entered. Ryder ran to the counter. "Cold cases, Royce. What happens when Tom Mason pulls some for review? Where's the assignment get noted?"

Royce started to protest. When Nautilus cleared his throat, Royce slipped a log book from beneath the counter.

"Lieutenant Mason signs them out. Usually he pulls the paperwork files first. If the detective or detectives he assigns to the cases need photos and physical evidence, I know the loot's approved the look-see. They can come down and root through the boxes."

Nautilus spun the log book his way and began flipping pages. "Lessee . . . I got jumped in mid June, so I'm looking for three cases assigned to me a few days earlier. Here we go." Nautilus copied down the ID numbers. "We're going back to the shelves, Leland. That fine with you?"

Royce side-eyed Ryder, like he was a rabid felon. Looked to Harry Nautilus.

"Uh, you're taking responsibility for everything going on tonight, Harry? You'll sign an authorization?" Royce nervously slipped a sheet to Nautilus.

Nautilus sighed and picked up a pen. "Here I am doing paperwork. Guess this means I'm back with the department."

They headed into the rear section, cavernous, boxes stacked to the ceiling. The air reeked of mold, mold-repelling chemicals, and the twice-yearly fumigation. Ryder ran ahead of Nautilus, locating boxes with case numbers. He pulled a box from the shelf, blew dust away, popped the top. He checked the attached review of contents.

"The case is ten years old. A wino found dead in an alley."

Nautilus shook his head. "Can't see it having any connection to anything. What's the next one?"

Ryder moved four aisles over. He dug amidst

tattered packages and removed a box held together by tape, barely. He checked the case description.

"It goes back to 1976."

"Too old. That leaves just the one."

Ryder jogged to another shelf, checking number sequences. He stopped in front of a set of boxes. He popped the front one and read the case synopsis. "Dates back eight years. A dead hooker . . ." Ryder read silently, then handed the synopsis to Nautilus. Nautilus stared at the sheet in his hand, eyes widening as he read.

"Jesus, Cars. It's Sally Harkness."

Ryder nodded. "One of the savaged red-headed prostitutes and one of the cases Sandhill was trying to protect." Ryder added the new information to his earlier thoughts. "It's making sense, Harry. It's fuzzy and discombobulated. But I'm feeling it all come together."

Nautilus scowled. "Ducky, right? He's connected?"

"He's been hiding something about the cases for years. I'll bet he was tampering with them when Sandhill found out."

Nautilus said, "But Sandhill got fired."

Ryder slapped dust from his palms. "And Ducks relaxed, felt safe. Until back in June, when he walks through the detectives' room and looks at your desk: There's the Harkness file pulled for review."

Nautilus frowned. "Why didn't Duckworth let it pass? The tampered files stood up under inspection before."

"Because this time it was Harry Nautilus doing

the review. You're the hound dog of detail, Harry. Everyone in the department knows if there was one fake blade of grass in a golf course, you'd smell it first, then get on your belly and track it down. Duckworth freaked because you were the one checking the case."

Nautilus stared at the box, thousands of pages of case history plus several accompanying parcels of physical evidence.

"What do we do? We don't have weeks for me to comb through three cases for inconsistencies."

Ryder studied the boxes. "Maybe you already have, Harry."

"Have what?"

Ryder pulled a parcel from the shelf and dropped it on the floor. "Go out front and call Bidwell, clue him in on what's about to happen. He'll listen to you. While you're there, get Royce to give you a hand truck. We'll need it to cart files to the car."

Atwan glared at Jacy. "Take off clothes, little girl."

"I don't undress in front of people, except maybe Aunt Nike."

"Take off clothes, go in bathtub. Clean."

"NO! Not in front of you."

"I say and you do. Get in bathtub."

"NO! NO! NO! Not with you looking!" Jacy stamped her foot. "GET OUT! GET OUT!"

Atwan growled and spun away. Jacy studied the bathtub, the strangest she had ever seen, the water swirling and bubbling and smelling sickly sweet, like old ladies' perfume. She started to sit in the water, but winced at a sharp pain. It hurt to bend. There was a washcloth set by the tub and she dipped it in the smelly water and washed herself off.

The towels were fluffy like sheep. On the sink was a toothbrush and a tube of toothpaste. Under it was a sign that said, *For Jacy*. She brushed her teeth. There was a pink robe hanging on a gold pole, another *For Jacy* note at the sleeve.

She wrapped herself in the robe and stepped through the door into the outer room just as a man slipped through the door. Jacy screamed.

"Pleased don't be scared, miss," the man said, a hand clasped over his eyes. "My name is Sajeem Ghobali. I'm here to assist you. Are you decent?"

"Decent at what?" Jacy said, staring at the strange man, small and brown and with a voice almost like singing. He had white clothes and a sailor hat. And a big golden box beneath his arm.

"Do you have your robe on, miss?"

"Yes."

"I'm here to help you get dressed."

"I do that by myself."

"I mean, I brought you a dress to wear. A new dress, just for you."

Jacy watched Sajeem Ghobali pull the top from the box. He reached through the folds of pink paper and pulled out a dress as white as snow.

"That's a dress like brides wear," Jacy said. Ghobali looked away.

"You like this kind of thing, buddy, watching guys take showers?"

Sandhill stood in a crew shower room, lathering under the watchful muzzle of Atwan's weapon. He let the steaming water pound his back and loosen rigid ligaments. He kept his legs straight as he bent to wash himself, stretching mobility into his back and thighs.

Atwan had come for Sandhill ten minutes back. Hearing Atwan's fast, clipped footfalls, Sandhill had rewound his legs with tape from the roll from the tool room, then reluctantly snapped the cuffs back on. They'd been easily snipped away with bolt cutters.

The shower room smelled of chlorine. Behind Atwan were two crewmen, one Oriental, the other vaguely Middle-Eastern; both holding H&K semi-automatics. They looked more like beer-soaked mariners than thugs, Sandhill noted, sloppy with their handling of the weapons, unfamiliar with the weight. Sandhill figured guard dog wasn't high on their list of duties. It was a small observation, but important.

Atwan glared. "Wash not talk."

Sandhill spun his head on his neck, arched his back. There'd been no way to hide the knife on his body; he knew they'd check for anything he might use as a weapon. He'd kept the useless badge wallet, just because it felt good in his pocket. He had no assets save for soap and a washcloth. He held up the sliver of blue soap.

"Guess there's not enough to carve into a gun, is there?"

Atwan trained the pistol on Sandhill's face. He reached in and tore the soaked hospital dressing from Sandhill's side, finding only a smear of bruise and crusted sutures.

"Hands high, turn in circle," Atwan ordered "Then bend over and open hole wide."

The full inspection, like Sandhill imagined. He did the turns and finished with the anal request.

"See any of you relatives up there, partner?"

Atwan shook the pistol emphatically. "You done. Get dress now."

Sandhill toweled off roughly, avoiding the swollen, plum-purple bruises on his thigh and the dressing on his side. Atwan gestured him into an adjoining room walled with gray lockers and pointed to clothing draped over a chair.

"Dress."

Sandhill stepped into a pair of outsized black pants, coarse wool worn shiny on the buttocks and knees. He pulled on a gray-green shirt with stamped-tin buttons.

"Where you get these duds, boys? Albania have a going-out-of-business sale?"

"Shut mouth. Dress."

A pair of box-square black shoes sat beneath the chair. Sandhill set his foot beside one and wiggled his toes. "I can't wear these brogans, they're four sizes too big. I'll fall on my face."

"Wear shoes now."

Sandhill produced his most reasonable look. "Come on, partner. Your boss isn't gonna like it when I trip and fall in the middle of his ceremony. Maybe my shoes aren't as formal as these rowboats, but they fit. How about it?"

Atwan kicked Sandhill's shoes to him. "Your shoes. Hurry fast."

Sandhill bent and tied on his battered cross-trainers. It was a small victory, but he could move fast in them. Out the porthole the eastern sky had lightened from cobalt to cerulean.

"Finish," Atwan said. "Time almost now."

55

Harry Nautilus sat in bed wearing red and black silk pajamas patterned with winged Oriental dragons breathing fire. They were Nautilus's favorite pajamas, his *lucky* PJs. He heard a car pull into the drive and rearranged the covers over his legs.

Downstairs the front door opened.

Nautilus pulled the rolling bedside table close, covering his lap like a desk. He shot a glance at the closed closet door. Studied the new additions to his wall. Pulled on reading glasses.

Whispered, "Go time."

Slow and heavy footsteps ascended the stairs. Ainsley Duckworth appeared in the hall outside Harry Nautilus's bedroom door. Nautilus was writing in a notepad, concentrating on the writing, like nothing else mattered.

"Captain Bidwell said you needed to talk to me, Nautilus. To meet you up here. What the hell you need at five thirty a.m? You're trying to talk me out of pressing assault charges against Ryder, right? Ain't gonna happen."

Nautilus kept his eyes to the writing pad.

"Nautilus?"

Harry Nautilus looked up, showing neither surprise or expectation. He laid down his pen. Took off his reading glasses, folded them, set them beside the pen.

"Step into the room, Ducks."

Duckworth entered and his mouth dropped. Paper was everywhere, surfaces piled high with files, pages strewn across the floor like autumn leaves. A card table in the corner held wigs, clothing, a purse, broken-off fingernails, eyeglasses, a rhinestoned high heel shoe – dozens of pieces of physical evidence from the murdered red-haired women and their crime scenes.

Nautilus watched Duckworth's eyes move from the evidence table to the far wall, completely covered with photographs relating to the crimes, a mural of suffering and death. There were photos from the crime scenes, from the morgue, from the autopsies. The largest photos, blown up to poster size, were of the women themselves – Sally Harkness, Tami Zelinger, Jiliana Simpkins – broken faced and sprawled across the ground.

Duckworth's confused eyes turned to Harry Nautilus.

Nautilus said, "I got bored, Ducks."

"What are you talking about?" Duckworth

whispered, shooting glances around the room. His eyes kept returning to the wall of photos.

"Six weeks back I got bored laying here. So I asked Tom Mason to send over the cold case files he'd left on my desk before I got knocked. For a month and a half I've lived with these girls, studied their cases. Every detail of their lives. Every detail of the crime scenes. Every detail of evidence. I've sent pieces to the local lab, the FBI lab, specialty labs."

"What did you find out?" Duckworth's voice was flat and dry.

"Things, Ducks. Sad things."

Harry Nautilus put the reading glasses back on his face. He picked up his pen and resumed writing on the notepad, as if Duckworth were inconsequential, already consigned to spending the rest of his life in a cell.

Duckworth said, "Why was I supposed to come here?"

Nautilus kept writing, didn't miss a beat.

"I wanted to see what you looked like walking in from the front instead of sneaking up from behind."

Ainsley Duckworth blinked his eyes as if Nautilus was moving in and out of focus. He turned for the door, leaving. Paused.

"They're waiting for me out there, aren't they?"

"Yep."

A long pause, the only sound the scratching of Harry Nautilus's pen. Duckworth couldn't see that Nautilus was writing gibberish.

Duckworth said, "It was that fucking Squill, you know. The bastard ruined my life."

Nautilus kept writing, his concentration on the notepad.

"Goddamn it!" Duckworth yelled. "Stop writing and listen to me."

Nautilus sighed. He slipped off the reading glasses. Set the pen across the pad.

"I married a worthless bitch, Nautilus," Duckworth said. "Patty was her name, *its* name. Lazy as a goddamn slug. Couldn't cook for shit. Ironed as good as a quadriplegic. She either dressed like a filthy whore or someone's grandmamma, couldn't get anything right. You've been around, Nautilus. You know how women need the control of a strong man. Without it they fall apart, nothing gets done."

Nautilus looked toward the window. The sun was rising behind the trees and the glass was orange as flame. He turned to Duckworth.

"You occasionally had to discipline your wife? That what you're telling me, Ducks?"

"Sometimes things got loud, nosy do-good neighbors called it in. There were cruiser runs to my house a few times. But things were cool, y'know. I'd make promises to Squill and the boys, they'd chill."

"The boys," Nautilus echoed.

"One day I found the bitch secretly transferring money from my account, getting set up to leave, like she thought she could make it

405

without me. I had to really set the bitch straight. Maybe I got a little excited. There was some stuff with her teeth, ribs. The slut's gall bladder had to be pulled out."

"What about the boys, Ducks?"

"Fucking Squill shows up at the hospital, tells me I was the best right-hand man he'd ever had. How much he needs me in Internal Affairs, keeping him tuned in to little opportunities, ways to move up, situations to exploit."

"But you were in trouble, right, Ducks?"

Duckworth waved the words away like a meddlesome fly. "Goddamn Patty was whining about going to the papers, making a huge stink. I told Squill she always said that stuff and I always kept her in line."

"But Squill couldn't take the risk."

"Fucking Squill says that, to keep my job and pension, I've got to shut her up . . . give her what she wanted: Divorce, house, savings, and three hundred bucks every paycheck for ten years. She sold the house, took off with everything. I'm still paying a blind account with money for that Irish bitch."

Nautilus added up what he'd heard. He went out on a limb. He figured it would hold.

"Patty was a redhead, Ducks. Right?"

"Hair like a goddamn fire truck."

Nautilus said, "And you got back at her, didn't you, Ducks? In your own way."

Duckworth smiled. His shoulders relaxed and

he faced his smile to the wall holding the photos of the dead prostitutes.

"In my own way."

Nautilus slid his right hand beneath the table. Closed it around the blanket-covered pistol in his lap.

"You couldn't vent any more rage on Patty. Hurt her, kill her, and you'd be suspect numero uno. But working over a stand-in, a proxy? Felt good, didn't it, Ducky? Cleaned the anger out. For a while, at least."

Duckworth jammed his fists into his sacrum and arched backward, clicking kinks from his spine.

"After doing whore number one, I relaxed for the first time in months. Sure, I knew the red-headed little street whore wasn't Patty. But for some long and tasty minutes, she was. It felt so good I did the other two. And a couple more in Florida when it got hot around here. But you know most of this, right, Nautilus?"

Nautilus nodded at the files and photos like he'd seen them a thousand times. "You left some loose ends, Ducks, missed a couple details."

Duckworth walked to the window, put his hands on the frame, looked out. He seemed pleased with the day. "I should have given you another pop in the head, Nautilus. I screwed up." His turned, his smile widening into a grin. "I did better with Sandhill."

Nautilus said, "Tell me."

Duckworth sat on the window frame and drummed his hands on his knees.

"Sandhill started looking into the cases. I figured he'd find something to front-burner them, a hair, a print. I remembered the property room shut down for fumigating twice a year, cameras shut off. On fume day I snatched the key from Chief Squill's desk. I was a hell of a lot better at taking evidence than Sandhill was."

"Where is Sandhill, Ducks?"

Duckworth winked. "About to follow the sweet little ladies."

"What ladies?"

Duckworth chuckled. His hand moved upward, nearing the shoulder-holstered weapon beneath his jacket.

"Freeze!" Nautilus yelled. He pulled his gun from beneath the table as Ryder emerged from the closet, his own weapon zeroed on Duckworth.

Duckworth's hand paused, his grin so wide it owned his face. He slowly brought his hand to his lips and kissed his fingertips. He blew the kiss at the photos on the wall.

Then bent his knees and launched backwards through the glass.

Ryder got to the window a half second before Nautilus. They stared at Duckworth's body on the drive, his neck at an impossible angle and a kiss still perched on his lips. Bidwell and the cops who'd been hiding in the garage ran to Duckworth, horrified faces looking between the body and the window.

"Sandhill?" Ryder whispered.

"He's on his own," Nautilus said.

56

Sandhill stood on the walkway outside the bridge as the blazing sun rose from a waking sea, the layered cirrus like contrails of fire. The breeze sang through the antennae atop the bridge. To the stern, the lights of Mobile had vanished beneath the horizon like expended candles.

A formally attired Mattoon appeared at Sandhill's side. He set his suited elbows against the railing and leaned forward, as relaxed as a man on a 1930s Cunard liner. Far below, the green water churned and foamed.

"You're looking well, Mr Sandhill."

Sandhill held up his arm, the floppy cuffs reaching to his knuckles. "Guess I'm looking as well as can be expected. I take it there weren't a lot of fashions to choose from?"

Atwan jabbed Sandhill with the gun. "Hands at side. Keep there."

Sandhill flicked his head at his guard. "Is this guy going to wave that piece during the ceremony? I can't think of a better way to scare my daughter."

Mattoon turned to Atwan. "I see nothing wrong with keeping the weapon beneath your jacket, Tenzel. We don't want my beloved to remember this occasion with anything but unblemished joy."

Atwan grunted and reluctantly jammed the pistol into his waistband, pulling the dark blazer tight to cover it. A small brown man in a white uniform appeared as if summoned by telepathy. He bowed slightly.

"All is in readiness, Mr Mattoon."

"Thank you, Mr Ghobali. Come inside, Mr Sandhill, Tenzel."

Sandhill fell in behind Mattoon, entering the bridge. A garden of floral arrangements was set amidst gauges and instruments and electronic screens. Lilacs and carnations interlaced through conduits overhead. A brilliant white carpet ran from a closed door at the back of the bridge to the center of the room. Mattoon reached to a microphone on the wall, keyed it. Sandhill heard the words booming outside, the public-address system echoing across the ship.

"Good morning. This is Mr Mattoon addressing you from the bridge. A very special event is about to occur, a ceremony of joy. Crews currently at the stations will remain so. Those not working are invited to the mess for champagne and hors d'oeuvres, working crews may partake at shift's end.

411

Thank you, gentlemen. I ask your good wishes extend to my life's new companion . . ." he paused, and his words gained the smallest inflection of command. ". . . as I know they will." Mattoon hung up the mike and positioned himself at the carpet's terminus, gesturing Sandhill beside him.

"Remember your vow," he whispered. "Bless this union and you will leave life quietly and with dignity. Anything else, and your screams will make a Torquemada faint."

Sandhill nodded, flexed his fingers, tapped them against his legs, and waited.

Sampanong entered the room from the side, dressed in full regalia and holding a bible. He positioned himself beside Mattoon.

The opening strains of Beethoven's Ninth Symphony began playing from the speakers in the overhead. Sandhill heard a moan seep from Mattoon as he stared at the closed door across the room.

". . . *seven, eight . . .*"

I was scared. The man named Oh Golly had told me to wait for the music, count to ten, open the door and walk across a rug to the people at the other end.

". . . *nine, ten . . .*"

I could feel my heart when I opened the door. I could feel something else, too. Something felt funny under my dress.

I stepped onto a rug as white as snow. The

room was gray and metal, with windows. At the far end of the room was my daddy, the Gumbo King. Beside him was a man with pointy hair and a face that looked made of rocks. He had on a black suit with a white flower on it. The scary bald man was by the pointy haired man. The man named Oh Golly was there, and a man in captain hat.

I took some steps. It hurt to walk. The man with the pointy hair was staring at me. His teeth looked like a smile but different somehow. It made my feet stop.

My toes felt wet.

I looked at my daddy and he nodded, like I was to come closer. He was going to lift me in the air like giving me away. He told me don't be scared when he did it.

I started to walk again. Someone whispered the word *Blood*. It was Oh Golly.

I kept walking.

Oh Golly ran over and looked down behind me. I looked and saw red dots on the rug. Then the pointy haired man ran over and looked down. He yanked up my dress to my knees and blood was running down from above.

The man screamed, "WHO DID THIS!"

The scary man ran over and bent down low to look. I saw my daddy move real fast and his foot kicked the scary man's face. Blood flew in the air. He fell on the rug. My daddy grabbed the pointy haired man and pulled him back hard, so his head hit the metal wall and bounced like a ball.

"Knife, Jacy. Knife!"

Back in the metal box my daddy had taped a knife on the leg by my panties. He said to be real careful so the point didn't stab me, but it poked me when I was stamping my foot to get the awful man from the bathroom so he wouldn't see it.

"Knife, Jacy!" Daddy's hand was grabbing by my face.

I pulled up my dress and peeled the knife off and gave to his hand. Oh Golly and the man in the captain hat looked real scared and ran out the door. When I looked back my daddy was grabbing the pointy haired man from behind and holding the knife at his neck. His face was purple and he grabbed at my daddy's arm.

"All we want is off, Mattoon," my daddy was saying. "You can be gone and free forever. Or you can die today."

"Yes, of course," the man was saying. "Don't hurt me. Please don't hurt me."

"Have your crew lower motorized lifeboats, Mattoon. Order them to stay back, no weapons. You're coming with us. When we get sufficient distance, we'll put you in a boat, you can come back to this floating perversion. Do you understand me?"

The knife in my daddy's hand was digging into the man neck. It was bleeding.

"Yes, of course. Please. You're hurting me. Please."

"All right, Mattoon, in a minute we're gonna samba outside and you'll start giving orders."

"Yes. Whatever you say."

"First we're gonna sashay over to your buddy on the floor and get his gun. I need a decent weapon. Jacy!"

"What?"

"Stand over by the table until we get outside. I'll call, you come out, right?"

"Yes sir."

My daddy moved the man toward the scary bald man on the floor. They were almost there when something bad happened. The vase on the table by my head exploded. Pieces flew everywhere.

I looked and saw the scary man still on the floor but pointing a big black gun at me. I could look into its eye.

I heard my daddy whisper a bad word.

The scary man stood up and made his hand get tight on the gun. My daddy closed his eyes. I saw his arm get looser on the pointy haired man's neck.

"Gutshoot Sandhill, Tenzel," the man started yelling. "Gutshoot the bastard."

The scary man moved the gun toward the Gumbo King. I saw the scary man smile and lick his tongue across his lips like a lizard.

I heard a strange sound.

57

Rrrrrrrrraaaaaaaaahhhhhhhhhheeeeeeeee . . .

The sound was like a lion crossed with a siren,
Sandhill thought, his face yanked to the door by
the insane howl. Atwan turned to the door.
Mattoon. Confusion in all eyes.

Rrrrrrrrhhhhhhhhhhhhhhrrrrrraaaaaaaaaaaaa . . . . .

Rose Desmond exploded into the room like a
rabid bull. Atwan whipped his pistol toward
Desmond, but it fired uselessly into the floor as
Desmond's shoulder hit Atwan like a cannon-
ball, blasting him sideways into the bulkhead
beside Sandhill. Desmond didn't stop, but
crashed through a chart table and into the side
bulkhead.

Atwan stumbled upright, stunned, shaking his
head to recover and moving the pistol up. Sandhill
wheeled in front of the man, his hand jabbing the
knife high, slashing across Atwan's eyes. He howled
and fired a blind shot that exploded through a
side porthole.

Sandhill swung the knife low. Slipped it through abdomenal fascia. Pulled hard upward as he stepped away.

Pink loops of intestine began to cascade from Atwan. The gun dropped to the floor. Atwan followed, kneeling in his innards before dropping face-first into the viscera and appearing to swim in them for several seconds before his engine shut down.

Sandhill scrabbled under the chart table for Atwan's fallen gun as footsteps thundered up the metal stairs to the bridge. Sandhill yelled for Jacy to crawl beneath a desk. He crouched behind the table as two crewmen ran inside waving weapons like B-movie cowboys.

Sandhill lifted his badge, yelled "Police!" and two-tapped the lead attacker's chest. The man dropped like a sack of wet flour. His companion screamed and fell, clawing his way back out the door. Sandhill let him escape, heard his footsteps scramble away. Sandhill grabbed the PA microphone.

"This is the FBI," he said, his voice reverberating throughout the ship. "Everyone on deck with your hands high." He paused, keyed the mike. "FBI operatives, hold your stations. US Navy at Pensacola reports helicopter strike force arriving in minutes."

Sandhill covered the door with the gun. Was it enough to confuse the crew? He hoped the man who'd run was now telling others about a badge-clutching lawman at the helm. They'd also heard the potent "FBI" over the PA, hopefully suggesting the shields were in charge if not in sight.

Believing the atmospheric cavalry was on the way might ice the cake.

It was silent until Sandhill heard a roar from port. He saw an inflatable cutting the water, moving away, a dozen men bouncing within the craft. *Thank God for cowardice,* Sandhill thought, watching the craft shrink in the distance.

There was no dark-suited man aboard the inflatable.

Sandhill studied Rose Desmond, sprawled on the floor, eyes focused either inside or on something at a great distance. Spittle was dripping down his chin. His clothes and skin were a motley of crusted blood. His legs were as loose as a rag doll, blue sneakers splayed on the floor. Sandhill stripped the belt from the dead Atwan and bound Rose's arms behind his back.

Sandhill slipped Jacy into a closet at the rear of the bridge. He bent and kissed her head. "I'll be back."

Mattoon's neck wasn't bleeding heavily, but enough to leave a trail. Sandhill tracked the drips to a suite of rooms on the level below the bridge. The trail led to a back bedroom. After five minutes of cautious searching, Sandhill found the ship owner's hiding place.

"I figure we're about forty miles from land, Mr Mattoon," Sandhill estimated, prone on the floor, steadying the gun at the figure quivering beneath the canopy bed. "Why don't you breast stroke out from under there. You'll need the practice."

58

Sandhill walked from his bedroom buttoning the vest Marie had crafted for the day: Purple velvet embellished with gold brocade. He winked across the room at Ryder. "Setting up Nautilus as already digging the dirt on Ducky was genius. You guys broke him open and out squirted a psychopath."

Ryder leaned back in the chair and pulled on a beer. "What about Clay's sentence? Accessory in Squill's death, you think?"

"Clay'll cop a plea by singing, but still draw heavy time in the iron-bar Hilton. Where it gets strange is muscle-boy. Roosevelt Desmond seems to remember nothing. Can't do much for the memory circuits to have a nine millimeter parked in your skull."

"A skull hard as yours, I guess."

Sandhill slipped on his crown, canted it to a rakish angle. "Wasn't his skull that stopped the bullet. It was his arm. When Atwan fired, Rose instinctively threw his arms out. The bullet went

420

in at his palm and popped out above the elbow. *Whap*. Smacked him right between the eyes. But after plowing through all that muscle, the bullet lacked the oomph to penetrate the cranium. It stuck halfway through."

Ryder shook his head in disbelief. "Then he came around and headed for the *Petite Angel*. A man on a mission."

"Climbed the stern rungs with one arm, Ryder. And a bullet in his noggin."

"You really sat beside Rose in the crapper?"

Sandhill grabbed a beer from the refrigerator. "I saw his blue shoes under the divider and thought he was a crewman. I figure he hid out, wondering what to do until Mattoon's announcement on the PA boomed through the ship. It pulled Rose to the bridge. He must have been right outside when Atwan shot the vase. It set Rose off and he came charging through the door."

"Must have been a sight to see."

"I'll hear that sound in my nightmares, Ryder: Rose Desmond screaming through the door like a banshee on PCP. Bulldozed Atwan down and ran right into a wall. *Bam*! Just laid there like he'd spent everything he had."

Ryder furrowed his brow. "He was trying to recapture Jacy, right? Or could someone like that actually . . ." Ryder let the words trail off.

"A rescue?" Sandhill shrugged. "I'm going to believe he'd had a change of heart. We'll never know, but it costs nothing, and makes me feel good."

The door below opened and Marie yelled up the stairs. "You boys joining the party or are you gonna stay up there and be heroes all day?"

Sandhill nodded toward the door. "Let's go, Ryder. Not every day a man watches his daughter turn nine."

They headed downstairs, Sandhill in the lead. He stopped midway and turned to Ryder. "I'm glad Nautilus came to the party. He's staying on the force?"

"Nailing Duckworth gave him new wind."

Sandhill started back down the steps. Ryder said, "Early on, Harry told me to watch you. I took it to mean you weren't to be trusted."

Sandhill paused. Frowned. "That so?"

"I misunderstood. What he meant was watch and learn."

A sign on the door of the restaurant said *Private Party, Open at 4 p.m.* Chairs and tables had been pushed aside at the rear and a dozen children played Twister. Etta James poured from the sound system.

Ryder looked to a nearby table and saw Nike studying the children, Nautilus studying Nike, Marie studying Nautilus. Ryder winced and headed over to distract someone, not sure who.

The front door jingled open. Norma Philips entered warily, a brown-bagged bottle jutting from her purse.

"Is this a private party?"

Sandhill ambled over, took her hand. "I sent you an invite, remember?"

"I thought it might be a mistake, given your views on politicians."

"I'm mellowing in my dotage. What's in the sack?"

Philips produced a bottle of Taittinger champagne. Sandhill's eyes widened. "What're we celebrating?"

"I just talked to Bidwell. Desmond's hidden computer drive led to Maya Ledbetter. She was hidden in the guest house of some millionaire pervert in Ohio."

"Maya, alive in Ohio? My God. How was she? I mean . . ."

"There's good news there, Mr Sandhill. The man hadn't touched her, still salivating or whatever. Maya's mother and aunt are flying to pick Maya up now. I made sure the city bought the flight. The poor girl's going to need counseling, but . . ."

"But Maya's alive, Mayor. That's more than LaShelle, or Darla, who was –"

Philips closed her eyes. "I heard. Just tossed into the ocean, according to the captured crewmen."

The two shared a long silence until Philips looked at the group of children laughing, contorting, falling, rising to play again.

"Look at the innocence, Mr Sandhill. Sometimes the world feels a bright and hopeful place. Then a rock moves aside and something like the Desmonds or Walter Mattoon crawls out." She paused. "Bidwell also told me that Mattoon's body washed ashore this morning. Guess he jumped overboard, right?"

Sandhill walked to the front window and studied the blue sky through the bright scrollwork of his new sign. "And the sea rejected the poison like vomit, purging itself on the white sands."

Philips said, "Coleridge? Homer?"

He turned to her and winked. "Sandhill. So how's the election coming now that Runion's ties to the scummy dealings are front-page news?"

"I jumped a couple points in the polls," Philips deadpanned.

"How many?"

"Around thirty-seven. Which reminds me, when I'm elected, I'll be in a position to make some changes. I'd like them to include you."

Sandhill watched Jacy skip across the floor in her new Marie-fashioned crown, a smaller and less battered version of Sandhill's. Jacy snatched a cupcake from a table and shot a wink at Sandhill.

"I don't know about tomorrow, Mayor. There's too much yesterday to deal with yet."

"I kind of figured that." Philips reached into her pocket and produced a sheet of paper, shaking it open and slipping on her reading glasses. "But just in case, I've spoken with the brass and they're prepared to offer you . . ."

The lady that just came in the door is the mayor. She's talking to the Gumbo King. I bet the mayor is asking him how to do things the right way, the King way. He'll probably say what I heard him tell Aunt Nike the other night: Sometimes it's hard but you just keep believing in yourself.

I'm going to live with the Gumbo King. I'll live with Aunt Nike, too. I can switch back and forth when I want.

I started out calling him Daddy, but something about it seemed weird. I think it seemed weird to him, too – when I called him by it, he frowned and crunched his teeth together. The way it came out is I call him King, he calls me Princess. That feels just right to both of us.

Like walking through a book that turned real.

ACKNOWLEDGMENTS

To my son, John, whose Father's Day gift of a homemade placemat sparked the book. To all of my family, who deal with my writing-generated preoccupations with grace and wit.

To Julia Wisdom and Anne O'Brien at Harper Collins, UK, who keep everything flowing. And to Robert Hunwick, who made me feel like the sole writer in his care.

Finally, to the marvellous folks at the Aaron M. Priest Literary Agency.

Coming soon from HarperCollins

BURIED ALIVE

The next thriller in the series featuring Carson
Ryder, the detective with a unique perspective
on serial killers

Enjoy an exclusive preview now

1

"R-rrrrrr."

"R-rrrrrr."

I felt the phone before I heard it, a rusty saw rasping over my forehead, trying to rip an opening into my dream-roiled subconscious.

"R-rrrrrr."

My eyes opened to slats of maple flooring. Chair legs. A crumpled sock. I was on the floor, head in the living room, feet in the bedroom.

"R-rrrrr."

Behind me I saw blanket and sheet following like a tangled umbilicus. I had tried to crawl from my dreams again. I rolled to the phone on the bedside table before the saw took another cut.

"Carson Ryder," I mumbled, cross-legged on the floor and leaning back against the bed. The bedside clock showed 7.25 a.m. on a Saturday morning. Outside, I heard gulls keening and Gulf waves slapping the shore.

"Detective Ryder, it's Nancy Wainwright at the

431

Alabama Institute for Aberrational Behavior. I need your help."

My mental Rolodex presented an image of a slender, fiftyish woman with long brown hair and intelligent eyes. I stifled a yawn.

"What can I do for you, Doctor?"

"Bobby Lee Crayline's here at the Institute."

I rubbed sleep from my eyes. "Again? Why?"

"He's going to be hypnotized."

It took a five-count for the words to enter my head, materialize into a grammatical pattern, and snap me bolt-upright with my feet on the floor and phone tight to my ear.

"Jesus. Bobby Lee Crayline?" I knew my heart was fully awake. I could feel it pounding. "Who's doing this?"

"Crayline's legal team. They want to regress Bobby Lee."

"Regressing Crayline could blow him off his hinges," I said, scarcely above a whisper. "Vangie told me Crayline was the tip of the one iceberg that she never wanted to see beneath the surface."

Vangie was Dr. Evangeline Prowse, psychiatrist, the former head of the Institute, which housed and studied several dozen of the country's most dangerous psychopaths and sociopaths. Vangie'd been murdered in Manhattan over a year ago, the circumstances strange and sad. After several acting directors at the Institute, Nancy Wainwright had been installed as full-time director a couple months ago. I barely knew her.

432

"You interviewed Bobby Lee in prison, right, Detective?" Wainwright continued. "I thought maybe you could stop the procedure."

Another mental Rolodex spun, one hidden in a far corner of my skull, and I saw Bobby Lee Crayline, his green reptilian eyes studying me the moment I entered Holman Prison's visitation room. I saw his flattened nose and his scarred hands on his side of the Plexiglas divider, hands skittering over the counter like restless tarantulas. I smelled the stink pouring like heat from his jittering, tattoo-smeared body. I'd gone home after the unsettling interview and washed my clothes. Twice.

"Crayline's legal team won't listen to me, Doctor," I explained. "I'm just a homicide dick from Mobile."

Bobby Lee Crayline had been arrested three years ago, at the age of twenty-four. His history was one of breathless violence. In high school he'd beaten two fellow students a half-inch shy of death, one student today confined to a wheelchair.

He left school and spent the next year winning amateur 'Toughest Man' competitions, often being dragged from his opponents. His reputation for crowd-pleasing mega-violence bought entrée into the Vegas-based XFL, Extreme Fighting League, a made-for-TV motley of pro wrestling, barroom brawling, and full-contact karate, two combatants fighting in a thirty-foot-square cage until one was vanquished in a shower of blood and teeth. I'd once watched three minutes of XFL before retreating from the television, wondering if the species known as *Homo Sapiens* – thinking man – had been hideously misnamed.

Bobby Lee Crayline's XFL career consisted of eleven bouts. He generally wounded his opponents in an early round, toying with them for several more, spitting insults and inflicting damage before the victim collapsed. One of his 'toys' died of a brain hemorrhage an hour after the match. Two opponents quit the league, humiliated.

Crayline had won all his fights but one, knocked unconscious in round three by what most thought a lucky uppercut by his opponent, an imposing and experienced fighter called Tommy 'Mad Dog' Dunkle. But after two years of wins, Bobby Lee Crayline disappeared overnight. No one knew where he went or why. One waggish sportswriter opined that "Hell summoned Bobby Lee to the home office."

Bobby Lee Crayline's next public appearance was eight months later, in court, arrested at a tucked-away house in the West Virginia mountains and charged with kidnapping. Chained inside a deep pit in a barn behind Crayline's house, barely alive, covered with flies and sores and his own excrement, was Tommy Dunkle, the one man to ever best Crayline in a fight.

Within a week of his arrest, three tormented bodies turned up in the countryside where Crayline spent his teen years, the corpses beaten like his high school victims, though nothing has thus far tied him to the killings.

For a month or so, Bobby Lee Crayline was the Manson of the moment, until replaced by a pretty teen girl who'd disappeared, the 24-hour media's gold-rush story.

Wainwright's voice brought me back to the present. "You know the danger of hypnotizing Crayline, Detective. Plus you're in that special unit."

She was referring to PSIT, the Psychological and Sociopathological Investigative Team. The team was me and my partner, Harry Nautilus. Few outside the Mobile PD even knew of the existence of the unit called *Piss-it* by everyone but Harry and me.

"When's this procedure supposed to go down?" I asked. "The hypnosis."

"Today at eleven."

"Grab the reins and stop the session, Doctor," I said. "Tell the fucking truth: Bobby Lee Crayline is a box that should never be opened."

"Can you help me convince the lawyers any hypnosis is too dangerous to their client?"

"You're giving me too much credit, Doctor. I can't just—"

"Please," Wainwright said. It was a plea.

The Institute was west of Montgomery, almost three hours away. I sighed and looked at the anxious eyes of my dog, Mr Mix-up, standing at the doorway with his bowl in his mouth, tail fanning behind. He wanted food and his morning walk.

"I'll come on one condition, Doc. I can bring my dog."

"Whatever it takes to get you here."

I hung up and went to my closet, almost empty. I'd been waiting for today to play laundry catch-up. I plucked yesterday's shirt from the basket to check the aroma index. The shirt got to my nose before my nose got to the shirt. I grabbed from the casual side of the closet: patched jeans and one of Harry's cast-off shirts, penguins in sunglasses sipping martinis. He'd found it overly conservative. I found it overly large by two sizes, but comfortable. My socks having missed the wash, I went without, jamming my feet into battered running shoes.

I checked the mirror and saw my hair had gotten long again—how does that happen? The man looking back at me resembled a thirty-six-year-old refugee from a Jimmy Buffet concert.

I fed Mr Mix-up, loaded him into my old pickup, painted gray with a roller. I took a deep breath, fired up the engine and raced north toward the Institute, hoping to stop the worst idea I'd heard in a long time.

The Hundredth Man
by J.A. Kerley

'Superb debut novel. A headless torso, the
heat-soaked Alabama nights, a detective with
a secret. Fantastic' *Sunday Express*

A body is found in the sweating heat of an Alabama night;
headless, words inked on the skin. To Detective Carson Ryder's
eyes it is no crime of passion, and when another mutilated
victim turns up his suspicions that this is the work of a serial
killer is confirmed.

Famous for solving a series of crimes the
year before, Carson Ryder has experience with psychopaths.
But he had help with that case – strange help, from a past
Ryder is trying to forget. Now he needs it again.

ISBN: 978-0-00-718059-2

Also available as an audio book

The Death Collectors
by J.A. Kerley

Thirty years after his death, Marsden Hexcamp's 'Art of the
Final Moment' remains as sought after as ever. But this is no
ordinary collection. Hexcamp's portfolio was completed with
the aid of a devoted band of acolytes – and half a dozen
victims, each of whom was slowly tortured to death so that
their final agonies could be distilled into art.

When tiny scraps of Hexcamp's 'art'
begin appearing at murder scenes alongside gruesomely
displayed corpses, Detective Carson Ryder and his partner
Harry Nautilus must go back three decades in search of
answers.

ISBN: 978-0-00-718061-5

Also available as an audio book

The Broken Souls
by J.A. Kerley

**Blood was everywhere, like the interior had been
hosed down with an artery . . .**

The gore-sodden horror that greets homicide detective
Carson Ryder on a late-night call out is enough to make
him want to quit the case. Too late.

Now he and his partner Harry are up to their
necks in a Southern swamp of the bizarre and disturbing.
An investigation full of twists and strange clues looks like it's
leading to the city's least likely suspects – a powerful family
whose philanthropy has made them famous.

Their strange and horrific past is about to engulf
everyone around them in a storm of violence and depravity.
And Ryder's right in the middle of it . . .

ISBN: 978-0-00-721434-1

Also available as an audio book

Blood Brother
by J.A. Kerley

Homicide detective Carson Ryder catches
killers. Jeremy Ridgecliffe is one of America's most
notorious murderers. But these two men with death in
their veins share a dark secret – they are brothers. And
now Jeremy's escaped and is at large in New York.

A mysterious video at the scene of a shocking
mutilation-murder demands Ryder be brought in on
the case. With Jeremy as the chief suspect, a man-hunt
begins – and the body count rises. Ryder is trapped in
a game of life, death and deceit – with an unknown
number of players and no clear way of winning . . .

ISBN: 978-0-00-726907-5

Also available as an audio book

In the Blood
by J.A. Kerley

'A chilling journey into a pitch-black mind' Michael Marshall

When it comes to murder, some things run in the family . . .

TV evangelist Reverend Scaler made his fortune
from firebrand rhetoric on the sins of modern America.
But Scaler has preached his last sermon after being bound
and beaten to death in an apparent S&M session.

Detective Carson Ryder has his own problems. He's edgy
and unpredictable, the crime scene barely seeming to affect him
any more than finding an infant abandoned in a boat – nearby,
a burnt-out shack, a body and signs of a struggle.

Scaler's tangled personal life reveals bizarre connections
between the cases. And it seems the baby fighting for its life
in hospital has powerful enemies. Ryder can't seem to save
himself – but can he save the life of an innocent child?

'The master of the macabre' *Guardian*

ISBN: 978-0-00-726909-9

Also available as an audio book

What's next?

Tell us the name of an author you love

| J.A. Kerley | Go ▶ |

and we'll find your next great book.